~~GU~~TTER
PRAYER

Carillon crouches in the shadow, eyes fixed on the door. Her
knife is in her hand, a gesture of bravado to herself more
than a deadly weapon. She's fought before, cut people with
it, but never killed with it. Cut and run, that's her way.

In this crowded city, that's not necessarily an option.

THE
GUTTER
PRAYER

Book One of the Black Iron Legacy

GARETH HANRAHAN

orbit

www.orbitbooks.net

ORBIT

First published in Great Britain in 2019 by Orbit

3 5 7 9 10 8 6 4 2

A CIP catalogue record for this book
is available from the British Library.

ISBN 978-0-356-51152-8

Typeset in Garamond by M Rules
Printed and bound by CPI Group (UK) Ltd, Croydon, CR0 4YY

Papers used by Orbit are from well-managed forests
and other responsible sources.

MIX
Paper from
responsible sources
FSC® C104740

Orbit
An imprint of
Little, Brown Book Group
Carmelite House
50 Victoria Embankment
London EC4Y 0DZ

An Hachette UK Company
www.hachette.co.uk

www.orbitbooks.net

For Helen

Who told me to write that novel . . .

But probably didn't mean this one

PROLOGUE

You stand on a rocky outcrop, riddled with tunnels like the other hills, and look over Guerdon. From here, you see the heart of the old city, its palaces and churches and towers reaching up like the hands of a man drowning, trying to break free of the warren of alleyways and hovels that surrounds them. Guerdon has always been a place in tension with itself, a city built atop its own previous incarnations yet denying them, striving to hide its past mistakes and present a new face to the world. Ships throng the island-spangled harbour between two sheltering headlands, bringing traders and travellers from across the world. Some will settle here, melding into the eternal, essential Guerdon.

Some will come not as travellers, but as refugees. You stand as testament to the freedom that Guerdon offers: freedom to worship, freedom from tyranny and hatred. Oh, this freedom is conditional, uncertain – the city has, in its time, chosen tyrants and fanatics and monsters to rule it, and you have been part of that, too – but the sheer weight of the city, its history and its myriad peoples always ensure that it slouches back eventually into comfortable corruption, where anything is permissible if you've got money.

Some will come as conquerors, drawn by that wealth. You were born in such a conflict, the spoils of a victory. Sometimes, the conquerors stay and are slowly absorbed into the city's culture. Sometimes, they raze what they can and move on, and Guerdon grows again from the ashes and rubble, incorporating the scar tissue into the living city.

You are aware of all this, as well as certain other things, but you cannot articulate how. You know, for example, that two Tallowmen guards patrol your western side, moving with the unearthly speed and grace of their kind. The dancing flames inside their heads illuminate a row of carvings on your flank, faces of long-dead judges and politicians immortalised in stone while their mortal remains have long since gone down the corpse shafts. The Tallowmen jitter by, and turn right down Mercy Street, passing the arch of your front door beneath the bell tower.

You are aware, too, of another patrol coming up behind you.

And in that gap, in the shadows, three thieves creep up on you. The first darts out of the mouth of an alleyway and scales your outer wall. Ragged hands find purchase in the cracks of your crumbling western side with inhuman quickness. He scampers across the low roof, hiding behind gargoyles and statues when the second group of Tallowmen pass by. Even if they'd looked up with their flickering fiery eyes, they'd have seen nothing amiss.

Something in the flames of the Tallowmen should disquiet you, but you are incapable of that or any other emotion.

The ghoul boy comes to a small door, used only by workmen cleaning the lead tiles of the roof. You know – again, you don't know how you know – that this door is unlocked, that the guard who should have locked it was bribed to neglect that part of his duties tonight. The ghoul boy tries the door, and it opens silently. Yellow-brown teeth gleam in the moonlight.

Back to the edge of the roof. He checks for the tell-tale light of the Tallowmen on the street, then drops a rope down. Another thief emerges from the same alleyway and climbs. The ghoul hauls up the rope, grabs her hand and pulls her out of sight in the brief gap between patrols. As she touches your walls, you know her to be a stranger to the city, a nomad girl, a runaway. You have not seen her before, but a flash of anger runs through you at her touch as you share, impossibly, in her emotion.

You have never felt this or anything else before, and wonder at it. Her hatred is not directed at you, but at the man who compels her to be here tonight, but you still marvel at it as the feeling travels the length of your roof-ridge.

The girl is familiar. The girl is important.

You hear her heart beating, her shallow, nervous breathing, feel the weight of the dagger in its sheathe pressing against her leg. There is, however, something missing about her. Something incomplete.

She and the ghoul boy vanish in through the open door, hurrying through your corridors and rows of offices, then down the side stairs back to ground level. There are more guards inside, humans – but they're stationed at the vaults on the north side, beneath your grand tower, not here in this hive of paper and records; the two thieves remain unseen as they descend. They come to one of your side doors, used by clerks and scribes during the day. It's locked and bolted and barred, but the girl picks the lock even as the ghoul scrabbles at the bolts. Now the door's unlocked, but they don't open it yet. The girl presses her eye to the keyhole and watches, waits, until the Tallowmen pass by again. Her hand fumbles at her throat, as if looking for a necklace that usually rests there, but her neck is bare. She scowls, and the flash of anger at the theft thrills you.

You are aware of the ghoul, of his physical presence within you, but you feel the girl far more keenly, share her fretful excitement as she waits for the glow of the Tallowmen candles to diminish. This, she fears, is the most dangerous part of the whole business.

She's wrong.

Again, the Tallowmen turn the corner onto Mercy Street. You want to reassure her that she is safe, that they are out of sight, but you cannot find your voice. No matter – she opens the door a crack and gestures, and the third member of the trio lumbers from the alley.

Now, as he thuds across the street in the best approximation of a sprint he's capable of, you see why they needed to open the ground-level door when they already had the roof entrance. The third member of the group is a Stone Man. You remember when the disease – or curse – first took root in the city. You remember the panic, the debates about internment, about quarantines. The alchemists found a treatment in time, and a full-scale epidemic was forestalled. But there are still outbreaks, patches, leper colonies of sufferers in the city. If the symptoms aren't caught early enough, the result is the motley creature that even now lurches over your threshold – a man whose flesh and bone are slowly transmuting into rock. Those afflicted by the plague grow immensely strong, but every little bit of wear and tear, every injury hastens their calcification. The internal organs are the last to go, so towards the end they are living statues, unable to move or see, locked forever in place, labouring to breathe, kept alive only by the charity of others.

This Stone Man is not yet paralysed, though he moves awkwardly, dragging his right leg. The girl winces at the noise as she shuts the door behind him, but you feel an equally unfamiliar thrill of joy and relief as her friend reaches the safety of their hiding place. The ghoul's already moving, racing down the long silent corridor that's usually thronged with prisoners and guards, witnesses and jurists, lawyers and liars. He runs on all fours, like a grey dog. The girl and the Stone Man follow; she stays low, but he's not that flexible. Fortunately, the corridor does not look out directly onto the street outside, so, even if the patrolling Tallowmen glanced this way, they wouldn't see him.

The thieves are looking for something. They check one record room, then another. These rooms are secure, locked away behind iron doors, but stone is stronger and the Stone Man bends or breaks them, one by one, enough for the ghoul or the human girl to wriggle through and search.

At one point, the girl grabs the Stone Man's elbow to hasten him along. A native of the city would never do such a thing, not willingly, not unless they had the alchemist's cure to hand. The curse is contagious.

They search another room, and another and another. There are hundreds of thousands of papers here, organised by a scheme that is a secret of the clerks, whispered only from one to another, passed on like an heirloom. If you knew what they sought, and they could understand your speech, you could perhaps tell them where to find what they seek, but they fumble on half blind.

They cannot find what they are looking for. Panic rises. The girl argues that they should leave, flee before they are discovered. The Stone Man shakes his head, as stubborn and immovable as, well, as stone. The ghoul keeps his own counsel, but hunches down, pulling his hood over his face as if trying to remove himself from their debate. They will keep looking. Maybe it's in the next room.

Elsewhere inside you, one guard asks another if he heard that. Why, might that not be the sound of an intruder? The other guards look at each other curiously, but then in the distance, the Stone Man smashes down another door, and the now-attentive guards definitely hear it.

You know – you alone know – that the guard who alerted his fellows is the same one who left the rooftop door unlocked. The guards fan out, sound the alarm, begin to search the labyrinth within you. The three thieves split up, try to evade their pursuers. You see the chase from both sides, hunters and hunted.

And, after the guards leave their post by the vaults, other figures enter. Two, three, four, climbing up from below. How have you not sensed them before? How did they come upon you, enter you, unawares? They move with the confidence of experience, sure of every action. Veterans of their trade.

The guards find the damage wrought by the Stone Man and begin to search the south wing, but your attention is focused on the strangers in your vault. With the guards gone, they work unimpeded. They unwrap a package, press it against the vault door, light a fuse. It blazes brighter than any Tallowman's candle, fizzing and roaring and then—

—you are burning, broken, rent asunder, thrown into disorder. Flames race through you, all those thousands of documents catching in an instant, old wooden floors fuelling the inferno. The stones crack. Your western hall collapses, the stone faces of judges plummeting into the street outside to smash on the cobblestones. You feel your *awareness* contract as the fire numbs you. Each part of you that is consumed is no longer part of you, just a burning ruin. It's eating you up.

It is not that you can no longer see the thieves – the ghoul, the Stone Boy, the nomad girl who taught you briefly to hate. It is that you can no longer know them with certainty. They flicker in and out of your rapidly fragmenting consciousness as they move from one part of you to another.

When the girl runs across the central courtyard, pursued by a Tallowman, you feel every footstep, every panicked breath she takes as she runs, trying to outdistance creatures that move far faster than her merely human flesh can hope to achieve. She's clever, though – she zigzags back into a burning section, vanishing from your perception. The Tallowman hesitates to follow her into the flames for fear of melting prematurely.

You've lost track of the ghoul, but the Stone Man is easy to spot. He stumbles into the High Court, knocking over the wooden seats where the Lords Justice and Wisdom sit when proceedings are in session. The velvet cushions of the viewer's gallery are already on fire. More pursuers close in on him. He's too slow to escape.

Around you, around what's left of you, the alarm spreads. A blaze of this size must be contained. People flee the neighbouring buildings, or hurl buckets of water on roofs set alight by sparks from your inferno. Others gather to gawk, as if the destruction of one of the city's greatest institutions was a sideshow for their amusement. Alchemy wagons race through the streets, carrying vats of fire-quelling liquids, better than water for dealing with a conflagration like this. They know the dangers of a fire in the city; there have been great fires in the past, though none in recent decades. Perhaps, with the alchemists' concoctions and the discipline of the city watch, they can contain this fire.

But it is too late for you.

Too late, you hear the voices of your brothers and sisters cry out, shouting the alarm, rousing the city to the danger.

Too late, you realise what you are. Your consciousness shrinks down, takes refuge in its vessel. That is what you are, if not what you have always been.

You feel a second emotion – fear – as the flames climb the tower. Something beneath you breaks, and the tower sags suddenly to one side, sending you rocking back and forth. Your voice jangles in the tumult, a sonorous death rattle.

Your supports break, and you fall.

CHAPTER ONE

Carillon crouches in the shadow, eyes fixed on the door. Her knife is in her hand, a gesture of bravado to herself more than a deadly weapon. She's fought before, cut people with it, but never killed with it. Cut and run, that's her way.

In this crowded city, that's not necessarily an option.

If one guard comes through the door, she'll wait until he goes past her hiding place, then creep after him and cut his throat. She tries to envisage herself doing it, but can't manage it. Maybe she can get away with just scaring him, or shanking him in the leg so he can't chase them.

If it's two, then she'll wait until they're about to find the others, hiss a warning and leap on one of them. Surely, between herself, Spar and Rat, they'll be able to take out two guards without giving themselves away.

Surely.

If it's three, same plan, only riskier.

She doesn't let her mind dwell on the other possibility – that it won't be humans like her who can be cut with her little knife, but something worse like the Tallowmen or Gullheads. The city has bred horrors all its own.

Every instinct in her tells her to run, to flee with her friends, to risk Heinreil's wrath for returning empty-handed. Better yet, to not return at all, but take the Dowager Gate or the River Gate out of the city tonight, be a dozen miles away before dawn.

Six. The door opens and it's six guards, all human, one two three big men, in padded leathers, maces in hand, and three more with pistols. She freezes for an instant in terror, unable to act, unable to run, caught against the cold stone of the old walls.

And then – she feels the shock through the wall before she hears the roar, the crash. She feels the whole House of Law shatter. She was in Severast when there was an earth tremor once, but it's not like that – it's more like a lightning strike and thunderclap right on top of her. She springs forward without thinking, as if the explosion had physically struck her, too, jumping through the scattered confusion of the guards.

One of them fires his pistol, point blank, so close she feels the sparks, the rush of air past her head, hot splinters of metal or stone showering down across her back, but the pain doesn't blossom and she knows she's not hit even as she runs.

Follow me, she prays as she runs blindly down the passageway, ducking into one random room and another, bouncing off locked doors. From the shouts behind her, she knows that some of them are after her. It's like stealing fruit in the market – one of you makes a big show of running, distracts the fruitseller, and the others grab an apple each and one more for the runner. Only, if she gets caught, she won't be let off with a thrashing. Still, she's got a better chance of escaping than Spar has.

She runs up a short stairway and sees an orange glow beneath the door. Tallowmen, she thinks, imagining their blazing wicks on the far side, before she realises that the whole north wing of the square House is ablaze. The guards are close behind her, so she opens the door anyway, ducking low to avoid the thick black smoke that pours through.

She skirts along the edge of the burning room. It is a library, with long rows of shelves packed with rows of cloth-bound books, journals of civic institutions, proceedings of parliament. At least, half of it is a library; the other half *was* a library. Old books burn quickly. She clings to the wall, finding her way through the smoke by touch, trailing her right hand along the stone blocks while groping ahead with her left.

One of the guards has the courage to follow her in, but, from the sound of his shouts, she guesses he went straight forward, thinking she'd run towards the fires. There's a creak, and a crash, and a shower of sparks as one of the burning bookcases topples. The guard's shouts to his fellows become a scream of pain, but she can do nothing for him. She can't see, can scarcely breathe. She fights down panic and keeps going until she comes to the side wall.

The House of Law is a quadrangle of buildings around a central green. They hang thieves there, and hanging seems like a better fate than burning right now. But there was a row of windows, wasn't there? On the inside face of the building, looking out onto that green. She's sure there is, there must be, because the fires have closed in behind her and there's no turning back.

The outstretched fingers of her left hand touch warm stone. The side wall. She scrabbles and sweeps her fingers over it, looking for the windows. They're higher than she remembers, and she can barely reach the sill even when stretching, standing on tiptoes. The windows are thick, leaded glass, and, while the fires have blown some of them out, this one is intact. She grabs a book off a shelf and flings it at the glass, to no avail. It bounces back. There's nothing she can do to break the glass from down here.

On this side, the sill's less than an inch wide, but if she can get up there, maybe she can lever one of the panes out, make an opening. She takes a step back to make a running jump up, and a hand closes around her ankle.

"Help me!"

It's the guard who followed her in. The burning bookcase must have fallen on him. He's crawling, dragging a limp and twisted leg, and he's horribly burnt down his left side. Weeping white-red blisters and blackened flesh on his face.

"I can't."

He's still clutching his pistol, and he tries to aim it at her while still grabbing her ankle, but she's faster. She grabs his arm and lifts it, pulls the trigger for him. The report, that close to her ear, is deafening, but the shot smashes part of the window behind her. More panes and panels fall, leaving a gap in the stained glass large enough to crawl through if she can climb up to it.

A face appears in the gap. Yellow eyes, brown teeth, pitted flesh – a grin of wickedly sharp teeth. Rat extends his rag-wrapped hand through the window. Cari's heart leaps. She's going to live. In that moment, her friend's monstrous, misshapen face seems as beautiful as the flawless features of a saint she once knew. She runs towards Rat – and stops.

Burning's a terrible way to die. She's never thought so before, but now that it's a distinct possibility it seems worse than anything. Her head feels weird, and she knows she's not thinking straight, but between the smoke and the heat and terror, weird seems wholly reasonable. She kneels down, slips an arm beneath the guard's shoulders, helps him stand on his good leg, to limp towards Rat.

"What are you doing?" hisses the ghoul, but he doesn't hesitate either. He grabs the guard by the shoulders when the wounded man is within reach of the window, and pulls him through the gap. Then he comes back for her, pulling her up, too. Rat's sinewy limbs aren't as tough or as strong as Spar's stone-cursed muscles, but he's more than strong enough to lift Carillon out of the burning building with one hand and pull her through into the blessed coolness of the open courtyard.

The guard moans and crawls away across the grass. They've done enough for him, Carillon decides; a half-act of mercy is all they can afford.

"Did you do this?" Rat asks in horror and wonder, flinching as part of the burning buildings collapses in on itself. The flames twine around the base of the huge bell tower that looms over the north side of the quadrangle.

Carillon shakes her head. "No, there was some sort of . . . boom. Where's Spar?"

"This way." Rat scurries off, and she runs after him. South, along the edge of the garden, past the empty old gibbets, away from the fire, towards the courts. There's no way now to get what they came for, even if the documents that Heinreil wants still exist and aren't falling around her as a blizzard of white ash, but maybe they can get away if they can get out onto the streets again. They just need to find Spar, find that big slow limping lump of rock, and get out.

She could leave him behind, just like Rat could abandon her. The ghoul could make it over the wall in a flash; ghouls are prodigious climbers. But they're friends – the first true friends she's had in a long time. Rat found her on the streets after she was stranded in this city, and he introduced her to Spar, who gave her a place to sleep safely.

The two also introduced her to Heinreil, but that wasn't their fault – Guerdon's underworld is dominated by the thieves' brotherhood, just like its trade and industry is run by the guild cartels. If they're caught, it's Heinreil's fault. Another reason to hate him.

There's a side door ahead, and if she hasn't been turned around it'll open up near where they came in, and that's where they'll find Spar.

Before they can get to it, the door opens and out comes a Tallowman.

Blazing eyes in a pale, waxy face. He's an old one, worn so thin he's translucent in places, and the fire inside him shines through holes in his chest. He's got a huge axe, bigger than Cari could lift, but he swings it easily with one hand. He laughs when he sees her and Rat outlined against the fire.

They turn and run, splitting up. Rat breaks left, scaling the wall of the burning library. She turns right, hoping to vanish into the darkness of the garden. Maybe she can hide behind a gibbet or some monument, she thinks, but the Tallowman's faster than she can imagine. He flickers forward, a blur of motion, and he's right in front of her. The axe swings, she throws herself down and to the side and it whistles right past her.

Again the laugh. He's toying with her.

She finds her courage. Finds she hasn't dropped her knife. She drives it right into the Tallowman's soft waxy chest. His clothes and his flesh are the same substance, yielding and mushy as warm candle wax, and the blade goes in easily. He just laughs again, the wound closing almost as fast as it opened, and now her knife's in his other hand. He reverses it, stabs it down, and her right shoulder's suddenly black and slick with blood.

She doesn't feel the pain yet, but she knows its coming.

She runs again, half stumbling towards the flames. The Tallowman hesitates, unwilling to follow, but it stalks her, herding her, cackling as it goes. It offers her a choice of deaths – run headlong into the fire and burn to death, bleed out here on the grass where so many other thieves met their fates, or turn back and let it dismember her with her own knife.

She wishes she had never come back to this city.

The heat from the blaze ahead of her scorches her face. The air's so hot it hurts to breathe, and she knows the smell of soot and burning paper will never, ever leave her. The Tallowman keeps pace with her, flickering back and forth, always blocking her from making a break.

She runs towards the north-east corner. That part of the House of Law is on fire, too, but the flames seem less intense there. Maybe she can make it there without the Tallowman following her. Maybe she can even make it before it takes her head off with its axe. She runs, cradling her bleeding arm, bracing herself all the while for the axe to come chopping through her back.

The Tallowman laughs and comes up behind her.

And then there's a clang, the ringing of a tremendous bell, and the sound lifts Carillon up, up out of herself, up out of the courtyard and the burning building. She flies high over the city, rising like a phoenix out of the wreckage. Behind her, below her, the bell tower topples down, and the Tallowman shrieks as burning rubble crushes it.

She sees Rat scrambling over rooftops, vanishing into the shadows across Mercy Street.

She sees Spar lumbering across the burning grass, towards the blazing rubble. She sees her own body, lying there amid the wreckage, pelted with burning debris, eyes wide but unseeing. She sees—

Stillness is death to a Stone Man. You have to keep moving, keep the blood flowing, the muscles moving. If you don't, those veins and arteries will become carved channels through hard stone, the muscles will turn to useless inert rocks. Spar is never motionless, even when he's standing still. He flexes, twitches, rocks – yes, rocks, very funny – from foot to foot. Works his jaw, his tongue, flicks his eyes back and forth. He has a special fear of his lips and tongue calcifying. Other Stone Men have their own secret language of taps and cracks, a code that works even when their mouths are forever frozen in place, but few people in the city speak it.

So when they hear the thunderclap or whatever-it-was, Spar's already moving. Rat's faster than he is, so Spar follows as best he can. His right leg drags behind him. His knee is numb and stiff behind its stony shell. Alkahest might cure it, if he gets some in time. The drug's expensive, but it slows the progress of the disease, keeps flesh from turning to stone. It has to be injected subcutaneously, though, and more and more he's finding it hard to drill through his own hide and hit living flesh.

He barely feels the heat from the blazing courtyard, although he guesses that if he had more skin on his face it'd be burnt by contact with the air. He scans the scene, trying to make sense of the dance of the flames and the fast-moving silhouettes. Rat vanishes across a rooftop, pursued by a Tallowman. Cari . . . Cari's there, down in the wreckage of the tower. He stumbles across the yard, praying to the Keepers that she's still alive, expecting to find her beheaded by a Tallowman's axe.

She's alive. Stunned. Eyes wide but unseeing, muttering to herself. Nearby, a pool of liquid and a burning wick, twisting like an angry cobra. Spar stamps down on the wick, killing it, then scoops Cari up, careful not to touch her skin. She weighs next to nothing, so he can easily carry her over one shoulder. He turns and runs back the way he came.

Lumbering down the corridor, not caring about the noise now. Maybe they've got lucky; maybe the fire drove the Tallowmen away. Few dare face a Stone Man in a fight, and Spar knows how to use his strength and size to best advantage. Still, he doesn't want to try his luck against Tallowmen. Luck is what it would be – one hit from his stone fists might splatter the waxy creations of the alchemists' guild, but they're so fast he'd be lucky to land that one hit.

He marches past the first door out onto the street. Too obvious.

He stumbles to a huge pair of ornate internal doors and smashes them to flinders. Beyond is a courtroom. He's been here before, he realises, long ago. He was up there in the viewer's gallery when they sentenced his father to hang. Vague memories of being dragged down a passageway by his mother, him hanging off her arm like a dead weight, desperate to stay behind but unable to name his fear. Heinreil and the others, clustering around his mother as an invisible honour guard, keeping the press of the crowd away from them. Old men who smelled of drink and dust despite their rich clothes, whispering that his father had paid his dues, that the Brotherhood would take care of them, no matter what.

These days, that means alkahest. Spar's leg starts to hurt as he drags it across the court. Never a good sign – means it's starting to calcify.

"Hold it there."

A man steps into view, blocking the far exit. He's dressed in leathers and a grubby green half-cloak. Sword and pistol at his belt, and he's holding a big iron-shod staff with a sharp hook at one end. The broken nose of a boxer. His hair seems to be migrating south, fleeing his balding pate to colonise the rich forest of his thick black beard. He's a big man, but he's only flesh and bone.

Spar charges, breaking into a Stone Man's approximation of a sprint. It's more like an avalanche, but the man jumps aside and the iron-shod staff comes down hard, right on the back of Spar's right knee. Spar stumbles, crashes into the doorframe, smashing it beneath his weight. He avoids falling only by digging his hand into the wall, crumbling the plaster like dry leaves. He lets Cari tumble to the ground.

The man shrugs his half-cloak back, and there's a silver badge pinned to his breast. He's a licensed thief-taker, a bounty hunter. Recovers lost property, takes sanctioned revenge for the rich. Not regular city watch, more of a bonded freelancer.

"I said, hold it there," says the thief-taker. The fire's getting closer – already, the upper gallery's burning – but there isn't a trace of concern in the man's deep voice. "Spar, isn't it? Idge's boy? Who's the girl?"

Spar responds by wrenching the door off its hinges and flinging it, eight feet of heavy oak, right at the man. The man ducks under it, steps forward and drives his staff like a spear into Spar's leg again. This time, something cracks.

"Who sent you here, boy? Tell me, and maybe I let her live. Maybe even let you keep that leg."

"Go to the grave."

"You first, boy." The thief-taker moves, almost as fast as a Tallowman, and smashes the staff into Spar's leg for the third time. Pain runs up it like an earthquake, and Spar topples. Before he can try to heave himself back up again, the thief-taker's on his back, and the stave comes down for a fourth blow, right on Spar's spine, and his whole body goes numb.

He can't move. He's all stone. All stone. A living tomb.

He screams, because his mouth still works, shouts and begs and pleads and cries for them to save him or kill him or do anything but leave him here, locked inside the ruin of his own body. The thief-taker vanishes, and the flames get closer and – he assumes – hotter, but he can't feel their heat. After a while, more guards arrive. They stick a rag in his mouth, carry him outside, and eight of them heave him into the back of a cart.

He lies there, breathing in the smell of ash and the stench of the slime the alchemists use to fight the fires.

All he can see is the floor of the cart, strewn with dirty straw, but he can still hear voices. Guards running to and fro, crowds jeering and hooting as the High Court of Guerdon burns. Others shouting make way, make way.

Spar finds himself drifting away into darkness.

The thief-taker's voice again. "One got away over the rooftops. Your candles can have him."

"The south wing's lost. All we can do is save the east."

"Six dead. And a Tallowman. Caught in the fires."

Other voices, nearby. A woman, coldly furious. An older man.

"This is a blow against order. A declaration of anarchy. Of war."

"The ruins are still too hot. We won't know what's been taken until—"

"A Stone Man, then."

"What matters is what we do next, not what we can salvage."

The cart rocks back and forth, and they lie another body down next to Spar. He can't see her, but he hears Cari's voice. She's still mumbling to herself, a constant stream of words. He tries to grunt, to signal to her that she's not alone, or that he's still in here in this stone shell, but his jaw has locked around the gag and he can't make a sound.

"What have we here," says another voice. He feels pressure on his back – very, very faintly, very far away, like the pressure a mountain must feel when a sparrow alights on it – and then a pinprick of pain, right where the thief-taker struck him. Feeling blazes through nerves once more, and he welcomes the agony of his shoulders unfreezing. Alkahest, a strong dose of blessed, life-giving, stone-denying alkahest.

He will move again. He's not all stone yet. He's not all gone.

Spar weeps with gratitude, but he's too tired to speak or to move. He can feel the alkahest seeping through his veins, pushing back the paralysis. For once, the Stone Man can rest and be still. Easiest, now, is to close eyes that are no longer frozen open, and be lulled into sleep by his friend's soft babbling . . .

Before the city was the sea, and in the sea was He Who Begets. And the people of the plains came to the sea, and the first speakers heard the voice of He Who Begets, and told the people of the plains of His glory and taught them to worship Him. They camped by the shore, and built the first temple amid the ruins. And He Who Begets sent His sacred beasts up out of the sea to consume the dead of the plains, so that their souls might be brought down to Him and live with Him in glory below forever. The people of the plains were glad, and gave of their dead to the beasts, and the beasts swam down to Him.

The camp became a village in the ruins, and the village became the city anew, and the people of the plains became the people of the city, and their numbers increased until they could not be counted. The sacred beasts, too, grew fat, for all those who died in the city were given unto them.

Then famine came to the city, and ice choked the bay, and the harvest in the lands around wilted and turned to dust.

The people were hungry, and ate the animals in the fields.

Then they ate the animals in the streets.

Then they sinned against He Who Begets, and broke into the temple precincts, and killed the sacred beasts, and ate of their holy flesh.

The priests said to the people, how now will the souls of the dead be carried to the god in the waters, but the people replied, what are the dead to us? Unless we eat, we will be dead, too.

And they killed the priests, and ate them, too.

Still the people starved, and many of them died. The dead thronged the streets, for there were no more sacred beasts to carry them away into the deep waters of God.

The dead thronged the streets, but they were houseless and bodiless, for their remains were eaten by the few people who were left.

And the people of the city dwindled, and became the people of the tombs, and they were few in number.

Over the frozen sea came a new people, the people of the ice, and they came upon the city and said: lo, here is a great city, but it is empty. Even its temples are abandoned. We shall dwell here, and shelter from the cold, and raise up shrines to our own gods there.

The people of the ice endured where the people of the city had not, and survived the cold. Many of them died, too, and their bodies were interred in tombs, in accordance with their customs. And the people of the tombs stole those bodies, and ate of them.

And in this way, the people of the ice and the people of the tombs survived the winter.

When the ice melted, the people of the ice became the people of the city, and the people of the tombs became the ghouls. For they were also, in their new way, people of the city.

And that is how the ghouls came to Guerdon.

CHAPTER TWO

"**W**ake up."
    Stone fingers prod her into wakefulness. Cari opens her eyes, looks up at blue sky. The sound of water lapping. She sits up, wincing as her shoulder complains. Someone has dressed and bound the knife wound the Tallowman had given her. Too neat for Spar's work.

"I got bored waiting for you to wake," says Spar, and shrugs. He starts to walk in a circle around their little island.

An artificial island, a pillar of stone in the middle of a water tank or cistern; an artificial lake, surrounded by high walls. Open to the sky. The water is stagnant and brown where it isn't iridescent with alchemical run-off. Green slime stains the rocks. Looking around, she spots a small iron gate in the wall.

"Where are we?"

"No idea. A prison for Stone Men, I guess."

That makes sense. Spar could break that gate down, but to get to it he'd have to cross the water, and he's too heavy to swim, and there's no telling how deep it is. And Stone Men still have to breathe.

"Is this the Isle of Statues?" She's heard of the island of Stone Men out in the bay, a colony established when the plague first appeared in Guerdon, where sufferers were exiled and left to pet-rify. She runs her hands over her own body and face, fearing that she too might be infected with the curse. She can't find any stony growths, but there are dozens of small painful burn marks across her face and hands, like she's been stung by fiery wasps.

Spar considers the question. "No. I heard the bells of Holy Beggar a few minutes ago, so I guess we're somewhere in the upper Wash."

Cari extends her hand. "Help me up?"

Spar doesn't move, just clucks his tongue disapprovingly.

"Right, right." Don't touch a Stone Man. Every city she's vis-ited had its own customs and rules and taboos, and the faster you internalised them, the better. Though Carillon was born in Guerdon, she grew up in the countryside, far from the plague. She stands up gingerly, careful not to put weight on her injured arm. "How did we get here?"

"Some thief-taker caught me. They threw me on a cart and drugged me." He stretches, stone scales scraping off each other. "They caught you, too. I don't know about Rat."

"Did you tell them we didn't burn down the hall?"

"Tell who?" asks Spar. "I haven't seen anyone since I woke up."

Cari cups her hands over her mouth, and shouts. "Hey! Turnkey! We're awake and need breakfast!"

Spar considers the position of the sun in the sky. "Bit late for that."

"And lunch!" shouts Cari. It's been a long time since she had three square meals a day, or even one, but it's worth a try.

Over the wall, someone laughs, but there's no other answer. Cari sinks back onto the least uncomfortable rock.

"Let's get our story straight," she suggests. "We tell them we didn't burn that place down. Hells, Rat and I rescued one of the guards from the fire."

"Some of them died, though."

"That wasn't our fault! You didn't hurt anyone, did you?"

"I tried to hit the thief-taker."

"You were running for your life from a burning building," says Cari. "And will you stop walking in circles?"

"No," says Spar.

"The point is, we didn't burn the place down. There was some sort of explosion, maybe an alchemical bomb." She's seen the weapons of war that the alchemists can make in other places – fires that never stop burning, animals warped into huge monsters, knife-smoke, ice contagions. Alchemical weapons are Guerdon's biggest export.

"We were robbing it, though." Spar shrugs. "No sense denying that."

"They'll hang me for that," says Cari. "I don't know what they do to Stone Men."

They can't hang Spar – his neck is armoured in stone – but doing nothing would be punishment enough. Deny him alkahest for long enough and he'll petrify, and that'll be worse than hanging. Dying of thirst, locked in the stone shell of his own living tomb. It's all ahead of him.

"Let me do the talking," he tells her. "You just stay quiet. The Brotherhood will get us out of this."

"I don't owe Heinreil my neck."

"It won't come to that. You have to trust him. Trust us." *Us*, he says. Trust the Brotherhood that his father founded, and died to protect. And he's right – there's a good chance the Brotherhood can buy their freedom with bribery. But that means she'll owe Heinreil even more, be beholden to the man for the rest of her life.

"Sod that," Cari throws an arm out, gesturing at the mucky lake and blank walls that make up their open-air prison. "I'm not risking everything for that slimy cock-faced goblin." She says that loudly enough to be overheard, and whoever's on the other side of the wall finds it absolutely hilarious. Cari turns to face the laughter and screams. "I want to talk to someone! Come on!"

"Don't tell them anything," insists Spar.

There's no answer anyway. The water laps against their little island, depositing a dead bird on the shore. Spar nudges it back into the lake with one stone-toed foot, and it slowly sinks into the mire. Cari sits fuming on the rock. She scratches at her neck, irritated by the absence of the necklace she usually wears. Throws pebbles into the slime, watches them sink. Patience is not Cari's strongest virtue.

"You were talking in your sleep again," he says after a few minutes.

"I don't talk in my sleep," Cari snaps.

"You were. Some story about ghouls and beasts. It didn't sound like you at all."

"I don't remember," she replies, but she does. Like a dream, all caught up in the bell tower collapsing around her and this strange, out-of-place vertiginous memory, like she'd fallen into the sky. Her head hurts. She rubs her temples, but it only replaces one pain with another as her fingers touch the scorched spots on her skin. Molten metal, Cari realises. That's what made these burns on her hands and face. Like a blacksmith's arms, gobbets of hot metal from the forge. She leans over the foul water, trying to see how badly she's been burnt. The water's more mud than mirror. She pokes at the larger burns with a finger.

"You'll live," says Spar.

"Until they hang me."

"They won't," he insists, but he can't be sure, and she can hear the lack of conviction in his voice. In Spar's father's time, the Brotherhood had enough sway to ensure that a case like theirs would never go to the gallows. But under Heinreil it's a different matter. Heinreil won't spend the money on bribes and lawyers until the return's worth it.

Cari looks at the distant gate. She could swim over – she's a strong swimmer, half her life spent around boats – but the gate looks sturdy and rust-free despite its surroundings. She checks for her knife and lock picks, but they've taken everything except for her shirt and trousers and, oddly, one shoe.

"Hell with it," she says, half to herself, and steps into the water. Her wounded shoulder means she can't swim easily, and all her little scars and cuts sting as if she's floating in lemon juice, and she's regretting the idea by the time she's swum ten feet, but her legs still work and she kicks forward through the slime. She twists awkwardly to keep her shoulder out of the water as much as she can.

"Cari!" hisses Spar, keeping his voice low to avoid being heard. "Come back!"

Halfway across, one of her her legs scrapes against some obstacle, like a reef. She stops, treads slime for a moment.

"What is it?" asks Spar.

Cari probes with her feet, rubbing against whatever's down there, trying to discern its shape. Four – no five spiky protrusions from a column, another one next to it, and something round between them.

A statue, arms upraised. She tries to swim around it, bumps into another one, and another, and another, too; a graveyard of Stone Men.

"You don't want to know." She swims on, using the dead men for support when the pain gets too much for her. She gets a mouthful of slime, chokes on it, spits it out. This was a mistake, she thinks, but there's no turning back now. All the marks on her face are afire now, a constellation of agony that almost eclipses the dull ache in her shoulder.

She glances back, sees Spar shuffling nervously on the shore. He's too far away to help. If he steps off the island, he'll sink and drown.

She's not keen on drowning either. She takes one last breather, balancing on the head of the last Stone Man, then swims the final stretch.

She makes it to the gate and pulls herself up onto the narrow lip. Spar exhales, his lungs rattling like a bag of pebbles. Cari pushes at the gate, rattles it, then starts to climb it. Maybe, if she balances on the top of the gate, she can reach the top of the wall around and climb up, even with one arm bound.

She can hear the sounds of the city now, muffled and distant but there nonetheless, the murmur of crowds, shouts and barks, the rattling hiss of train engines, the tolling of the bells of the Holy Beggar—

The Tallowman is burning low now. Guttering. It makes it hard to concentrate. It leaps to another rooftop and misjudges the distance, landing badly, sprawling on the roof tiles and slipping towards the street far below, but it's so light, so much waxy flesh burned away, that it can easily catch itself. Like a spider skipping across the surface of a pond. *I'm a spider*, it thinks, with some part of its brain grown soft enough for whimsy.

It laughs and leers at the meat people down below. They look away, or cower, or hasten their pace. They fear the Tallowman, and that's good. It could go down there, have fun down there. Be faster than them, stronger, better – brighter.

The smell of blood reminds it of the mission. It cut the ghoul, so there's a blood trail to follow. Its nose, though, is drooping, melting, and blocked with its own wax. It jams two fingers up its nostrils (remembering to put the axe down first; wouldn't want to chop its own head off) and wiggles them about, opening channels from the outside to its hollow inside where its flame-self burns. It adjusts the nose, remoulding it so it's more dignified. In a rare moment of self-reflection, the Tallowman acknowledges that it's burnt for too long and needs a good long soak in a tallow vat. Needs a new wick threaded through its body, for this one's nearly gone. The Tallowman must buy each new life with the good deeds of the previous one. If it doesn't catch the ghoul, maybe the alchemists won't remake it. Naughty candle, reduced to a puddle with an axe.

Focus.

The Tallowman inhales sharply. The candle flame in his head flares with the rush of air. Bread-baking, cattle shit and blood from the slaughterhouses, soot from a thousand thousand chimneys and smokestacks, salt and oil engine oil, fruit smells and melting sugar that might make it hungry if it still had a stomach – and ghoul blood, slow and thick and sweetly rotten. The ghoul came this way, and the trail's pointing straight to Gravehill. The boy's going to earth.

Gravehill, the old city quarter of the dead, is on the far side of Castle Hill. It's a long climb for a ghoul, especially in the daylight. Especially a wounded one. Castle Hill is like a wall, dividing the portside districts and the old city from the newer suburbs beyond. Not that Gravehill is new; it's old, but, as Guerdon expanded, people built houses in and atop the tombs of their ancestors, and now the living and dead crowd together in that slum. Ghouls are common there, unlike the rest of the city.

If the Tallowman were fresh, it would spring up the long zig-zagging rows of steps that ascend the south face of Castle Hill. Take them at a run, six or eight at a time, flashing past the red-flushed faces of servants and clerks climbing towards the homes of their betters, past living guards and watchmen. It might even dare to scamper up the cliff face itself; some previous iteration of city folk carved into the sides of Castle Hill, excavating tunnels and halls in the hard rock, so the climb is steep but not impossible for a mere human, and easy for a fresh Tallowman. But it's not fresh, so he looks elsewhere.

Down there, off to the right, there's a tunnel cutting, a place where the subterranean train lines that run beneath the city come to the surface. The Tallowman leaps from rooftop to rooftop, skittering across tiles. It might be a rat, or a bird, or a ghost to those below, whose sleep is disturbed by strange noises from above. One last scramble, then a spring, and the Tallowman clings to the side of a stone tunnel mouth that swallows the train line.

There it waits, inhaling the smell of the ghoul's blood so it'll be able to follow the trail on the far side. Each inhalation makes the Tallowman's wick flare brighter, melting more of its body.

The train thunders by, and the Tallowman leaps onto the roof as it passes. Stumbling now – one side's a little softer than the other – but still lightning-quick, it swings over the edge of the carriage roof and through a narrow window. The carriage is half full of sailors and night workers on their way home, but no one dares question the Tallowman's sudden entrance. Hands muffle shrieks of alarm; shouts are swallowed. It's guild business, always guild business – best not to cross their path.

It takes a seat between a tattooed sailor and a grey-robed student, who pretends not to notice the grinning, glowing wax effigy that sits next to her. It crosses its legs, resting its long knife across its knees. It trims the worst of the melted wax off its fingers to keep them nimble.

The train rattles and screams under Castle Hill. It smiles politely at his fellow passengers and doesn't cut any of their throats. The brakes squeal as they come to Gravesend Station. Passageways lead off deeper underground, for those commuters whose business brings them down below here. A branch line, the

Mortuary Line, to one of the big churches and its corpse shaft. Instead, the Tallowman takes the stairs, leaping up them in two bounds, past the shocked face of the ticket inspector in his booth and out into the cold morning air of Gravehill.

It takes too long, too long to catch the ghoul's scent, too many minutes scuttling along drainpipes on Leavetaking Square, too long poking amid the coffin-pocked dirt piles near the new Last Days mausoleum. The smell's coming from the oldest, deepest part of Gravehill, the catacombs and warrens of the ghouls. The Tallowman can't be afraid – it's not capable of such an emotion – but it can fret, and flicker at the thought of taking on many ghouls at once. Ghouls are tough, like old leather instead of the soft juicy gushing meat of humans. Still, a blunt knife offers its own amusements, too.

As it turns out, it needn't have worried. The ghoul didn't take refuge in the main warren, where the majority of the city's ghouls live. The rat's hole is down in another crypt. The Tallowman laughs. Find the ghoul, kill him, then go back to the alchemists, beg for another turn in the mould, a fresh body. It dares to hope.

It stalks down dusty marble stairs into the crypt. The blood smell is strong here. Soon, it'll get even stronger.

The Tallowman turns a corner into another chamber, and there's a woman there. Human, not a ghoul, her features illuminated only by the light that shines through the Tallowman's thin shell. Skin like cracked leather, close-cropped hair, eyes of brilliant blue.

It leers at her with its misshapen face, brings the knife up to threaten her, but she doesn't flinch.

"Are you the fuckwit that scared off all the bloody ghouls?" she asks. "Place is quieter than—"

Flicker-quick, the Tallowman is at her side, knife at her throat.

"Just don't," she says, and there's not a trace of fear in her voice. It doesn't have the energy left to be curious about this strange woman. She's not its quarry. It tries to speak, to question her about what she saw, but its vocal cords melted hours ago and it can only gurgle. Instead, it points at the blood trail, gesturing angrily.

"Leave the ghoul alone and sod off, please."

Infuriated, the Tallowman releases the woman and ducks around her. Moving on all fours now, nose-hole pressed to the ground, following the blood trail. It leads through a stone door that's slightly ajar, and the Tallowman wriggles through, leaving the edges smeared with soft wax. Beyond, a short passage that ends at another stone door. Heavy, but even in its diminished state the Tallowman should be able to force it open quickly. It throws itself against the stone, feels the door give very slightly. It can smell the ghoul on the other side, so close it can almost taste the blood. The ghoul pushes back, trying to hold the door closed, but even stringy ghoul muscle cannot compete against the strength and speed of a Tallowman for long.

And then, behind it, the first door starts to close, scraping along the floor. The Tallowman moves, lightning-fast, knife whipping out to cut at the arm of the woman in the outer crypt. The blow scrapes off armour hidden beneath her clothes. She gets the door shut, and now the Tallowman's trapped in the narrow space between the two crypts.

It bounces back from one door to the other, slamming into each one, testing the strength of the person on the far side. The ghoul's weaker, it decides, and starts pushing on that door. It hurls itself against the door again and again, but the ghoul holds firm.

The Tallowman's flame dwindles, yellows, darkens. The stone doors are air-tight, it thinks with its last thought.

Then the flame goes out, and the Tallowman is just a wax statue, as lifeless as any other corpse in Gravehill.

*

"So it is what we choose to rescue from the burning house that matters. It is only in moments of crisis and despair that we reveal what we really value."

Olmiah clasps his hands together and smiles at the congregation. It was, he thinks, one of his best sermons to date – topical, insightful, relevant, but carefully calibrated to be understandable by the mob. He only wishes that his superiors had been in the church to hear it – such things are always best experienced firsthand – but Bishop Ashur is off at some emergency civic meeting, and Seril is ministering at hospitals, so while his audience is scarcely diminished in size, its political sway is grievously diminished this morning. The Church of the Holy Beggar is one of the seven oldest Keeper churches in Guerdon, and thus supposedly one of most prestigious, but while all men may be equal in the eyes of the gods, here in the mortal realm things are more subtle and complex.

This sermon, with its political overtones and witty allusions to the previous day's fire, would go down far better at the Church of St Storm or the Church of the Holy Smith, or the golden chapel in the alchemists' guildhall – which isn't one of the seven but has a lot more influence. So Olmiah is told anyway, usually by his mother, whose knowledge of church hierarchy and politics bewilders him. At the very least, he can tell his mother about this sermon when it's done.

His eyes scan the crowd beyond the line of flickering candles, and alight on a woman in the front row. Gods above and below, she's beautiful! Young and slim, richly dressed, yellow hair glimmering in the candlelight, jewels glittering in her bosom, and, best of all, an expression of rapt attention. She's transfixed by his words, her spirit lifted.

Who is she? Without being at all obvious about it, he directs his speech towards her, preaching and praying in her direction so he can admire her as he talks. She's clearly the daughter of some wealthy aristocrat or guild master, although he can't see any sigils that might indicate what family she comes from. Nor, to his surprise and concern, can he see any bodyguards or chaperones by her side. She's there surrounded by the poor folk, a jewel in the mud, seemingly heedless of the criminals and beggars that press on her from either side.

Clearly – and the thought strikes him with such clarity that he nearly loses his place in the litany – she is a young woman of such burning, passionate faith that she sought out his church. She endures the stench and filth of the commons, of those beneath her, in order to hear the words of the charismatic young priest whose reputation has clearly spread beyond the walls of the Holy Beggar to whatever glittering palace this beauty calls home. But oh! – she is in peril, terrible peril. Her spirit is so bright, her soul so pure, that she has walked into this den of corruption without realising the danger. There are alleyways not two minutes' walk from this church that Olmiah himself is scared to go down alone. What must it be like for this beautiful girl, so slim and delicate? Why, the instant she leaves the protection of his church, she'll surely be assailed by brutes, stripped of her finery, her nakedness revealed to the world. Their rough peasant hands will tear at her dress, ripping it away from her legs, her breasts.

Olmiah loses his place in the litany again. His voice is no longer a clarion trumpet of faith, but a tortured squeak. The congregation breaks into laughter – all except the woman, who smiles encouragingly. Even, dare he say, lovingly.

The church bell rings, throwing him off even more. Olmiah frowns, wondering if some filthy urchin has crept into the bell tower and started playing with the ropes, but he realises that his sermon waxed somewhat longer than it should have, and the noon hour is upon them. The bell-ringer of the Holy Beggar is blind and half deaf. His employment, like many others in this parish, is an act of charity, so Olmiah must forgive him for interrupting.

"Let us bow our heads in prayer!" shouts Olmiah, grateful for the brief respite that he can use to find his voice and place again. Fifty heads bow down – all except the girl, who defiantly looks straight at him, a rebellious angel in microcosm.

Gods below, what a creature! Thoughts so impious that he would scarcely have believed himself capable of conceiving them gush through Olmiah's mind.

Obviously she cannot be allowed to leave. It wouldn't be safe. She must stay within the walls of the Holy Beggar until suitable transportation can be arranged. After the ceremony, he'll bring her into his private quarters – insist on it, tell her that there are theological matters to discuss with her – and then he'll send out for a carriage to take her home. Though it's hard to find a carriage on market day, so she might have to wait for hours. Perhaps even overnight.

Like a drunk, he staggers to the end of the ceremony. It lacks the grace and conviction it possessed before he saw the girl, but she doesn't seem to mind and the unwashed masses can't tell the difference anyway. You could dress a donkey in gold cloth and teach it to bray in time with the litany, and they wouldn't know the difference between it and Bishop Ashur.

He dismisses the congregation. They rise and flood out of the doors. First the sick ward, kept separated from the rest by blessed red ropes, plague sufferers, god-cursed veterans, Stone Men. Then the rest, the common folk of the Wash. It reminds Olmiah of the opening of a sluice gate that empties a pool, the muddy waters of the crowd swirling and churning before pouring into the river.

Leaving gold behind. She remains seated, eyes fixed on him, bright and beautiful.

He stumbles towards the angel. She rises to greet him. Without a word, she takes his hand, leads him back towards the private chambers at the back of the church. He fumbles with the door lock, feeling the heat of her body through his cassock.

It's all going so much better than he expected. For a moment, he wishes his mother was here to see it. She won't be able to sniff dismissively at him now!

The door opens. They step inside into the private darkness.

He turns to the girl to beg her name, but she's not there anymore. She's unfolded like a flower, all her beauty and wealth peeling away, unravelling, leaving only a tangle of chaos and hunger. He's unravelling, too, strips of his skin detaching painlessly from his arm, his face, to fall into the whirling vortex of the Raveller. Nerves, muscle, bone follow, threads of cassock, too, glittering cloth-of-gold merging into the whirling chaos that is all that remains of the dress she wore.

The unravelling reaches his torso, his head. For an instant, his vision is impossibly elongated as she devours his eyes.

Then all he can think about, forever, is her. He understands, in that moment, that she too was a victim of the Raveller. Multiple victims, even – her beauty taken from one woman, her grace from another, her clothing from a third, her eyes from another, all knitted together. Now he adds his threads of existence to the Raveller's collection, and in that he finds some measure of union with the girl.

The bells continue to ring, drowning out whatever noises he might be able to muster.

Spar watches Cari swim away from the little island. He steps to the very edge, to the precipice that drops away into the murky waters. He has learned to manage frustration and anger since succumbing to the plague, as it stole portions of his life, one by one. He knows that if Cari starts to drown, there is little that he can do to save her. If he plunges into the water, he'll drown too and there'll be two bodies in the lake instead of one. He watches helplessly from the edge. He doesn't pray to any gods, but with all his soul he wills her to make it across.

She drops beneath the surface once, twice, choking on the slime, but with a final kick she reaches the gate. She grabs it one-handed and hauls herself up. Shouts out in the hall, then starts climbing.

Ever since becoming stone, he'd had a dread of heights, of falling. He grinds his fingers nervously as Cari clambers up the gate, using the bars as a ladder. She's too short to reach the top of the wall, but she probes for handholds, for cracks in the mortar. She finds one, digs her fingers in, pulls herself up. Another foot closer to the top. Spar groans – at this distance, he can't see the cracks, he can't tell if she's got a secure handhold or if it's going to give way and let her fall.

She stops abruptly, her whole body freezing in place. "The young priest is dead," says Cari. Her voice is distant, as if she's reciting something learned by rote.

Then she falls backwards off the wall, and splashes into the mire, still in some sort of a trance.

Spar roars at her to wake up, to breathe, to grab onto the gate, but she sinks beneath the surface and vanishes. He bellows for whatever guards there might be in this strange prison.

Running footsteps, and figures appear at the gate. One's the thief-taker, the man who so thoroughly beat Spar the night before – or however long ago it was; Spar realises that days could have passed while he was unconscious and drugged with that potent dose of alkahest.

"She's in the water," roars Spar, and points. The thief-taker has his hooked pole, and plunges it into the water, swirling it back and forth until it catches on Cari's shirt. He hooks her and pulls her to the door, then lifts her out. She splutters, throws up brown slime, but she's alive. The thief-taker carries her away, and another guard, a fat man, relocks the iron gate.

"Is she all right?"

No answer.

Spar is left alone again.

Hours pass. The sun vanishes behind rain clouds. He catches enough water in his hands, cupped like a stone basin, to slake his thirst, but he's still ravenous. Older Stone Men, he's heard, stop feeling hungry or full, and have to remember how long it's been since they last ate, or they risk their stomachs petrifying or bursting.

He's got nothing to eat, so he takes pleasure in his hunger. It's a mark of pride that he's still alive on the inside.

As dusk falls, the thief-taker returns. He unlocks the gate and pushes a small boat, a skiff, onto the water, then punts across the lake. When he's close enough, he throws a sack to Spar.

"Thought you might be hungry."

Spar doesn't move. "Why don't you join me? Plenty of room on my island for two."

The thief-taker laughs. "I'm fine here on my little boat. Miss Thay is well, by the by."

He doesn't know that name. "Who?"

"The girl. Carillon."

Spar knew Cari was short for Carillon, but she'd always been evasive about her family, and he didn't pry. She was a runaway, he knew that much. Thay sounds distantly familiar, but he can't place it.

"Interesting young woman," continues the thief-taker, "but she's not a thieves' guild member, is she?"

Spar shrugs. "I hardly know her," he lies.

"Oh, some would disagree with you," says the Thief-taker, laughing at some private joke. "You met her through Heinreil, of course, and the brotherhood."

Stony silence. It was Rat who introduced Cari to Spar — brought her to his door one night, sick and shivering like a stray kitten. But Spar's not going to implicate Rat unless . . .

"You must have known the ghoul well, though. The third member of your little gang."

Spar crosses his arms, and it's like the stone door of a tomb slamming shut.

"Or were the ones who blew up the vault part of the gang, too?"

"I don't know anything about that." That much is true.

"Just a coincidence it happened at the same time as your break-in?" The thief-taker scoffs. "I think you've been set up, boy, and they're counting on you being a noble fool to take the blame. Like I told Miss Thay, I don't give two shits about you or the ghoul or her, or whatever you were doing in the Hall. I want Heinreil."

"I don't know anyone by that name. I do want a lawyer. It's my right."

The thief-taker sighs. "This was one of the first quarantine hospitals, before they sent your lot to the Isle of Statues. Shameful place. I don't want to keep you here, but I don't have a choice — not unless you give me Heinreil."

"No."

"Ah, I forgot. You're Idge's son, aren't you? The great man himself, the hero who stole from the rich and gave to the poor. The man who didn't talk. What happened to him? Remind me, what became of his courage and conviction?"

Spar doesn't answer. Turns his back on the man.

"Well then." The thief-taker reaches inside his jerkin, holds up a brass syringe, tipped with a steel needle big and thick enough to punch through the stony crust above Spar's flesh. "How often do you need alkahest? You're pretty far gone from the way you walk. Every week? Every five days? Probably more often if you're cooped up in here, with shit to eat and no space to move."

He dangles the syringe above the waters. "I can wait until your legs seize up. Wait until there's nothing left of you but a mouth and eyes. I don't even need eyes, really, I suppose. Just a tongue to give me a name."

He throws the syringe onto Spar's island. It clatters and bounces, but Spar snatches it up before it can roll off into the waters.

"My name's Jere," says the man. "I'm telling you that so you can thank me."

Spar stands there, unmoving, the alkahest cupped like the precious thing it is in his left hand.

"All right," says Jere, "we'll see if you thank me next time. And you will, sooner or later. Don't be a fool, lad. Your friend Cari's no fool — and she's not coming back here."

CHAPTER THREE

"My name's Jere," said the man, "I'm telling you that so you can thank me."

Cari's teeth chatter, she's shaking like she never has before. She's half drowned and soaked, but it's not nearly drowning that scared her.

It was whatever caused it. Like something had reached in across the city and carried her mind away. The particulars of the vision are fading fast, like a dream forgotten on waking, but she remembers being inside a church, old and dark, and some horrible thing taking the young priest apart. It hadn't felt real at the time, either. She'd seen things from every angle, from above and below and the sides. Maybe not seen. It felt like seeing at the time, but ...

"I was a fly on all the walls," she says to herself.

"You're welcome." Jere shakes his head in disbelief. "Here, before you freeze." He drops a bundle of grey cloth in her lap.

"What's this?"

"A change of clothes." He sits down in the chair across the desk from her, and reclines, watching her, waiting for a show.

"Turn around," she demands. She's changed her clothes in public, been naked in front of strangers before, there's no room for modesty on a small ship, but she's not going to let this thief-taker win at everything.

"Turn my back on a girl who carries this?" he asks, and produces her knife, her treasured little dagger, from a pocket. The last time she saw it, it was going into her own shoulder, driven by the wax hands of the Tallowman. "You'll get it back if you behave."

"Well, you've got my knife now, and I haven't, so turn your damn back."

Jere laughs at that, spins his chair around. She wriggles out of her wet clothes, wincing at the pain in her shoulder. The bandage over the wound is soaked from within and without, the brown-green stains of the slime meeting the red-brown of dried blood. She unwraps the old bandage.

"I'll need a new wound dressing," she says.

"Someone else will see to that."

The garment he's given her is a grey robe, belted at the waist, like a monk's habit. She's seen other people in the city wearing them before. She pulls it on over her head, wriggles into it. It's too big for her, but it's warm and dry. There are undergarments, too, and a pair of sandals.

"Is there any food?" she asks.

"Someone else will see to that, too."

"Thank you, Jere," she says, mockingly.

He turns back to her. "Normally, a little sneak like you isn't worth my time. You're not even a citizen – they'd let the candle-makers have you, not that there's enough of you to make a nightlight. But here's the thing."

He reaches into a desk drawer and pulls out a big leather-bound ledger. It's just like the ones in the library in the House of Law. She saw hundreds of books identical to that one burn.

Jere notices her surprise. "It wasn't in the archive. Strange thing – someone had consulted the book with your birth records in it the day before, so it was down at the reading room in the south wing, and so it survived. Like you, Carillon Thay."

He flips the book open to a marked page.

"Born here in Guerdon twenty-three years ago. Father Aridon Thay, of *those* Thays. Mother unknown — normally, it's the other way around, so we'll assume the stork delivered you to the family mansion. If I'd known you were quality when I arrested you, I'd have put you in a nicer cell."

"Give that one to Spar," she suggests. "I like the water."

"Clearly you do. I spent the morning asking about you, Miss Thay, when I should have been finding out who blew up the Tower of Law. Your family packs you off to an aunt out in the country as soon as they can. It seems you don't like it there much — at twelve, you're reported missing. Of course, the Thays have other things to worry about than one wayward daughter, what with them all being murdered."

He pauses, looks at her for a moment. "If you confessed to that crime, you'd definitely be worth my while."

"I was four," she says. She scarcely recalls most of her old family, other than her Aunt Silva. Her memories of her stern-voiced grandfather Jermas are stronger than those of her father, who she remembers only as a pale, distant presence.

Jere continues. "Not much in the way of an inheritance either — turns out the Thays were in debt up to their eyeballs, although that only came out afterwards. But you're off at sea. Off in Severast, and Firesea, and the Twin Caliphates, according to some tales I heard down the docks today. I'd have called you a beggar and petty thief, but because you're quality, we've got to say *adventuress*, haven't we?"

He closes the book, gently, keeping the page marked.

"So, four months ago, you come back here."

"Not by choice. There was a storm and the captain took shelter here. Then they wouldn't let me back on board."

"Because you were a stowaway."

"I offered to work my passage."

"Why so eager to leave?" Jere asks. She doesn't have a good answer. She never felt comfortable in Guerdon, or anywhere near it. The whole city feels like it's pressing in on top of her, burying her beneath its mountains of masonry, its history, its crowds. She doesn't like it.

When she doesn't answer, he continues. "Now, here's where I take notice. You fall in with that ghoul boy. He introduces you to the Stone Man, Spar. And Spar is one of Heinreil's brutes. So, you know Heinreil."

She keeps quiet, as Spar told her, but it's hard to swallow her venom. Heinreil stole from her, but, more than that, he humiliated Spar, and she hates him for that. It rankles to see her clever friend treated like a filthy dog, and rankles even more to watch Spar enduring it, taking Heinreil's lashes and cruelties without complaint, out of loyalty to his dead father. Family has never meant much to Cari, and dead family even less.

"He sent you to rob the House of Law," says Jere.

She forces herself to shrug noncommittally, but she knows she isn't fooling anyone.

"He set you up."

She bites her lip.

"So give him to me."

She wishes she could. She'd do it in a heartbeat – but she doesn't know enough. She's not Brotherhood, so she's not privy to those secrets. And Spar would never forgive her. She shakes her head.

"All right," says Jere, "who arranged it all? Spar? Was it Spar?"

It was Spar, but she doesn't want to let him take the fall. It's clear from the way the thief-taker's acting that something else is going on, that she's in much less trouble than she should be. She's got lucky, but can't see how. Maybe she can carry Spar with her.

"It was Rat," she lies, "he knows Heinreil. Spar was just there in case we got spotted and had to fight our way out."

Jere clicks his tongue. "Pity about that ghoul boy, then."

"What happened to him?" She had assumed that Rat had got away across the city, made it back to the Brotherhood safe house.

"Ask the Tallowman." Jere picks up her dagger and slips it into a sheath. Then he pulls a sticky black cord of some kind from a drawer, and knots it tightly around the dagger and sheath, binding it in place. "Clever stuff, this. The alchemists make it. You can only cut it with a special blade, or dissolve it with chemicals. We use it on prisoners, these days." He hands her the bound knife. The black cord is springy and slightly damp to the touch.

"Miss Thay, you're guilty as sin, but I'm neither judge nor jury so I don't care. Your bounty's been paid, so you're free to go."

"What about Spar?"

"His bounty hasn't been paid. He's not free to go." Jere raises his voice. "Come and take her, if you really want her."

Cari's trick to appearing calm is to make herself hollow. She swallows herself, pushing all her nervousness and fear deep down inside and pretends she's a metal statue, a model of a girl. Then, when the time comes to bolt, she lets it all out and it's like the whip of a line under tension, this elastic explosion of speed that gets her out of trouble. She's run away from strange men and monsters in a dozen cities and ports across the seas. She moves too fast for trouble to catch up with her.

This time, though, she can't judge the right moment to bolt. This situation isn't like all the rest.

He says his name is Professor Ongent, this man who bought her bounty from the thief-taker. He's old but not frail, with a round belly, beard like an unkempt hedge and little owlish glasses that she's not sure if he really needs, the way he peers at her over their rims. Like her, he's wearing a shapeless grey robe, although he's got a woven belt of gold-and-blue threads and a silver chain around his neck. He smiles warmly at her.

"I'm afraid you'll have to leave the name of Carillon Thay here, child," he says, "it would draw attention to you – and to me, and I've just invested quite a lot of money in you."

The last time anyone did that, it was to sell her to slavers in Ulbishe. "I don't use it anyway." Her robe doesn't have pockets, so she fumbles around for a place to put her peace-bonded knife. It keeps slipping out of the belt.

"Shall I keep that for you?" offers Ongent.

"S'fine." She manages to roll the sleeve of the baggy robe back over itself to make a sort of pocket for her knife. It's not like she can use it anyway, with Jere's clever alchemical rope holding it in its sheath, but the familiar weight is comforting.

Ongent and Jere have a brief, whispered conversation – they obviously know one another. Cari can't quite figure out who's in charge, or if they're friends or just have a common interest.

Jere growls at Cari. "You'd best not make trouble, girl."

She nods, pretending to be cowed. She doesn't make trouble, it finds her.

"I've arranged accommodation for you at the university," says Ongent, "and a position as a research assistant."

The sheer weirdness of that is enough to make her follow Ongent out onto the street. It's twilight, so he produces a little alchemical glow lamp from his bag and shakes it. It sheds a bubble of greenish light that throngs the deserted street with eerie half-shadows. He leads her up a steep flight of stairs out of the Wash towards Phaeton Street. Dark alleyways and lanes lead off the stairs, into a maze of small houses and tenements, and she tenses as they pass each entrance. Ongent just keeps huffing and puffing up the steps, as if he's out for an afternoon constitutional and his only worry is getting to the top of this little hill, not getting robbed and left in a ditch.

She contemplates robbing him and leaving him in a ditch.

"We'll take a look at that wound on your arm tomorrow," says Ongent. She flexes her shoulder, and it aches.

"I'll be fine," she says, "I just need to wash it out and bind it again. It's not a deep cut."

"It wouldn't be, no. They like to play with their victims."

She wonders why an academic would know so much about how the Tallowmen behave, or maybe it's common knowledge these days in Guerdon. They pass one at the arched entrance to a subway on Phaeton Street. This Tallowman is made from a young girl, younger than Cari, but grotesquely stretched to fill the six-foot-six mould used to make the monsters. The wick's light shines through her fang-like teeth as she examines Ongent's pass. Cari gives the creature a wide berth – the monsters turn violent when they feel trapped.

"And the wounds on your face?"

She'd almost forgotten the constellation of little burns, where the molten metal from the burning tower struck her. She brushes her fingers over them. "It's nothing."

The professor clucks his tongue as if disappointed. He pauses halfway down the stairs. She can hear the rattle of the trains below, the hiss of steam. The walls of the stairwell are covered in posters and bills, thickly plastered one on top of the other. Advertisements for sovereign cures and fortune tellers, recruiting posters for mercenary companies, notices of city ordinances and curfews. He peels them away, burrowing through the papery shell to the stone wall beneath.

"Can you read?" he asks.

"Yes." One legacy of living with her Aunt Silva, that country house was full of books. Her cousin Eladora always had her nose in a book. Only a year or two older than Cari, but always giving the impression of having been born middle-aged and dully dependable. At times they'd been close, allies against Silva or the neighbour who rented the land when Eladora's father got sick. Mostly, they'd quarrelled.

Ongent pulls down the last scab of parchment, revealing the wall of the stairwell. It's made from a greenish stone that looks wet to the touch. It's carved with symbols.

"Can you read these?"

She peers at them, then shakes her head. "No."

"Few can. These are ghoul tunnels. There are thousands of them beneath the city. Many are flooded or abandoned. Others are used only by the ghouls. Others, like this one, have been reclaimed for civic purposes, their origins forgotten except by those who study the history of the city." He touches the symbols, almost reverently. "That's my vocation, my field of study. I lecture in the history and archaeology of Guerdon."

He starts down the stairs, expecting her to follow. She looks at the symbols again. There is something familiar about them, but she can't place it.

"Come along, please," he calls. Her instincts tell her to run – she could dart back up the stairs and vanish on Phaeton Street, maybe follow it down to the docks and stow away on board a ship bound for distant lands. Be gone by dawn. But she owes Rat, and Spar, and maybe even this strange professor. Owes Heinreil something else, even though her knife's wrapped in that alchemical bond. And, anyway, there's a Tallowman right there at the top of the stairs.

"One of your friends is a ghoul, I believe," says Ongent. He keeps his voice low, pitched for her ears alone, even though the station's nearly deserted. "I had Jere do a little investigating today," he adds apologetically.

She shrugs.

"Did he ever discuss history with you?"

She scoffs.

"Have you ever discussed topics like the ghoul anarchy or the Varithian Kings with him or anyone else?"

"I don't even know who they are."

"I take it you haven't read, say, De Reis' *A Critical Assessment of the Pre-Reclamation Era*. I wrote the preface for the second edition you know," he adds, blushing slightly.

"No."

"Then we have a mystery," he says. "When Jere found you in the ruins of the House of Law, you were talking in your sleep. Specifically, you were reciting the tale of 'How The Ghouls Came To The City'. That's a story known only to the ghouls – and the few scholars who bother to study their culture, of course."

Before she can answer, the station fills with clouds of acrid chemical steam and the train rolls in. They step on board into a nearly empty carriage. Cari flinches; she's never been on an underground train like this before, and it unsettles her. The thought of being trapped deep below a city, carried forward against her will, getting further and further from the open air . . . it's like a nightmare of being buried alive.

"Maybe I heard it somewhere before," she offers as explanation, more to herself than to him.

"Possible," admits Ongent, "if unlikely. Tell me, Cari, have you . . . heard any other stories?"

"I had . . . I blacked out in the prison, before I fell in the water. I saw something then, too."

"*Saw* something?" asks Ongent. "Did you also see things before, when you told the ghoul story?"

"I can't remember. I think so, but I don't know what." Green stone tunnels, like this one. The taste of corpse meat. Freezing cold. Huge figures, squatting on gigantic stones.

"And what about the second time? What did you see then? Another story?"

"No – it was like I was seeing some young priest in an old church. There was a woman in the crowd, and he wanted her – but she . . . she sort of fell apart and ate him, and became him."

"Well then, that's a task for another day." The train huffs and groans as it drags itself out of the low-lying Wash, climbing some steep subterranean incline.

"What is?"

"Finding that old church, and seeing if the young priest is really dead."

He says it like it's a perfectly sensible, normal thing to do.

"What if it was just a dream?" she asks. Though it didn't feel like a dream, and dreams don't make you black out at the worst possible moment.

"Then perhaps, in time, you can be Carillon Thay again. I have friends in many places in Guerdon, including parliament, and they can be your friends, too. Or, if you prefer, we will part on good terms, and you can leave the city again and never return." He smiles at her. She doesn't like it. "But I don't think it was a dream. I think you contacted something – or, rather, the reverse. It contacted you."

"Like what?"

"I have no idea," he says happily, as if glad to have a mystery.

"Have you heard of anything like this happening before?"

"Oh, there are certainly all manner of gifts and curses. Psychical prodigies, saints, sorcerers, wild talents, god-touched and the like. I'm sure that, with study, we can learn more about your . . . condition. Be thankful that I found you before the alchemists did – that would not have been pleasant for you, believe me."

The train emerges from a tunnel mouth and crosses the Duchess Viaduct, high above Glimmerside, the city's pleasure garden. Ahead is the University District, sprawling down the east and north sides of Holyhill like run-off from the shining cathedrals. Cari peers out of the window. She's far from the parts of the city she knows, and wants to get the lie of the land in case she needs to run. The Keepers' cathedrals catch her eye – three on the crest of the hill, all made from the same white stone and so similar that they could have been made by the same architect – and below and around them, a riotous confusion of other temples and churches. Beyond the temple precincts are the halls and theatres of the university, crammed wherever they'll fit, driven by immediate necessity instead of some divine plan.

Both Temple Quarter and the university flow into Glimmerside, creating a strange borderland where the theological and spiritual realms mix with the unbridled commerce of the lower city. She looks down on streets of coffee shops, of suppliers of rare goods and curiosities, of backstreet temples and bawdy theatres catering to both the intellectual pretensions and base lusts of the students. On the far side of Glimmer, above the docks, is a haze of multicoloured smoke, marking the edge of the Alchemists' Quarter.

She catches sight of a temple like a rose, sharp crystals of quartz catching the last rays of the setting sun.

"There's a temple to the Dancer." She's always liked those temples, when she visited them in other cities. The cult of the Dancer sought their divinity in movement, in ecstatic dance, in the ceaseless whirl. Cari was even an initiate of the temple in Severast for a few months.

"Guerdon has had many gods in its day. You were born during the years of the Holy Strife, but when I was young, the only churches in the city were those of the Keepers, and foreign faiths were suppressed. That couldn't last, of course, not with so many immigrants and foreign traders gaining influence in parliament, and the scandals with the relics. The disestablishmentarian bloc had the votes to push through a reform bill, but the adherents of the Kept Gods fought back on the streets. Riots, civil strife, even assassinations, but underlying the religious debate were tensions between the established wealthy families and the powerful newcomers. It might be . . . " He trails off when he notices Cari staring at him. "Well, you'll have to attend my lectures if you're to pose as my research assistant."

That, she can predict without any mysterious gifts of foresight, is not going to happen.

The train screeches to a halt, and Ongent pulls himself upright, grunting with the effort. "Come along."

Leaving Pilgrim Station, they follow a winding street that skirts the edge of the university. It smells of money – still rundown, but they've hosed off the cobblestones recently and the buildings are in good repair. Ongent toddles along ahead of her, moving quicker now that he's on familiar ground. He turns a corner, onto Desiderata Street. He brings her to a townhouse. Small by the standards of the rich folk who can attend the university, of course – the place Cari shares with Spar is a tenth the size of these places, and she only had that much space because no one else risks sharing with a contagious Stone Man.

She wonders how Spar is doing in that flooded prison cell. She wonders if Rat's alive or dead. She doesn't trust her own run of luck. It feels like a betrayal.

Ongent raps on the door. Cari hears running footsteps. The sound of two bolts being drawn back, the crackle of a magical ward disarming, then the door opens and a girl peers out at them. Her round face is familiar to Cari, but it takes her a moment to place it.

"Carillon?"

"Don't use her name," cautions Ongent as he hustles Cari inside. "Remember, Eladora, no one can know she's your cousin."

CHAPTER FOUR

R at, in a tunnel.

Ghouls can see the dark, see all the colours beyond black. The rich variations of shadow, the subtle shades of empty tunnel, and the yawning, blazing, darkness of the deep places below. There's more to Guerdon below than above, in cellars and passageways and dungeons and sewers, in the buried forgotten pasts of the city, and all its unseen arteries and bowels, and more below the city than its inhabitants can imagine. The surface folk are insects crawling on skin.

He lingers in the darkness, but he cannot remain here. He needs to get back to the surface. He's hungry, and he can smell dead flesh down in these tunnels. He should get back up to the sunlight, pay coin for bread and meat in the market, or maybe just catch some of his namesakes and choke them down whole, live and wriggling. Ghouls are corpse eaters by nature. Rat wants to eat dead flesh.

But it's also in the nature of ghouls to change, and he doesn't want that. So he pushes away his hunger, thinks of sunlight, and goes back to the door to the surface tomb. He has to drag it open, stone scraping on stone.

With ghoul eyes, he considers the form of the Tallowman. Its waxy flesh is luminescent in his vision, shedding a sickly glow from the melted scars. He bends down and touches the wick that protrudes from the creature's spine. It's cold and slimy, but when his skin makes contact there's a spark, a tingling thrill that numbs his arm, and the wax form twitches. The thing isn't wholly dead.

Experimentally, he tries digging his claws into the Tallowman's neck, wondering if he can dismember it without too much effort, but the congealed wax is now harder than marble. He sits back and licks his fingers while he considers his options. He could try burning it, but that might relight the wick and bring the monster briefly back to life, in which time it'll kill him a dozen times over.

The door at the far end of the little passageway is smeared with waxy marks after the Tallowman tried to force its way out. It's a heavy stone slab, the lid of a tomb, but suddenly it's flung aside like it's made of wicker. The woman shines her alchemical lamp into the darkness, pinning Rat in the harsh light. "Oy, you. Stop where you are," she says, and then she raises a hand and recites a phrase in the tongue of the dead. Her pronunciation is terrible, but the meaning is clear to Rat, to all ghouls. *We who attend to souls call ye who attend to bodies.* She's an agent of the Keepers. "Also," she adds, "I helped you with that candlefucker. So you owe me, right?"

Rat hesitates. After the debacle at the Tower of Law, he needs to find Spar and Cari, to report back to Heinreil, maybe even get paid, but he can't ignore the Keeper woman's invocation either. He eyes her warily: "What do you want of the ghouls?"

"Church business. For the lugholes of yon ancient horrors only."

"Find another guide. I'm busy."

"Fuck you," she says, "if you think I'm freezing my arse off in this graveyard all night. Anyway, you don't want to go back up yet. The hill's crawling with Tallowmen, and I don't think you want to be out there now." Rat freezes, wondering how much she knows about his ties to the Brotherhood. *"We call ye and command ye"*, she adds in dead-speak, "so pay heed to your betters and show me the way down."

Heinreil's only a man. There's worse in the world than him. The ghouls will punish him if he pisses off their allies in the church of the Keepers.

"All right," agrees Rat, "but stay close and keep up. And I'm just bringing you down to them below – getting back is your own affair. I'll not wait for you."

"Right," she says, and extends a gloved hand. Her grip is incredibly strong. "Aleena."

"Rat." Half the ghouls in the city call themselves Rat.

"That's not your—" and she says a word in dead-speak that roughly means your real name, your ghoul name.

"It's not, but that's not *church business*, now is it?"

"Fair enough."

Aleena gathers up her belongings, stuffing a blanket and the remains of a meal into a bag. Rat spots a gilded, ornate scroll case among her belongings, nestled next to a massive pistol. He licks his rough tongue over his broken teeth, wondering what the Brotherhood would pay for that. Aleena stretches, rubbing her neck, then her wrist. She flexes it experimentally, and seems satisfied that she's not hurt. "Beaten up by a fucking table ornament. I'm getting old."

Rat starts off down the tunnel.

"Wait." She takes out the pistol. "There's more of them candle-fuckers around."

Rat hoots, and says, "They're like the rest – they go in, but they don't come out. You won't need that thing, but keep it in hand if it makes you braver. Just don't shoot me in the back." The door grinds open. Aleena puts the pistol back in her bag and picks up the lamp.

"Not that," says Rat. "Trust me, there are things you don't want to see. Things you mustn't see, too. If you bring that lamp down, you'll be leaving your eyes below." He puts just the right lugubrious notes of menace and wicked humour into his voice; it's a spiel he's given before. The elders are picky about their privacy.

"I've been down here before. And if anything wants to take my eyes, I'll shove theirs up their arse if they have one." Still, she puts the lamp back away.

They descend into the darkness. He leads her by a circuitous route, for there are no straight paths down here, just a choice of labyrinths. She stumbles on rough floors and loose bones. She tries keeping one hand pressed to the tunnel wall, so he brings her under one of the city's sewage works, down paths where the walls ooze black, and after that she keeps her hands to herself, her only tether to the surface Rat's infrequent commands. Alchemical waste slithers past her legs, half-alive piles of pus that sprout blind eyes and hairy whiskers. They pass through abandoned sections of the city, and through still-inhabited ones. A door leads them into the cellar of a tavern, and he whispers to her to stay quiet as they pass beneath a room full of dock workers breaking their fasts. She can move surprisingly quietly when she has to, but otherwise she's loud as a sewer boar in the tunnels. He can tell when she bumps or brushes against a new obstacle by each fresh profanity.

Down through subway tunnels and sewer lines, tracing Guerdon's growth like rings in a tree.

Down through the old ghoul tunnels – the upper, abandoned ones. As the city above grows, those below dig deeper and deeper, maintaining the distance between them, and forcing those things that dwell even further below to retreat into earth. There are wars in the dark that the surface folk never know about.

Down through temples to old and forgotten gods, past empty

plinths where the darkness is stained, darkness so deep that even Rat is unsettled.

They come to one of the corpse shafts, and Rat calls for a stop. "You can have a little light here," he says, and grins in anticipation.

The alchemical lamp flares, brighter than the sun. Rat expected a scream, but he's disappointed. Aleena's expression is unchanged beneath the encrusted dirt and cobwebs; she doesn't flinch or recoil at the sight. She raises the lamp, letting its lights beams explore the heights of the circular shaft. It's not strong enough to reach even halfway up, but it's clear that far above is one of the city's mausoleums. Dozens of corpses dangle from ropes or hang from meat hooks. Chemical sluices keep the flies away and mask some of the stench. The floor is a carpet of gnawed knucklebones.

"I thought we'd stop for a spot of lunch," says Rat, grinning.

Aleena turns the lamp down so it's just a little bubble of light around her, then trudges over to a stone block. "Aye, you know how to show a girl a good time. Lucky I brought my own."

He can smell her food. It's vile, chalky and gritty and thin and tasteless. He should eat it, beg a few crumbs of surface food instead of taking from the grisly bounty that surrounds him. But he's not that strong.

Rat vanishes into the darkness and finds himself a juicy thigh bone. The ghoul-hunger is on him now, primordial, deep and dark, like there are endless tunnels in his guts that can only be filled by cadavers. There have been times when pickings have been slim indeed, when all they send down is withered, grey-fleshed old men and women, with nothing on their bones but ash and the memory of sorrow. There have been times of plenty – times of plague, or war – when these shafts get choked with so many bodies, and the ghouls swell up like the fattest of maggots, their bellies so swollen they can scarcely fit through the tunnels.

Things are good enough right now, but Rat knows the elders are unsettled. There are more churches in Guerdon now, temples to foreign gods, and they don't dig corpse shafts like the Keepers do.

As he eats, he watches the human. The lamplight makes her skin sickly white. Her cloak's wrapped tightly around her to keep out the cold of the tunnels – although the heat of decomposition makes the shaft as hot as a sauna. She eats with gusto despite her surroundings, shovelling the food into her thickset form. She's missing two fingers off her left hand, and the puckering of the flesh around the old wound tells Rat that a sword blow took them. Ghouls are natural anatomists.

Rat wrenches a finger off a hanging corpse and sucks it, the little gobbets of meat and tendon sliding off the bone into his mouth. It's another three hours to the elders, maybe four or five if he has to drag a blind human all the way. Then another ten hours' slow climb back up to the surface. There are short cuts, though, that would bite two or more hours off that tally. He chews the knucklebones contemplatively, rolling them around his cheeks as he thinks back to the previous night's mission. The Tower of Law collapsing, wreathed in roaring fire, the ground quaking and splitting as something lashed out furiously from below. The Tallowmen everywhere, like rivulets of molten wax dripping over the city. Spar, outlined against the fire, lumbering across the courtyard. Rat doesn't give much for his friend's chances, not these days. Not with the plague. The thought of Spar's meat petrifying makes Rat suddenly nervous; every piece of gristle on those finger bones feels like a pebble between his teeth. Ghouls usually can't get the plague, he reminds himself, but it can still poison them. He spits out a particularly hard lump, which rings as it strikes the floor.

Aleena looks up at the sudden noise, peering into the impenetrable darkness of the shaft. She peers straight at Rat, but obviously can't see him. He grins to himself, then bends down and finds the lump of fingerbone. His fingers probe it, pick it apart, and find an unexpected treasure. A little golden ring. The undertakers must have missed it. An old ring, bought in youth, lost in the fatty folds of middle age. Humans, he thinks, get weaker as they age, slower. Ghouls are different.

Carillon's another matter. She might have made it clear, if she was quick. She doesn't know Heinreil, or how to contact the master of the Brotherhood. She might go back to Spar's place, or she might just run. Rat found her on the streets when they'd both gone for the same dropped purse, and took ... pity is a surface word, unused by ghouls. An interest, maybe? Like Spar, she was a lump of gristle he could chew over and over. She's been good to Spar, too – treats him like he isn't dying, and that kindness counts with Rat.

He recalls evenings in Spar's little room, when Rat would crouch in the corner by the fireplace and listen to Spar rumbling on about some issue of the day, about some scandal or news from the war. Spar talks like he's in parliament, or addressing a mob in Lambs Square. Cari, wine in hand and boots up on the table, asking questions despite herself, or punctuating Spar's oratorical flights with gentle mockery. Rat rarely speaks in those evenings; he likes to close his eyes and listen to his friends talk, like voices echoing down from above. The warmth from the fire softening his leathery muscles, heating his sluggish blood.

If those evenings have been taken from him, it's one fewer tie to the surface. He wants to be done with this errand, wants to know if his friends are alive or dead. Impatient, he circles around behind Aleena. His hooves are silent as the tread of a ghost, but she still tenses when he draws near, that three-fingered hand closing around a weapon beneath her cloak. He stops at the edge of the light. "Time to go."

She looks around at the hanging bodies and sighs. "Holy Beggar, cherish your children," she prays, invoking one of the Keeper gods, and then she douses the lamp. Something rustles in the distance, a limp limb falling into place, maybe, and they both freeze for a moment, listening for some distant danger. Rat grabs her hand and pulls her towards the next door.

"Down."

Down again. The path now is well-trodden by ghouls climbing up from below to visit the body shafts. Rat is an outlier among his kind; these days, only a few ghouls bother with the surface. Still, the going is treacherous, slick with corpse fat and fungi. Great broad-headed mushrooms, fruiting from the tunnel floors, and patches of hairy tendrils that glow a million colours in Rat's dark-adapted eyes, but would bleach to a ghastly pale furze if Aleena's lamp touched them.

He chooses a route that's faster, but harder. Slipping and sliding over rocks. Squeezing, at times, through natural caves, the edges worn smooth by the passage of ghouls. Through corridors of cut stone, built by forgotten peoples. Through abandoned sections of the city, and tunnels he hasn't visited in years.

Aleena stumbles, and stops. She reaches down with her free hand, and her fingers touch a metal rail along the floor.

"This is a train line!" she hisses angrily. "We've gone in a circle, you little shit!" She wrenches free of Rat's grasp and grabs at the lamp.

Light flares in the darkness. Rat stumbles back, suddenly blind.

Aleena sees. A train car, grubby and battered like all the rest, but disconcertingly familiar in this chamber of warped shapes and slithering colours. Rune-etched rails run off into the distance, vanishing into a wet-lipped tunnel mouth. Stalactites of slime or jelly hang from the ceiling, glistening in the sudden brightness. There's no platform, just a carved promontory that runs up like a gangplank to the train's doors. Beyond it, a shape rises and moves, a rolling tide of fat yellow-white worms, knotted together.

Rat grabs her, pulls her behind the train. "Not *your* trains," he hisses through broken teeth. He curses himself for risking this short cut.

"It's a Crawling One," she whispers, "they're not—" She's going to say "dangerous", but Rat interrupts her.

"Different down here." He paws at her lamp, turns it down, but it's too late, they've been spotted. There's a wet squirming noise as the worm-colony rolls towards them. Scout-worms range ahead of the main body, crawling over Rat's hooves, Aleena's worn boots, dripping down from the roof of the train car and slithering down Aleena's back.

Aleena steps out around the corner, right into the creature's path. The Crawling One engulfs her like a wave, its million writhing fingers pouring over her. She vanishes from sight beneath the slimy horde without a moment to scream. Then the worms part, withdraw. Rat half expects to see Aleena's picked-bare skeleton emerge, but she's still alive. Slimy and annoyed, but otherwise unharmed.

The worms pile on each other, knot together, build shapes. Two towers rise, then intertwine into a thicker torso, an approximation of the human form. Arm-knots dangle limply down for a moment, then spring into animation, producing an all-encompassing black cloak that it wraps around itself. Thick worm-fingers pull a white porcelain mask from nowhere and lift it into place, concealing the horror beneath. Crawling One sorcery – the worm-colonies are much better at withstanding the stresses of spell casting than any human, so they've carved out a niche as sorcerers for hire.

"Forgive me," says the Crawling One, "We did not expect to meet a representative of your most holy church down here." Its voice is oddly musical and warm, but behind it she can hear the flapping and slithering of the worms, like hot fat on a frying pan.

"What, may we ask, brings you walking in the places beneath?" It extends a cloth-wrapped "hand" to Aleena and helps her up. She feels worms pop and squish beneath the cloth as she pulls herself upright.

"Clearly, I'm down here for my health. My doctor told me to spend days wading in shit. Wish I'd know I could have taken the bloody train," says Aleena, casting an angry glance at Rat.

"Do you like our conveyance? It's exceedingly swift. Not on the public maps, of course. We have an arrangement with the authorities." The Crawling One leans forward, conspiratorially. "It's a terribly long commute without it, you know."

The porcelain mask swivels to look at Rat, still crouched behind the train car. "Your guide led you astray, we see. The fault is not yours, but that of your feckless ghoul." The Crawling One advances towards Rat. "The ghouls know better than to cross us."

"Leave the little shit alone," says Aleena, "I told him to make haste. I've got a message for his elders."

"What, may we ask, is the substance of this message?" The Crawling One rises up, more than seven feet tall now, swaying as it looks down at Aleena.

"Church business," she replies. "None of yours. We'll leave you be."

"We are exceedingly well-informed on many matters," reply the swarm. "Perhaps we can be of some assistance?"

Rat sidles away from the Crawling One, out of the dim sphere of light from Aleena's slime-encrusted lamp, backing away towards another exit. The mask isn't facing him, but the Crawling One has ten thousand eyes, and their dark vision is even better than a ghoul's.

"You can tell us, or we can take it from his meat." There's a flash of sorcery, and Rat goes sprawling on the ground, a smell of scorched ghoul hair from the burn on his chest. Worms wriggle towards him, little sharp-toothed mouths snapping. Crawling Ones and ghouls both feed on dead flesh, but for very different reasons. Ghouls do it out of hunger, but Crawling Ones do it to consume the memories – or perhaps, the souls – of the deceased. Every one of those thousands of worms contains a lifetime of knowledge stolen from the dead.

"Wait!" Aleena holds up her hands, an unexpected note of fear in her voice. "I don't know the message. It's on a fucking scroll. Here." She unslings her backpack and kneels down. The Crawling One stops advancing towards Rat. Limbs and torso reknit so its approximation of a human form faces towards Aleena again. Rat exhales in relief. Maybe, if she gives the sealed scroll to the Crawling One, it'll let them go. They can walk out of here and go down to the elders so Rat can discharge his cursed responsibility to her then go off to find Heinreil and get paid. Or, better yet, Aleena hands over the scroll, decides she can't continue her errand, and they both go back to the surface. A cautionary tale, no real harm done, and Rat will never, ever go near the Crawlers' territory again. He can see a safe way out of here.

And then Aleena pulls that pistol from her bag.

Shit, thinks Rat.

"Said it was none of your business."

The gun roars, far louder than any weapon its size has a right to do. The porcelain mask shatters, and the head of the Crawling One explodes. That won't kill it, of course, won't even really slow it down. It swipes blindly at Aleena, but she rolls back and draws what looks like an antique short sword as she springs to her feet. *Swords won't do much either*, thinks Rat. It's a colony, not a single creature. Killing one or even a hundred worms just annoys the swarm. The best way to really hurt a Crawling One is—

Aleena's sword bursts into flame. That's handy.

She swings it at the Crawling One, trying to set its robe alight, but the monster recoils out of reach, its knotted body elongating obscenely. She darts forward, sword blazing brighter than her lamp. The Crawling One retreats, momentarily confused. She gives it no time to use its sorcery, no space to work magic. It tears off the encumbering robe and rears up, shying away from the burning brand.

Aleena steps forward, the light of her sword reflected in her eyes. She seems taller now to Rat, growing in stature as she advances until it is she who towers over the Crawling One. "Back, you fucking great pile of willies!" She moves with terrible deliberation, one heavy tread after another, her broad feet picking their spots one after another, always stepping to stable ground. The Crawling One slithers, slops, flows ahead of her. Rat scuttles and darts, dodging between the two combatants. He's outclassed here. He runs for a hiding place.

Lightning erupts from the Crawling One's limb. The flash lights up the chamber, driving away the shadows. The force of the bolt disintegrates the Crawling One's arm, causing it to unknit and fall apart, worms tumbling hither and yon or burning up in the backlash. Aleena gets her flaming sword between her body and the spell-bolt just in time, but she's still driven to her knees as her miracle contends against the sorcery of a multitudinous, eldritch thing on its home ground.

The flames on her sword gutter and die. The light fades. Now the only illumination comes from her discarded little lamp.

Aleena struggles to her feet and stands at the edge of that circle of light. Blood streams from her nose, her ears. "You think that was clever, do you? My nephews will go fishing with you as bait, you hear me? Come on, stop skulking there!"

From out of the darkness, the Crawling One replies. Without its shattered mask it speaks in a fuliginous chorus of voices, whispering in a thousand other languages beneath its words. "Haste not from the charnel clay, but fat and instruct the very worm that gnaws, subsumed in the totality, ever-birthed ever-consumed by the dead hand that moves the blind eye that sees . . . "

To Rat's eyes – but not to Aleena's – the colour of the darkness changes. He can see shapes in it now, creatures of shadow, gathering around the black tower of the Crawling One. It has more arms now, and they sway and gesture, weaving a greater spell.

Power gathers around it. The darkness falls towards it, drawn in by sorcery. There is no longer any air in the chamber, and Rat struggles to breathe. The dark shapes close on Aleena.

And then Rat finds the brake lever on the train carriage, and pulls it. With grinding solemnity, the train starts to move, slowly at first, then faster and faster down the slope as if it too is drawn in by the Crawling One's spell. Little sparks of blue leap between the train's underbelly and the rails on which the Crawling One stands. Rat flings himself out of the side door, landing heavily, scrambling forward on all fours.

The Crawling One collapses before the train rolls over it. It falls into its constituent worms, dropping from a nine-foot-tall figure to a thick writhing carpet in an instant. The sound of some of the worms popping as the train rolls over them is lost in the general clamour and roar.

Rat grabs Aleena. "Run!" she screams in his ear, and he's not going to argue. Hand in hand, they run down corridors at random, trusting in Rat's instincts to find ones that slope down.

After an unknown time, they slow by mutual consensus, catch their breath.

"God's shit," says Aleena. "That's your idea of a fucking short cut? Let's save time by getting sodomised by magic worms?"

"If you hadn't lit that lamp . . . " hisses Rat, but he's still gasping for air and can't finish.

"Well, aye." Aleena says ruefully. "I wasn't expecting a bloody train station down here, now, was I? When you descend into the bloody bowels of the earth to consort with elder fucking horrors from before the dawn of history, you don't ask if there's a convenient transport option, do you?"

Rat shrugs. There are stranger things down here. He warned her of that.

"Ah, fuck." Aleena holds up the tattered remnants of her backpack. The scroll is gone.

Cari doesn't do reunions. She doesn't do returns in general.

It's equally awkward for Eladora. Cari quickly works out that Ongent hasn't told her cousin anything about Cari's life since leaving the house they shared as children, or about her strange condition. Eladora seems to think that the professor took Cari in out of charity, that he's a soft-hearted old duffer who's lying to the university to put a roof over Cari's head. He just plucked Cari out of prison, and dropped her here, in this quiet house of books and closed doors and neatly folded clothes, and then toddled off home up the hill towards the university, leaving her alone with Eladora.

Almost alone – there's someone else in the house, in an attic room. She can hear footsteps, the creak of movement, but this housemate remains unseen.

Eladora uses politeness like a caulker uses pitch, slathering hot shovelfuls of it over every crack in the conversation. She starts off babbling about mutual relatives, and people they knew in childhood. Cari didn't care much for any of them at the time, and the intervening years haven't made her grow any fonder. There's also the conversational reef of the Thay murders, which Eladora has been trained not to mention and Cari doesn't want to talk about, so any discussion of family requires careful navigation.

The university starts off as a safer topic. Eladora's one of Ongent's students in the department of history. Professor Ongent's a wonderful teacher. Isn't it wonderful to be here in the great city of Guerdon, with all its sights and strangeness? Why, it's even a little bit wild – sometimes, Eladora and her friends go slumming down in Glimmerside.

It becomes clear that they have lived in very different Guerdons. Eladora's polite smile freezes in place as she listens to Cari casually describe bits of the city she never knew existed. At one point, Cari mentions how the Tallowman stabbed her, and Eladora drops her teacup. It smashes on the floor, though Eladora's expression doesn't change in the slightest.

It's too much fun. Cari starts telling her dear cousin more stories about her travels overseas. Some are true, some aren't, but Eladora has no way of telling which. Eladora mentions the fighting pits in tones of horror; Cari was once chased by a death worm in the swamps. Eladora has a blue jade bracelet; Cari remembers helping a steal a cargo of blue jade off the coast of Mattaur. There's a boy in her class that Eladora likes; Cari was a temple dancer in Severast for a while, and so on.

The *pièce de résistance* is when Eladora asks where Cari was staying in the city before Ongent brought her here, and Cari replies that she was sharing a small flat with a Stone Man. Eladora suddenly remembers something urgent she has to do, and retreats to the bathroom. There's the sound of frantic scrubbing, and Eladora doesn't come back for half an hour. (The next morning, when Cari gets up, she discovers that the kitchen has been scrubbed with a chemical cleaner, and the teacups they used have been hurled into the fireplace, crushed and burnt.)

Eladora shows Cari up to her room. First floor, next to Eladora's. There's another room on the floor above, up a narrow staircase. There are new locks on the door, but no key. No books on the shelves. Sheets freshly laundered, and another three robes like the ones she's wearing folded on a chair.

"It's almost like we were back in mother's house in Wheldacre," says Eladora, even though it's nothing like that. "It's so good to see you again, Carillon", even though it clearly isn't, "but you must be exhausted."

The last one's true.

Cari's bed is larger and softer than any she's had in years. Her belly's full for the first time in months. She's warm and dry and safe, but sleep is still hard to find. She worries about Spar, about Rat. Every time she nearly falls asleep, she hears voices at the edge of her consciousness, whispering to one another, calling out across the rooftops. Sometimes, it's like they're right outside her window.

Finally, she gives up. Gathering her blankets, she goes downstairs into the cellar and makes a bed for herself in a dark corner.

Finally, she sleeps, and does not dream.

CHAPTER FIVE

Jere watches the Stone Man sleep. Stone Men have to be restless sleepers, changing position every few minutes to ensure they don't calcify through stillness. Jere's known sufferers who employ elaborate solutions – servants who prod them awake every hour, slanted beds they slowly roll down, clocks and time-candles and other aids to wakefulness. Others just train themselves to snatch sleep in brief naps throughout the day, never staying still for more than half an hour at a time.

Most sleep standing up, in case they can't get up again. Nothing kills a Stone Man quicker than getting stuck lying down.

Trapped on his little island, Spar has nothing to lean against, nothing to wake him up if he sleeps too long – nothing except his own terrors. He jerks awake every few minutes, dragging himself painfully upright to shake out his stony limbs and check to make sure no joints have locked in his slumber.

The boy jerks awake again, and spots Jere sitting offshore in the little rowing boat.

"Breakfast," shouts Jere, and throws a parcel of food. Spar tries to catch it, but he's still dull and slow with exhaustion, and he fumbles it. The parcel lands in the water with a splash. It sinks in the shallows at the edge of the island. Jere could paddle around and pull it out, but he has no intention of getting that close to his prisoner. He has too much respect for the Stone Man's strength.

Anyway, hunger might push the boy into giving up Heinreil.

Spar drags himself over to the water's edge, fearful of slipping on the slimy rocks and sliding into the depths. He fishes the soaked package out of the water. The wet paper separates under his grasp, and chunks of bread float out across the green sea.

"Feel like talking?" asks Jere.

Spar sits down with his great granite back to the thief-taker and starts to eat what remains of the already paltry meal.

"I'll be back this evening," calls Jere, and paddles back to shore. He checks the box of alkahest syringes in his office before leaving. Just one left. He'll need to find more. Jere prides himself on being able to break the will of the toughest prisoner, but this is Idge's son. Idge, who defied the city and the watch and took the noose to protect the Brotherhood he founded.

The Thay girl's file is still on his desk. He picks it up and leafs through it in irritation. A day wasted on a spoiled runaway who doesn't know the first thing about the Brotherhood. Still, the professor owes him a favour, so it's not a total loss. He shoves the file into a cubbyhole and takes the ledger of births and deaths from the ruined hall of records with him. He's not sure what to do with it – officially speaking, he shouldn't have removed it in the first place, but he's learned to trust his luck. Finding the relevant records intact, instead of incinerated with all the rest – it has to mean something, even if he can't discern what that is yet.

Jere's next appointment is at a coffee house on Venture Square. It's an upmarket place, so he pulls his good coat on over his leathers. He leaves the hook staff hanging on the coat stand, and instead takes a sturdy walking cane with a hidden blade. The coat has nice big pockets, big enough to hide a small gun, big enough to hide Jere's own hands, with all their scars and calloused knuckles. He shaved this morning, another concession to the quality. It pays to look respectable when mixing with members of parliament.

He sticks his head into Bolind's room. The big man is slumped on the cot-bed like a beached whale, reading a newspaper.

"I'm off. Keep an eye on Idgeson in there."

"Right you are, boss. Bring me back one of them little sweet rolls, would you?"

"Do I look like a waiter?"

The newspaper twitches aside as Bolind appraises him. "Naw, more like an ape dressed up as a man-whore."

The coffee shop has been Effro Kelkin's de facto office for more than forty years. Every morning, the old man still stomps through the market, glad-handing his supporters and glowering at rivals, checking prices and the cargo listings of ships the same way a beggar counts the coins in his bowl. Then, he goes to his table in the back room of the *Vulcan*, where, the legend insists, he's still nursing the same cup of coffee, endlessly refilled.

Jere knows more about Kelkin from Professor Ongent's habit of spouting lectures on political history than he does from the man himself. Kelkin can be famously charming when he wants to be, but Jere is an employee, not a potential supporter, so he gets the other side of the man, sour as bad vinegar.

A generation ago, Kelkin was the most powerful politician in the city. He was the architect of the industrial-liberal coalition that broke the theocratic hold on parliament, the champion of the merchants and investors whose fortunes ebbed and flowed through Guerdon's docks. Once in power, he led a crusade against "crime, corruption and dissent". As Ongent put it, instead of trying to heal the wounds of the Strife, he cauterised them with fire. The Keepers still hate him for that, and there are always rumours that Kelkin's secretly a member of some underground sect or cult. After observing his employer of nearly four years, Jere the Thief-taker suspects that Kelkin's only gods are Money, mated to the holy bride Trade, and their twin sons Order and Power.

This is the city you made, thinks Jere, *a city that overtook you*. These days, Kelkin's old industrial-liberal faction is a neglected minority in parliament – the power's in the hands of the guildmasters, especially the alchemists, and Kelkin's feud with Guildmistress Rosha is famously bitter. A few years ago, Kelkin tried to outflank the alchemists on law and order, and in response they brought the Tallowmen out onto the streets, leaving Kelkin struggling to catch up.

Still, it puts Kelkin's money in Jere's pocket, as the old politician tries to make any impact he can on the city's organised crime. Already, there are calls for the Tallowmen to be taken off the leash, to give the waxy horrors more authority to hunt down criminals.

Jere steps into the welcome warmth of the coffee shop, shoulders his way through the press of customers up to Kelkin's table. Normally, he has to wait in line for an audience, but not today.

"I should have you strung up by your thumbs," hisses Kelkin. "That was a debacle."

"I haven't had breakfast yet, boss," objects Jere, "so give me a moment before you have your tantrum."

"I'll feed you your own fucking entrails. You think it's funny that the House of Law is still burning?"

"Of course not. Of course that's a disaster – but it's on the alchemists more than you. They had candles burning all over the place last night, and they still didn't stop the attack. If they can't protect the highest court, then they can hardly argue that the security of the whole city be put in their hands, can they?"

"I'm not paying you for policy advice," snaps Kelkin. "What about Heinreil?"

Jere catches a waitress's eye, mouths an order. She nods. Kelkin raps Jere across the knuckles with a spoon. Inwardly, Jere laughs – he appreciates the old man's insolence. Kelkin has to know that Jere could break his old neck in an instant with his bare hands, not to mention the dozen or so weapons the thief-taker keeps concealed under his greatcoat.

"There were two gangs of Heinreil's thieves in the House last night. One group, I guess, were trying to break into the treasure vault under the tower. They're the ones who set the bomb, and it looks like they underestimated how big a blast they made. I haven't got an alchemist's report yet – I will – but I'm guessing that first group died in the blast.

"The second lot were supposed to be a distraction, to pull the guards away from the vault. A Stone Man, a sneak-thief and a ghoul. The Tallowmen got the ghoul, but I caught the other two."

"Who was the thief?" asks Kelkin.

Jere considers his answer carefully. The Thays were part of Kelkin's coalition at one point, weren't they, but that doesn't mean they weren't his bitter enemies, too, and Kelkin keeps meticulous track of debts and favours and punishment owed. If he mentions the girl's true identity, it could cause further problems. Anyway, Kelkin is paying him to track down Heinreil, not Carillon Thay. She's Ongent's bounty. The champion of free trade can hardly blame Jere for having multiple clients.

"Just some human girl, fresh off the boat from Severast. Not even a Brotherhood initiate. Disposable."

Kelkin grunts in irritation. "So you have nothing."

"I have the Stone Man, locked up in the old lithosarium down by the Wash. He was the leader of their group, and he knows Heinreil."

"Directly, or through an intermediary?"

"Directly, I think. I haven't cracked him yet, but—"

"But he'll need alkahest, yes. You know the Keepers are giving it even to criminals in prison now? Charitable dolts. Pennies in the collection plate for the poor going right into Rosha's pocket, and for what? Another few miserable days of life for the walking dead?" Kelkin snaps his fingers. "I'll make arrangements with Vang or one of the other magistrates, get a writ so you can keep the Stone Man in custody for another month. If you haven't broken him by then, he'll have to go to the regular courts ... or are you thinking he won't testify against Heinreil ever?"

Heinreil isn't the only person who considers Spar disposable.

"I think I can get to him. He's stubborn, and loyal to the Broth— the thieves' guild, but I can work on him, convince him that Heinreil sold him out to distract the guards, that it's not like the old days."

Kelkin nods. "I'll get you an extended writ."

Jere can almost hear the clack of abacus beads behind the bushy eyebrows, the quill scratching in the great ledger of debts. A favour owed to a magistrate to keep Spar in Jere's custody for longer; another debt to Jere, to be repaid with silver. And always, the continuous accumulation of compound interest on the vast debt that Kelkin considers the city owes to him.

"What was in the vault?" asks Jere. "Knowing why they wanted to break into the House of Law might help."

"Well, let's get you a list."

They leave the coffee shop. For an old man, Kelkin sets a frightful pace, hobbling along like an angry beetle. Jere spots Kelkin's carriage waiting in Venture Square, but the old man marches off on foot towards Mercy Street.

The smell of ash. Soot stains on windows and walls. The strangeness of the skyline without the Tower of Law rising like a sentinel over the district.

They pass the gallows.

They pass a memorial erected by the Keepers, marking the spot where condemned prisoners were once auctioned off for human sacrifice to various cults, during one of Guerdon's previous flirtations with religious liberties, long ago. The Keepers used gory tales of that blood market as an argument against Kelkin's plan to open the city to foreign gods.

They pass a line of watchful Tallowmen, like a row of burning torches marking the edge of the incident.

Inside, workers pick through the rubble. Many, Jere notices, are Stone Men. When the disease first broke out, thirty or so years ago, Kelkin ordered the infected to be rounded up and imprisoned in a salt mine outside the city. Thousands calcified to death there, and the Stone Riots brought down the government of the day. Even Jere feels a chill when one of the ailing monsters spots Kelkin and recognises him. A rumble of discontent runs through the crowd.

Kelkin ignores them, walks past them as if they're already calcified.

Stone Men are being used to dig through the remains because the ruins are still hot. Definitely an alchemical bomb – the weaponmongers have perfected fires that never go out, acid that can eat through a ship's hull, gases that blind and choke. Lycanthrope serums, transmutation clouds. The Philosopher's Bomb.

A large crowd has gathered on Mercy Street, on the far side of the Tallowman line. A smaller, but much more exclusive crowd has also gathered on this side, on the blackened grass of the central courtyard. Guildmistress Rosha, the most powerful woman in the city, and her proxy in parliament, Droupe, arguing with a bunch of robed Keepers over custody of the remains of the bell that once rang from the top of the tower. The Keepers argue that it was a blessed relic of the church, despite being installed in a civic building; Rosha says that analysis of the metal will reveal much about the sort of weapon used. The decider, in the absence of a higher or more competent authority, will be the head of the city watch, Arthan Nabur. Jere lurks at the back of the crowd, eavesdropping, while Kelkin heads off to make some police inspector or clerk miserable.

Which way will Nabur go? Jere's more used to betting on which cockroach will reach the top of the tavern wall first, or on the fights down in the Wash, but it's the same concept. Will Nabur make a stand against the guild's takeover of the city watch, make a stand for men of flesh and sinew against monsters of wax, or will he scuttle towards retirement in Rosha's good graces?

It's no contest at all. Nabur waffles about how much he appreciates the guild's help, how important a quick resolution is to the city's reputation, how the Keepers, while a valuable and esteemed part of the city's spiritual hierarchy, can no longer presume to dictate to the secular authorities. He goes on so long that Rosha loses interest and snaps that the watch will have a report as soon as the analysis of the remains are complete. Stone Men load bits of twisted masonry, shattered bell fragments, broken stones and still-soft gobbets of metal onto fireproof covered wagons. They remind Jere of a line of hearses.

He'll need a copy of that report, ideally before it gets into the hands of the watch. He marks the faces of the junior alchemists overseeing operations – one of them may be his way in. The problem with alchemists is that you can't bribe people who can turn base matter into gold – in this case, by selling weapons and cure-alls overseas, but the principle's the same. Still, he'll find a way.

Kelkin emerges from the crowd and hands him a jotted list. "A few thousand in coin. Ceremonial chains and maces. One of the bane swords. Copies of treaties and other legal documents. Evidence relating to cases on trial – the squid cult, the

Beckanore incident . . . " Kelkin mutters, "all of it destroyed, of course. Idiots."

Kelkin turns, about to reignite the argument and crucify Arthan Nabur — something Jere would quite enjoy watching — when there are shouts and hisses from outside. The line of Tallowmen charges forward, driving the mob back like a burning torch thrust into the faces of snarling wolves. The line becomes an angle, pointing at an alleyway off Mercy Street.

Guildmistress Rosha and Nabur lead the way, followed by a crowd that includes Jere and Kelkin.

Left briefly unsupervised, the Stone Men stop working but do not rest. Instead, they stomp around the ruins, shaking out stiff limbs or injecting one another with precious alkahest. One roguish half-statue steals her neighbour's syringe, and their brawl is a sideshow for the crowd.

With great solemnity and pomp, Nabur examines the alley wall.

"What is it? What can you see?" demands Kelkin, who is unable to see over the others. Jere, though, is tall enough to read the message scrawled on the brickwork.

THIS IS NOT THE LAST.

Down and down.

Down until it's rotting warm, thick with decay. Down to tunnels gnawed by nameless things, boring through the stone like grave grubs through decaying flesh.

Rat is a young ghoul. He doesn't come down here ever if he can avoid it. There are stages in his kind's growth, stable plateaus in the otherwise headlong degradation. As a young ghoul, he can pass for surface folk in dim light, think for himself, find pleasure in worldly things. As long as he stays on the surface, stays among the living, immersing himself in the wild free-flowing life of the city above, he can prolong his youth, for ghouls do not age as humans do.

Older ghouls grow animalistic, vicious, driven by their hungers. Incapable of communication other than yelping and roaring, interested only in finding carrion to eat – or fresher meat, if they've no other choice. The sunlight burns them, the city above repels them. Rat detests the senility of middle ghouldom, hates the thought of joining the countless hordes of feral ghouls who throng the caverns of this region of the underworld. The corpse thigh he ate earlier sits uneasily in his belly, an anchor dragging him down.

The heat sinks deep into his flesh, accretes around his bones. The rot-smell is pervasive, sinking into his brain. His stomach grows, and he remembers exactly how far it is to the nearest corpse shaft. It even takes him a moment to remember that those shafts were sunk by the folk of the city above as tribute – payment – to the ghoul folk and aren't a natural part of the world. His thoughts are slow as pitch.

Aleena walks behind him. These tunnels are too narrow for her to wield her sword, but she's got a knife, and a gun, too. The latter's empty, but still intimidating. The older ghouls shy away from her, respectful of the barking magic of the alchemists – and of the violent flames of sainthood that flicker around the knife.

She glances down a side tunnel, where a hundred pairs of hungry eyes reflect the light of her blade. One of the ghouls pushes forward into the light, snarls at her. She grins and takes a step towards him, and the ghoul vanishes back into the shadows.

"Are we nearly fucking there yet?" she asks, "'cos your cousins are acting like I'm dinner, not a duly recognised emissary of the most holy bloody church."

Rat shakes his head to clear it. "Not long now," he says. In truth, he has no idea. Navigating these trackless tunnels is done on instinct. He has no idea if the paths do change, or if he simply has no conscious memory of which way is best. He has to let instinct guide him, let his surface mind drift away into ghouldom. Lose himself, piece by piece.

Turning feral isn't the worst part. It's what comes after.

A fetid wind blows down the corridor, and he knows they're close. The passageway widens. Behind them, the older ghouls meep and hiss at one another, but they dare not follow any further. Aleena and Rat walk out into the wider tunnel, which soon becomes a huge cave, much larger than the light from Aleena's burning blade can illuminate. Bigger than the inside of a cathedral.

Gigantic pedestals rise from the bone-strewn floor of the cave, and on each pedestal squats an elder ghoul.

Rat fights the urge to cower or to prostrate himself before these monsters. On the other side of the ghoul life cycle, beyond the feral maze of blind hunger and instinct, there is elderdom. The smallest of them must be ten or twelve feet tall, skull hideously elongated into a canine muzzle, hands twisted permanently into claws. Eyes glowing with an orange light. Instinct leeches into sorcery for them; they cast spells like younger ghouls rip throats, wounding reality. They are soul-eaters, psychopomps, eaters of the dregs of the dead. Their magic is like congealed fat, rendered from the thousands of corpses they've consumed. They sit cross-legged, staring at one another, communing in ways that Rat can't begin to comprehend.

Nostrils flare as they smell Aleena. One of them leans forward, growls something in a language older than the city that neither Aleena nor Rat not any living soul can speak.

Aleena sheaths her knife, puts away the gun. "The Keepers sent me," she begins.

The elder ghoul snarls, angry at the lack of respect. Beyond it, other elders stir from their reverie. Sorcery hisses through the air like mustard gas, stinging Rat's eyes and nose. He wants to run.

"Buggering monks with their shitty scrolls. Er. I had all this written down," mutters Aleena, and she tries to recite the correct greeting from memory. The words aren't meant for human tongues, and she stumbles over them, like she's trying to gargle with finger bones in her mouth.

The orange-eyed elder unfolds, one obscenely long hoof-footed leg extending down to the cave floor, then another, crushing skulls to powder as it stands up and towers above them. Its jaws open much too wide as it yawns and roars. The elders may be the protectors and priests and gods of their race, but they think nothing of swatting an individual ghoul. Rat cringes in anticipation of the killing swipe.

"Fuck this."

Aleena blazes with sudden light. Angelic, transfigured, her physical body is a stained-glass case for the burning lamp within. Her voice like choirs of angels.

"I DROPPED THE BLOODY SCROLL, ALL RIGHT? I CAN'T SODDING MAKE NICE." Every word a resounding trumpet. "BUT NOTHING'S CHANGED. THE BARGAINS YOUR KIND MADE WITH MINE STILL HOLD. I'M NOT YOUR FUCKING ENEMY." She cocks her head.

"YOU DON'T WANT ME AS YOUR ENEMY."

The elder ghoul flinches, then settles back onto its pedestal. A yellow tongue, scaly like a lizard, licks over its sharp teeth as it considers the saint's words. Then it points a clawed finger at Rat, and suddenly his mouth isn't his own. The elder ghoul is speaking through him, words wriggling up through his throat and out of his mouth.

"The bargain holds. What do you want of the first dwellers?"

Aleena's fires die down. "The Keepers are worried. They said to say that prisoners are banging on their cage. That they're restless. Do the prisoners know something we don't?"

A gelatinously, inhuman amusement comes with the command to speak, and Rat smirks unwillingly as he says, "Many things. They are older than your Keepers. But we keep watch on the gates. The Ravellers remain contained. Furious, very angry, but contained."

"All of 'em?"

Rat finds himself shrugging. "Count them if you can. Is your city empty? Do you still have a face to call your own? We have done our part. Look to your own."

As he speaks, Rat catches a glimpse of the elder ghoul's thoughts. Memories of an older war, of hooded holy warriors with blazing weapons, burning ghoul and Raveller alike, burning any unclean thing from the depths. They were not always thorough. Some things were left behind, to fester in the ruins of temples and to grow in charnel ground. Images of Ravellers clawing at the stone seals that hold the rest of that vile horde prisoner.

They're scared, thinks Rat.

That's a mistake.

The elder ghoul is in his head and can read his thoughts much faster and more thoroughly than he can read theirs. Flash-image of himself as a rat, a little scrap of cowering, pissing fur and meat, furtively scurrying in the corners, and the elder ghoul as a gigantic predator, snarling, sniffing the air, about to pounce. *Shut up and stay out of affairs that don't concern you*, that's the message, and it's one Rat understands. Peripheries are the safest – he's not a full-fledged ghoul or a thief or a bully-boy or, now, an agent of the Keeper's church, but he's on the fringe of all of them. Uncommitted, where it's easy to run, and he has every intention of staying there. He has no idea what Aleena and the ghouls are on about anyway.

The elder ghoul lowers its finger, and Rat's body is his own again.

"The Keepers will do what we promised. The faithful dead are yours," says Aleena. Her fires go out, and she scowls as she adds, "Not that they get a say in the matter."

The elder ghoul actually laughs at that, a gurgling noise like a sucking drain, and climbs back onto its pedestal. It closes its eyes and joins with its brethren in their strange communion.

Aleena sighs. "Let's go." She sounds exhausted.

"This way," says Rat, to his own surprise. He leads them out via a different tunnel. The route back to the surface blazes in his mind. Apparently, the elders want to be rid of Aleena quickly, too.

They climb in silence, trudging up endless ghoul tunnels that spiral towards the surface.

Despite herself, Cari finds some of the lecture interesting. She spends the first few minutes pulling at the alchemical rope around her dagger, wondering if by some chance it weakened overnight, but it's just as strong as ever. Then, she observes her fellow students, sitting quietly in grey rows, like cultists at some church of learning. Most are human or kin enough to pass for it; a Crawling One sits near the front, one gloved hand pressed to its porcelain mask to keep it in place. She's seen stranger things in Severast.

Some of the other students glance at her, wondering who the newcomer is. She stares back at them until they drop their gaze. Her grasp of Guerdon law is limited to the practicalities of a street thief, which is to say, 'don't get caught'. Now, she's unsure where she stands. The thief-taker let her go free, thanks to Ongent's intercession – but he's a private bounty hunter, not an official member of the watch, so she's still technically a wanted criminal. And there are the Tallowmen . . . but she hasn't seen many of *them* in the University District, and she's fine with that.

Ongent doesn't address the audience. Half the time it's like he's talking to himself, or having a one-on-one argument with a questioning student, but his enthusiasm for the topic carries the class with him. Cari only grasps fragments of his talk – it's about how buildings can change function over time. She's seen that herself, over in Gravehill, where the tombs have become houses for the living. Rat sheltered her there for a night or two, before sending her to Spar.

She wishes Spar was here. He'd get a lot more out of lectures like this. He's got a mind made for studying architecture or oratory or statecraft, instead of shaking down shopkeepers for protection money.

The professor talks about the Seamarket, which used to be a temple to some gods that they kicked out of Guerdon long ago, and how you can still see traces of the building's original function beneath the fish guts and the trestle tables. He talks about the Barbed Gardens in Serran, how they turned the old king's palace into a maze of death traps to stop anyone claiming the crown, about the decline of parts of Castle Hill and how people colonised derelict palaces and made them into communes – and then he's on about architecture and kings and dynasties she's never heard of, and she loses the thread of the lecture.

She falls asleep, until a red-faced Eladora elbows her in the ribs. Cari's instinctive reaction is to go for her knife, but fortunately it's tied in its sheathe, so no one gets stabbed and few people notice. Cari mutters a half-apology. On reflection, she hasn't slept well since she arrived in Guerdon, although last night she got a solid few hours in the cellar. She misses the sound of the wind, the motion of the waves. She yawns, covering her mouth with a hand that's so clean she barely recognises it as her own. Eladora insisted that Cari scrub up before coming to the university, to wash off the Wash and any trace of the Stone Plague. Eladora waiting outside the door with towels. Like old times in Aunt Silva's house, the pair of them falling back onto habits learned in childhood.

Ongent sweeps out of the lecture theatre, followed by a retinue of students and assistants. Eladora drags Cari along with them. One by one, Ongent deals with them – answering this one's question on Varithian kingship rites, telling another when to submit an essay, counselling a third on what books to consult. One by one, they drop away, until only three remain – Cari, Eladora and a young man who trails after Ongent like his shadow. There's a definite family resemblance, close enough that Cari guesses he must be Ongent's son, but where the professor is all beard and enthusiasm and wild gestures, his son is reserved, even sullen, and moves with an economy of motion that makes Cari think of a scorpion. She can tell he's armed. Like her, he's wearing the grey robes of a university student, a relic of the days when this was a seminary – see, even she can pick up things from a lecture – but he's got a leather knapsack that he instinctively keeps close to his right hand.

Cari watches the boy, and notices Eladora staring at him too, sizing him up in a very different way. Cari catches Eladora's eye and smirks; Eladora turns an even brighter shade of red and hurries after the professor, staring at her shoes instead of the boy.

Ongent leads the trio to his study. They wade through piles of papers and tottering piles of books to find places to sit. Glass-fronted display cases hold insects pinned to boards, broken chunks of ancient statues, old leather-bound books, things in jars. A row of maps, all of Guerdon at different stages in its evolution, hang around the walls. On the desk is another statue, an ugly squat thing of iron with a leering face that scares Cari for reasons she can't understand. The room isn't small, but it's so crammed with Ongent's people and papers that Cari feels alarmingly confined. This is not her place. Eladora notices her distress and moves a stack of books off a hidden windowsill, so Cari can at least see out of the narrow window onto the university quadrangle beyond.

"Miren, go and fetch us some tea," orders Ongent. The boy slinks out of the door. Eladora volunteers to help him – too quickly, too eagerly – leaving Cari alone with Ongent.

"How are you today, Carillon?" he asks. He's smiling, but she's one of the insects pinned to the board.

"All right," she says, then adds hastily, "I didn't have any dreams." She knows that she should be stringing this out, running it as a con. Have visions for money – Ongent's clearly got plenty. But it's too close to her, with her cousin and her family coming into it.

He doesn't seem disappointed by her admission. He just nods. "The absence of visions is important, too. We need to study you as if you were a phenomenon, you see? What I want to do you, my dear, is keep careful track of, well, everything. When you have one of these visions and what you see, of course, but also where you are when it happens, what you're doing. Note your sleeping habits, what you ate, who you associate with. Anytime you feel the slightest inkling of, ah, revelation, record it."

"I don't like writing things down."

"Well, it's time to learn a new habit." He reaches into a drawer, pulls out a blank notebook and a pencil.

She takes them, sword and shield of a gladiatorial bout she's ill-equipped to fight. Ongent beams.

"Now," he declares, "you described how, in one of your visions, you saw a young priest in an old church, and how he encountered a delightful and alluring young woman, who, as you put it, fell apart and ate him. I had Miren do a little snooping this morning, starting with the nearest church to your former . . . residence in the Wash. And there, in the old Church of the Holy Beggar, are three priests. One of them is named Olmiah, and while the other priests there are old and bent like myself, he is scarcely older than you are. Furthermore, several people remember seeing a mysterious beautiful woman who attended a single service at the church, never to be seen again. Obviously, there were no witnesses to confirm if this woman did devour Olmiah and take his form – no witnesses except you, that is – but I certainly think it supports what you saw."

Cari shivers. "He didn't talk to the priest, did he?" If the thing in woman's form knows that she saw it killing this Olmiah and taking his form, it might come after her.

"No. I asked him to be discreet. However, he did learn something else interesting – the woman was at Olmiah's service when you fell from the wall. That was not a vision of the past, Carillon – it was, I think, something that happened at that very moment."

"What's next, then? Wait for it to happen again?"

"Precisely. Eladora or my boy Miren will always be at your side, watching over you."

"I don't like being watched. It makes me uncomfortable."

Ongent sits down on the corner of the desk and lays his hand on Cari's shoulder. It's meant to be reassuring, but she shies away. "Of course, but remember, these visions can be overwhelming. You fell off a wall and nearly drowned. Maybe you'd have escaped the House of Law instead of falling down unconscious in the middle of a burning building if you hadn't had that first one. Think of it as a medical condition, and Eladora as your nurse."

That doesn't sound much better to Cari.

"Which reminds me," says Ongent, and he pulls a box of bandages and surgical tools off a shelf. "Miren has some training as a doctor. Let's get him to take a look at your shoulder."

When Miren and Eladora return, Cari lets him change the dressing on the wound. She watches him closely as he does so. His movements with the scalpel are quick and deft, cutting away the soaked bandages with the grace she'd associate with a cutpurse. His fingers, though, are rough and uncaring as he pulls her this way and that – he knows his way around anatomy, certainly, but she doubts he's ever treated a patient before. Once he's changed the dressing, he smears ointment on the scars on her face.

"Much better," proclaims Ongent, examing Miren's work. "Much better indeed."

CHAPTER SIX

T HIS IS NOT THE LAST.

A threat? A warning? A declaration of war?

Or a distraction? Jere had assumed that the destruction of the tower was an accident, that the thieves had overestimated the power of the bomb they used on the vault. Was he wrong, or is someone else trying to take advantage of the accident by making it seem deliberate? The city is already unsettled after the fire; another disaster like that one, and things could tip into a chaotic state.

An internal foe, then? Who profits most from catastrophe? The alchemists, trying to solidify their control of parliament and push their Tallowmen onto the streets? Religious fanatics? Monarchists, praying that the city's long-vanished kings will miraculously return in its hour of need?

Or is it some external foe? Guerdon, for all its wealth, is vulnerable. The standing army is small; the navy famously well-armed, but still far smaller than the forces fighting in the Godswar.

This isn't my problem, Jere tells himself. Kelkin hired him to catch the crime boss, not to save Guerdon from some sinister conspiracy, but the two may be intertwined.

He rereads the list of vault contents that Kelkin obtained for him. Money, a bane sword, copies of treaties, evidence relating to cases on trial.

He's tempted to dismiss the money instantly – if you had an alchemical bomb that powerful, you could sell it for more than the monetary contents of the vault. But what if the thieves didn't know the vault's contents? He runs through that scenario in his head – they get an alchemical bomb, decide to rob the city's court instead of a bank or treasury, thinking it contains far more money than it actually does. It doesn't make sense. Spar and the ghoul and the Thay girl were there as distractions, to draw the guards and Tallowmen away. Heinreil planned it, and Heinreil isn't stupid. They knew what they were going for.

The bane sword . . . He tries to recall – the bane swords were forged in *lo the year something because verily a dread thing arose*. Demons. Something something. He can't even remember who made the things. They're just kept around for ceremonial purposes. The old joke: *how do you know they're demon-bane swords? I don't see any demons around here, do you?*

A collector might pay a fortune for a bane sword. A crazy demon cult might pay for a sword to be destroyed. THIS IS NOT THE LAST . . . and there's more than one sword. He'll have to ask Ongent. The professor's his go-to expert on matters historical and supernatural.

Copies of treaties and legal documents – it doesn't fit. There's often profit in learning secret information, but only when it's secret. If the thieves had planned on unlocking the vault door and leaving no trace of their presence, that would make sense, but they used an alchemical bomb. No way for that to be subtle.

The evidence, then. It's an old trick, destroying physical evidence before it can be presented in court. It works best, of course, when the reliability of the city watch is already in question – and that's certainly true these days. Tallowmen don't need evidence if they catch you red-handed. That would only make sense, though, if the cases in question were ones involving the sort of crime the Tallowmen can stop – murder, rape, theft, arson and the like. The squid cult case is on the borderline, with its ritual drownings and offerings to the deep; the Beckanore incident is a territorial squabble between Guerdon and the nearby nation of Old Haith, and isn't obviously relevant. Although one of the disputes regarding Beckanore is that the army of Old Haith got hold of new alchemical weapons that weren't sold by the guild's regular brokers. Probably middlemen or smugglers, and while Heinreil doubtless has his hand in smuggling, none of the evidence there has any chance of connecting him to the crime.

None of it clicks. Not only does it get him no closer to Heinreil, the criminal's involvement makes it all more confusing. Heinreil isn't a fanatic, he isn't an idiot, and he's not prone to making mistakes. Jere jams the list into his pocket and sets off downhill, towards the docks.

Professor Ongent isn't the only expert that Jere can call upon.

When it comes to matters alchemical or military, he's got Dredger.

Dredger's main yard is out on Shrike Island, one of the archipelago of small rocky islands that dot the bay, near the Isle of Statues. He couldn't ply his singular trade in the city, after all. Dredger specialises in second-hand death. The alchemists guard the secrets of creating their alchemical weapons closely, but the effects are out there in the world. Ever-burning fires, poison clouds that linger for weeks or longer, metal-eating slime. After a battle or siege won with alchemical weapons – and if you've got the money to buy alchemical weapons, you've probably won – the battlefield is scarred with poisonous residues. The alchemists, of course, can sell you counter-agents, but it's cheaper to call in Dredger. Sometimes, he'll even pay you.

He drags the remains off to his yards, where his workforce — mostly dying Stone Men, or other desperate unfortunates — sift the debris for still-usable remnants. Pockets of poison gas. Still-blazing chunks of burning metal. Transmutations that haven't stopped yet. Unhatched eggs. They collect these leftover bits of death and repackage them, and Dredger sells them on.

Though his main yards are out on Shrike Island in the bay, Dredger rarely sets foot on that hell. He works from a much less contaminated complex down on the shore; the protective rubbery suit with its articulated gauntlets, its brass helmet and wheezing breathing apparatus is just to impress the customers, or so Jere guesses. He's never actually seen Dredger take it off, and, for all he knows, there could be a Crawling One or some alchemy-rotted monstrosity beneath that helmet. He's worked with stranger things.

Seeing his fine clothes, one of Dredger's staff mistakes Jere for a potential buyer, and ushers him into the boss's office post-haste. Dredger laughs when he sees him. It sounds like someone drowning in a sewer.

"This man," says Dredger, "has no money. Never has money. Only brings trouble. Shoot him on sight next time."

Jere produces a bottle of nectarwine, a sickeningly sweet liquor that Dredger has a taste for.

"Strangle him on sight," amends Dredger, "then search the body. Sit down, Jere."

The servant retreats. Dredger clomps around the desk, grabs the bottle, holds it up to the light and lets the viscous liquid slide around inside the glass.

"Have you tried the stuff they're brewing out on Shrike?" Dredger asks. "It's mostly fermented seaweed and chemical run-off, but the Stone Men can't get enough of it. They can actually get drunk off it. Even the ones with calcified stomachs."

"Gods, no. I like having eyes."

"I asked if you'd drunk any, not smelled any. It's best drunk by means of a funnel, so you don't risk getting any near your skin." Dredger locks the bottle away in a drawer. "So."

"So. The House of Law."

"I guessed you'd come calling about that." The weapons dealer pulls out an ornate sphere of metal, about a foot across, made of interlocking plates. His gloved fingers manipulate them, pressing at hidden catches and clasps, then twist and the sphere comes apart in his hands. He spreads its metallic guts across his desk; an augury, with hoses and tanks instead of entrails and organs. "This is a siege charge. Phlogiston and elemental fire, kept in separate tanks, released when the fuse *here* burns down, see? Makes a mighty big bang, enough to take down a city wall, and then you get a lot of really hot and nasty fire."

"That's what brought down the House of Law?" asks Jere.

Dredger's helmet clacks and hisses as some flow of gas switches on. "If you set one of these off under the House of Law, you wouldn't just topple the bell tower – Mercy Street would be a crater deep enough to drown a whale."

"Don't whales live in water?"

"The crater, in this hypothetical, is full of fire, remember?"

"Roast a whale, then."

"The point is, it's overkill. Far too much blasting power." Dredger shakes his head, as if bemoaning the inefficiency of certain nameless parties.

"So did they use something else, then?"

"They should have – but no. I felt the earth shake, and I saw the flames. That was a phlogiston blast, and no mistake."

Jere hefts the casing of the bomb. "A smaller version? Or can you set this to a lower yield?"

"They don't come any smaller. Normally, phlogiston just burns – it uses anything as fuel, it can burn on ice, even in a vacuum, but you don't get that lovely bang. To get that, you need to be very clever." He waves a glove at the complex assembly of little tanks. "That's what all this stuff does – synchronises the release so you get phlogiston burning itself, and that gives you your blast."

Dredger mimes the action, fingers standing in for phlogiston spraying into the central void of the sphere, intertwining, meshing into clasped fists, and then spreading to indicate an earth-shattering explosion.

"You're right, though. You can get a smaller boom out of one of these – but only if you know what you're doing."

He takes the sphere from Jere, flips it over, points at a panel. "You need to drill in here, and at eight other places on the sphere, and remove exactly the same amount of fire-water from each tank. Elemental phlogiston is nasty stuff and requires special handling gear. Bastard stuff wants to escape, and it's a tricky prisoner. Has to be kept under pressure, but not too much. Lighter than air and sets the sky on fire if it gets out. Let me put it this way – when we have any out at the yards, I take a little holiday, just in case the wind's blowing the wrong way when ..." Again, the hands unclasp. Again, the catastrophe.

"All right. Say you could do all that, and you wanted to blow open a bank vault. Would it make sense to use a phlogiston charge?" asks Jere.

"If you can do all that, you can also do a hundred easier and safer things that'll open a vault. It's like trying to quietly shiv some fucker in an alleyway with a ... a siege howitzer. It's madness."

THIS IS NOT THE LAST, thinks Jere. "So, assuming he knew what he was doing ..." he begins.

"He?"

"They," corrects Jere. He. Heinreil. "Assuming we're not dealing with idiots, they picked this bomb for a reason, and that was because they wanted to blow up the House of Law – but just that building. They didn't want to cause massive damage to the rest of the city."

"That'd be my guess," says Dredger. "I know the alchemists took away the ruins of the vault for analysis and decontamination, and it'll take them weeks before they make a pronouncement, but I'll wager that bottle of nectarwine against all the rot-gut in this city that they'll agree with me."

"Could the bomb be part of the same shipment of weapons that was smuggled to Old Haith?"

Dredger's mechanical eyepiece clicks and whirs, the equivalent of giving Jere the stink-eye. Anytime smuggling of alchemical weapons is mentioned in parliament, the watch make trouble for Dredger. He's under suspicion of being involved. Which is only fair, given he's a smuggler of alchemical weapons.

"Maybe," says Dredger finally. "That was all top-quality stuff from the factories. I haven't heard of the Haithi using phlogiston bombs, though – they're siege weapons. They need sea-mines, howlers, acid seeds, that sort of wide-area defensive stuff." He waves his gloves over the table, as if it's some wide swathe of land or sea and he's burning it all with a poison cloud. Jere fought in the Godswar when he was younger and stupider; he remembers bombardments like that, as bad as the wrath of any god.

"One last question," says Jere. "How easy is it to get your hands on one of these bombs?"

"Hellishly hard unless you're willing to pay. They don't exactly fall off the back of a wagon."

"Figured as much. You haven't heard of any more going missing, I presume?"

"I wish. There's a lovely little war down in Mattaur that's crying out for one. You tell Heinreil that if he wants to make real money, talk to me."

"I never mentioned that name," says Jere.

"I'm in competition with the alchemists. I need to stay sharp. For that matter, tell Kelkin that if he wants to save the city money, hire me to clean up the Tower of Law ruins instead of the guild. My lads will do it for a tenth the price. Tell him to ask that question in parliament, eh?"

Jere stands up. "If I ever see such an august citizen, I'll let him know."

"I'm a respectable businessman, me," says Dredger.

Jere snaps his fingers. "Oh, you don't have any alkahest to spare, do you? I've got a late-stage Stone Man sitting in a cell, and I need to keep him flesh until he starts talking. I've got a vial left, but the boy's stubborn."

"To spare? No. Half the Stone Men in the city come calling at my door, looking for work. I need all the vials I have." Dredger considers the request for a moment, toying with the disassembled bomb. "I can give you a good deal on a few shots if you give me a day or two's notice."

"Nah, if I haven't got him in a week, he'll be Nabur's problem. Thanks anyway." Dredger doesn't need to know that Kelkin promised to arrange with a magistrate to get an extension on the usual one-week limit that a thief-taker can hold a prisoner.

Jere takes his leave of Dredger, hurries down the stairs and out into the alleyways and narrow wynds of the Wash. THIS IS NOT THE LAST, the graffiti promised, but the bomb used on the House is rare and expensive. Is the next going to be something else? Or is he putting too much weight on some joker's graffiti?

Heinreil knows. Find Heinreil, and the answers will fall out of him when Jere hits him hard enough. He's a simple sort of investigator.

Jere climbs away from the docks, passing a row of temples.

He passes the Church of the Holy Beggar. The faithful cluster in the doorway, fewer in number every day, as proselytisers for other faiths draw them away, luring them with promises of easier paths to salvation, with gods more ready to intercede.

Nearby, a temple dancer cavorts and twirls, naked despite the cold drizzle that falls across the Wash. The Dancer's simple ecstasy has found little purchase in the mercantile city of Guerdon.

A Crawling One addresses the crowd with whispers, beckoning the curious to come closer and learn the secret wisdom of the worms. The worms are a relatively recent phenomenon in the city; they only showed up about, what, twenty years ago? A wizard's experiment gone wrong, some say, or a plague dug up in some archaeological dig in the Archipelago. The worms don't even have a religion or a temple – they peddle a cut-price afterlife, where some of your thoughts and memories get to survive as worm fodder instead of joining with the Gods. Of course, it's an open question how much of you lives on in the worms, and how much is just a squirming pile of worms pretending to be you long enough to liquidate your estate. The alchemists must really be cutting into the sorcery business, thinks Jere, if the Crawling Ones have to sell themselves on the street corners like this.

Drums and cymbals herald the approach of a group from the Last Days Temple, and that means trouble. He glances up at the rooftops, and, as he expected, spots several flickering shapes drawing closer, hopping from building to building. The Tallowmen, gathering in advance of any fighting, as if the city's religious strife is a boil that can be lanced with their sharp knives.

It's not my problem either, he tells himself. He takes a side alleyway to avoid the Last Days, cutting down the back of the warehouses on Fish Street. He's aware that his good clothes mark him out as having money, but everyone in the Wash knows Jere the thief-taker. No one's going to be stupid enough to—

—he dodges, but the stone still catches him in the side,

stinging, knocking the wind out of him. Attackers move in. There are three of the bastards, one on a rooftop, two more at ground level. He doesn't recognise any of them – that big one's definitely new to the city, and the one on the rooftop has the bronzed skin and purpled lips of Jashan. A sailor, he guesses, hoping for extra tavern money. The third's rake-thin, lips drawn back over jagged teeth, in the coils of addiction to crow or vat-gin or some other drug.

They picked the wrong mark.

He lets himself sink down in the gutter, groans as if unable to move. Big Man glances at the Addict, then advances, club in hand, greed evident on his face. The Sailor hefts another chunk of brick. Addict hangs back, nervously.

Big Man gets close enough, and Jere springs up, drawing the blade from his sword cane. He keeps the hollow cane in his other hand, using it to parry Big Man's panicked swing, while he drives the blade into his foe's thigh – not deep enough to cut an artery, but enough to make the man squeal like a stuck pig. Then Jere twists the short blade, and Big Man staggers to the left, straight into the path of the incoming brick from Sailor. Big Man goes down.

Addict drops into a crouch, backs off. Jere thumps Big Man with the cane, just to make sure he stays down. No sign of Sailor.

From behind, Jere hears a hiss. Hot breath steams in the air. The stink of fish and carrion.

Gullhead.

He throws himself forward, out of reach of those curved hook blades the beast favours. It shrieks in anger and charges after him. He gets a glimpse of rank, matted feathers, a thickly muscled humanoid body, crazy hateful little black eyes. Beak drooling bloody saliva. Gullheads don't live long – they're not natural creatures but the product of discontinued alchemical experiments.

After a few years, they just fall apart. Constant pain makes them brutally aggressive, so they often find employment as mercenaries, leg-breakers, killers for hire.

And assassins.

Jere pulls the pistol from his pocket and unloads it into the Gullhead's chest at point-blank range. It's only a small calibre, and, anyway, Gullheads cling to life with the crazy tenacity of a creature that shouldn't exist in the first place. The shot barely staggers it, but it's enough for Jere to get his sword between the monster and himself.

It screeches, frustrated. It feints right, left, but the sharp point of the sword tracks it unerringly. Jere's got a longer reach, so if it charges, it'll get skewered before it can get to him.

Where are Sailor and Addict? Jere can't take his eyes off the monster for an instant to check.

The Gullhead circles, clawed feet clicking on the wet cobble-stones. Jere matches it step for step, knowing that if he slips or stumbles it'll kill him in a flash.

They like, he knows, to rip open the throat and suck on the spray of hot blood that gushes forth. Those curved blades are used like meat hooks, to hang bodies upside down so all the blood runs down and out.

"Jacks!" shouts Sailor from above. The sound of running feet in the alleyway behind Jere, matched by the sound of Sailor scrambling across the warehouse roof – Addict and Sailor are fleeing. The Gullhead hesitates, then joins them in their retreat. It grabs Big Man as it runs, hoisting him up like a sack of potatoes. Jere doesn't know if it's rescuing its fallen cohort or snatching a potential meal.

His attackers vanish. A moment later, the alleyway floods with candlelight as three Tallowmen arrive, heads burning brightly. Then they're gone, too, in pursuit or off on some other errand.

Jere retrieves his cane, slides the sword home and tries to make sense of the encounter. If they just wanted money, why not roll him in an alleyway instead of ambushing him like that? And why bring a Gullhead?

Bolind rolls around the corner, breathless. Face like a ripe tomato, but the big gun in his hand doesn't waver as he scans the alleyways nearby. "Boss? You all right?"

"Yeah. Candles scared them off." He frowns. "How'd you know I was in trouble?"

"Street kids ran by the office, shouting that the big thief-taker was getting his head kicked in down back of Fish Street. Who was it?"

"Three humans, and a Gullhead. All strangers."

Bolind kneels, examines the trail of blood left by the wounded attacker. "I'll get a dog, we can follow—"

"Leave it," says Jere, "the Tallowmen were right behind them. Let's let the city's finest deal with it for the moment."

Bolind frowns, doesn't let the gun drop. "You sure?"

"Yeah. I've got work to do."

Back in his office, and there's something off. Papers have been moved – very slightly, but enough for him to notice. There's an unfamiliar smell in the air. He draws his sword, moving cautiously through the deserted building. He checks his weapons cabinet, his document safe, his files.

He checks it all again. And again.

Nothing. Nothing's missing, nothing's changed.

He walks down the corridor of empty cells, opens the door to the flooded chamber. The Stone Boy's still there, still walking in endless circles around the little island.

"Hey," shouts Jere, "did you see anyone today?"

"No," answers Spar.

"Did you hear anything strange?"

"No."

"Do you want to talk about Heinreil?"

"No."

"Then goodnight."

The artificial island is forty-one steps in diameter. A little more if he wades into the water, risking the slimy edge along the precipice. Risk is something a Stone Man has to judge at every turn. Healthy flesh heals. Stone is harder to break, but never mended. Still, the water is thrillingly cold and painful against the crust of his left leg, where it finds its way between the plates and chills his flesh. His right leg, though, drags behind him, a dead weight, and is insensate to the cold.

Next time the thief-taker brings the alkahest, decides Spar, he won't bother injecting it into his thigh. He'll find another site, higher up his torso. Risk, again – the chemical, the poison, that holds back the progress of the disease has only so much potency, and he must weigh the possibility of restoring his leg against the risk of losing more of his body. The disease will win in the end – there's no cure – but properly managed, and with enough alkahest, he can hold out for years.

Compared to that, holding out against Jere's interrogation is easy. Spar scarcely pays the words any heed, lets them whistle past his stone-deaf ears, threats breaking like gentle waves on the granite cliffs of his resolve.

The thief-taker feints and dodges in his questions. One time it's threatening to withhold alkahest if Jere doesn't cooperate. Next, it's a promise of a reduced sentence, hints of employment. Or maybe Jere's claiming that they caught Rat, that the ghoul has already told them everything, and that Spar's punishing himself for nothing. Tricks so old that Spar hardly even listens. He's not going to give the master of the Brotherhood up to the thief-taker, and that's that.

His loyalty was bought by the Brotherhood long ago, after the city hanged his father. Old men, smelling of liquor and cologne, shaking his hand firmly and telling him that his dues were paid, that his family would be taken care of. Sad eyes, all of them, sad and tired. One of them would visit that house on Hog Hill, modest but better than most in the city, each month to pay their respects to Spar's mother and to hand him a cheque or a wad of notes. They always put it into his hand, even when he was a child. The man of the house, a man of the Brotherhood.

Once, that meant something. His father told him the Brotherhood's history like a bedtime story, making it sound romantic and heroic. Champions of the common folk. The Brotherhood's older than the churches that once ruled the city, older than the guilds, older than the alchemists. There were thieves fencing stolen goods when Guerdon was a stinking pirate haven, not the semi-respectable industrial port it is now. There are districts where the Brotherhood is still respected, where people still remember what the thieves did for their families in generations past. Where people remember loyalty.

The Brotherhood stood by him even when no one else did, when the first patches of irritated skin flaked away and the flakes glittered in the sun, like chips of quartz. They stopped putting the money into his hand, then. He had to leave the respectable neighbourhood of Hog Close then, move down with his sort, down with the monsters and strangeness of the Wash, but the guild found him a place. Found him work. And alkahest, the caustic angel.

Keeping his head down and plodding doggedly on came naturally to Spar, even before the stone. Imperturbable to impenetrable. The city wheeled and changed around him, and so did the Brotherhood. The old men went away. In their place were creatures like Heinreil, faster, like lizards. Handshakes limp and moist, eyes glassy and unfeeling, but better able to survive in the new environment. The last act of a long drama that began many years before Spar was born.

Heinreil wasn't the master that Spar would have chosen, but he was master nonetheless, just like the squalid flat in the Wash wasn't the modest house on Hog Hill, but it was the Brotherhood all the same, taking care of its own.

He remembered an evening, only a few days ago. Heinreil came to his flat at night. A soft tap on the door, a summons that managed to be dismissive at the same time. He pushed past Spar without looking at the Stone Man, slipping in and spinning around, surveying the room. Spar remembers how he'd swallowed his irritation, how he'd reminded himself that it wasn't his room, not really, it belonged to the Brotherhood.

Heinreil's bodyguard followed the master in. Spar had to back away to give the monster space to pass through the room. The Fever Knight hauled his armoured bulk through the gap, glaring at him from behind eyeholes of thick glass. The steel containment suit he wore kept his rotten frame together, or maybe protected everyone else from the toxins in his body. Dribbling fluid leaks encrusted the steel plates with patches of vile slime. That horrific facemask, a polished brass skull decorated with melted flesh. They say that the Fever Knight was hurt in the war, by an alchemical weapon or divine wrath, and that the rotten mask of loose skin he wears over his helmet is actually his own face, that he tore it off in his agony. Whatever else the Fever Knight was, he was terrifyingly strong and immensely cruel. Spar had never seen the Knight fight, but he'd seen the aftermath. Skulls crushed with such force they'd popped open, brains spilling out like beer from a broken barrel.

"You're alone here?" Heinreil knew the answer, of course,

and it wasn't really a question, but everything Heinreil said was somehow rhetorical, a joke that the rest of the world wasn't in on.

"You're here," said Spar.

"I'm reliably informed that you have a houseguest," said Heinreil.

The Brotherhood took care of its own.

And if you weren't part of the Brotherhood, they took care of you, too.

"She was sick, Heinreil. Rat found her on the docks and took pity on her. She'll be moving on soon."

"She's been pickpocketing, my boy. She's on our territory, and not playing by our rules. You know what has to be done."

"I'll sort it out."

"That's why we're here," said Heinreil mildly. He pottered around the flat, examining Spar's belongings with his gloved hands. From a heavy box, he drew out a bundle of handwritten papers. "Gods below." Sitting down, he leafed through the pages, turning each one reverently. "I haven't seen this in years. I had no idea you kept it."

Spar wanted to rush across the room and tear his father's manuscript out of Heinreil's hands, but the Fever Knight blocked his path, as if daring him to try. He turned his flash of anger into a disinterested shrug.

"I reread it, sometimes. To remember him."

"Ah, Spar, so you should. So you should indeed. A great man." Heinreil turned a few more pages, and stopped. The handwriting had changed halfway down the page, from Idge's tight but legible hand to a clumsier scrawl.

Before the master could ask a question, the front door of the flat rattled. Heinreil slipped the manuscript back into the box as the Fever Knight tensed for action.

The door opened. Cari, eyes too bright, a bottle in her hand half empty.

"Shit. Spar, what's going on?" Her gaze fixed on the Fever Knight, an uncharacteristic quaver in her voice. The Knight's reputation for brutality makes Tallowmen sound like gentle lambs. The bottle slipped from her fingers as she reached for her knife.

"Try it," said the Fever Knight. Steam hissed from his armour in anticipation.

Heinreil rose from his chair. "Cari, isn't it? Don't be afraid, lass. You're among friends." He picked up the unbroken bottle and put it safely back on a shelf.

"Uh-huh. I'm friends with lots of monsters, me."

"I'll pay her cut, Heinreil," said Spar. "There's no need for this."

"I'm afraid there is," said Heinreil. "The Brotherhood has arrangements and understandings with the powers that be. We can't have little gutter thieves running around like stray cats. Cari, you can either pay us our due—"

"Fuck you."

"Or we can take our due."

"I'm not staying. There's a ship leaving for the Archipelago in three days. I'll be on it. I'll be gone and I'm not coming back, ever."

"You've already stolen from us," said Heinreil. Without warning, the Fever Knight lurched forward and grabbed Cari by the forearms with his massive gauntlets. She shrieked as he twisted his grip, forcing the knife out of her hand and crushing her wrists. He lifted her into the air with one hand.

Heinreil picked up the knife, ran his thumb along the oiled blade. "I'm afraid what you've done can't go unanswered."

"Don't," rumbled Spar. "I said I'll pay."

"You're in good standing with the Brotherhood. She's the one who committed the offence," said Heinreil.

Then: "Oh. What's this?"

He pressed the knife blade against Cari's throat, and then

used it to fish out the cord of a necklace she wore. The knife tip followed along the cord, pulling it taut until an amulet emerged from Cari's shirt. To Spar's eyes, it looked to be a jewel of jet or some other black stone.

"Not that. Fuck no, not that! It's mine! Spar, please, stop him!"

Heinreil jerked the cord, pulling it free. "I'll consider this partial payment." He let the amulet dangle for a moment, gleaming in the lamplight, then it vanished, a conjurer's trick. Cari tried to wriggle free of the giant's grip, kicking and spitting at Heinreil.

"Stop him!" she begged.

"Move," said the Fever Knight, "and she breaks."

"Spar, take hold of your guest," ordered Heinreil.

"I can't."

"How conscientious." Heinreil grabbed a blanket and threw it to Spar, who wrapped it around his hands and gently restrained Cari.

"They'll kill you," he whispered. "It's not worth it."

"It's mine. My mother gave it to me, it's all I have left of her."

"It belongs to the Brotherhood," said Heinreil, "and in time, if you are worthy, it may be returned to you. Spar will tell you what his father did to those who defied the Brotherhood. He did what had to be done, and so have I."

"It's all I have," said Cari. Her voice caught in her throat.

"I'll get it back," promised Spar. "But now's not the time."

The Fever Knight sneered and backed away towards the door, watching both Cari and Spar warily. Armoured gauntlets flexing, daring Spar to strike.

Heinreil sighed. "Ach, boy, don't make promises like that." He turned to leave, hunched as if carrying a heavy burden. "I'll be in touch. Things are in motion. Forces are aligning." Quoting Idge. "I'll be in touch."

And then, a few days later, the summons to the Tower.

CHAPTER SEVEN

When Eladora is nervous, she talks. She clutches Cari as they walk, arm in arm, just a couple of students out for a walk around the University District. Nothing to see here, just two girls aimlessly wandering, waiting for one of them to have an impossible vision, waiting for the city to rise up and tip itself into her brain. Nothing to see, just two girls, and Miren sloping after them like a sullen watchdog. Cari tries to keep track of him, but Eladora distracts her.

Right now, it's an account of what happened after Cari ran away, with a veiled accusation that Cari was an ungrateful cow for not appreciating the home Aunt Silva gave her. It's the third time Cari's heard this story in the last two days. "We wrote to the watch, of course, to see if you'd turned up *here*. We even hired a thief-taker to go looking for you, as if you were some common burglar, and of course mother was absolutely mortified at having such a thug snooping around the house asking questions. He seemed to think that we were somehow responsible, can you believe that, as if we'd been keeping you in the cellar and making you skivvy for us . . . "

"I left a note," mutters Cari.

"Well, that was hardly an explanation, was it? You just said you felt restless. Felt *uncomfortable*. What was really uncomfortable, let me tell you, was attending the ten-year remembrance ceremony and everyone mistaking me for you. Lots of people I didn't know coming up and offering me condolences on the death of my *father*, while he's sitting right there next to me, glowing like a beetroot candle. And other people whispering that we were somehow *responsible*, like we'd crept in and murdered them all."

"Did you?" She's not sure if she means it as a joke or a barb, but Eladora clearly has little sense of humour about the topic. Cari guesses she shouldn't either, it being her father and close family and all, but they were strangers when they were alive and are strangers dead.

Eladora clearly wants to flounce off, but has to keep hold of Cari for Professor Ongent. She compromises by jerking Cari painfully down a side street, making her stumble painfully. "That's a horrible thing to say. Mother was *devastated*. And where were you? Off doing gods-knows-what on some foreign ship."

To be honest, Cari can't quite recall why she was so driven to leave. It was so long ago, and all she likes to recall of Aunt Silva's house is the attic, and the warren of outbuildings around the back where she'd spent hours exploring. Broken tools, empty casks and crates. Other strange objects from the house's previous existence as a working farm, now utterly out of place in its new incarnation as a country home. Cari recalled being fascinated by the leftovers; rusty scar-things beneath the skin of the place. She's reminded of Ongent's lectures on archaeology, but he reduced the past to something that had happened, to a dead litany of deeds already done and cities already ruined. It felt like the professor was burying someone alive. It makes her think of Spar.

Whatever she sought, she'd known even then she wouldn't find it in Silva's country house, or in the books of well-meaning instruction and philosophy her aunt had forced Cari to read. The only books she'd enjoyed were those that described other lands across the sea.

Miren appears at their side, quiet as a shadow.

"Do you feel anything, Carillon? I can't help but f-feel you're not *trying*," says Eladora. "I don't pretend to understand this, but I do think you could be more diligent about trying. Have you written in your journal? Your handwriting's atrocious, but that's no reason not to keep diligent notes. You're not qualified to say what's significant."

"No," admits Cari. She should lie, she thinks, make something up, in case Miren reports back to his father and he puts an end to this strange indulgence. Miren, she's learned, is also a resident of the house on Desiderata Street – though he must have some way of coming and going in secret, because she's never sure when he's home, when he's listening. The strain of deception is beginning to wear on her. She's been stringing this along for two days now, and escaping the thief-taker's creepy prison only barely outweighs having to not strangle Eladora. Acting like a well-bred student makes Cari more nervous than any heist, but she knows she'd be a fool to give it up for nothing, and without understanding what happened to her that night when they broke into the Tower. Maybe she could make up something else about the ghouls.

"Well, there you are," Eladora sniffs.

Angered, Cari deviates from their planned walk around the outskirts of the university, turning right instead of left at a crossroads. Eladora's black shoes clip-clopping on cobbles to catch up. Miren like Cari's shadow, effortlessly keeping pace. The momentary darkness of an archway, then a shift in the buzz of the crowd as they emerge onto a street in Holyhill. The grey of the robed students diluted by the black of priests. Noises of street barkers, relic-sellers, beggars by the cartload. Cari pulls up her hood; any of those cripples begging for alms could sell her out to Heinreil. She quickens her pace, marching along St Barchus' Street as it clings to the steep eastern side of the slope; the buildings on her right have two sets of main entrances. One set opens here on St Barchus, but go inside and descend several stories and you would find a second set opening onto the Way of Flowers. Cari turns right down an absurdly steep set of stairs.

"It's nearly noon," complains Eladora. "We should stop."

WHERE IS THE OPENER WHERE IS OUR SIBLING OUR SELF OUR SHADOW

The noise shatters Cari. Infinitely louder, infinitely closer than a thunderclap. She staggers, knowing that she must have been shot at close range in the head. Nothing else could make such an all-consuming noise. That, or the city was struck by some alchemical doomsday weapon; a dragon bomb, like the one that hit Jashan. She paws at her face, searching for blood, a gaping entry wound. Maybe all her bones have been reduced to powder by the blast.

"for", says Eladora, heedless of Cari's utter annihilation.

Five hundred and ninety-four pairs of feet walk on Cari's body. Worms wriggle beneath her skin, gathering in a great convocation in her stomach. Scurry through her outstretched arms. Shuffle through the hollows of her legs. Her spine is a rope that giants tug, making her head ring. She's four hundred feet tall, swaying dizzily across the city. She can smell the acrid smoke from the alchemists' foundries, see the islands out in the bay, the tiny dots of ships black against the dazzle of the noonday sun on the waters.

"lunch"

Two figures, one very old and blind, one a man, one a woman. Priest's robes again. Are they going to be murdered, unravelled before her eyes? She can't bear to watch. The woman wears mail beneath her robes. She can feel every ringlet, every rivet. Feel the weight of the shortsword at her belt, the gun strapped to her right leg. She knows the woman is tired, and has bathed recently, washing off the dust of the streets and the tunnels below; she can smell the fresh water, the lingering incense that surrounds the older man, and the fainter scent of urine from his shameful incontinence. She knows the weakness in his legs, the fragile aching bird bones that scarcely support him, the thumping panic of his heart as he listens – but she cannot hear what the woman is saying. Words are lost to her.

The woman looks up at Cari – how can she, when Cari's perspective is splintered a millionfold, but she does it anyway – and turns to fire in the vision.

Cari's lying on the ground. Her legs feel like wet string. She's aware that she's hurt, bleeding and bruised. Did she fall all the way down the stairs? No – Miren's there, he caught her before she fell to her death. She tries to speak, tastes vomit. Eladora, shocked, fumbles for a notebook as if Cari were a specimen to be observed. A crowd, whispering, gawking.

The sickening feeling of a million ants crawling through her belly, her veins, crowding her heart, marching in solemn procession up her spine. **HARK HERALD BLOOD OF MY BLOOD CHILD OF MY CHILD RETURNED TO RETURN**

"Get me out of here," Cari begs. Her skull is about to split. She's seeing triple, or more, as if the world's been shattered into prisms. Another wave of nausea rushes over her, a triple wave, overlapping, conflicting. She thinks she screams, but can't tell. She can't feel her body anymore, she's too big, with unnatural stone-hard shapes pushing her flesh and bone out of the way. In her confusion, all she can think is that she caught Spar's plague.

Miren and Eladora lift her, start to carry her uphill – it's the shortest route to the university, but the pain grows intolerably worse with every step. Three hammers rain blows down on her head, over and over again.

"Down, down," she hisses. She's not sure if they heard her, not sure if she still has a tongue to speak. She's gone blind, but she feels the sun's heat on her face shift, change position, and she realises they understood. She'd thank the gods if she could.

They stumble down the hillside, down steep streets and cascades of stairs, down into Glimmerside. Visions war and clash inside Cari's mind, but with each step the pressure lifts until, suddenly, it's gone and all is silence.

Miren senses her relief, and drops her. Eladora stumbles under the sudden weight, and Miren pushes them into an alleyway. His hands, free, hover near his knife as he watches the few people in the crowd who followed their hasty descent, who might have seen more than a student drunk at noon in the shadow of the holiest churches in the city.

Cari spits to rid her mouth of the taste of vomit. Her heart's racing, and she feels exhausted, but whatever that – those – visions were, they don't seem to have had any other effects beyond a pounding headache. Still, she lies there in the trash, feeling like a vase that had been smashed. All her pieces are back together, but she's not sure if they hold together like they once did.

Eladora scribbles in her notebook. "Precisely . . . noon."

"Was I talking?"

"Sort of. Nonsense, mostly. I wrote it all down."

"Let me see."

Eladora snatches the notebook away. "Professor Ongent should see it first."

Cari's too weak to argue for the moment. "Fine."

"Did you see anything?" asks Eladora, pen trembling.

"A choir . . . more church stuff. Why am I seeing churches?"

"The gods are calling the wayward home," suggests Miren. It's the first time he's spoken in Cari's presence. His voice is squeakier than she expected, younger, with more humour.

"I'm not convinced." Cari looks up towards Holyhill. The sunlight reflecting off the white marble of the three great churches dazzles her, and she can't bear the thought of returning to the university that way.

Miren helps her upright. She leans on him and lets him bring her to a corner café. Eladora orders for the three of them, and the food helps. Cari wolfs it down. Eladora daintily nibbles a sandwich and leaves half of it on the plate. Miren dissects his meal, dividing meat from bread from filling, pushing the entrails around his plate so all the elements are discrete and nothing's touching anything else, then eating them one by one. Cari steals Eladora's leftovers and eats them, too. After a while, she feels more like herself again.

"Let's go back to the university," insists Eladora, rising from her chair. One of the staff darts over, and she settles the bill with a coin that would have paid Cari's share of the rent on Spar's place for the better part of a month.

"Not yet," says Cari. She sets off down through Glimmerside, taking the long way home, away from the terrible presences on Holyhill. Eladora follows her like a nervous puppy, initially pleading with her, frightened of the dangerous streets. Cari takes a bitter pleasure in her cousin's fears; Eladora would run screaming from the Wash. Miren follows them both at a distance, apparently lost in his own thoughts.

They come to Philosopher's Street, the main thoroughfare, and the crowds are thick there. A procession of carts rattles through the streets. Each cart is marked with the symbol of the alchemists' guild. Red flags warn of danger, and the crowds part to let the carts through, like thin ice melting away in the presence of a hot brand. Cari feels a strange echo of what affected her when the church bells rang. The carts are covered, but she can guess what's in them – the rubble and debris from the House of Law. The little wounds on her face start to burn as this terrible sick feeling rises from her stomach.

Eladora's looking at her strangely.

"What?"

"You're crying," says Eladora. Cari touches her cheek, finds it wet, the salty tears running over the burns and scars. She hasn't cried in years, not like this. *It's a funeral procession*, she thinks, and she has to force herself to stare at the carts to remind herself that they're full of rubble, not the corpse of someone important to her.

As if she had people important to her.

The carts push through, moving sedately through Glimmerside, heading down the hill towards the Alchemists' Quarter. The smokestacks and cooling towers of the district rise from that promontory of stone that spits out into the harbour. Clouds of yellow smoke hang over the towers, reflected in the muddy waters of the bay. The city's new cathedrals of industry, grander and greater than those little shrines on Holyhill, eclipsing the gods of the Keepers. Flare of phlogiston. Hiss of acid.

Fear seizes Cari, terror like she's never known before, an unnatural, *external* fear. With a sneak-thief's instinct, she bites her lip to keep from screaming. Blood runs down her chin as she stares at the reaching fingers of those chimneys, and for a moment her skin burns with an impossible heat, a blazing bath so hot that she feels she must be melting. The sun goes out, and she starts to topple again.

Then Miren's grabbing her by the arm, pulling her back into an alleyway as Tallowmen march by, ruddy faces scanning the crowd for known criminals. The professor's son takes no chances with his charge, leading her through the backstreets and secret ways of Glimmerside, back to his father's musty office overlooking the green square of the quadrangle.

*

Eladora's positively overflowing with information. "Her *first* attack was at noon, Professor. She collapsed and fell down the steps near Fenton's Bakery. She was vocalising again, but it wasn't anything I understood. It might have been proto-Taenian, so maybe if we wrote it down phonetically, you could—"

Ongent smiles indulgently. "Eladora, be a dear and fetch me the library's copy of Thalis's *Sacred and Secular Architecture in the Ashen Period*, please."

"But I took notes." Eladora holds out her sheaf of papers, a bribe to buy entry into the professor's office.

Ongent gently but firmly takes the papers from her and shows her to the door. "No need to hurry. We have all afternoon."

Eladora shoots a pleading glance at Miren, who's taken up position beside the door and is cleaning his nails with his knife. He doesn't look up as his father shuts the door on Eladora.

Ongent turns back to Cari, who stands nervously in the middle of the room. Her pounding headache is gone, but she still feels weak, and her eyes still sting with tears.

"So, it happened twice then," says Ongent. "No more than that?"

"Dreams, maybe. I don't remember them. Today was the first time since the prison that I . . . " Cari searches for the right term. "Lost myself."

Ongent gestures to her to sit down. She has to clear piles of papers and other junk off the couch to find a spot. Ongent stands with his hands clasped behind his back at the window, then inhales sharply. It's a gesture Cari recognises from the previous morning as marking the start of a lecture. She yawns involuntarily.

"There are elemental and spiritual forces beyond the strictly physical realm," begins Ongent. "Different cultures have a range of ways of both describing and channelling or using these forces. You might call them magic, or sorcery, or the blessings of gods, or the work of demons. Uncontrolled, these forces interact destructively with the physical realm, so they must be carefully contained or shaped into beneficial forms. Sorcery, for example, is the art of imposing structure on raw elemental force. A sorcerer draws these wild forces into the physical world, and, as he does so, he channels them through his mind where he shapes and guides them to a useful configuration, which the layman would call a spell. Similarly, alchemy involves evoking the latent magic in certain physical residues and – in conjunction with catalysts and the alchemist's own will – causing reactions that shape and channel that energy."

Ongent sounds amused, like he's telling a long joke with no discernible punchline. Cari knows that this sort of magical theorising is new and controversial. A generation ago, Ongent the heretic would be burning at the stake. Still would be, if he said this sort of thing in Ishmere or Ul-Taen. Instead, Ongent the professor gets well paid to put everything into nice little abstract boxes. Cari mistrusts simple answers. The streets taught her that there's always unseen complexity tangled up in the simplest thing.

"Now, we turn to the gods – not for guidance or protection, but as experimental subjects. Deities, demons and other supernatural entities can be considered as self-perpetuating structures in the elemental chaos. They might be naturally accreting structures, or perhaps they were unconsciously shaped over many generations by blind faith. These self-perpetuating structures can channel elemental energy through congruent souls – or, to put it another way, saints manifest the sacred blessings of the gods."

"You think I'm a saint?" snorts Cari, trying to make light of it, but the thought scares her. There was a saint in the temple where she danced in Severast. When the Dancer took him, he'd rise into the air, limbs twitching wildly, eyes rolling back into his head.

He wore a special ritual mask to stop him swallowing his tongue. The older priests would interpret the lines and curves his dancing limbs traced through the air, discern the future in his unwilling movements. She'd been there when the Dancer broke the young man. She'd heard his spine crack, his head loll back, but he kept dancing and dancing through the air for hours, a grisly puppet for unseen forces.

And the Godswar — she's never dared get too close to it, but she's heard stories. How some gods went mad with bloodlust and terror, and turned their miracles and saints into terrible weapons. There's no power without price, and she needs to know the true cost of these visions.

"It's a possibility. Most saints are adherents of one faith or another, but the ways of the gods are strange and unfathomable. You might have attracted the attention of one of them. Like, a lodestone picking up a pebble that happened to be rich in, ah, iron."

"I do keep dreaming of churches," she admits. "The Holy Beggar . . . and some other Keeper place." The Keepers were the dominant faith in the city before the reforms. A generation ago, they'd have been the ones burning Ongent.

"Quite." Ongent sits down next to her, uncomfortably close. "Carillon, I won't lie to you. This gift of yours is dangerous.. The city authorities frown on unknown saints and unlicensed sorcery. More importantly, unless you learn to control and channel it correctly, it may even endanger your life, and the safety of those around you. If I continue my research and Eladora keeps taking such diligent notes, I may be able to discover the nature of your gift, to learn what power is trying to speak through you, but it will take time."

"There's an 'or'." Cari can hear the hesitation in his voice.

"There is an alternative. I myself have some small magical

talent. With your permission, we can try a divination together. A ritual to, ah, make manifest any spiritual connections you might unwittingly be party to."

Every instinct in Cari is to run. Ongent is too close to her, too pressing. She can smell him, dust and old man sweat masked by tobacco smoke. The Cari of a few days ago would have gone for her knife, or for the door, but she can't run from this, can she?

"All right."

"Good, good. Bear with me a moment." Ongent heaves himself off the couch and potters around the room, collecting bits of ritual paraphernalia. A skull, some glass jars, a brass instrument with lots of lenses and levers, a golden pen. "Clear off that table, please?" He gestures at a pile of books and papers next to the couch. Cari lifts one of the books and discovers there is indeed an old battered table underneath. She shoves the papers onto the floor. The surface of the table is polished wood, marked with silver runes.

"One doesn't like to advertise," mutters Ongent. "Thaumaturgy is still seen as a questionable field of study, even in these liberal times. Go into alchemy, that's what they tell the most promising students, neglect the fundamentals and the historical theory and just follow the money. Feh!" He's talking to himself now, as he sets up his equipment on the table. He cranks a wheel on the brass contraption, and the skull's eye sockets begin to pulse with a flickering purple light.

"Say you do work out which god's trying to talk to me. What then? Can you stop it? Do I go to their church and present myself and get them to help me?"

"Excellent questions, my dear, all of which are predicated on this working. Let us take matters one step at a time." He douses the lamp above his blackboard, plunging the room into darkness apart from the purple glow from the skull. Its light makes Cari's

skin look ghostlike; Ongent is a dim shape. She can hear whispering voices, very quiet and low, but that must be her imagination.
Something scuttles through the papers she pushed off the table.
The room becomes thronged, numinous, like a temple in the
moments before the manifestation of a deity. Cari sits on the edge
of the couch and fights the overwhelming urge to kneel.

She is very close to understanding.

She is reminded of some stairs in Aunt Silva's house, a back
stairway that went up to an old suite of rooms built by some
previous resident that were now superfluous to the needs of the
household. Those rooms were crammed with strange things: old
farm tools, old books, old treasures, the scattered bones of thought.
Some of the tools were rusty and sharp, and Silva told her not to go
exploring. As a child, Cari lay in her bedroom and imagined wonders in the forbidden rooms above, but when she actually climbed
and opened the door at the top of the stairs and looked, there was
nothing left but dust and junk. As a child, she believed that some
power or presence had fled at her approach. The wonder was too
fragile to endure, or she had not made the proper preparations or
offerings to entice it to stay. She has that same feeling, now: that
she is approaching a thing both terrible and fragile and divine.

Ongent moves through the darkness. She hears a bang as he
barks his knee on his desk. "Ouch! Ow, ow ow." He limps over
to the window and throws it open. Light floods in. The mood of
wonder vanishes, replaced by something else. She's exposed, discovered. She blinks, and sees the after-images of strange insects
the size of her fist writhing on the table next to her, pinned by
bright spears. They're not real, and neither are the faces that
peer in the window behind Ongent. She guesses that the skull's
making her more able to perceive invisible forces.

He sits down heavily on the couch next to her. "Are you ready,
Carillon?"

She closes her eyes, screwing them so tightly shut the pressure is painful. When she looks again, the hallucinations are gone, and there's only Ongent sitting there holding the glowing skull, his face a mask of tender concern.

"Yeah. Let's try this."

"Hold this talisman, please. Don't let go." He hands her the skull. It's hot to the touch. Little tendrils of crackling arcane energy crawl from the eye sockets and twine around her fingers.

Ongent mutters some words. Nothing happens. He adjusts the brass instrument, opens a little vial of some caustic unguent and smears it across the skull's polished pate, and tries again.

Again, nothing.

"Should something . . . "

"Ssh."

Ongent gets up, walks back to the window, apparently deep in thought. He stares out at the city. "Keep holding the skull," he orders her.

She sits there, absurdly, clutching her skull and listening at the sounds of the university quadrangle outside through the window, to Ongent's heavy breathing. Nothing continues to happen.

Then it hits her, drags her down and up simultaneously. She sees the city from a dozen different angles, overlapping. Tiny many-legged things scuttle around her bones. Water laps at her stomach. Her left hand is on fire, but the right one next to it on the skull is untouched. Voices scream and roar in her ears. And there's *more* of her than there should be, like she has limbs or organs that she didn't know about, a tail that uncoils and reaches into the darkness far below.

Cari's perspective becomes detached and confused. She's looking out of the eye sockets of the skull in her hands now, looking up at her own face. She can see her mouth moving, words hatching from it like great maggots, but she has no ears and can only see.

She barely recognises herself, with her clean face and brushed hair and the grey student robes. The little scars blaze with an unnatural light. She wants to scream a warning to herself, but this skull doesn't even have a jawbone. Ongent comes up behind Cari – behind her, an instant out of her body and she's already forgetting who she is, subsumed in this flood. He lays his hands on her shoulders, whispers something to her or to the thing that's speaking with her mouth.

She tries to return to her body, but she falls. Everything goes not merely dark, but absent. Eyeless. She descends through Guerdon's strata, feeling the waves crash on the bulwarks of her spine, the weight of the warehouses, the hallowed temples, the swarming markets, and below them all the underworld, grave-cold and labyrinthine. Then deeper. She has the sensation of falling at terrible, terrible speed into the depths. She tastes mud and dirt, a flash of some metallic, chemical tang, then stone and stone and stone and blood. There's a rushing in her ears like a million subway cars screaming through tunnels. Worms crawl over her skin, then under it, stripping the flesh from her bones.

And then she's in a strange hall, a temple, lightless yet she can see through too many eyes. A presence is all around her, like a shadow on her soul. Her skin grows cold and hard as iron. Her mouth – mouths – speak without moving.

COME DOWN, DAUGHTER

It's her voice, a chorus of her voice, but it's also oozing and thick and completely inhuman. The presence threatens to overwhelm her. She's drowning in it. Panicked, she kicks back—

—and there's a knife at her throat, the cold steel digging into her neck, blood trickling from the wound. Strong young hands grabbing her. Miren drags her off Professor Ongent, who's lying stunned on the floor of his study. His nose is broken, his face clawed by Cari's fingernails. Shards of the magic skull crunch underfoot.

Miren pulls her upright, then does something with his leg and knee that sends incredible pain shooting through her lower back, and her own legs go numb. He presses the knife deeper, and snarls – literally, snarls, an animal noise that's somehow a question – at his father.

"It's all right, Miren. Let her go. Slowly." The professor hoists himself into a chair and dabs at his bloody nose with a stained handkerchief. Miren twists Cari again, grabbing her shoulder with one hand and driving his knuckles into her back, and her right arm goes numb and limp. He throws her back down to the couch and stands there between her and Ongent, eyes bright, nostrils flaring with his shallow breaths, a guard dog daring an intruder to cross the threshold.

Silence, punctuated by the professor noisily catching his breath, by Cari quietly swearing. Miren is part of the silence, indistinguishable from it. He crosses the room like a ghost and shuts the window, blotting out the outside world. His knife is still in his hand, and Cari watches it warily.

"Well," says Ongent, "that was illuminating."

"Was it?" says Cari. "I just saw … I don't know. Could I have a drink?"

"Certainly." Ongent grins at her, but the blood caking his face makes it less than reassuring. "Miren, please take Carillon and – wait, no. Go and fetch Eladora and have her take Carillon home. Then come back here immediately. We have work to do."

Miren slips out, the dagger vanishing beneath his grey robes. Cari's own robes are covered with blood – mostly the professor's, some hers. She tries to hide it in the folds. "Sorry about your nose," she mutters. Apologies have never come easily to her. "And your skull."

"No matter, no matter. The Ul-Taen Dynasties used to sacrifice a child before each invocation, as a defence against wrathful deities. The Ghost Walls were raised around Khebesh to protect against similar intrusions. In the grand scheme of things, child, considering the forces involved, one used nose and a little thaumaturgy fetch are very small sacrifices indeed."

"So did it work? Did you figure out which god is ..." Cari hesitates, as if asking would complete some incantation and make her fate inescapable.

"Oh, no, I'm afraid not," says Ongent, "the energies involved were far too potent for my little apparatus here to contain them. I'll need to repeat the experiment on a larger scale, I fear. But," he grins again, and it's even more gruesome, "this does prove my theory! Some divine force speaks through you, Carillon Thay, and I can help you tame it."

CHAPTER EIGHT

Rat, in the walls.

The clubhouse is crowded tonight. The air is thick with the smells of humans, scents clinging to them and marking them. To the ghoul's heightened senses, each person is shrouded in their past doings. The sailors are easy to spot. Salt-drenched, wind-whipped, and beneath those smells the exotic traces of distant ports. Spices and hashish from Severast. Fish and cheese and sour milk from Old Haith. From Ishmere, from the Godswar, battle-field incense, the tang of sorcery. Locals from Guerdon — dock workers, mainly — have a different smell beneath their sweat, a harsh alchemical stench belched out of the factory chimneys. It's everywhere in Guerdon these days.

He can spot the thieves, too. They're the ones that stink of fear.

He skulks around the edges of the big loud room, away from the crowded bar in the middle, away from the ring of wooden tables in the half-light. Heinreil told them to meet here after the House of Law job, but he's a day late for that appointment, thanks to his unexpected detour into the depths with Aleena.

He's been antsy ever since he parted company with the Keeper's saint, after they made it back to the surface. Stepping from another nameless, lightless ghoul tunnel into a familiar subway track, pressing against the walls as a train rumbled by, blue sparks spitting from its alchemical engine. She'd thanked him for his service, muttered that all her money was gone with her torn backpack, and stomped off towards the lights of the nearest platform. And that was that, his duty to the elder ghouls done.

The elder's invasive thoughts still wriggle like hot threads in his head, as though thinking them scarred Rat's brain tissues. He wants a strong drink – or better yet a nice hunk of dead meat – to put him right, but they don't serve ghouls here.

Rat doesn't like this place. Too many people, too many eyes. And he's got to look out for worm-eyes, too, thanks to Aleena. What was he thinking, pissing off the Crawling Ones?

He scans the crowd from his hiding place. Spar should be easy to spot if he's here. Everyone gives the Stone Man plenty of space – some out of respect, most out of fear of contagion. Spar used to come here a lot, when Rat first knew him. A young man, looking for his father's ghost. Lots of friends here, once. Old family friends, inherited from Idge. So many retellings of tales about Spar's father, and his sacrifice. Rat grew bored, half slept in the corner, but young Spar was always rapt, always attentive, like he was paying his respects in the only way he could.

It wasn't only the disease that drove all those friends away. Heinreil's star rose, and Spar didn't fight for his place. His circle dwindled, until there was just a few old men and a ghoul left. Pulchar retired to run a restaurant. Starris, toothless and drooling, sitting on a bench somewhere up on Holyhill. Daj got into a fight with a Gullhead and never woke up.

Cari doesn't like the place either. A bad first impression – some lecherous sailor grabbed her when Spar first brought her here, and she was quick to go for her knife. Too quick, maybe, thinks Rat. She didn't need to do that, not with the Stone Man there to guard her. They have few enough friends left as it is without trying to make more enemies.

Cari's a lot harder to spot than Spar, but he's sure she's not here either. Rat called by the little room the two share down in the Wash, but there was no one there, and it didn't smell like they'd been back since the Tower came down. Where are they?

Some sort of boom, Cari said.

Rat hisses softly through sharp teeth. Did the Tallowmen get his friends? Was he the only one to escape? Is that why they're not here? No one in the crowd knows anything – and if Idge's son was arrested and hauled off to Queen's Point jail, everyone would know. Something else happened to them.

Upstairs, a door opens for a moment, spilling light and laughter into the main room, and Rat hears a familiar voice for a moment. Tammur, one of the old hands with the guild.

Rat sneaks upstairs. By custom, the upper ring of rooms is reserved for important members of the guild, for Heinreil and his cronies. Just like the lowest tunnels, and that giant cave with the hexagonal pillars, are for the elder ghouls, thinks Rat, which would make the taproom the warrens of hungry-eyed feral corpse eaters, and the streets outside the upper crypts of Gravehill. The city consumes and repeats itself.

He opens the door a crack, slides in like a rat, quiet and boneless and impossibly thin.

Inside, old thieves play cards. A casual game to pass the time, the same unremarkable hands going round the table, the pot waxing and waning but no one's winning big. Their attention is held by the game so most of the players don't notice Rat.

One of them does. A Crawling One, gloved pseudo-hands of knotted worms pulsing gently as it looks through its cards, holding each one up to its masked face as if that's the only place it has eyes. From the purple sigils on its robe, its name is Nine

Moons Falling. It's a Brotherhood sorcerer. Worms wriggle free from its sleeves, its collar, and point their blunt heads at Rat as he circles the room. Like ghouls, the Crawling Ones are a nation unto themselves in the city, above and below, not really part of this surface realm of mortals and sunlight and life. Carrion eaters, both of them. Mystics, both of them, in their way, freelance ex-psychopomps grown fat on the spiritual energy of the godless dead.

Of course, no one would hire a ghoul as a sorcerer. Ghouls only get properly mystic when they grow old and weird, like the elders. Crawling Ones are sorcerers, all of them, weaving spells like they weave humanoid shapes out of worms.

Does it know that Rat tried to kill one of its brethren? For all the ghoul knows, it could even be the same Crawling One. They all smell alike, all the same sickly-sweet rot and faint hint of ozone. It doesn't move, though; it just plays the Six of Knives and scoops the pot. Mimics human laughter so perfectly it's eerie. Probably the laugh of some dead man that the worms ate. Everything he was, consumed and digested by the Crawling colony.

Rat sidles up to another card player.

"Hey, Tammur."

Tammur nearly fumbles his cards in surprise. "Gods below. Don't interrupt me when I'm playing, please."

Tammur. The last of Idge's inner circle to remain active in the guild. These days, Tammur's an adviser, a fixer, almost legitimate. Owns lots of ships and warehouses along the Wash – few of them in his name, of course, and none that could be traced back to the guild. He threw his lot in with Heinreil years ago, but Spar still counts him as a friend.

He throws a coin into the empty space in the middle of the table, then turns to Rat.

"We all thought the Tallowmen had caught you. You were the only one to make it out, you know."

"Spar?"

"He's in custody. Jere Taphson, not the watch – for the moment. There's little that can be done for the boy right now, I fear."

One of the other players grunts. "He's gone to stone. What's Heinreil going to do for him? You can't bribe the plague to let the boy go."

"The Brotherhood looks out for its own," replies Tammur, quoting the scripture of the streets. "When he comes before a magistrate, we'll do what we can for him – as we would for any fellow in good standing. Play your cards, Hedan."

Hedan growls in frustration, then picks up the minimal possible bet and throws it in. Nine Moons Falling puts in twice that without hesitation, smoothly confident in its cards. The fourth player, a tattooed woman Rat doesn't know, takes her time to think.

"What about Cari?" asks Rat.

"The Tallows or the gallows," laughs Hedan. "And no waiting."

"I heard tell sweet Cari found a benefactor," says Tammur. "Any ideas who that might be?" The last directed to Rat, but Hedan provides his own wordless response, lewdly thrusting his crotch against the table and grunting.

Rat tries to think what Tammur could mean. All he can guess is that she's running a scam on some mark. At least she's out of jail.

"Your turn, Tam," says the woman. A sailor, Rat guesses, one of Tammur's business partners from across the ocean.

"Spar said I'd get paid," insists Rat.

"I'll tell Heinreil that—" begins Tammur.

"Tell him what?" The door opens and Heinreil swaggers in. Two bodyguards flanking him, another two in the corridor outside. Behind him comes the Fever Knight, armour clanking, clear liquids hissing through pipes and tubes or spilling onto the floor, scarring the wood. Glimpses of scarred, translucent flesh through the cracks. Heinreil's leg-breaker, here to scare the troops into line.

Heinreil pulls over a chair, puts it between the woman and Tammur, deals himself into the game, and throws in three gold coins without even looking at his cards.

"The ghoul wants to be paid for the Tower of Law," says Tammur mildly, without looking up.

"Did the ghoul get what he was sent for?"

"Circumstances change. Towers explode."

"Did he get what we asked? No, he did not." Heinreil glances in irritation at Rat. "What are you still doing here? You smell like you fucked a sewer. Get out."

Rat fades into the shadows, but doesn't leave. If Heinreil notices, he gives no intimation of this.

The turn comes around to Tammur again, and he raises. "We need to make it known that the Tower wasn't us. The watch are spreading it around. Saying that it was revenge for Idge, maybe, or a botched job on the treasure vault."

"This is not the last." Hedan's bravado is in full retreat, driven from the field by the presence of Heinreil and the Fever Knight. "That's what it said. On a wall. Everyone's saying it."

"Are they now? Oh well," mutters Heinreil.

"Fanatics," adds the woman. "That's how the Godwars start. Madness breeds madness, breeds ... unwelcome divinity." She flexes her wrist. Her tattoos resemble magical wards. Some of them almost seem to glow in Rat's eyes. He blinks; some lingering after-effect of communing with the elder ghoul, maybe.

"Is that it, Heinreil?" asks Tammur. "The Godwar coming to Guerdon?"

"Not a prayer." Heinreil draws a card, then leans back and shows his hand to one of his bodyguards, who smirks. "Bad for business. Still, put more men on the warehouses – if things kick off and there's panic, make sure our places are safe. I'm going to move more cargo through to the Archipelago."

"We'd do better moving people," says Tammur. Guerdon is crowded with refugees fleeing the Godwar, eager to buy passage to the safe, unspoiled frontier of the Archipelago – a chain of islands across an ocean so storm-wracked that they can be reached safely only by ships with modern alchemical engines. "Myri here has a line on an old passenger liner we could refit."

Heinreil yawns. "Not interested."

"Tam promised you'd give me a fair hearing," says the woman hastily. "She's a good ship, seaworthy. She can make a run to the Archipelago in—"

"I don't repeat myself," says Heinreil. "If you want to do business in my city, remember that." He turns to Tammur. "What I need from you is a full audit – how much cash do we have on hand, and how much can we raise if needed?"

Myri sits back, seething, teeth clenched, clearly signalling her displeasure. Rat narrows his eyes – she's overacting, putting on a show. Tammur sighs. "I'll look at the books. How much should I put aside for the magistrates?"

"Nothing. It'll be foreign investment, through local agents there. You don't need to worry about our home-grown leeches."

"Not about the audit. Spar."

"If Taphson doesn't beat him or break him, and he actually reaches court alive – put aside twenty, but don't touch it unless we know the boy can still work. We can plead compassion and have him sent to the Isle of Statues for five thousand if he's gone to stone."

Tammur draws another card, then folds. The turn goes around the table again twice. Hedan tries to stay in, tries to brazen it out, but it's clear he has nothing and the other three bleed him dry. Myri's still in the game, but has only a few coins left in front of her.

"I shouldn't play with Crawlers," spits Hedan. "Can't read a bloody mask."

Obligingly, Nine Moons Falling reaches up and removes its porcelain face. Worms writhe in the shadows of its hood. It forms them into a pallid, thin-lipped smile.

Heinreil doesn't flinch. "What's it to be? Call or raise?"

The Crawling One reaches inside its shadowy robe. It pulls out a bag and upends it on the table. Rubies and emeralds tumble from it, a fortune in stones.

Without a word, Myri lays her cards face down on the table and clasps her hands, head bowed. Again, her tattoos ripple and glow faintly.

"I don't carry that sort of money," says Heinreil. "And Crawlers don't play cards. Not unless there's a good reason for it. What do you want?"

"A trinket." The worm's voice is like a slithering chorus. "A thing of nothing."

"When a sorcerer says something's a trinket, it means it's worth a lot more than it looks. Wizards could take lessons from street magicians. Learn how to play a mark." Heinreil thinks for a moment, then reaches inside his jacket and pulls out a small token on a string.

Rat recognises it. Cari's amulet.

Heinreil dangles the little talisman over the pot. "Add one more thing – tell me why you want it."

"If you win," gurgles the Crawling One.

The talisman drops. "Call."

The Crawling One lays its cards down on the table, and, as it does so, it whispers a spell. Reality squirms and bends under the force of its magic. Probabilities warp. The wave of change passes over Tammur, over Hedan, over the bodyguards without any of them noticing. Most humans can't perceive subtle sorcery like this. Rat couldn't either, usually, but his senses are somehow heightened after his experiences in the tunnels.

That's why he can see Myri's tattoos glow dimly, as though her blood's on fire. He can see her strain against the change, see her grab it and hold it, then swallow it, forcing the spell to wreak its reality warping effects inside her instead of on the cards. She gasps in pain, then smiles bloodily through clenched teeth as Heinreil reveals his cards.

A winning hand.

Shielded against the Crawling One's magical attempt at cheating by Myri. She was a plant, Rat thinks, and he wonders how Heinreil anticipated the Crawling One's scheme. He shivers, aware of forces moving around him invisibly, connecting his friend to greater events.

Heinreil scoops the pot. Pockets Cari's talisman and rolls the three biggest rubies to Myri. He stands, addresses the Crawling One. "You and I need to have a little chat. Everyone else, out."

Apparently, everyone else doesn't mean the Fever Knight, or Myri, both of whom remain with Heinreil. Rat follows Tammur like a shadow.

He wants to listen at the door, lurk and see if he can make out anything of Nine Moons Falling's confession, but another of Heinreil's bodyguards grabs him first, leads him downstairs, out of the hall and back onto the streets.

"The boss has another job for you."

CHAPTER NINE

Entering the house on Desiderata Street by the front door still feels wrong to Carillon. All her instincts tell her to go around the back, to the servant's entrance, or to scale the side wall and climb in through that little window. It's a place to rob, not a home. Eladora walks arm in arm with her all the way down from the university, though, grip like a vice, chattering all the time, a nervous rush of words that Carillon doesn't bother pretending to hear. Although she's grateful for Eladora's literal support. She still feels horribly weak and unsteady.

In the door, and down to the little kitchen. Eladora places her heavy satchel on the table and bustles around; it's Aunt Silva in the kitchen at Wheldacre, projected twenty years across space and time. Tea brews, soup bubbles on the stove.

Cari sits there in domestic normality and thinks about falling into that lightless chasm. Some god tore her soul from her body and dragged her down. A leaf getting washed down a sewer, that's what she was. Tiny in the face of the divine. She grips the rough wooden edge of the table tightly, as if she can hold onto the material world by sheer force alone.

"Tell me, did the professor find my notes useful? You will tell me if you have another episode, won't you? Actually, I should really have my notebook to hand. Best be prepared." Eladora rummages through her satchel, stacking books on the table next to Cari until she finds what she seeks. She stares at Cari and vanishes off to another room, returning with a cushion. "In case you have a fit and fall off the stool, aim for this."

Cari briefly contemplates smothering her cousin with the cushion.

"Well, tell me, what did the professor say?" asks Eladora.

Cari tries to make light of it. "You were right. I'm a saint."

"Oh." Eladora takes a step back, as if expecting Cari to burst into flame or start manifesting ectoplasm all over her kitchen. "How . . . unusual. No doubt it's some f-foreign god." She makes it sound like it's a lover's pox that Cari picked up in some distant port.

"Maybe. All this only started after I came back to this fucking city," says Cari. She rolls that thought around in her head. It makes a lot of sense. She's had more than her share of weird experiences since she fled Guerdon all those years ago, but none of them involved head-shattering supernatural visions sent by some old blind god. Maybe it even explains the antipathy she's felt towards the city all her life; as a child, in Grandfather Thay's mansion, she'd always been uncomfortable. A feeling like the constant buzzing of bees that only she could hear. Going to Aunt Silva's house in the country had been a blessed relief – but even there, a few miles outside Guerdon, she'd been restless, uneasy, like there was something chasing her.

Invisible fingers fumbling across the countryside, looking for a dropped plaything. Lifting her like the dancing saint in Severast. Snapping her.

A plan forms.

She announces, "I'm wrecked, El. I'm going to bed."

"But I'm making soup," protests Eladora.

"I'll heat it up later."

Down to her little nest in the basement, where thick walls blot out the sounds of the city. It's barely even evening, the clocks haven't yet struck six, but Cari curls up and closes her eyes, and tries to ignore the city as it breaks over her.

Midnight. The house is silent and still; she can't hear anyone on the street outside, except some distant revellers down in Glimmerside.

Cari steals up to the kitchen. Eladora's satchel is still on the table, but her notebook's gone. Typical – her cousin can't be helpful even when she's being robbed. Cari glances at the stack of books next to it – some of them might be worth a fortune, she reflects, but she has no idea which, and they'll all too heavy.

She flips through one of them while she drinks cold soup. Architectural drawings of churches and cathedrals, sketches of Guerdon in ruins. A few pictures of some civil war, fighting on the streets, the city burning. Sword-wielding knights bearing the Keeper's mark, patrolling lines in the ash that were once grand thoroughfares. Some of the buildings Cari recognises. On the page they're ideals, perfect forms. She wonders what their long-dead architects would say now to see them, soot-stained and graffitied, overshadowed by the smokestacks and towers of industry.

Turning a page, she comes across an illustration of a vertical shaft, lined with marble, extending from the crypt of some great church down into the earth below. At the base of the shaft dance a pack of hungry ghouls. The artist, perhaps sick of drawing endless geometric shapes and sweeping architecture, lavished attention on these illustrations, and their canine faces are alive with glee and hunger. She worries about what's become of Rat. Did the Tallowmen catch him? She remembers Ongent asking her questions about her ghoul friend, asking if he'd talked to her about the previous ages of the city. And Spar, still—

Stupid girl, woolgathering when she should be acting. Angrily, she closes the book and pushes it away across the table. She finds a sharp knife in a drawer, and spends a minute trying to cut the alchemical peace-bond off her own dagger, but the black stuff regrows as fast as it's damaged. Fine. She stuffs her dagger into Eladora's satchel, then slips the knife into her belt. She ransacks the kitchen cupboards for food and slips upstairs, bypassing her own room. There are two others – Eladora's, and Miren's attic room at the top of a narrow stairs.

Miren's not worth the risk.

Eladora's room, then. Pressing her ear against the door, Cari can hear her cousin breathing evenly. She tries the handle. Locked. Her lock picks are scattered across the ruins of the Tower of Law, she realises, or maybe in the thief-taker's place. The kitchen knife might work, but it's not ideal.

Inspiration strikes. She returns to the kitchen, makes one small adjustment, then comes back up.

She knocks on the door.

"Eladora?"

Stirring, mumbled confusion.

"Eladora?" she asks again.

"Carillon," mutters Eladora in half-sleep. Then, bolt awake: "What's wrong? What's happening? Did you have another attack?"

"I can't work the stove." She puts just enough pathetic whining into her voice, mimicking Eladora's own.

"Oh, for heaven's sake. Give me a moment." Shuffling, then the click of the lock.

"Sorry," says Cari, "I'm starving."

"I did offer earlier, but never mind." Eladora smiles and rubs her eyes. "It'll take a few minutes."

"I'll be down in a moment," offers Cari. Still half-asleep, Eladora stumbles downstairs. Cari hears her fumbling with the stove, cursing as it fails to light. It'll take her a few minutes to find the stopcock that Cari turned all the way off.

Clothes first. Cari raids Eladora's wardrobe, rifling past half a dozen identical grey robes and dresses that were unfashionable even in Aunt Silva's day. She's not looking for fashion, just practicality. Neither frumpy dresses nor grey robes are suitable for what she has in mind. She finds a pair of trousers that might fit, some other clothes that she can adapt. Into the bag with them. She can wear them until she pawns them and finds something better, or technically worse but more like Cari's preferred outfit. And, hey, what's this – a box of coins, hidden where no one would ever think to look, at the back of the wardrobe. Into the bag, too.

A quick sweep of the room. More coin, enough to buy passage to Severast maybe, if she doesn't mind eating bilge rat. And in a drawer next to the bed, a little alchemical pistol. Cari pauses at that – it doesn't square with her mental image of her cousin. The gun's been fired a few times, from the stains on the muzzle. A safety talisman for a nervous country girl in the big city? Something Aunt Silva insisted on? Or connected to her work with Professor Ongent?

Into the bag with it.

Then out of the window, into the night. Cari perches on the little windowsill, scanning the street below, breathing in the night air. She looks across the shrouded city. Moonlight on the harbour, turning the fumes over the Alchemists' Quarter to a purple haze. The great bulk of Holyhill to her right, with its white cathedrals like three skulls lined up on a shelf. The bulk of the city to her left, Glimmerside sloping down to the docks and the Wash. She looks for the tell-tale flicker of candles in wax heads, for traces of the Tallowmen. That's her one last fear – that one of those horrors will find her before she gets out of the city.

She sways unsteadily on the windowsill as another vision rises within her brain, but she's ready for it, or maybe it's less intense this time. Either way, she's able to tighten her grip as she sees—

Another street in the city. Not too far. Still in Glimmerside. Her perspective's horribly skewed, like she's seeing it from a dozen angles at once, and feeling it, too – the trickle of rainwater in the gutters, the hissing heat of the gas lamp, and the heavy footsteps of the night watchman. Human; it's Glimmerside after all, almost genteel. No freakish gull monsters or psychotic waxworks here, thank you very much, but if the watchman comes around the corner and looks up, he could look straight at Carillon.

With a strange doubled vision, she can see the distant light of the guard's lantern with her own eyes, reflecting in shop windows at the end of the street, and she can see the lantern directly through this divine vision or whatever it is.

The street – the other street, the one she's not on but can still, impossibly, see – is nearly empty. Just one other person, coming up the long steep stairs from the subway. A youngish man, also human, in the robes of a priest.

She recognises him instantly. It's the priest from the Church of the Holy Beggar, the one she saw before – being devoured by a shadowy monster-thing.

The watchman approaches the thing that looks like a priest. The priest smiles and speaks a greeting, and Cari, from her divine perspective, can feel the thing change as it does so. She can feel it form lungs and throat even as it opens its mouth, taste the acid on its newborn tongue.

"Good night to you." The watchman nods and passes by.

The thing turns and walks towards Desiderata street, towards Carillon. It looks right at her, and it recognises her.

In that instant, she knows its name, its title: Raveller.

For a moment, she's outside the city. She's nothing more than a shadow of a shadow, a residual darkness hiding under a stone. The stones are cracked and worn, part of some old ruin. Frost on the ground – it's winter, last winter, around the time Carillon arrived back in Guerdon. The darkness writhes, consumes insects, and from them learns to grow legs. It scuttles out of its hiding place, snatches up a bird, takes wings and eyes, knitting a form together from strands of dissolved flesh and spirit. From afar, the Raveller saw her then. It came to the city to find her.

The vision ends, and she's back entirely in her own form, her consciousness back crammed down into the thief on the window-sill. Looking down to the end of the street, she sees the figure of the priest standing in the shadows, scanning the fronts of the houses. She presses herself against the wall, sliding back into Eladora's bedroom without being spotted. From the Raveller's hesitation, she guesses that it can't sense her now that she's out of that divine perspective, now that she's no longer in communion with whatever deity likes to send her sightseeing across Guerdon and tell her stories about long-dead ghouls.

"Carillon?" hisses Eladora from the corridor. "If you're going to get me up in the dead of—" She comes to the door, sees her ransacked room, and shrieks. "What in the gods' name have you done to my things?"

Cari slams the window down. "Shut up! The thing from the Holy Beggar's here. It's looking for me."

Eladora's face clouds in confusion. Clearly, Ongent and Miren don't share everything with her.

"Get Miren," she says.

"He's gone out. On an errand for Professor Ongent."

"Bolt the doors," orders Cari. When Eladora doesn't move fast enough, Cari grabs her by the arm and shoves her in the direction of the stairs. "It's saint stuff. Something unholy. Move!" Finally obedient, Eladora stumbles downstairs. Clack of the heavy bolts. The door's double-bolted and reinforced, which struck Cari as suspicious when she first arrived. Now, it seems also prudent.

Cari checks the street outside, peering out of the window from the side, careful not to reveal herself. The priest moves slowly up Desiderata, going door to door, zigzagging from one side of the street to the other and back again. Outside each door, he just pauses for a long moment, pressing against it. He's doing something, and Cari can't figure out what that is until he's closer. The priest-thing comes to the door, covering the keyhole and letterbox with his body, and then shudders. Cari sees shadows moving inside the house, whip-quick, smearing blood against the inside of the windows. She once saw an octopus in a glass tank in the market at Severast, and its tentacles slithering over the glass reminds her of those shadows.

The priest-thing gathers itself, sucking its tentacles back into its form. Cari's sure that everyone else in that house, and every house along the street from here to the corner, is dead.

The priest turns and starts to cross the street towards Cari. All the bolts in the world aren't even going to slow the Raveller down.

Run, then. She checks the little window in the hallway that looks out over the back of the house, over yards and alleyways to the distant bulk of Gethis Station. Little lights crawl over the rooftops. The Tallowmen are out in force tonight, knives bright in their hands, looking for criminals to gut and slice, blind to the far worse danger on Cari's doorstep.

Her decision's made before she even really knows it. She returns to Eladora's bedroom, leans out of the window. Eladora's little pistol has a hell of a kick for its size. The priest's head explodes in a spray of colour-smeared slime. Translucent tentacles like flowing glass sprout from the ruin of its skull, lashing up blindly at the house. Cari falls back onto the floor of the bedroom, landing awkwardly. She crawls into the hallway and kicks Eladora's door shut with one foot, then braces it, holding it shut as tentacles scrabble at it. She hears shrieks from downstairs, but it's the sound of Eladora freaking out in terror, not being sliced to ribbons by the thing outside.

Cari doesn't expect the little pistol to do much to the Raveller. She knows – but doesn't know how she knows – that it would take a much bigger gun to do any real damage. She knows – instinctively, intuitively, like a childhood memory – that the Raveller borrows shapes because it is inherently shapeless. It doesn't have bones to break or organs to burst. It doesn't bleed. In the dark, endless catacombs beneath the world, the Ravellers writhe and slither and feast. It's a spirit made flesh, the shadow cast by a dark god, a stolen form assembled from dried blood and the leavings of sacrifices. A thing of nightmare.

But this is Desiderata Street. The edge of the University District, bordering on the good part of Glimmerside. This is perilously close to being a quality part of town. Break the peace of the night with a pistol shot down in the Wash or Five Knives and no one cares. Let off a gun here, though, and someone notices.

And these days, some*things*.

Light pours in over Cari's shoulder for an instant, as though someone lit a bonfire right outside the window. Footsteps run across the roof of the house, an inhumanly fast drumbeat. The Tallowmen are here.

Cari races down the stairs. Eladora's still standing by the front door, frozen like a statue, making this keening screech. She's right next to the letterbox. "Get back!" shouts Cari, and she runs forward, but it's too late.

A slim white hand pushes through the letterbox and dissolves into a thousand flailing tentacles, reaching for Cari and Eladora. Some of the tentacles have human eyes, Cari notices in that split second between seeing them and being devoured by them. Others have teeth.

The letterbox suddenly blazes with arcane power.

The door of the house explodes in blue light. Eladora's wail is drowned out by the Raveller's inhuman roar of pain from a hundred different mouths. The force of the blast sends Cari sprawling against the end of the bannister. It picks Eladora up and throws her down the hallway like a doll. The door was warded, Cari guesses, some of Ongent's sorcery. She knows fuck-all about magic, and after tonight really doesn't want to get any closer to it.

She gets up. Sways. Blood's pouring from her mouth, her nose, and she feels like she's been kicked in the stomach, but nothing's broken. She grabs Eladora's satchel, then hauls Eladora to her feet. Her cousin's stunned. Red stains spread across her once white nightdress. She's still alive, though.

Outside, through the burning wreck of the door, she sees the seething colourless pool of the Raveller writhing in the middle of the street. It's lost all shape – there's nothing left of the priest from the Holy Beggar, or the beautiful woman, or any of the other faces it stole before it came to Guerdon. Three Tallowman stand around outside, like copies of each other from the same mould, every one of them with the same manic grin, the same upraised knife. Waiting for something fleshy to stab. The Raveller obliges, taking on the shape of some underworld ogre, a hulking brute with insect eyes. Glassy razor-edged tentacles burst from its arms and flanks, and slice through waxy flesh.

The Tallowman's wounds seal as quickly as they are opened, just like the alchemical goo on Cari's dagger.

The waxworks stab back, lightning-fast, a hundred little cuts in the Raveller's belly. Those too heal almost instantly.

It's not that they can't hurt each other. It's just going to take a great deal of effort.

The Raveller lunges forward, grabs one of the Tallowmen, spreadeagles it, pulling waxy arms out to the left and right. Then it sprouts a bigger tentacle from its chest and cuts the waxwork clean in two, exposing the treated spinal cord of its wick. The Tallowman's light goes out, and it dies.

The other two go into a frenzy, driving their knives as deep into the mutable substance of the Raveller as their inhuman strength can muster, raking deep gouges into the monster faster than it can heal. All three creatures move faster than the human eye can follow – it's like a catfight with knives and tentacles.

Cari's not going that way. Nothing's going out of that door without being turned into bloody ribbons. She runs down the hallway to the back of the house, pulling the stunned Eladora with her. Out into the little cobbled yard at the back of the house, ducking under a washing line, up over a low wall into the alleyway behind. More lights race across distant rooftops as more and more Tallowmen are drawn by the fray. The two surviving ones in the fight are blazing brightly now, like beacon fires.

The alleyway's shadows are cool and concealing. Cari half carries Eladora as far as she can, down past the end of the row and across Pilgrim Street to another sheltered yard. It's safe enough. She unwraps her cousin's limp arms from around her neck and lays Eladora down in a quiet corner. Eladora's face is horribly bruised and blood's oozing from a gash on her forehead, but her colour's good and she's breathing steadily. She's even half conscious.

"Carillon?"

"Sssh, ssh. Just lie there, all right. Everything'll be fine."

"That's my bag . . . " Eladora paws at the leather satchel on Cari's shoulder.

"I just need to borrow it."

"You'll ruin it," mutters Eladora dreamily. "You ruin everything nice."

Charming, thinks Cari.

"It's your mother in you. Silva always said so . . . up from the dark, and whispering . . . " Eladora slips back into unconsciousness. Cari straightens up. Glances right, back up Desiderata, just in time to see a white flash of light like a thunderbolt, and then another and another. Screaming, and glass shattering. So many Tallowmen it looks like the whole city's on fire.

Not her problem.

Not her city.

She vanishes into the night. Down, down towards the docks and the sea and escape.

CHAPTER TEN

Y ou learn to sleep anywhere on campaign. When you don't know when you'll next get a chance to rest, you make the most of every opportunity. There was this one guy in Jere's old company, a little Severastian named Marlo, who claimed that he'd slept through most of the Battle of the White Forest while on the front lines. The Bloody-Handed Saint came crashing through the trees, swinging his holy death sword that slays twenty men with every blow, and twenty-one fell down. It takes a special dedication to lie down and fall asleep while surrounded by the god-blasted corpses of your comrades, but Marlo managed it.

Jere learned the trick from him, but he's lost it in the last few years. A soldier has it easy – there's someone to tell you where to go, what to do, and you can just put your head down and follow orders. Thief-taking is a different business. Jere is bone-tired after a day traipsing around the city, but he can't quieten his mind.

The morning, checking into the Beckanore case – talking to contacts in the army, visiting the people from Old Haith that lived in the city. The Old Haithers wanted to build a sea fort on the island of Beckanore, and claimed that the city of Guerdon had ceded the island to them in some ancient treaty. Parliament had told them to go shove their claims up the Crown of Haith's necrotic arsehole, only in more diplomatic language, and now Old Haith was making all sorts of threats. Sabre-rattling, warships sailing suspiciously close to Guerdon's trade routes, the "mysterious" burning of the mostly abandoned monastery on Beckanore. Most of them would come to nothing – Old Haith had bigger problems elsewhere. They wanted the sea fort to defend against the Ishmere or whoever they were fighting this month in the war; against saint-blessed armadas of wave and storm. The last thing Old Haith wanted to do was piss off the neutral city of Guerdon, and the last thing Guerdon wanted to do was have to give up its immensely profitable weapon-selling neutrality and get involved.

Blowing up the whole House of Law to make the dispute go away, though – however satisfying – didn't seem likely.

Dredger was looking into the alchemical bomb, so Jere tried to push that out of his head for the moment. Large-scale alchemical weapons . . . worse than the fucking gods, thought Jere. At least when a saint or sorcerer or even a bloody actual living manifestation on the battlefield takes a shot at you, you can see it coming. They mean to kill you. It's honest. Alchemy kills indiscriminately and invisibly. No swords or bullets, no blasting spells, just a little pinch of dust in the air that gets into your lungs and strangles you, or rain that seeps through your skin and turns your guts into sticking black rotten mush.

Marlo, Jere suddenly recalls, died in his sleep. Took a nap on ground tainted by some alchemy bomb, and never woke up. When they poked him, their fingers punched right through his ribcage. The poison in the ground had leeched all the strength from him, turned him into something with the consistency of wet paper.

THIS IS NOT THE LAST on walls around him, or in his mind's eye.

Alchemy bombs going off in the city. He turns that thought over in his mind. Even Kelkin, worst-case Kelkin, never suggested that idea in their conversation yesterday. The House of Law bombing as a trial run, a pre-emptive strike for some other city or country attacking the fat prize of Guerdon. The whole city like Marlo, going to sleep and never waking up again, poisoned in their beds. Invisible dust in the air, poison in the water. Unseen horrors.

Finally, he'd gone back to Pulchar's, to the alley beside the restaurant, with its bins full of scraps and rats, with its smell of frying meat and onions. Pulchar had been a guild thief once, years ago, before Heinreil took over. He'd come through the purges and the bad nights pretty well. Retiring to run a cookhouse was a lot better than choking on your own blood in an alley. Jere had waited until the old man came out for a smoke. The conversation ran through Jere's mind over and over.

"What's the special tonight, Pulchar?"

The old man spat. "Again? Gods below. Go feed a ghoul."

Jere tapped his iron-shod staff on an overflowing bin. "Maybe I will. Maybe I'll come back with a few of my lads. Who's eating here tonight? How many bounties?"

Pulchar closed the door to the kitchen behind him, moved down the alleyway, lowered his voice. "I gave you the House of Law job, didn't I?"

"The House of Law, yeah. Picked up some street trash girl, the Tallows got another. And, aye, I've got Idge's boy sitting in one of my cells." Pulchar flinched at that; he'd been part of Idge's inner circle, back in the day, and still owed some loyalty to Idge's memory. "Of course, you said it was a break-in. Not that the whole fucking building was going to explode. I nearly got my beard singed, you know."

"I don't know anything about that," hissed Pulchar. "I heard a robbery, not a bloody bombing."

"Do you reckon it was Heinreil?"

Pulchar glanced back, took a long drag on his cigarette. "I don't know. What was the score? What were they after?"

"You tell me."

"Maybe. Maybe. I know Heinreil's moved alchemical weapons. We never touched the stuff when I was working, but these days, with the war so close . . . " The cook paused. "Is this the war? Are they going to attack Guerdon?"

"Where's Heinreil getting the weapons? Where's he moving them to?"

"I just hear what's said at dinner. I'm not in the Brotherhood anymore, am I?"

"If you hear anything . . . "

"I'll keep it to myself. Fuck it, come back with your bully-boys. Bring the waxworks too for all I care. I'm sick of this!"

Jere tried another tack. "Fair enough. I've got Idge's boy. Let's see if he can live up to his father. Gods, stone, though. Horrible way to go. Like I told him, all I need is a tongue to speak, and the rest of him can go cold . . . "

"The alchemist's cure—"

"Is expensive, and I've got to eat same as your customers in here. Give. Me. Something." Jere's staff thudded into the ground three times, underlining his demands.

"This is all I have, all right? I don't want to see you ever again after this."

"You can't cook for shit, so I won't be back here to eat."

"The word is that Heinreil's looking for Ven the Goat."

"And who," asked Jere, "is Ven the Goat?"

"Call yourself a fucking thief-taker . . . Ven the Goat, man. He robbed the fucking High Cathedral, didn't he? Stole all these sacred cups and jewelled robes and the like. Biggest haul in a hundred years."

"Oh, right." Long before Jere's time. "What happened to him?"

Pulchar shrugged. "If I knew that, I'd have told Heinreil, not you. Drank himself to death would be my guess. Although . . . "

"Go on."

"Ven used to say that what he stole wasn't a fraction of the real treasure. Said the biggest prize in Guerdon was in the church, right in front of everyone, but no one ever saw it. Maybe he found religion."

"Right." Jere rolled his eyes. "Hear the phrase 'this is not the last' recently?"

"Someone wrote it on a wall up near Mercy Street after the Tower came down. Yeah, everyone heard that." Pulchar flung the end of his cigarette into a corner, startling a mouse. "So, where's next to burn?"

Shouts outside. The wild ringing of distant bells. Jere rolls out of bed and peers out of the grimy little window. A cluster of fast-moving lights in the distance, and then a bright blue flash and a sound like thunder. Up at the church end of Glimmerside, by the looks of it, by the university. Another bombing? The next to burn?

He groans as he rises. Fuck, he's old now. His side aches where that stone hit him yesterday. He pulls on his boots, grabs a cloak. Debates taking the staff, but he doesn't want to aggravate the injury to his ribs hauling that big stick around, so he goes for his trick cane instead. Loads his pistol, and his spare. Knife in his boot, too, ready for a night on the town.

From next door he hears the steady footsteps of the Stone Man, still circling endlessly around his island prison. Shit, thinks Jere, he does owe Pulchar. Jere hurries over to a chest and pulls out a vial of alkahest. It's his last one – he'll have to get more, maybe get Kelkin to pay for it. He weighs in it in his hand in one of those moments of exhausted philosophical reverie one gets just after waking, when you're still half wandering the paths of sleep. He imagines the city as a Stone Man, fear freezing it, locking it down, entombing its living crowds within the dead stone of the buildings. Is he the alkahest or the weapon that wounds?

He moves next door, shoves his little boat onto the water and punts across on the heads of dead men. For the first time, he's unsettled by the thought that he sleeps thirty feet away from a mass grave. It's hard to remember that those eerie statues were once human.

The Stone Man – the still-living Stone Man – pauses when he sees Jere.

"What's happening?" asks Spar.

"More of your friend Heinreil's devilry. Feel like talking about it?"

"No."

"Have some more time to think about it. I may be gone for a good while, maybe all of tomorrow." Jere throws the alkahest vial to Spar. "That's the last one I have. You may want to hold off using it. Maybe you don't really need that leg. Maybe you can get by with only one arm. I don't know – how much more are you willing to give that man?"

"Not him," said Spar thickly. "The Brotherhood."

"Like there's a difference." Jere leaves the Stone Man with his thoughts; maybe this will be the night when he finally cracks, but it's looking less and less likely. Jere's learned to read Spar's body language, and the Stone Man seethes whenever Heinreil's name comes up, but he won't speak. He's Idge's boy through and through beneath that stony shell. His father protected the Brotherhood from Kelkin by refusing to talk, refusing to deal after his arrest. If Spar does the same, THIS IS NOT THE LAST. If Heinreil's behind the bombing, THIS IS NOT THE LAST.

From the streets, he's got a better view of the carnage up at Glimmerside. Half the city's woken up to look at the fireworks. The flashes of light are less frequent now, but there's a ring of burning buildings. The city map, traced in red flames across the dark face of the hillside: Pilgrim Street, Desiderata, Redoubt.

He hails a cab. The raptequine – the horse-derived thing in harness – snarls at him. Alchemists brew them up in vats, same as the Gullheads. Faster and stronger than horses and, more importantly for city work, they shit less. Have to be fed on meat, though. Jere's pulled belongings of more than a few murder victims out of the feeding troughs. Nothing of the bodies remained, not even bone.

He pays the cabbie double to get up there quickly. The beast hisses and roars as it thunders through the streets, snapping jaws clearing the path of drunks and gawkers. Jere rechecks his pistol, slides the blade from the cane to make sure it doesn't stick. He's girding himself for war, he realises, like he used to do before a battle. He can almost hear Marlo snoring beside him, the old mercenary's battle cry.

Up the high street and into Glimmerside. Distant bells of fire engines, answered by the frantic ringing of church bells on Holyhill. Streets more thickly crowded here, the cab slowing to a crawl despite the raptequine's growling. The cabbie shouts at people to clear the road, but they've nowhere to go. Up ahead, there's a cordon of city watch blocking the roads, with a few prowling Tallowmen to back them up.

Jere dismounts and pays the cabbies, then shoulders his way through the crowd, using his size and strength to force his way up to the guards. One of them recognises him, and lets him past, waving off the Tallowmen who flicker towards him, murder in their unblinking waxwork eyes. The street beyond the cordon is thick with ash, sticky with lumps of white-red slime that Jere recognises finally as chunks of Tallowman flesh, chopped from the bodies of the destroyed wax men by some tremendous force. The lumps soften when the heat from the burning buildings touches them. Some of the remains twitch and seem to move away from the fires, but he can't tell – and doesn't want to know – if they're just sliding downhill as they melt, or if there's still some ghastly approximation of life in those dismembered bits.

Desiderata Street is a battleground.

Ankle-deep in wax. The whole east side gutted by fire, houses stripped to black skeletons. The firefighters' alchemical slime drips, pungent and caustic, from the smouldering ruins to pool and puddle with the rivers of melted wax. All the alchemists' works mingling together as they pour down a storm drain. A few figures in the alchemists' livery move through the ruins like wading birds, carrying handheld slime thuribles, looking for lingering hotspots. *They're not using Stone Men*, thinks Jere absently – is this less dangerous in the aftermath than the Tower of Law, or do they just not want to bring the plague up to this part of the city?

Halfway along the street there's a big hole or crater. It doesn't look like a bomb blast. More like something broke through the street and clawed its way frantically down towards the sewers below. Smoke rises from the still-hot edges of the hole; slime bubbles on the scorched and broken cobblestones. Through an open doorway, Jere can see into one of the houses near the hole. A guardsman kneels by a red mess on the floor, and pokes through it with his truncheon, retches when he finds a face. Jere can't be sure in the dim light, but he'd lay odds that those remains are the butchered giblets of the people who lived there, chopped up by the same thrashing blades that dismembered all those Tallowmen.

He moves on. He hears the sound of weeping coming from an alleyway. At the end, seated on a step, two people. A young woman in a nightdress, a guard's cloak draped around her shoulders. She's weeping and clinging to her companion, a slight young man in dark clothes. When he sees Jere, he detaches himself from the girl, slipping out of her grasp. She sniffles, wipes her nose and tries to compose herself when she realises that they're no longer alone. She takes her hands away from her eyes and Jere spots a huge welt on her forehead, like she's been smashed with a mace.

Miren. The professor's son. No wonder the girl's weeping, if she's looking for comfort from that cold boy.

"What happened?" asks Jere.

"My father's been arrested." Miren says it matter-of-factly; no trace of worry. "He told me to look out for you. He wants to see you."

"Who's arrested him? The watch, or ...?" The Tallowmen don't have the authority to arrest anyone, not officially. They're backup for the watch, made to prevent crimes and keep the peace, nothing more. But half the Tallowmen in the city must be clustered around these few streets, or in pieces underfoot.

"The watch."

"Right. What happened? Do you know?"

The girl on the doorstep rises, but Miren's back by her side before she can speak, abruptly solicitous and soothing, pressing her back down and quietening her. Miren looks up at Jere and shakes his head. "I wasn't here when it started. Some sort of monster, like a tide of black slime."

Whatever the fuck that is, thinks Jere. For obscure supernatural threats, Ongent is his go-to informant, but the professor's in custody. He makes a mental note to check with Dredger when he gets a chance.

"What about the thief girl?" He nearly says *Thay*, but Ongent asked that he not mention that bit of her history, and Tallowmen have ears like bats.

"Sh-she ran off," stammers Eladora, shivering. "I don't know where. She stole my bag," she adds petulantly.

"I'll keep an eye out for her," mutters Jere. The Thay girl is a small problem compared to the devastation on the street outside, but it's an annoying one. He released her into the professor's keeping; both he and Ongent are liable for her future misdeeds. She'll probably crawl back to Heinreil and beg for another job, or else fuck off again with the morning tide.

Back up to the main street. The fires are mostly under control, and the Tallowmen – both the dead and the quick – have melted away, one set into the gutters and the other into the shadows. There are only a few nervous watch standing around. Black robes gathering the dead, and firefighters washing the slime away.

The watch won't let him into the professor's house. It's empty anyway. The professor's been taken down to the watch's keep, over on Queen's Point. Jere hitches a ride with one of the departing watch-wagons. The crowds have mostly dispersed, too, but there's still a sick energy in the air, sour adrenaline running through the streets. The city's sleep has been disturbed; like some giant animal with stone sinews and nerves made of living people, Guerdon paces back and forth, testing the limits of its cage. There's going to be more trouble tonight. Fighting down in the docks, maybe. Tavern brawls and looting, especially if most of the city's Tallowmen seem to be running around rooftops in Glimmerside. Worse, if people think that whatever happened at Desiderata was another bombing.

At the keep they refuse to let Jere see the professor. He wheedles, calls in favours, threatens, all to no avail. Even old friends of his won't help. Frustrated, he goes out into the courtyard to clear his head – and there's the answer. A carriage, bearing the arms of the noble house of Droupe. Droupe, member of parliament; Droupe, in the pocket of the alchemists. From talking to Kelkin, Jere knows that the only thing that would get Droupe down to the low city after midnight is a command from the alchemists' guild. The alchemists want to talk to Ongent before anyone else.

Jere heads back inside, finds a quiet bench in the waiting room and lies down. Sleep comes easily. He's still got a thousand questions running through his mind, but now he's got a battle to focus on. A battle to win.

Not even the host of guards and prisoners tromping through the keep in the aftermath of the dock riots wakes him.

CHAPTER ELEVEN

Slip-sliding on rain-slick cobbles down the hills towards the harbour. Cari keeps to the back alleyways, the thief's paths, staying off the main streets. Tallowmen run past every few minutes, leaping from rooftop to rooftop on their way to Glimmerside. The monsters' lights are burning bright with alarm, and they burn the shadows away as they pass and force Cari to crouch low or press herself into a wall to avoid being seen. The Tallowmen have other business tonight, though.

Thunder rolls across the city.

The Raveller isn't following her. It's still fighting the Tallowmen. She prays to every god she knows that the two horrors will cancel each other out, black slime versus fleshy wax, shapeless shapes cutting and slicing each other until the rain washes them away. It's not her problem. It's not her city. Every step takes her closer to the sea and escape. There are always ships coming and going from Guerdon. Refugees come on ships from the lands wracked by the Godswar, and the ships go back laden with mercenaries and war-chymists plying their trade. Grain haulers from Severast and its sunny plains, ships carrying furs and amber from Varinth, traders from Paravos and the Sunset Lands.

Any one will do. The satchel she stole from Eladora is reassuringly heavy, enough to buy passage. The city sticks to Cari's skin. The grit burrows into her pores and poisons her blood. She wants to wash it off, to slough free of Guerdon and her unwanted sainthood. The open ocean will cure her. She will be anonymous again, forgotten, able to be whoever she wants to be. West, she decides. She'll sail west, away from Guerdon and away from the eldritch terrors of the Godswar, off to the new lands of the Archipelago. She clutches her knife for reassurance, and her hand brushes against the texture of the rubbery cord. She can get another knife, she reminds herself.

She skirts around the edge of the New Docks. The ships that moor here are big freighters, run by the guilds. She might be able to stow away on one, but she's not willing to risk it, not when there are better options. The dockland taverns and flophouses have vomited their contents onto the street, as people come out to look at the pyrotechnics up in Glimmerside. Flashes of light, and flames. Bells ringing in the distance to sound the alarm. With luck, Eladora's out of the line of fire. Ongent will have to find another fascinating prodigy to experiment on; if Cari's curse goes away as mysteriously as it manifested when she leaves the city, she'll be happy never to come back to Guerdon.

Cold tendrils slither across her brain, freezing the inside of her skull. Her skin crawls. This time, she recognises the onset of the vision, and can prepare for it. She skids to a halt, crouches in the shadows of a door and wraps her arms around her head as some forgotten god reaches down from heaven and breaks into her mind with a sledgehammer. This one's not a vision, it's a plea, a blast of raw emotion, of longing and loneliness and terror. Cari is in the belly of a ship a thousand miles from anyone she's ever known, in a strange and terrifying land. She has no friends, no money, nothing to fall back on. She's going to starve on the streets, get raped and murdered in an alleyway, going to die cold and alone. Cari is young again, in the darkness of the Thay mansion. Her father, pale and nervous, refuses to look at her, talks to her as he'd soothe a wild dog. She is alone. Cari is sick, feverish, huddled in sweat-soaked blankets in the stinking hold of a ship. Through the thudding pain in her head, through the thick fog, she hears two crewmen talking about whether they should throw her overboard before or after she dies. She's weak, friendless, alone.

Come back, the visions say. Come back to us. You're nothing without us.

The howling in her ears must be a hallucination, she tells herself as she staggers down the hill. No one else can hear the howling. A few people laugh at the drunk girl, or the mad girl, stumbling blindly towards the sea.

She rejects them again. She doesn't need anyone, has never needed anyone. Once she gets to the ships, she can go wherever she wants. Leave Guerdon with all its entanglements and strangeness behind. Seek her fortune in the wide world beyond.

And then, almost as an afterthought, one last vision slithers across her mind.

Spar, in the prison. Still walking around that little island to keep his limbs supple. In the centre of the island, on a little shelf of rock, lies a vial of alkahest, only it isn't alkahest. To her eyes, it's stained black, corrosive and poisonous, like a coiled viper. It's horribly wrong. Even at this remove, even seen through some weird divine revelation from a distance, just looking at it sickens her. She wants to look away, to escape this contagion, but the vision holds her there.

With three thunderous footsteps, Spar crosses the island and picks up the vial. He flexes his blocky fingers, causing little scales of stone to fall from the joints. Those hands are strong enough to break iron, and even though the vial is made of tough brass, he picks it up as gingerly as he can. He rotates it so the steel needle points down, then positions it over a crack in the stone armour of his hip.

Cari screams a warning to her friend, but she's not there, not then. He doesn't hear her. One miracle, but not another.

The needle punches through the softer skin beneath the stone, through the hardening encrustation like grey warts that presages pet-rification. He presses the plunger, and the liquid floods into his veins.

She sees him tense in anticipation of the alkahest. He described it to her once as warm acid, a good pain beneath the skin. It reminded him that he was still alive, still flesh, not all cold stone yet. He welcomed the pain.

Not this time. His back arches. His limbs flail like falling pillars in an earthquake. He topples, smashing into the ground like the Tower of Law falling on Cari. The noises he makes are nothing human. He thrashes, rolling and rumbling around. If he rolls to the edge of the little island, she realises, he won't be able to stop himself from drowning.

The vision fades.

"Out of the way, idiot!" Four big men, dock workers, carrying heavy boxes, stomp past her. Ahead, smokestacks limned in moonlight, is a ship. Stink of rotting fish and oil, sweat and salt. She's at the docks.

Her vision's still doubled. She shakes her head to clear it. All her visions so far have been real. She was right about the death of the priest in the Holy Beggar, about the Raveller coming to find her at Ongent's house. Ongent claimed that her story about the ghouls was correct, too. The other visions she doesn't understand, but has no reason to doubt them. Whoever these gods are, they're playing fair when they invade her brain. They haven't tried to – or couldn't – lie to her.

So Spar's dying. Poisoned. Up in that stinking prison at the back of the Wash. She didn't see anyone else in that vision. No sign of the thief-taker or his goons. Spar's dying alone.

He can walk out, she tells herself. All he needs to do is tell the thief-taker how to take down Heinreil. All he needs to do is talk. Buy himself out of jail and destroy that bastard Heinreil at the same time. Spar hates him, too, this should be easy. This shouldn't be her problem.

She saw the needle punching into his living skin, tasted the poison as it entered his blood. Sensed his stupid, frustrating, misplaced courage. He's not going to yield.

The dockers deposit the boxes with a pile of their fellows, and join the chain of labourers passing boxes up the gangplank. The ship's being loaded in the dark so she can catch the early morning tide. From the look of her, bound for the new lands to the west, for the Archipelago, for the Silver Coast and the Hordingers.

She unslings her satchel, digs out the bag of coins. It's heavy in her hand.

At the end of the gangplank is a man in an oiled rain cloak, barking orders. All she needs to do is walk up to him and hand him the money, and ask for a cabin. She can go on board, curl up on the bed and listen to the creaking of the hull and the waves until she sails out of Guerdon. The visions will fall away the further she gets from the city. She'll be free.

She doesn't have to stay. She chooses to do so.

Faster now, not stumbling anymore, walking uphill into the warren of the Wash. Accelerating into trouble.

From the outside, the old lithosarium looks abandoned, but Cari knows from her experiences on the streets, as well as Professor Ongent's lecture, that the city finds new uses for old shells. Palaces become communes; watchtowers get turned into smokehouses or shanties. When the cold rains sluice down on the city, they wash the people from the streets into whatever shelter they can find. So, there are two reasons why this building might still look abandoned.

First, it's a lithosarium. The days of panic over the Stone Plague may be in the past, and the curse of the Stone Men is now just another hazard, another fact of life, but people still fear the contagion. The alchemists have their cure, yes, but alkahest is expensive. A jar of cautic paste, applied to the skin, guards against contagion but even that jar costs a month's wages for a labourer. The lithosarium's empty of Stone Men now, all save one, but people might still fear invisible motes of sickness ingrained into the rough stone walls.

If that were the case, though, there wouldn't be graffiti on the walls, and the inner corridors of the building would have been choked with rot and fruiting bodies and spreading slime from the pools. There were people sheltering there, she guesses, only a few homeless vagrants with nowhere else to go. Like she was, when she arrived in Guerdon. It's the Wash; anywhere dry is all right on cold nights.

There's no one there now, though, which implies the second possibility – that the building's guarded. She never saw anyone except Jere the thief-taker there during her brief incarceration, but he's been holding Spar for several days now. He must have help.

She watches the closed front door of the lithosarium from across the street, with its little viewing slit and speaking grill so people could visit their afflicted relatives without risking touching them. The bust of a stern-faced man stares out from its place above the door. Another sort of stone man, this one made beautiful and perfectly smooth, but someone has smashed out his eyes and tried to scrape away the name beneath the bust. She can read only the first letter, a K. It's not something Cari would have noticed before, but she's clearly absorbed something of the professor's lectures because she notes that there's no religious symbology around the bust. It's a civic response to the horrors of the plague, built thirty years ago at its height.

There are no windows on the ground level of the lithosarium, and all the second-storey ones are bricked up. The place could hold an army of guards.

Cari circles around the building. This part of the Wash is quiet now. There are still fires burning up on Glimmerside, but they're under control. The streets and alleyways nearby are mostly empty. This is the thieving hour, when honest people sleep.

A moment of doubt — what if Spar's not there? She's basing all this on a vision. They've checked out so far, but she still fears to rely on them. Jere's a thief-taker, a bounty hunter, not part of the city watch. He hunts wanted criminals and sells them to the watch. As a member of the Brotherhood — a real member, not Cari's loose association — there's a price on Spar's head. If Jere's cashed him in, then Spar will be down at Queen's Point. Unreachable behind the towering walls.

She completes her circuit of the lithosarium. It's bigger than she expected, a sprawling warren of rooms. One section's been reclaimed by the city and turned into a tenement, but it's still a large warren of wards and cells, chapels and assembly halls. Feeding rooms, where they used to crack open the frozen jaws of plague victims to pump them full of onion soup and keep them alive once they'd lost the use of their limbs, their mouths. There are several other entrances on the ground floor, but they're all bricked up, all except one, which is securely locked. The door is new and sturdy. She's not getting in that way. This is taking too long. There are too many suspicious eyes in the Wash. At least if she gets caught by Jere there's a chance he'll hand her back to Ongent. If it's the watch, she might get away with a beating. A Tallowman, or Heinreil's lot, and she's dead in a gutter.

She creeps back around to the tenement, worry fluttering in her stomach. The tenement has no front door, just an archway into an unlit stairwell. She slips in; she knows that the way to avoid being noticed is to act like you belong. Walk like you own the place, but the people who live here don't walk with pride either. Like her, they slip and hunch and hide. The stairwell smells of piss. Obscene graffiti on the walls mixed with religious ravings. This place is better than where she stayed when she first arrived in the city, worse than the little flat she stayed in with Spar. Up three turns of the staircase, and she finds a boarded-up window that should look out onto the roof of the lithosarium. No doubt they boarded it up to avoid the reminder of the plague hospital next door.

Voices echo up the stairwell from down below. Drunks out on the street, arguing. She freezes until their voices fade as they pass by the archway. In one of the tenement rooms, someone stirs, shouts a groggy curse down at the revellers, then goes back to sleep.

Cari's knife is still useless as a weapon while bound with the alchemical cord, but she's got the little kitchen knife she borrowed from Eladora's. She manages to prise one of the boards off the window before the cheap blade snaps. She lowers the board carefully to the ground once she loosens it, then pulls another plank free. She wriggles out through the gap, twists around and lower herself onto the mossy roof of the lithosarium.

Scrambling on hands and knees. The green sliming her fingers, her palms, the cassock of her stupid grey scholar's robe. Her shoulder aches where the Tallowman stabbed her, but the bandages that Ongent gave her hold and she doesn't think the wound's reopened.

She wonders how she's going to get Spar out of this place even if she rescues him from the island prison. It's not like a Stone Man can climb out over the roofs like this. His weight would smash right through these rotten old tiles, even if she somehow got him up here. Going out on ground level may be the only option. Spar can deal with a few guards, no problem, those great rocky fists could smash a Gullhead into paste with one blow, but they'll make a lot of noise. Bring a lot more attention, a lot more trouble.

Maybe the Tallowmen are all dead. Maybe every waxwork in the city converged on Desiderata Street and got chopped up by the Raveller. Maybe she and Spar can just walk out of the door.

Distracted, she puts her weight on the wrong tile.

Slip-slide, falling, slithering towards a sheer drop. Three storeys down to splatter on the cobbles of the Wash. She catches herself as she hits the old gutter, arm now caked in more slime and pigeon shit. Cari pulls herself back onto the roof, moves more carefully this time.

The roof is a wilderness of angles and old chimneys. She was unconscious when Jere carried her out of the water cell. Hell, she was unconscious when they put her in there, too, both times struck down by her visions. If she'd been awake, she might have noticed the route that Jere took, been able to work out where the open ceiling of the flooded chamber is relative to the front door. Shit shit shit. She can't even be sure that Spar's in this lithosarium at all. Jere could have brought her from some other prison to his office when he sold her to Ongent.

Far away across the city, the bells chime. Three in the morning.

The Holy Beggar isn't ringing. It's the closest church. She should be able to hear its bells clearest of all, but it's silent. The last time she heard those bells was just before her vision of the Raveller consuming the fat priest.

The answer hits her like one of the visions, but there's no pain, no disjunction, just recognition.

The bells. It's the bells. The bells are somehow giving her the visions. The other churches, like the three up on Holyhill and the ones beyond, they're too far away to hit her like they did before. She can feel them, the chill night air crackling with their unwanted power, their painful inhuman sight, but it's not hammering into her head this time.

Carefully, she stands up. The slimy tiles make for unsteady

footing, but she cannot bring herself to kneel or prostrate herself for this. Not now.

Then she listens to the bells. Opens herself to their vision. Trying to control it this time, now that their cacophony is diminished.

She's looking at herself from across the city. She can see herself as if looking through a telescope, despite the distance, despite the darkness. It's like the building she stands on, all its brick and stone and wood and frankly shoddy roof tiles are just phantoms, and she's the only real and living thing there. She has no eyes, but her attention shifts fractionally. There, across the roof, behind that ridge, is a square open to the sky. And there, surrounded by water that appears cloudy and pale in her vision, is Spar.

She's too late.

Her perspective snaps back to her own body. She's Cari again. Somehow, the distant chiming of the bells sounds to her like a frustrated snarl.

She races across the rooftop, scrambles over the ridge, and stands on the lip of the water cell. It's too dark to see, though lingering after-images from the vision superimposed on the blackness show her the outline of the little island. She can hear him, his stifled whimpers of agony through frozen lips.

She's too late, but she tries anyway. The wall of the cell is too slick to climb, up here, but she gets as far down as she can, dangles for a moment, thin legs poking out of her lumpy grey robe, then lets herself drop into the water. It's like slamming into a wall of ice, but it breaks her fall, and she kicks back up to the surface and treads water, hiding amid the frozen crowd of dead Stone Men. Spar moans, a sound like an earth slide, plates in his throat grinding off one another. She can't make out any words. He tries to roll towards her, but another spasm catches him and slams him back down, as though invisible hands forcibly restrained him. She watches the iron gate for a few moments, wondering if any of

Jere's guards heard the splash of her landing in the water, but the corridors outside are silent. She swims over. The gate's locked, as before, but there's a narrow gap between the top of the gate and the bottom of the arch, wide enough for her squeeze through.

Drawn up against the wall is the small wooden boat and an oar, and hanging from a hook above is a key. She lets herself hope it's going to be that easy.

She punts the boat over to the island.

Spar tries to say something, maybe her name, but he's convulsing inside his stone shell. His eyes keep rolling back. She glimpses his tongue, and it's gone scaly, covered with thin plates of stone.

"It's me," Cari whispers, "Cari. I came back. I'm breaking you out of here. Hold still, okay?"

She's not sure how she manages it – it's more like she wrestles the boat under him than anything else – but she gets him in. Just before she shoves off, she spots the syringe of alkahest from her vision. It looks just like the rest. She picks it up. Still half full of poison. She pulls the plunger back so the needle retreats into its housing, like a snake withdrawing its fangs, and carefully places it in her satchel. It might be important, later. Spar groans when she puts it near him, instinctively trying to roll away from the poison.

Crossing the little lake is nerve-wracking. One convulsion and Spar could smash the boat to flinders, or roll over the edge into the cold black water below. He's too heavy to float, and there's no way she could drag him out alone. One convulsion and he drowns.

Reaching the gate raises both their spirits. She gets him out of the boat, like the great invalided boulder he is, and halfway down the corridor before she can't support his weight any longer. Cari snarls in frustration – to have got so close to rescuing Spar despite everything, and all she's managed to do is get him twenty feet clear of his cell. And all because he wouldn't roll over on the fucking thieves' Brotherhood like he should have.

"I'll be back in a minute," says Cari, lowering him to lean against the wall. Her skin tingles where his stone arm was draped across her shoulder, the back of her neck, her cheek. She runs her fingers over it, they come away bloody from tiny abrasive scratches. The burn marks from the Tower of Law sting, too, painful again. A sudden fear of contracting the Stone Plague comes over her, for which she irrationally blames Eladora.

Spar manages to lift his head, grind out some words. "Did you . . . make . . . deal?" His voice is horrible, like it's coming from deep underground, buried alive in sucking mud and weighed down by boulders.

"No," she spits. "And even if I had, fuck you. I'm trying to save your life." She darts away, glancing left and right through empty archways into empty rooms. Then she comes to a wooden door set into an old arch. Jere's office. She presses her ear to it, hears nothing. It's unlocked.

Papers and books and other junk on the desk. On the wall, two hooks supporting a heavy iron-shod staff that looks perfect as a crutch for Spar. She takes it down and lays it next to the door while she keeps searching. Cabinets with more papers. The desk, next. She remembers Jere consulting a big red ledger, rescued from the ruin of the House of Law. That book contained birth records. Was it those records or her visions that attracted Professor Ongent's attention?

She checks the desk. The ledger's gone. There's a box containing a ball of black gunk there, soft as warm butter, the same alchemical substance that Jere bound her knife with, and a little vial of purple liquid that must be the solvent, which she pockets. A gun. Other tools she doesn't recognise.

"You're the Thay girl."

An unfamiliar voice. Male. His breath smells of booze but he's not that drunk yet. Her right hand finds the gun.

She turns around. A man, balding, paunchy but with big shoulders, leather stab vest. His hands are raised, arms open, like he's trying to avoid threatening her.

The reverse isn't true. Cari's never fired a gun before, but at this range she can't miss. She aims the gun at fat man's fat face.

"I'm here for my friend," she says. She nods at Jere's chair beside the desk. "Sit down." She can use the alchemical stuff to tie him up, she thinks, that's what it's for.

The fat man doesn't move. "No, love, you're not. He's staying put until he cracks, and that dragon ain't loaded."

He grabs for her. She pulls the trigger, but nothing happens, and then his hands clamp around her like manacles. She twists, kicking and biting at him as he lifts her into the air. He wraps one strong arm around her waist, trapping her left arm, turning her away from him, and his right hand is at her right shoulder, fingers probing at her knife wound, ripping open the stitches. The useless gun falls to the ground.

Fat man slams her down on the table, winding her, and then straddles her chest, pinning her down with his bulk. She can't move, can't breathe. "Hey now, hey now," he says, like he's trying to soothe her. She wriggles, wrestles, but can't get free. She even turns her mind inward, bargaining with whatever supernatural force sends the visions. What's the fucking point of being a saint if they won't help you in times like this?

But she's not blessed with supernatural strength. She doesn't conjure hellfire.

"Hey now." Keeping her pinned, still astride her stomach, he reaches down and scrabbles in the desk. He's going to tie her up with that alchemical stuff.

The whole building shakes with Spar's roar. The wooden door is smashed to splinters as the Stone Man staggers into the room. Fat guy is so terrified, he pisses himself right on top of Cari. His weight lifts off her as he goes for the gun on the floor instead, fumbling to slot an alchemical cartridge into the weapon.

Exhausted by the effort of dragging himself along the corridor, Spar topples like a pillar in an earthquake, but even as he falls Cari's moving. She shoves up, and Fat Man half slides awkwardly off the table, their legs tangled. He's still going for the gun, but she gets her fingers into the ball of black goo in the drawer first and slams it down, gluing her hand and his hand and the gun to the floor all at the same time.

She twists and rips her hand free as the black slime hardens. She skips over Spar's form even as he hits the floor with an earthquake crash, and grabs the heavy staff. Her hand, still encrusted with the slime, is now glued to it, but that's all right. Fat man struggles to rise, but the goo has him tight. Try as he might, he can't defend himself with one arm glued to the floor. The staff's unwieldy for someone Cari's size, but she brings it down as hard as she can across the back of fat man's head, and he's down.

"Alk," groans Spar. Alkahest. He needs alkahest.

There's a small chest near the door. Locked, but she searches the unconscious fat man and finds a matching key. It's empty. The poisonous vial was the last one.

"There's none here. We'll find some once we're out of here." Spar groans again, in wordless agony, but, with her help, he manages to pull himself upright.

A few droplets of the purple liquid dissolve the bonds holding her hand to the staff. She pushes the metal head of the staff under Spar's armpit, so he can lean on it. It creaks as he puts his full weight on it, but it holds.

"Come on."

As they stagger towards the door, towards the city, she pours the rest of the purple vial on her dagger. The black slime melts away, revealing the pure sharp steel of the blade beneath.

CHAPTER TWELVE

The sewer mouth is an old one, connecting the deep channel that runs under Castle Hill to the harbour. These days, most of the city's waste is shunted to newer tunnels that catch the sewage of Guerdon's millions and carries it away off east, dumping it into the sea beyond the Shad Rocks. This tunnel is mostly dry now. Rat crouches next to a rusted gate and watches the ships. Even with ghoulish night-vision, the cold waters are an all-consuming blackness, pockmarked with flotsam and trash.

Rats – four-legged furry ones – scurry past Rat's hooves. Rats don't fear ghouls. It's the presence of the other thieves that spooks them. He led six of Heinreil's rogues through the sewers to this place.

Their target is a cargo ship, the *Ammonite*. She's moored to a buoy on the edge of the deep-water channel. Wallowing low in the water, fully loaded. Competition for space at Guerdon's docks is fierce, so the *Ammonite*'s owners had her moved to this mooring, like a neglected dog chained up in a yard, to wait until they're ready to depart. With the Godswar in full swing to the east, ships usually travel in convoys for protection against divine wrath and holy sea monsters. Kraken saints, their once-human bodies grossly warped and swollen, bones soft as mush.

If the *Ammonite* was carrying anything of real worth, she'd be at a guarded dock, not left exposed out here. Rat doesn't know what they're doing out here, but that's the modern Brotherhood for you. Heinreil has his plans and his orders, and you follow them or the Fever Knight comes calling.

The other thieves clamber out of the tunnel. By their standards, they're being quiet. Rat hunches against the cacophony. The only one of them with any stealth at all is Silkpurse. The ghoul has shed her usual absurd finery, the dresses and feathered hats on which she spends every coin she can steal, so that maybe, just once, she can pass for human in a dark room. Instead, she's dressed like Rat, in rags and tatters scavenged from the dead, although her face is slathered in powder and filler to disguise her ghoulish features. Rat doesn't know if play-acting human helps her stay on the surface, helps her delay going feral – but she's a ghoul, and that means she's quiet. She's bringing up the rear, making sure none of the rest go astray in the dark.

Rat wishes they'd managed to lose Myri. Her tattoos glimmer in the darkness as she clambers over the gate. He wonders what magic she's working – and how long she can keep it together. Every human sorcerer has to have a death wish. Humans aren't made to work spells, and it kills them one way or another. Right now, Heinreil's new pet seems calm and controlled, but that's a surface impression. Rat suspects she's here just to keep an eye on the other thieves, remind them that Heinreil's not to be questioned.

The other three are Cafstan and his sons. A Brotherhood family, four or five generations now, and no doubt Cafstan's grandchildren are being taught to pick pockets before they can walk. All three are laden down with heavy packs that clank when they set them down.

"What are those?" hisses Rat.

Cafstan shrugs. "Boss wants us to swap out these dummies for the real thing. So they don't know they've been robbed till they're long gone to sea."

Rat rolls his eyes. This sort of overcomplex, controlling detail is typical of Heinreil. No simple robberies anymore.

Silkpurse joins him at the tunnel mouth. "Darling, pay it no mind. Unanswered questions will only give you wrinkles."

"No guards," says Rat. He's been watching the ship's deck for several minutes now, and hasn't seen the slightest bit of activity.

"Well, get on with it," orders Myri. She pulls off her right glove and flexes her hand. Fat purple sparks crawl around her fingers, and there's a sudden sizzle in the air.

"Moonlight." Rat waits until the clouds pass in front of the moon again, and then he and Silkpurse scrabble down the slime-slick, wave-licked edge down to the sea. Just upstream of the tunnel mouth, there's a pile of rocks, and hidden there in a nook is a small wooden boat. The two ghouls untie it, check it, then float it on the water. The Brotherhood usually use this tunnel mouth for smuggling.

With Silkpurse's help, the other four manage to climb down to the boat.

"We left the packs up top," whispers Cafstan. "You get them."

The two ghouls scramble back up. The heavy packs are there. Spar sneaks a look inside. Metal gas cylinders, capped with valves and spigots. They look brand new. From their weight, they're full, too. A very elaborate deception for little gain.

They lower the packs down. The boat's only big enough for four; the ghouls' job now is to wait until the others come back. Cafstan's boys grunt with effort as they push off into the filthy waters of the harbour, and row towards the outline of the freighter.

"They'll be a while," says Silkpurse. She sits down on the edge of the sewer tunnel, dangling her bare legs in the slime. She produces a cloth-wrapped bundle from a satchel. "Sandwich?"

Rat's nose wrinkles at the stench of scorched grains, of gut-clogging plants, of dumb bovine meat, sickeningly bland and soulless. He should take the surface food, but he can't bring himself to stomach it. "I'm not hungry."

Silkpurse nibbles on the crust of one of her sandwiches, daintily, fussily brushing away any crumbs that fall on her rags. She doesn't talk with her mouth full. Finally, she swallows with effort, then says, "You've been below. I can smell it on you."

Rat nods. "All the way." All the way to the elders.

"Go below too much, you stay below, remember that. You're still young, darling. I remember you when you were sucking finger bones and the teats of them who died in childbirth. You'll go feral quick if you go visiting the elders." She shifts uncomfortably, glancing down the tunnel behind them as if expecting one of the fabled giants to climb out of the underworld right there. "You should stay away from them. You've got friends up here, not down there. Idge's boy, I like him. And that foreign girl, the angry one. What became of her?"

"Gone." Rat's irritated by the thought. Still no word from Cari, and Spar's still in prison.

Silkpurse finishes the last of her sandwich. She takes out a small mirror and checks her thick makeup. "Pity. Pity."

Out in the harbour, he spies figures moving on the deck of the *Ammonite*. The two carrying heavy bags must be Cafstan's boys, heading down to the hold to make the switch. Dummy alchemical caskets for real ones. A third must be Myri, the sorceress. She's at the stern of the ship, and Rat's elder-touched eyes pick up the glimmer of magic. He strains to see, wondering what mischief she's working now.

"Why'd you go below?" asks Silkpurse.

"Church messenger needed a guide."

Silkpurse hoots softly in amusement. "A good little errand boy, you are. Me, I spit on the church. Can't buy me with a few stringy grey carcasses tossed down a well. I remember when the church wouldn't let folk like us go above ground, not never. Many's the time I got beaten by the Keeper's fucking holy warriors for setting foot outside Gravehill. Blessed be the liberator, Mr Kelkin. He put things to rights, he did."

"I won't be doing that again. I took a short cut and ran into a Crawler nest. It didn't like that."

"Just the two of you, and you're not dead?" Silkpurse sounds surprised.

"The church woman was a bloody saint, as it turned out. Flaming sword and everything."

"Ugh." Silkpurse shudders. "They used to have lots of the bastards, and they were the worst. You could sneak past most of the churches, but not saints. Not their miracle workers. Few of them around these days, and thank the gods below for that. No Godswar here, thank you very much."

Rat shrugs. The Godswar is always distant from Guerdon. It takes in alchemist weapons and mercenaries, spits out money, refugees and bad news. The idea of the Godswar coming to the city is as absurd as a river flowing backwards.

Humans are slow. So very slow. What are they doing on that ship? What takes so long? Rat frets, scurrying back and forth along the lip of the tunnel. Sniffs the air, and smells burning. Distant shouts, and bells ringing wildly. There's some sort of disturbance in the city. Silkpurse hears it, too.

"Rioting," she guesses. Unconsciously, she rubs an old scar on her shoulder. Parts of the city are waiting for an excuse to erupt, to turn fear and hatred of the Tallowmen into action. And when the city does riot, ghouls often come off the worst. There are few of them on the surface, and the corpse eaters are mistrusted. Rat bares his teeth. Let them come. He has excess energy of his own to work off, frustration and worry and the lingering effects of his contact with the elder ghoul. His mouth floods with black bile.

"Keep an eye out for a watch ship," says Silkpurse, then she clambers down to the edge of the water, waiting for the other thieves to return.

Rat scans the harbour. The city watch has a dock at Queen's Point, and gunboats they use to patrol the river and harbour. If the riots bring them out, there's a good chance they'd spot the thieves on the *Ammonite*, because Cafstan and his boys are so fucking slow they deserve to be caught.

Finally – finally! – there's movement on the freighter. One of the Cafstan lads, climbing down a rope to the boat below. Then the other, and he's half carrying something. It's Myri. Rat can't tell if she's injured or sick, then realises that she must be drained by whatever magic she cast. The Cafstan boy helps her down the rope, then follows himself.

Off in the direction of Queen's Point, Rat hears a ship's horn blaring, the coughing choke of an engine. Lights, a searchlight blazing brighter than the dawn.

Cafstan's boat starts moving, but they're going the wrong way. They should be heading straight back to shore, back to the tunnel mouth where Rat and Silkpurse wait, but instead they take a detour to the mooring holding the *Ammonite*. They only spend a moment there, just long enough for Myri to touch it with an outstretched hand. There's a flare of energy and Rat nearly panics, thinking that they've given themselves away. Then he remembers that the spell was invisible to everyone else – assuming the watch ship doesn't have any sorcerers on board, or thaumic lenses. He rubs his eyes, wondering if this knack for seeing magic is ever going to fade or if his contact with the elder has triggered some permanent shift in him.

The searchlight plays over the shore, but merciful gods below, the watch gunboat turns her nose upstream. She's heading towards the city docks, towards the riots. Her engine roars as she cuts through the water, sending white moon-scar wakes out behind her on the black waters.

In comparison, Cafstan's little boat is a ghost. It reaches the shore. Rat reaches down and helps haul them up. First Myri – she's cold and shivering, fists clenched tightly, but she's not injured. "Come on, get the others," she snaps. "We need to get back quick."

"What's happening?" asks Rat.

"The warehouses along Sedge Street are on fire." Sedge Street runs parallel to Hook Row. Tammur – and through Tammur, the Brotherhood – owns most of Hook Row. Warehouses crammed full of stolen goods. If the fire doesn't get them, the looters might.

Below, the Cafstans unload the boat, and as soon as they're clear Silkpurse pulls it out of the water and stashes it back in its hidden nook. The Cafstan brothers hand up the first satchel to Rat. They're grinning, laughing to one another, joshing and pushing with glee.

Old Cafstan climbs up next, huffing with the effort. One of his sons starts to follow, but the weight of his pack makes him slip on the slimy rocks. He twists and falls awkwardly, scraping his pack against the rock face. There's the crunch of breaking glass, and suddenly the boy is on fire.

The flames burn blue and green. Phlogiston, the alchemist's fire. The same impossible heat Rat remembers from the Tower of Law. The Cafstan boy's screams are unutterably loud in the sheltered cove. His brother, stupid and brave, grabs him and pulls him back into the water. If this were normal fire, maybe that would work, but this is one of the alchemist's weapons. Water only feeds the flames.

The search light on the gunboat tracks back towards them, like the finger of an accusing god. Cafstan stares in horror, frozen as one of his sons thrashes in the water, blue fires and steam like wraiths that devour his flesh. The other boy and Silkpurse are still down there, but the fire's between them and the tunnel entrance. The other boy's screaming, too, all their laughter forgotten.

Distantly, Spar realises that the boys must have lifted some of the *Ammonite*'s cargo for themselves, filled their pockets with a little extra. Decanted phlogiston from the canisters into glass bottles, deviated from the plan. The time for recriminations will come later, though – if they don't get clear before that watch cutter closes on them, nothing will matter.

The heat from the burning man is tremendous. Through the flames, Rat can see the brother stumbling in the shallows, half-blind, cradling his maimed hand. If Silkpurse can get to him, maybe they can rescue one of them. Cafstan throws a leg over the edge, as if climbing down into that inferno will help matters.

"Hold him," snaps Myri, and Rat obeys, locking his arms around the old man. He has to strain to hold him back.

Myri steps to the edge. Her tattoos glow, their light pale and washed out against the blue-green hellfire. She points to the burning boy, and he slides backwards, pushed by an invisible force. He slithers, still screaming, out into the deeper water, and then he sinks like a stone, the black waters swallowing him. He's still visible for a few moments, like a shooting star falling into the darkness.

The other boy's maimed, half blind, but still alive. Maybe Silkpurse can carry him up.

But she can't carry the stolen goods *and* the boy.

Myri makes the decision for them. The sorcerer points at the other Cafstan boy, and invisible forces drag him out too, scudding across the waves and then abruptly plunging beneath them.

Unlike his brother, he's not limned in blue fire, so he vanishes instantly.

Rat muffles Cafstan's screams.

Silkpurse scuttles up the cliff, carrying the three satchels. Between the two ghouls, they're able to hustle both Cafstan and the stolen goods back into the shelter of the tunnel. Myri follows behind, her hands flat in front of her like she's holding something down, something that's straining to rise back up. Her left hand smokes, and the skin blisters as though burnt.

The gunboat's beam lights up the tunnel mouth behind them, but there's no trace left of their presence, save a few fresh burn marks on the rocks, invisible at range.

Once they're clear, Cafstan falls into the sewage and stays there, weeping. Rat shoots a glance at Silkpurse, but she just shrugs. Nothing can be done. All that's left is to keep going to the warehouse, pitch in there. Without the Cafstans to help carry the satchels of stolen alchemy, they have to split the load between the two ghouls.

The satchels are noticeably lighter than the supposedly empty ones they brought over.

CHAPTER THIRTEEN

E ven with the staff, walking is agony. His limbs are stone, unmoving, unresponsive, or they are burning, blazing, searing liquid, no strength or control just agony racing through him. All his muscles turned to angry serpents, ripping and biting him from the inside. He tries to croak, to tell Cari to leave him to die, to get out of here, but his tongue rebels and his jaw locks.

His father held out. His father was tortured by the watch. Poisoned, drugged, beaten. He didn't talk. Hanged, and he didn't talk. Up until now, Spar could hold onto that, emulate his father's martyrdom. He knew he was going to die, but at least in Jere's prison he could be like Idge, and not give the bastards the satisfaction of breaking him.

Now, Spar is faced with the terrifying prospect of not dying. Two minutes in the open air do more to shatter his resolve than all the deprivations of the prison cell. He clings to Cari like a drowning man.

Down streets that surge and fall back like stone waves on the night shore. Distant voices, shouts, and he cannot tell if he's really hearing them, or just remembering them. The channels of his thought are calcifying, he thinks, the Stone Plague creeping into his brain.

His father held out. His father was tortured by the watch. Poisoned, drugged, beaten. He didn't talk. Hanged, and he didn't talk.

He didn't give up the Brotherhood. Idge didn't. Or Spar didn't – which is it? And which Brotherhood? He's nine years old, sitting on the stairs of the big house, listening to his father playing cards with the others, desperately wanting to be part of their circle. Hearing them make plans for changing the city. New buildings springing up in the Wash, in the shadows of Castle Hill. Protecting people from the cruelties of parliament. Even changing parliament. Laughing, but not completely denying, the idea that one day Spar or someone like him would be in parliament, a voice for the oppressed.

He's nine years old, and he sneaks around the bottom of the stairs and looks in, and all the faces are Heinreil's, red-flushed and grinning. All except Idge, still at the head of the table, but there's a noose around his neck, tongue bloated like a purple slug pushing out of his mouth, eyes bulging, waxy yellow-green and the smell of shit.

Down streets that surge and fall back like stone waves on the night shore. Distant voices, shouts, and he cannot tell if he's really hearing them, or just remembering them. The channels of his thought are calcifying, he thinks, the Stone Plague creeping into his brain.

His father held out. His father was tortured by the watch. Poisoned, drugged, beaten. He didn't talk. Hanged, and he didn't talk.

They're asking him to do something. He won't – he won't talk. He won't give in. Better to die here. Stone men don't bend.

The channels of his thought are calcifying, he thinks, the Stone Plague creeping into his brain.

He hears a voice, echoing as if shouted down a very long tunnel. Cari.

"Push!"

He's leaning against something solid and wooden. A door. He pushes, and the lock splinters, the doors open, and he falls heavily onto a marble floor. Echoes inside and out. Cari drags him across the marble, getting him off the street, then the doors close again. He hears a bar drop, then darkness.

Cool silence and stillness. Restful. He knows he should get up, that lying down is death for a Stone Man and that he's risking more of his joints calcifying, but the pain's bearable for the first time in an eternity and he's very tired. The channels of his thought are calcifying, he thinks, the Stone Plague creeping into his brain.

He wants, very much, for the Brotherhood to say the same things about him that they said about his father. He wants quiet old men in dark suits to go by his mother's little house, and tell her that her son died well, just like his father. But one of them will be Heinreil, or all of them maybe. He'll lie. Tell Spar's mother that her son was a coward, or a traitor. Tell her that he's still alive, alive forever in a stone prison. Throw her out in the streets, cut her throat, anoint himself master of the Brotherhood in the blood of Idge's widow.

"You still there?"

Cari's voice. He can't see. Have his eyes turned to stone? It happens, scaly fragments that spread out from the edges, then turn into this blank white film over the whole eye, sealing the socket. Blindness is a new horror.

"I've got alkahest. Roll over."

She pulls at his chestplates, but he's too heavy for her to move. With a tremendous effort that opens up new sorts of pain, he pushes himself over.

He's not blind. Moonlight through some high window plays over a carved ceiling depicting gods and saints. They're in a church.

Cari finds a gap in the plates, right above his heart. There's a sharp but welcome pain, and then alkahest – real alkahest, not the poison Jere gave him – flows through him. He shudders and convulses, but when the shakes pass, he feels better.

"Where are we?"

"The Holy Beggar. They had a shot of alkahest in the vestry. For the poor faithful, I guess." She puts her bag on a nearby pew, and it jingles with coin. "Not sure if you qualify on either count, but fuck it."

Spar tries to sit upright, but that's not happening for another few minutes. "What if – discovered?" he manages to say. Speaking's easier than it was, but he still feels like his lungs have to push against boulders lying on his chest.

"Yeah, about that." Cari looks around, then up towards the bell tower. "I'm pretty sure everyone here has been eaten by a monster."

"How – know?"

"I'll be back in a minute, okay?"

Her footsteps recede into the cool darkness.

Spar closes his eyes, feels his heart beat, pumping blood and alkahest through him. Feels the alchemical cure dissolving the stone, softening sinews and joints, eating away at the leading edge of the plague. It runs into his brain, and with sharp knives of pain it digs away at the channels of his thought, letting him think clearly for the first time in a long time. Like pure rainwater washing away debris in a gutter.

And underneath the debris, beneath the calcification that pressed on his mind, he finds something hot and bright. Anger.

The spire of the Holy Beggar is a stunted thing. Two smaller towers flanking it rise almost as high as the belfry, giving the church a hunched look. A church for the Wash as the city thinks it should behave – humble, plain, simple, pathetically grateful for the benedictions given to it from on high. The spire faces up towards the three great cathedrals up on Holyhill, a paltry, earthbound approximation of their celestial glory.

The staircase up to the bells is very narrow and rickety. Spar would never make it up here. Cari doesn't mind – she wants to make this pilgrimage alone. In a small anteroom at the bottom of the stairs, she finds an old coat and some other clothes. She hastily changes, glad to be rid of the piss-soaked student robes. She feels more like herself again – but even the Cari of the streets, the sneak-thief and wanderer, has to deal with her changed circumstances.

Even if she's right, and the Raveller killed everyone else in the church, they still can't stay here. They can't go back to their little hovel either. Spar's an escaped criminal, and she's – well, if the watch catches her she'll be at Ongent's mercy, and she doesn't know how far she can trust the professor. She doesn't trust this gift either, this strange power.

It's the bells. It happens when the bells ring. So, let's go and look at a bell, she thinks.

Then back to the original plan – down to the docks, down to a ship. Maybe Spar will leave with her. The money she stole from Eladora isn't enough to cover both passage and a supply of alka-hest, but they could steal or stow away if it came to it.

One more twist of the staircase, and she's out in the open air, on a narrow balcony that runs around the bells.

Bright moonlight, stark and white across the rooftops. From this perspective, Desiderata Street is hidden behind the shoulder of Holyhill, so she can't tell if there's anything happening up there, although she can see a thin column of smoke. Closer, fires burn in the docklands. A warehouse, set alight in the riots.

She takes a deep breath, then turns around.

A single bell hangs there, forged from some black metal that's crenellated and ridged. It was once something else, she guesses, another metal shape that was melted down and cast in the form of a bell.

Greatly daring, she reaches out towards the metal surface. She touches it gingerly, expecting it to be hot or painful to the touch, tensing in anticipation of some magical discharge or revelation, but nothing happens. It's just a bell, still and cold.

She runs her fingers over the metal, feeling every imperfection. It didn't melt neatly. Traces of its previous shape can still be felt even in the thing's new form. That was a hand, she can tell. Those were runes. They couldn't destroy whatever-it-was, so they imprisoned it.

She's the saint of a trapped, truncated god.

Not just a god. A pantheon. There are dozens of church bells in the city. What sort of god, though?

One way to find out.

Cari braces herself against a wall, puts one foot on the bell, and shoves. She shouldn't be strong enough to ring the bell, but it moves, swinging smoothly away from her until it can go no further and the clapper slams into the bell . . . and Cari falls to her knees. This close, it's not images, it's feelings, tastes, sensations exploding beneath her skin.

In her vision, the city burns. A tide of Ravellers rise, slithering up from the depths. Black iron gods squat on impossible towers, howling for worship, for offerings to their terrible glory. Robed priests, elbow-deep in the blood of sacrifices, red knives cutting out the hearts of their enemies to be thrown on burning braziers. The smoke from a million burning hearts hangs over Guerdon like a ruddy pall. Death fuels death. A woman kneels before these idols, a high priestess, beautiful and terrible. She clasps a medallion in her red-stained hands, and it blooms with a ghastly light, a colourless fire. Transfigured in the bloodshed, made divine by slaughter, Carillon recognises herself.

She feels the overwhelming urge to prostrate herself before this divinity. To worship it. Become its vessel, its channel to the mortal world. More than a saint; an avatar.

Fuck that.

If the thing in the bell wants to keep her in Guerdon, it'll have to do better. *Show me Heinreil*, she demands.

She doesn't see anything, but it's not like nothing happens. It's the difference between having your eyes closed and opening your eyes in the darkness. Heinreil's somehow blocked from her, occluded. She snarls with anger and shoves the bell again. *Show me something!*

The bell tolls, and Carillon sees everything.

The sound of the bell dies away slowly. Vibrations ripple through the bones of the Holy Beggar, through his stone skin. Spar lies and recovers his strength. He can already feel the dose of alkahest wearing off, which is much too quick. A vial should last him a week, more like two if he's careful and doesn't aggravate the disease. If he's working, maybe three days minimum. If his disease has progressed to the next stage, where he needs nearly constant supplies, that's going to be a problem.

He hears Cari's footsteps as she circles around, checks the bar on the door, listens for anyone coming to investigate the noise.

"Did you ring the bell?" he asks. He can tell his voice is stronger.

"Yeah." She sounds drunk, or dazed. She can't stop scratching at her collar, her neck. A nervous twitch.

"The 'why'," he wheezes, "was implied."

She kneels down next to him in the darkness, careful to keep her bare knees away from his skin. "A weird thing's going on with me, Spar," she begins, and starts with that moment he witnessed, when she tried to escape from the lithosarium by climbing out of the lake of dead men, but was struck down by a vision. Four nights and a lifetime ago. She tells him about Ongent buying her freedom, her family and what happened to them, the visions, the professor's experiment, the Raveller and the Tallowmen, and her vision of the poisoned alkahest.

When she's done, Spar lays his head back on the hard floor and stares up at the distant ceiling. He's silent for a very long time.

"Do you want to use this?" he asks at last.

"Yes!" she hisses, eyes bright in the darkness. "We take down Heinreil. He sold us out, poisoned you."

"You can't prove that," says Spar.

"I will. We will. We prove that he sold us out, tried to poison you, and the Brotherhood turns on him. You take over. And then . . . gods, what couldn't we do then, with the Brotherhood behind us? Once I work out how to use this without it breaking my head—"

"If."

"Maybe we cut a deal with Professor Ongent, or find someone else who knows about saint shit. I don't know yet. But I can do it."

"And I can punch through walls or wrestle a Gullhead, but I'm still sick, Cari."

"You didn't give up, though, did you? You could have just sat down and never moved again, gone to the Isle of Statues, stopped taking alkahest. It's the same with this. Fuck the gods, or the bells, or whatever, but I'll take their stuff and make it into a weapon."

"It's never that easy." He grabs the butt end of the staff, holds it out to her. "Help me up."

She wraps two slim hands around his wrist instead, pale flesh touching stone. "You know better," he mutters, but he can almost feel her touch through his skin. He reverses the staff, digging its iron-shod butt into the ground and pushing against it. With Cari's help, he drags himself upright. His head spins, but the pain's mostly gone for now.

"We're not staying here."

"The priest's gone."

He uses the creature's name hesitantly. "The . . . Raveller might come back. Or the . . . bell-ringer, come to see what's wrong. And I'm starving. I can walk far enough to find some food, anyway. Let's go."

Cari hesitates. "We'll need money. I have some, but I saw silver and jewels when I went looking for alkahest. Give me two minutes to clear this place out."

"It's bad luck to rob a church. It's not the Brotherhood way. Come on, I know people who'll help us." He lifts the heavy bar away from the door with one hand, and ushers Cari out.

They leave the church behind them almost empty.

CHAPTER FOURTEEN

The coffee at the watch headquarters on Queen's Point is just as bad as Jere remembers it. No matter how much Guerdon changes, there are fixed truths you can rely on. Everything else seems to be spinning into chaos, so he takes a maudlin comfort in the acidic taste. He imagines that it must be mostly run-off from the alchemists' vats. The fire-fighting wagons have been out in force this morning, if you can call this pre-dawn hour a proper morning. The city hasn't slept. It staggers, drunk-tired, into the new day, uncertain of everything and looking for a fight.

Jere stretches. He's glad not to be on the watch roster any more. Keeping order in this city isn't his problem these days. What did Droupe call it, a stew pot that needs to watched in case it boils over? More like one of the alchemists' dangerous mixes of unstable elements. Waiting for a match to set it off.

A guard. Bridthen. Jere worked with him, years back. Knows he likes gambling on cards more than he should. Bridthen's always in need of a little extra coin.

"You can see him now," whispers Bridthen, "five minutes, all right?"

Jere drains the last of the coffee, knowing he'll regret that in a few hours, knowing he needs it now. He follows Bridthen down familiar corridors and stairs, down into the cells. They're crammed to bursting with those arrested in the rioting last night, twenty prisoners crammed into a space made for two, but Ongent rates a room on his own. An ageing professor of history doesn't fit the profile of the watch's usual guests.

Ongent's lying on a little straw pallet, arms folded behind his head, but he's not asleep. He's staring at the ceiling, eyes a little glassy. Drugs? Not Ongent's usual vice. Jere doesn't know if the professor has any usual vices. For an . . . informant? Consultant? Friend? Whatever word applies to their relationship, Jere realises he knows little about why Ongent would be willing to cultivate an association with a thief-taker. Jere can buy someone like Dredger with coin, Pulchar with threats. What does Ongent want?

"You don't want to lie on that," says Jere, nodding towards the bed. "You don't know what's crawling around in there. Things with too many eyes and ears." He hopes the professor gets his meaning, that this place is bugged. "Are you all right?"

"Never better, dear fellow," says Ongent. "Positively exhilarated."

"I went by your place up on Glimmerside last night. Lots of dead waxworks, and burnt buildings, and a big hole in the ground. Miren and that student of yours are fine, by the way. Just shaken."

Ongent sits upright, stares right at Jere. "You will ensure that *all* my students are safe, won't you? Some of them are so nervous, especially in the wake of the recent attacks. There were two girls staying in that house, along with my boy."

He's more worried about Carillon-bloody-Thay, realises Jere, than he is about being in prison himself. "They're fine," says Jere. "I'll keep an eye on them. Now, tell me, what happened?"

"I really don't know. Miren came running to me with warning of some sort of supernatural attack on Desiderata Street. The Tallowmen were already there when I arrived, fighting — I have absolutely no idea what, though. I told Miren to go make sure Eladora was safe, then I — well, you know that I dabble in sorcery. It came into my mind that I could possibly help with a little magic. Foolish, absolutely idiotic in retrospect, but I was overcome with excitement. I've never gone to war, Jere, or done anything dangerous in my life, so when the opportunity arose I couldn't resist the temptation."

Jere winces. "Did your spell cause all that damage?"

"Oh, my, no. I don't have anywhere near that kind of power. I'm afraid that whatever the attacker was, it responded in kind and with vastly greater force. Fortunately, it struck at the Tallowmen, not me. I was on the periphery of its blast, and survived with only a few bruises." Ongent actually grins. "To be honest, it was rather fun."

"What was the attacker? Describe it."

"I don't know what it was. It kept changing shape. I can't recall ever seeing anything like it. It was horrific." The professor's voice quavers. "Is it gone?"

"Like I said, there's a big hole in front of your house. To me, it looks like something was trying to escape, but I've no idea if it got away or got killed."

"The Tallowmen will know."

Jere shakes his head. "There weren't any survivors. I counted more than two dozen waxworks, all snuffed out. The alchemists might be able to reconstitute some of them, get at their memories that way, but from what I've heard that takes time. You're the only surviving witness." *Apart from Carillon Thay.*

Bridthen knocks on the door. "Time's up."

"Tell them exactly what you just told me. Try to remember everything you can about the attacker."

"Certainly. Civic duty, and all that. Jere, I am terribly sorry for all this fuss. I know it was idiotic of me to try my little sorcery. Do you think I'll be here long?"

"They'll question you, then other guards will question you, and then they'll let the alchemists have a go. It'll be a few days, but I can put in a word with the magistrates, and make sure the guards know you're a witness and not a criminal. Get you moved to somewhere better, with fewer bugs."

"Thank you. That's very reassuring," says Ongent. "You will look in on my students, won't you? And do me one last favour, Jere. In my office at the university there's a book, *Sacred and Secular Architecture in the Ashen Period*. Miren can show you. I'll need something to read while I'm helping the watch with their inquiries." Ongent winks, obviously finding the whole situation much funnier than Jere does. Twenty dead Tallowmen is no laughing matter, even without the threat of some unknown monster stalking the city, or the bomber that destroyed the Tower of Law. And Carillon Thay, the common thread between both incidents. He'd like to know exactly why Ongent was so willing to pay the girl's bounty, take her in under his roof, but he can't ask now without giving too much away to the watch.

"I'll be back with it when I can," says Jere.

He takes a side exit from the cell block, a backstairs used only by the watch. It leads out through a portico onto a wind-chilled yard overlooking the harbour. A pair of ornamental cannons long since fallen into disuse point out to sea, guarding Guerdon against vanished foes. The alchemists build better guns now, and, anyway, who's going to attack a city that makes weapons for all sides in the Godswar? The alchemists and weaponsmiths are scrupulous about staying neutral and selling to anyone with the coin to buy their bombs and poisons and monsters.

Jere watches the gulls wheel above the harbour and thinks about monsters.

Something old, some predator from a past age drawn to the blood and meat of the crowded city? Or something new? They make their own monsters these days, Tallowmen and Gullheads and other things, breeding them in great profusion in the vats. The alchemists' industrial complex is off to the east, across the bay, and the seas out there are stained yellow and red from run-off. Did something escape from a lab and slither out onto the city streets?

This isn't your problem, he reminds himself. He's not part of the watch anymore. Until someone puts a bounty on the monster's head, this is all just a waste of his time.

A narrow steep staircase, cut into the cliff-side, zigzags down from this perch to the dockside below. From here, he can see a cargo ship bound for the Silver Coast wallowing in the harbour, waiting for the tide to turn and carry her out to sea. A few smaller tugs and fishing boats, and a barge heading out towards one of the isles. He wonders idly if that's one of Dredger's boats.

Jere hurries down into the morning hubbub of the fish markets, as boats that were out all night come back in with the morning tide. The smells are flashes of childhood memory; any of those kids running laughing through the crowd could be the Jere of thirty – gods, more like forty – years ago, before the wars and the watch and too many late nights. He stops at a little stall to buy fresh-baked bread and better coffee.

Picks up a newspaper left by another customer, and it's there on the front page. THIS IS NOT THE LAST, scrawled in chalk across a brick wall in an alleyway.

Thing is, Jere recognises that wall, that alleyway. It's around the corner from where he found Ongent's son and that student of his last night.

And last night, there wasn't anything written on that wall. Which means it was added *after* the attack, when the whole street was crawling with watch and Tallowmen.

Which means all this is an inside job.

The university offices are nearly empty at this hour of the morning, and the door to Ongent's study is locked. Jere spends a few fruitless minutes searching the old stone corridors and musty stairs for a porter, then spots Ongent's assistant, that pale girl, crossing the lawn outside. Her face is stained black and blue by bruises. He ducks down to a side door to meet her.

"Morning."

She jumps, nervous as a stray cat. "What are you doing here? Is the professor here?"

"He's still in custody, Miss . . . ?"

"Duttin. Eladora Duttin."

"Jere Taphson. Look, the professor wanted me to have a look at some book that's in his office. Do you happen to have a key?"

She does. "I was just going there myself. I-I honestly don't know where else to go. Desiderata Street is all closed off, and the professor's in jail, and Miren went off to look for Carillon." The last name carries a lot of venom.

"I'm looking for her, too."

"She stole my bag. And nearly fifty sovereigns. I don't know if you should look in an ale house or a ship or a . . . dancing-girl temple." They come to the door of the study, and Eladora rams the key into the lock like she's shivving someone in an alley. "She shows up, ruins things, and then vanishes. Twice now."

"Twice?"

Eladora pales beneath the bruises. "Never mind me," she says.

"You knew her already?"

"Which book?"

"Something about ash. Sacred and secret architecture?"

"*Sacred and Secular Architecture in the Ashen Period.* This place isn't usually so messy." She searches through the remains of Ongent's thaumaturgical experiments.

He works it out. "You're her cousin?"

Eladora snorts. "How did you know?"

"You come from money, but not too much. You knew Carillon Thay a long time ago, but she's only been back in the city for a few weeks. You're not her friend, but you grew up together. And she doesn't have any living siblings."

"She ran away when I was fourteen."

Jere settles himself against the side of a desk as Eladora combs through the bookshelves. "Your mother is a Thay?"

"She never talks about that side of the family. She didn't, even before the murders." Eladora says it matter-of-factly; the tragedy is old. Tough scar tissue or merely scabbed over, wonders Jere.

"What do you think happened?" he asks.

"The thieves' guild murdered them over unpaid debts." The official story.

"You know," says Jere, "I know a few people who were in the Brotherhood back then, and they all swear blind that it wasn't them."

"They're thieves, Mr Taphson. Why would you expect honesty from them?"

She finds a heavy book under papers on the couch and carries it over to him in triumph. Jere takes it from her and flips through it. Eladora squeaks in horror at the cavalier way he treats the book. Endless pages of dense text, interspersed with a few architectural diagrams, pieces of buildings diagrammed like cuts of meat. What possible relevance could this book have? Then he sees it, and opens the book wide.

Near the beginning, there's an engraved copy of what Jere

dimly recalls is a famous carving from one of the big Keeper churches. On one side, heroic knights and fiery-haloed saints fight their way through burning streets. On the other is a host of fanatics and madmen, eyes bulging, whipped into a frenzy by the screams of their hellish priests. In the vanguard of this unholy army, though, are horrible demons, depicted as mishmashes of limbs, crazed patchwork anatomies, all fangs and claws, or else as twisted human figures with leering faces. Around those demons is a mesh of fine lines, like a child's scribble. Like threads. *It kept changing shape*, Ongent said.

"I'm not one for reading," says Jere. He turns the book around so Eladora can see what he's looking at. "What's going on here?"

"It's the Black Iron War. Year fourteen fifty-four of the city?" She recites from memory. "The blessed army came to cleanse the wicked city, and only blood could wash away the sins of the Black Iron Gods. The saints entered Guerdon girded in holy fire, and put a third of the people to the sword. The Black Iron Gods waxed fat on suffering, and lent power to their blood-sworn priests and from the deeps they called the Ravellers, eaters of form, who fell upon the armies of the blessed and caused great confusion, for those who fell rose again in semblance, though they were but hollow shells in thrall. Yet the saints were not dismayed, and came to the place called Mercy, and there they threw down the temples of Black Iron."

She turns a few pages and shows him a sketch of a statue. It's humanoid in shape, forged from some dark metal, and though its features are those of a beautiful woman, he feels an instinctive revulsion.

"The cult of the Black Iron Gods ruled Guerdon until the Keepers overthrew them. The city was very badly damaged in the war – whole districts destroyed by fire and siege. It laid the foundations for the modern city, though. They cleared away all the burnt parts, and tore down the twelve temples, and built the seven churches of the Keepers and some of the greatest civic buildings in their place. The post-Ashen Reconstruction is really a fascinating period, historically speaking. It rejuvenated Guerdon under Keeper rule, although De Reis argues that the Keeper theocrats were actually more of a hindrance to the city's growth. Professor Ongent agrees with him, but most people still cling to Pilgrin's *History of Guerdon* as – ha! – holy writ."

He wrestles the book off her before she can start in on architectural styles.

"I've got to go. Thanks for this."

"What about the professor? Miren said that you'd be able to sort everything out with the watch, get him released."

"That's where I'm going. To meet a man who knows magistrates."

"I shall come with you," declares Eladora. "And make it clear that the professor is an innocent victim in all this. Give me a moment to leave a note for Miren." She grabs pen and paper from a drawer on the desk and starts writing. Even in haste, her penmanship is excellent.

Jere slips his newspaper into the book as a place-mark, and prowls around the room. He pokes at the fragments of skull from the professor's experiment, at the other books on the desk. Looks out of the window. Down there, in the shadow of the archway, watchful eyes. A priest's cassock, bald head, broken nose. A Keeper. As if one of the little figures from the engraving had come to life, although Jere can't imagine that little man following behind some fire-girded saint, full of faith and vigour. No, Jere guesses that priest is as cold as a tomb.

Jere piles bone on circuit. Puts a book at a particular angle on the desk. Leaves loose papers in a pile that slopes towards that window.

"Miss Duttin? There's someone watching this office. They may try to break in. I want you to take a good look around, and memorise the place of everything that you can. That way, if the professor does have guests we'll know."

Eladora's fine penmanship disintegrates into a nervous scrawl. "Shouldn't we call the university porters, or the watch?" Her voice quavers.

"No." The door has sorcerous wards on the inside, no doubt drawn by the professor. Elegant curlicued lines of silver connect them to the lock. Jere moistens his forefinger with his tongue, touches the runes, feels them sizzle. They're still live.

"What about my note? They'll know I was here."

"They know already. I wonder when they started watching."

Eladora's fingers brush against a heavy desk lamp. "We could wait for them, and . . . "

"I make it a habit not to contemplate assault on an empty stomach. And to not piss off powerful people unless I have to. Anyway, I might be wrong." He's not, but he wants to play this out rather than confronting the priest.

Eladora takes her note and folds it. "I'll leave it with one of the clerks." She picks up a bundle of papers from the desk – she didn't come in with those, and Jere can make out Ongent's crabbed handwriting on them – locks the door behind her and pockets the key, then drops off the letter with a sleepy-eyed young assistant lecturer, who stares blearily at it and promises to give it to Miren. Then they're off, down side corridors and back doors, and then through morning crowds down into the train station. Jere watches to see if they're being tailed, but it looks like the priest was working alone.

"Which stop?" asks Eladora.

"Venture Square."

*

A palpable wall of irritation, stronger than any magical ward, surrounds Effro Kelkin. No petitioners today; no one dares approach his table in the back room of the coffee shop. His current assistant hovers near the door like a man caught in an open field during a wild thunderstorm, terrified that any movement could draw a bolt of lightning. Kelkin goes through assistants and secretaries like firewood.

Jere grins and shoos the boy out. "He'll want to see me."

Relieved, the boy flees into the main room of the crowded coffee house. Kelkin looks up, but his instinctive roar of invective dies on his lips when he sees Jere and Eladora.

"Morning, boss," says Jere.

"Gods below." Improbably, Kelkin's attention focuses on Eladora. He frowns in thought, then snaps his fingers. "You're Silva Thay's girl. What did she name you? Something weedy. Elsinore, Elamira, El . . ."

"Eladora Duttin, sir." Eladora curtsies in confusion. "But you are correct, my mother was Silva Thay before she married." Her voice drops as she says the last sentence, as if unwilling to admit her relation to the infamous Thays in public. Unfortunately, the coffee shop's loud and Kelkin's half-deaf, or at least he pretends to be.

"Speak up. And yes, yes, Duttin. She married some pious yokel and went off to raise chickens. Delightful to meet you." *Of course,* thinks Jere. The Thays were among Kelkin's biggest supporters back in the day, when he was bringing in all his reforms and remaking the city. Breaking the church of the Keepers' stranglehold on everything. Kelkin must have known Eladora – and Carillon Thay, for that matter – when they were babies. Now that it's been pointed out, Jere kicks himself for taking so long to see it – Eladora and Carillon resemble each other enough to mark their kinship.

Kelkin points Eladora to a chair, shoves a plate of pastries in front of her. "Now sit there and be quiet. Taphson, bring me good news. Tell me that Stone Thief has cracked, and given you Heinreil."

"Not yet." Kelkin groans, but Jere presses on. "First, I need a favour. Eladora here is a student of Professor Ongent."

"Who?"

Eladora pipes up helpfully from behind a scone. "He holds the Derling chair of history at the university, and lectures in ancient urban . . . "

Kelkin cuts her off. "So?"

"He owns the place on Desiderata Street that got attacked last night. The watch picked him up for throwing sorcery. Can you have a magistrate step in before they break out the thumbscrews?"

Kelkin makes a note. "I'll look into it. The committee on public order is meeting this morning in emergency session to discuss Desiderata Street. I'll talk to someone about your professor afterwards."

"On that topic." Jere slides the newspaper over to Kelkin, with the news story about the Desiderata Street attack face up.

"I do read the fucking headlines," he snaps. "My dog can bring me the morning newspaper, Taphson, and he's a damn sight cheaper than you are. He pisses on the floor less, too. Why am I employing you, again?"

"I was there last night," says Jere mildly. "So was Eladora." He taps the photograph, the wall with THIS IS NOT THE LAST written on it. "And that wasn't there."

"When were you there?"

"Right after the fight. Eladora was there the whole time, from when the attack began. There when the Tallowmen showed up, when the professor tried sorcery, when the creature fled or blew up and it all ended."

"Desiderata Street," says Kelkin carefully, "was cordoned off. No one was allowed in or out without the watch and the Tallowmen's permission."

"Yes. So whoever left this message did so with the collusion of one or the other group. Either the watch knew, or the candle boys did."

Kelkin's face is very dark now. His eyes like flints beneath his bushy eyebrows. His rage focused, like a swordsman who puts all his strength and fury into a single controlled thrust.

"You have no proof, though. Just your testimony."

"Not yet, no. Look, boss, Heinreil and his thieves I can handle. I'll get Heinreil before the magistrates one day. He's a slippery bastard, but I know where I stand with him. Corruption on this scale in the watch, that's something else. And the Tallowmen, the alchemists – danger money is only the start of it. I'll need double the usual rate." The money is important to Jere. One reason he and Kelkin work well together is that they both know the virtue as well as the value of payment. When Jere was a mercenary, he risked his life for coin. He's willing to do the same here, but the deal has to be sanctified. The pay shows that Kelkin appreciates Jere's courage and sacrifice. Professor Ongent may have only a fraction of Kelkin's wealth, but he doesn't value money in the same way. Ongent's always been well off, Jere can tell, so he deals in favours and secrets and a veneer of friendship, and precious little coin. Kelkin offers an honest transaction. It's a cynic's oath.

Kelkin nods imperceptibly, then snorts with anger. He takes his irritation at Jere's higher price out on Eladora.

"You shouldn't have brought her along," he snaps. He takes a swig of coffee; his hands are shaking. He's more rattled than Jere's ever seen him, and it's about to get worse.

"You're an expert on pre-Ashen history and holy wars, are you, boss?" Jere shows Kelkin the book from Ongent's study and points to the illustration of the Raveller. "That's the thing that attacked Desiderata Street last night – and carved up a few dozen Tallowmen on the way."

Kelkin stares at the illustration, then closes his eyes. For a moment, he's an old man. Kelkin's mouth moves, his tongue licks grey lips, whispers something that might be a prayer. A strange sight on the lips of the man famed for breaking the church's hold on Guerdon. He brushes his hand over the book, flips through it.

In the distance, bells ring out across the city. Ten o'clock in the morning. Parliament is open for business. On any other day Kelkin would be rushing out, stomping off in the direction of the squat drum on Castle Hill, trailing supplicants behind him like fallen leaves carried on the hurricane of his annoyance. Right now, though, he's frozen in his chair like a terminal Stone Man.

"Are you certain?" he says at last. "Are you absolutely *fucking* certain that it was a servant of the Black Iron Gods?"

"Eladora here saw it."

"Hmm?" Jere pokes Eladora. Stupid mooncalf girl.

"I didn't see very much," says Eladora, "but ... but I think that's what it was. The professor would know for certain. Once you get him out of custody, I'm certain he'd be able to help you."

"How is your MOTHER?" roars Kelkin, rounding on Eladora with such unexpected fury that Jere instinctively half rises, hand going to his sword cane. "Is she well? Tell me, did she give you a RELIGIOUS EDUCATION?" So angry that spittle flies from his mouth.

Eladora's stunned. She stammers, but can't find words. She starts to weep with great racking sobs.

"Gods below, Effro. What was that?" asks Jere. He hands Eladora a napkin.

Kelkin grunts and tries to ignore the crying girl. "I misspoke, perhaps."

"I think you did."

"I'll talk to a magistrate. Come by the house tomorrow night. No," Kelkin corrects himself, "the night after. At nine. Keep working on that graffiti, the threat of more attacks. And Heinreil. Leave the professor to me for now. I must rush."

He hurries out. His long-suffering secretary follows after, leaving Jere alone with Eladora. Her sobbing subsides to quiet shaking.

"I'm s-s-sorry," she manages, fanning herself with one hand. "It's just, just . . . everything. The professor, and, that thing, and Miren, and . . . f-f- Carillon, and my mother, and . . . everything."

Jere seizes on the one part he can trust to bear weight. "Kelkin will get the professor out. He's a big man in parliament."

Eladora scavenges another napkin. "I know very well who Effro Kelkin is, Mr Taphson. I pay close attention to politics." She wipes her face, dabs at her nose. The napkin comes away red with blood from her bruises and cuts. She folds it over in distaste. "And his stature is much diminished of late, so forgive me if I don't share your f-f-faith in his influence."

"Why did he ask about your mother?"

Eladora starts to tidy up Kelkin's plate, lining up knife and fork, brushing the crumbs of his scones into a pile. "I have no idea. My mother is, ah, fervent in her faith. She's a Safidist."

The Safidists are an offshoot of the Keepers, Jere recalls. When he was a boy growing up in the city, there was only the church of the Keepers. Kelkin's reforms opened the city to other faiths, and also allowed a hundred splinter sects of the Keepers to bother and harangue people on the street. These days, Jere's main interest in religion is purely professional. He just cares about which ones are likely to inspire crimes, or start street fights, or murder people. Safidists don't fall into any of those categories, unless you count accidental arson. He vaguely recalls a few incidents where Safidists set themselves on fire with phlogiston-infused swords. And they burn their dead, too, instead of handing them over to the priests like other Keepers do.

"Safidists . . . want to be saints, right?"

"To offer up the soul entire to the will of the divine." He guesses she's quoting something. She probably got that from Ongent; half of what the professor says is a quote from some book, or sounds like it is.

"Was she always a Safidist?"

"I don't know. She became more committed after Carillon left. She decided that it was her fault that Carillon was so, um, wayward. So, I got the benefit of her . . . determination."

"And did she give you a 'religious education'?"

"Ha. She tried. You think a Safidist would have anything to do with Professor Ongent? Safidists believe we should all be subservient slaves to the gods of the Keepers. That there's only one true faith, and it's theirs. The professor studies the whole history of Guerdon. All its many gods. And they're all the same."

Jere looks down at the illustration, still open on the table. Keeper saints and underworld devils of the Black Iron Gods, fighting to the death. He realises, suddenly, that the battle depicted took place roughly where this very coffee shop stands. " 'And they came to the place called Mercy'," he says. Quoting is catching, apparently. "How are their gods the same?"

"They're all self-sustaining magical constructs. I don't pretend to understand the sorcery of it, or the mathematics, but it's true. Gods – all gods, I think – are just spells that keep going. Like waterwheels powered by the passage of souls, maybe. Prayer strengthens them, and so does *residuum*, the portion of the soul that remains in the corpse after death. The gods are not omniscient or omnipotent, just very different from us. More powerful in some ways, but locked into patterns of behaviour they cannot change, so they're not really sentient, I suppose. Saints are p-p-points of congruency between our world and theirs." Eladora pauses, takes a breath. "That's what the professor says. I suppose that's one sort of religious education, but not quite what my mother had in mind."

"You're underselling the gods."

"Are you among the faithful, Mr Taphson?"

"No. But I've seen the Godswar." Cities melting like ice under a blowtorch. Armies of the dead. Wild saints wielding lightning like spears. "Omnipotent sounds about right."

"If their gods were all-powerful, they wouldn't need to their worshippers to fight a war," says Eladora quietly.

"And they wouldn't need to buy weapons from the alchemists, or hire mercenaries, I suppose." The city's wealth and its neutrality in the Godswar are two sides of the same coin. Jere wonders what it would be like if the gods of the Keepers joined the conflict. The thought is absurd, even laughable. It's mixing up a cannon with a chimney pot just because they're both tubes that belch smoke.

"I suppose not." Eladora closes the book, then speaks hastily. "Mr Taphson, my mother strongly disapproves of my studies with Professor Ongent, so much so that we are no longer on speaking terms, and have not been in some time. She no longer supports me financially. I have some savings, but Carillon took all my coin and everything else is in Desiderata Street and they won't let me go back there. The professor's in prison, I . . . I don't know where Miren is. He often vanishes for weeks, and I, I . . . " The tears threaten to come back, but she collects herself. "I don't know where to go, and I have no money."

Commotion outside. Jere stands – he's taller than most of the customers by a head – and can see right to the door. Bolind's there, clutching the back of his head, shouting at one of the coffee shop's waiters. Bolind's supposed to be watching the prisoner. Jere swears under his breath, then digs a handful of coins out and drops them on the table in front of Eladora.

"If Miren doesn't show up today, come down to my offices. They're in the old plague hospital in the Wash. Come down before dark, mind you. There's plenty of space there."

"The lithosarium?"

"I'd bring you down there now, but I need to attend to this. Keep good care of that book."

She gathers up the coins. "I am in your debt."

"Aye, you are. You can thank me later. Good luck – I hope Ongent's boy turns up, but I wouldn't count on it."

The Stone Boy is gone. Carillon Thay was here.

Bolind's lucky to be alive. Spar could have smashed every bone in his body. Jere's tempted to do the same. Two prisoners, both of immense value, and he lets them stroll out. They even stole Jere's staff, and he can see the bloody symbolism himself thank you very much.

He's trailed them to the Holy Beggar church, where they'd forced the door. After that, they could have gone anywhere in the city. He'll find them again, if they're still in Guerdon, but it'll take time, and things are slipping out of his grasp.

Bolind emerges from the shadows of the bell tower, clutching a grey robe.

"I found this. Looks like she changed clothes."

Jere grunts in acknowledgement. He shakes out the robe, but there's nothing of interest in it.

"And this," says Bolind. He holds up an empty syringe of alkahest. "Looks like one of 'em broke into the back room to find it."

"I gave Spar a shot just last night. Bloody thieves." Jere drums his fingers on his cane, missing the familiar weight of his staff. Bolind, still swearing that his skull is fractured, sits down on a pew and gingerly probes his purpled head with black-stained fingers. The theft and immediate use of the alkahest might mean that Spar's in worse shape than Jere had suspected, if he needs a second dose of the drug so soon. Alkahest isn't that hard to come by in the city, but if the Stone Boy needs a dose every day or two, maybe he'll slip up and reveal himself. And if the Thay girl sticks with him instead of bolting, Jere can catch her, too.

Go after them, or work on the mysterious THIS IS NOT THE LAST message? The one that implicates either the city watch or the Tallowmen in the bombing of the Tower of Law and the Desiderata Street murders?

The church darkens suddenly. A figure in the doorway, outlined against the morning light streaming in from the Wash. Portly and robed.

"My heavens, what happened here?"

One of the priests. "You had a break-in during the night. A pair of thieves. One of them was a Stone Man, and they robbed your alkahest."

"To profane the house of the gods, even when one is in dire need, is a terrible thing. Terrible indeed. The Holy Beggar is humble and unassuming. He asks for charity, but does not expect, and thus draws out the best in the hearts of others." The priest approaches Jere, extends a pudgy hand. "I am Olmiah, one of the Keepers of this church. What can you tell me of them?" The strong scent of a woman's perfume, and beneath it a foul stench, like the priest's trodden in a pile of dung.

"Jere Taphson, thief-taker", says Jere, bowing rather than clasping that hand. He doesn't want to get caught in a long conversation. "I must hurry in search of them, Keeper, but my associate Bolind here has some questions for you. We know they took alkahest, but if you notice anything else missing ... "

"Of course, of course. Oh, but you are injured," says the priest on seeing Bolind. "Come into the sacristy, I have bandages and healing salves somewhere." Bolind offers groans as gratitude.

"All right," says Jere, "once you're done here, fetch as many of the old crowd as you can and get them to report in. We're going to need bodies on the streets." The old crowd are a mix of fellow veterans, ex-watch, adventurers and the like that Jere knows he can trust, at least as long as Kelkin's coin keeps flowing. Bolind nods and winces. "Go, go."

The big man follows the priest into the shadows of the sacristy. Jere pauses on the threshold, suddenly troubled by a sense of foreboding.

Above him, the bells of the Holy Beggar ring out, marking the noon hour.

CHAPTER FIFTEEN

Mother Bleak's home is an old barge turned into a houseboat, tied up at the edge of what was once a canal, but is now so choked with weeds and garbage that it's almost solid ground. Still, the weight of Spar made the boat lurch to one side when he stepped on board, and Mother Bleak insisted on making him sleep right in the middle, in the little galley. Cari curled up on a bench nearby and slept like the dead. It's not much of a boat, but she's spent half her life at sea, and the cramped cabin feels more comfortable than Desidirata Street ever did.

She's woken by the sound of gulls walking on the roof overhead.

Spar's almost invisible in the darkness, an unmoving lump. She can't tell if he's asleep or just brooding.

"Morning," she says.

"Can't move," whispers Spar. "Stone."

"Shit." She kneels down beside him. She has to press her ear to his mouth to understand him.

"Seized up. Tried calling for help, but can't speak."

"Gods, I didn't hear. I'm sorry."

"Alkahest." He spits the word, sounding ashamed and furious.

"I'll find some," she promises, though she has no idea where.

She scurries up on deck. There's no sign of Mother Bleak, who seems to be some old family friend of Spar's. She took them in without question last night, and fussed over him like proper aunts are supposed to do. There's a little framed portrait of a man who looks like Spar – or like Spar would if he wasn't covered in rocky sores – hanging on the wall of the cabin. It must be Idge. They're trading on old debts to stay here.

Three other boats, equally weed-locked. A canyon of tenements, overhanging the canal. Faces in windows stare at her, at this new intrusion into their neighbourhood. Cari keeps her head down, letting her hair hang over her face. The burn marks from the melting bell in the Tower of Law are still fiery red, an easy distinguishing mark for anyone searching for her. Ongent, Heinreil's thieves, the watch, the Tallowmen . . . the Raveller.

She climbs off the boat and crosses the concrete bank, follows the old horse-track upstream a little. Passes a rusting alchemical engine that once dragged boats along the canal. Its smokestacks remind her of the petrified, drowned Stone Men in the lithosarium, their mouths open in silent screams, their hands outstretched towards the surface as they drowned.

Into a maze of alleyways, the west end of the Wash.

Turn right, and she'll be in familiar territory. She can see the spire of the Holy Beggar in the distance there, a landmark that's haunted her dreams and her waking hours for the last five days. Go past that and turn down towards Pollard's Square, and she'd come to the little tenement flat she shared with Spar. There's a backstreet potion shop near there, selling fake cure-alls and patent medicines; that's where Spar bought his alkahest. She can't go back there. Heinreil will have someone watching it.

So, she turns left, along the city-ward spur of Queen's Point. New lines of regimented terraced houses, in serried ranks along the slope. Cari kicks herself for dumping her student's robe back in the church – the grey robe would draw less attention here than her current garb.

There are gates and choke points between the Wash and Newtown, where the watch turn back undesirables. Sneaking past them used to be easy enough, but she's heard stories that there are Tallowmen in the side wynds now, waiting there to catch any pickpocket or footpad who might rise out of the scum-sump of the Wash to trouble the not-quite-gentry-but-better-than-you of Newtown.

Cari took very little with her when she ran away from Aunt Silva's house. She took some clothes and money – just like she did when she ran away from Silva's daughter, she realises, and the thought is both funny and sad. She took the black amulet, the only physical reminder she ever had of her mother. She also took years of Silva's lessons on proper behaviour, on posture and diction and how to be a lady. *Act like you belong, and most people won't look at you.* So she straightens up as she approaches the gate, brushes her hair back, and adopts the proper sneer. She practically dares the guards to stop her, to ask about her business or her scarred face.

And if that doesn't work, there's the comfortable weight and sharpness of her knife.

Neither social grace nor her knife would work on a Tallowman, but she's lucky, and all the guards are human. Only one gives Cari a second glance, but she doesn't stop her.

A neat row of shops, and at the end an apothecary. Inside, a fat woman stares at her from a high stool behind the counter, like a glassy-eyed gull watching fish flop in the shallows. Rows upon rows of jars behind her, all neatly labelled. A door to a back storeroom.

The woman initially assumes that Cari wants an abortifacient, and frowns down at her with feigned pity. "No, alkahest," Cari corrects her.

The apothecary produces a heavy glass jar, brimming with a clear slime. It's the wrong sort of alkahest. The substance comes in two forms – the injectable liquid that Spar needs, in its metal syringes with rock-punching needles, and as a caustic ointment, a purging stinging slime meant to be rubbed on skin that's come in contact with Stone Men, to avoid infection. Cari never bothered with the precaution before, she just washed after brushing against Spar when she remembered to, and has got away with it so far.

She doesn't know the technical term for the injectable form, though. "The sort in the syringe." The woman's frown grows. Buying the ointment isn't that unusual – many people in Guerdon are obsessive about avoiding contact with the plague, even now. Carillon remembers seeing a half-empty jar of the ointment in Eladora's medicine cabinet back in Desiderata Street. The syringe is only for Stone Men with the incurably advanced form of the plague. Not the sort of people, these days, who'd be found in a shop like this.

The woman names the price, and Cari nearly chokes. It's three times what she expected. She can pay with the money stolen from Eladora, but not for long, not if Spar needs the drug almost daily now. She hands over the money, praying that this is some after-effect of Heinreil's poison that will soon wear off, and he'll be back to one dose every week or two if he's careful.

"You must sign for it," says the woman. She pushes a large ledger across the desk. The last entry in it dated four years previously. A printed notice at the top of the page talks about plague ordinances passed by parliament, about how every outbreak must be reported to the watch.

Eladora Duttin, writes Cari, and gives the address as simply the university.

"This perfume, too." Cheap but not unpleasant, and necessary. The smell of the stagnant canal already clings to Cari's clothes, marking her out. If she needs to move in other parts of the city without attracting attention, she may need to mask it. "And willowfyne. And a cup of water, please."

Willowfyne is a common painkiller, for headaches and fevers. Cari's shoulder still hurts, but what she really wants is water from the back room. The woman scowls, but obliges. She leaves the door ajar so she can keep an eye on Cari, and that lets Cari spy on her, too, marking the layout in case she needs to come back here and steal alkahest instead of buying it, to conserve her funds.

The apothecary comes back with a finger of water in a cup, and the all-important syringe. Cari stuffs perfume and alkahest into her bag, careful to keep the full syringe away from the one she took from the lithosarium, the one that still has a small residue of poison in it. Careful, too, not to let the apothecary see that. Cari feels she's drawn too much attention already.

A Tallowman walks behind her down the street, dogging her footsteps so close that she can feel the candle heat on the back of her neck. Following her until she's back down in the Wash.

Mother Bleak must be back. Condensation rolls down the inside of the windows of the houseboat, and when Cari opens the door she's greeted by a wall of steam and Spar's earthquake laughter. He's still stuck on the ground, unable to move, but the old woman has propped him up on a box so he can sit up a little. Mother Bleak cleans around him, scrubbing every surface with a rag dipped in a bucket of scalding-hot water. Lined face as red-flushed as her scarlet headscarf, little silver rings in her nose jingling as she scrubs. She's wearing an astonishing pair of black rubbery gloves that come up to her shoulders, the sort worn by glassblowers or foundry workers. Cari remembers seeing men wearing gloves like that down at the dockyards as they handled alchemical waste.

"Have you got it?" Mother Bleak snaps. "Give it here."

Cari hands over the alkahest syringe. Expertly, Bleak twists off the cap, exposing the bright steel of the needle. Kneels down next to Spar.

"There's another pair of gloves on the counter," she tells Cari, "put those on and help push him forward."

Cari kneels down next to her and puts her shoulder to Spar's broad back. "It's all right, I can manage."

Bleak snorts, but doesn't argue. The two of them together lever Spar's dead weight forward and up, exposing a crack in his skin-paving. Bleak drives the needle through the softer crust without hesitation and presses the plunger home. Spar winces in pain, shudders, then lies back and smiles. "It's good. It's good. I can feel my knees. Give me a moment."

"You've done that before," says Cari to Mother Bleak.

"My husband, and one of my girls. Long gone away, now, but I still have the knack. You should be more careful, dear. It just takes a little touch to spread, and you might not have the cure to hand." Mother Bleak puts the cap back on the syringe. "A scrap dealer used to pay two coppers for an empty one. Might be more now, with the war. Are you feeling better, Spar?"

Spar reaches down and takes hold of his right ankle, then pulls the leg towards him so the knee bends sharply. There's an audible crack as pebble-like scabs crack, and little trickles of watery pus mixed with grit cascade down his calf. He smiles through the pain. "Like a new man."

Satisfied, Mother Bleak starts to mop up the liquid. "There are some clothes there, too, for both of you. Cari, there's stew on the pot there. Spar and I have already eaten."

Cari finds a stew-stained funnel next to the pot. The narrow end is bright with the blood of recent scrapes. They must have had to force it between Spar's locked jaws. She fills her own bowl with the thin fish stew and sits down at the table, suddenly ravenous. "We have money," she remembers to say between mouthfuls. "For the clothes, and for letting us stay here."

Mother Bleak waves a hand dismissively. "Idge's son is always welcome here."

Spar pulls himself upright, causing the boat to rock violently.

Hot stew spills onto Cari's hand. She licks it up, unwilling to lose a drop. Spar leans against the stove, testing his ability to stand. He flexes both feet, then starts pacing back and forth. The cabin of the houseboat is only three of his big paces long, and he has to duck almost double, but he's moving again.

"Idge's son doesn't fit here," he mutters.

"Is it the watch you're hiding from?" asks Mother Bleak. "Or the candles?"

"Both," admits Spar, "but also the Brotherhood. For the moment."

Cari glances at Spar. She met Mother Bleak less than ten hours ago, and while the old woman has given them every possible shelter, she doesn't know her or trust her. If Bleak betrays them to Heinreil before they're ready . . .

"Ah, Spar? Are you sure you know what you're doing? Seven or eight years ago, when everything was uncertain, that was the time. Back when they were casting around for a leader after old Bill the Skinner died. You were the prince-in-waiting, but you didn't do anything." Bleak clucks in disappointment and worry. She scrapes at a spot of dried fish stew with a yellowed fingernail.

"I was sick," said Spar. "And, anyway, now I don't have a choice. Heinreil tried to kill me."

"The Tower of Law?" For an old washerwoman, Bleak's remarkably well informed, thinks Cari.

"Not just that. He smuggled poison into the thief-taker's place. That's what nearly finished me off last night. Show her, Cari."

Cari produces the poisoned syringe. Bleak doesn't even bother examining it. "I've never heard of a poison that mixes with alkahest. All that's worth maybe two coppers," she snaps. "He'll just say it was the thief-taker, or that the alkahest was a bad batch, or something. Can you prove it was him?"

Cari holds her breath. Right now, all their proof hangs on her supernatural visions. Her unwanted, uncertain sainthood.

"Not yet," says Spar, "but I can't back down from this." There's a doleful sense of duty in the way he says it that Cari doesn't like. She's spoiling for this fight, eager to bring Heinreil down. Spar has a much greater reason to hate the leader, and much more to gain from the conflict, but he's dragging his feet. Cari knows there's a spark of anger somewhere behind that grey face, but it's smothered by stone.

"Well," says Bleak, "I suppose it's none of my business." To Cari, conversationally, like they were two old friends nattering away, "I'm not Brotherhood, dear, you see, not really. After the plague, though, we owed Idge, not that he'd demand it, mind; no, he was a generous man. Saw the Brotherhood's thieving as balance. Taking from them that had everything."

Cari sorts idly through the pile of old clothes as Mother Bleak and Spar talk. Gossip, mostly, about people Cari doesn't know with undertones of business. Listing Brotherhood members and thieves who aren't happy with Heinreil, or don't trust him, or still have stronger loyalties to Idge. Setting up meetings, but Bleak's right, it's all hollow until they have proof.

Cari's visions, assuming she can get them under control, aren't enough on their own. She's not a Brotherhood member, so her voice carries no weight with the other thieves, and, anyway, what's she going to say? That the recast remnant of a dead god whispered unseen truths straight into her brain? They need proof everyone can see.

"Where did you get those gloves?" asks Cari. The clothes in the pile are old and threadbare, passed down many times. The rubber gloves on the counter look brand new.

"One of my daughter's boys works down at Dredger's yard."

"Does he know any alchemists?" asks Cari. *The poison,* she thinks. *There must be a cure.*

CHAPTER SIXTEEN

It takes Eladora Duttin two days to solve a mystery that's haunted Guerdon for centuries.

She leaves the coffee shop, clutching the precious library copy of *Sacred and Secular Architecture* in one hand and her purse in the other. She won't get paid by the university for another ten days, but she spends two of her few coins – borrowed coins, she won't take charity from a thief-taker – on a train ticket back up to Pilgrim Station. Eladora prefers to think of the city as a few islands of safety linked by train lines and brightly lit thoroughfares. She never goes down alleyways or backstreets if she can help it.

Desiderata Street is still closed off. From the corner, she can see her bedroom window, see the blasted wreckage of the front door – and the still-smouldering crater in the road outside. No city watch here, just Tallowmen with their translucent skins and permanent leers. The closest one is partially melted and looks like it's slouching. Uncouth even in undeath, or half-death or whatever horrific state they exist in.

She can't go home.

She instinctively heads towards Professor Ongent's office, but then remembers Jere's warning that the seminary is being watched. He told her to look for signs that some intruder had broken in and searched the office, but the thought of opening the door and finding someone there terrifies her. In her imagination it's a Gullhead, filthy and shrieking, beak drooling with bloody spittle, little eyes black and mad as it hacks her to pieces.

No, she's not going back there.

She wanders through mid-morning crowds. Shopowners brushing debris from the pavements outside their stores, cursing the riots of last night. Students, disappointed that lectures aren't cancelled after the battle on Desiderata Street. She imagines Miren appearing out of the crowd, sliding up to her like a lithe shadow, never speaking but saying so much with his . . . well, perhaps not saying, but implying with the absence of . . .

She just wants Miren there, as some vestige of her nicely ordered world of academia. She misses the days when she and the professor would talk for hours about the history of the city, or about news from abroad, or college gossip – Ongent has a wicked appetite for scandal and rumour – and Miren would sit there in the corner, lost in his own thoughts. At times, Eladora even envisages a day when Miren comes out of that dark introspective labyrinth and sees her waiting there for him. No doubt the professor was much like his son at that age – brooding, with the weight of the world on his slim shoulders. It probably takes time and wisdom to cultivate the professor's jovial lightness. She just needs to be patient and understanding.

It would be so much easier if Miren was here, to protect her from the crowds. Five – no, six years she's lived in Guerdon, and she still finds the city nerve-wracking. Even here, just down the road from the university, she feels like an intruder. She wants to go back to the college, to hide among familiar rooms and places, but that safe cocoon's gone, too.

Footsore and thirsty, she stops at a coffee shop. Another few coins gone. Eladora came to the city with enough money to see her through her first few years, although she had to be frugal. She started tutoring other students before the money ran out, and then Professor Ongent recruited her as an assistant. She's never had to worry about running out of money. Now, she's adrift. Invisibly shipwrecked. Penniless, apart from a few borrowed coins.

She realises, as she sits down, that this is the same coffee shop where they took Carillon after she had her strange attack at noon. At the time, her pride at being initiated into some deeper level of Ongent's research outweighed her irritation at her cousin's return. Now, she wishes Carillon had never come back. Why couldn't she have drowned at sea as a punishment from the gods, as Eladora's mother claimed had happened to her?

Carillon, a saint. That's the strangest joke of all.

After Carillon left, Eladora's mother Silva grew more fervent in her beliefs. Silva believed that sainthood was a blessing from the gods, a reward for the pious. She fasted, and prayed, and sometimes even hurt herself in her devotions, and she made sure her daughter did, too. From the ages of fourteen to seventeen, Eladora cried every night in shame at not being chosen by the gods of the Keepers, as though it was her own fault that her soul was not ablaze with divine light.

She started reading books other than the *Testament of the Keepers*. Modern books, books that talked about the gods as another mode of being instead of being ineffable and eternal, books that assigned numbers and statistics to the divine. Works on reification, on thaumaturgy. Books that argued that sainthood was the result of spiritual congruency or aetheric permeability or simply the blind, groping attention of the unthinking gods, that it was no more a blessing than being struck by a thunderbolt.

The noon bells ring out again in chorus from the triple crown of spires atop Holyhill, and Eladora has an idea. It's so obvious, so simple, that she mistrusts it. She reads *Sacred and Secular Architecture*, rereads certain passages, consults the notes she prepared for Ongent. She searches for a flaw in her idea, probes it with every tool she possesses, but she can find nothing to disprove it.

She imagines herself delivering a lecture on her idea. At first she imagines that she's giving the lecture to Miren, but he feigns disinterest even in this. Instead, it's the professor listening to her, clapping his hands with enthusiasm as his pupil takes flight. She can almost hear his voice, asking her:

"What is the greatest unsolved mystery of the Ashen Period?"

Guerdon fell under the sway of the terrible Black Iron Gods – so named because these deities were incarnated – *inferated*, perhaps – as statues made of metal. By taking physical form, they were able to feast on the souls of those sacrificed to them and grow more powerful. Carrion gods, so hungry they could not abide the slightest gap between mouth and meat. Wallowing in murder.

They grew hungry. They demanded more and more sacrifices, until the people of the city rose up against them. The gods of the Keepers – until then minor rustic gods of the hinterlands – rose up and blessed the land with many saints, whose flaming swords and divine wrath drove back the worshippers of the Black Iron Gods and their hideous servitors, the shapeless Ravellers. And thus the city was delivered from the tyranny of the carrion gods. By the standards of the modern day, it was a civilised, sane little war. Worshippers and saints fought and died, but there was little direct divine intervention, none of the contagious madness that marks the Godswar across the seas.

But what happened to the Black Iron Gods? The Testament says they were destroyed, and that was accepted as truth for centuries, but modern theomantic theory suggests that's impossible. The Godswar proves it – look at the devastation of Khenth and Jadan. Their belligerent deities destroyed one another, but gods are immortal. They kept coming back, each time becoming more twisted and diminished in stature, both pantheons tearing at one another until the gods were shambling horrors and all their worshippers were ruined beyond the point of resurrection. Gods do not die easily, their death throes are the stuff of nightmare, but the defeat of the Black Iron Gods was marked by a period of prosperity, rebuilding and expansion.

"But," scoffs her imaginary Ongent, "where then are the Black Iron Gods? If they were never destroyed, where did they go?"

She thinks of Carillon stumbling at noon, as the bells rang out from the cathedrals up on Holyhill. Her cousin buckling under the sound, the visions crashing through her. A stab of jealousy at the thought that the Kept Gods, the gentle and wise gods of Eladora's youth, had chosen Cari as their vessel – and then an equally unworthy feeling of smug superiority when it became clear that Cari's gods were something savage and wild and sordid.

These gods of hers must be close at hand here in Guerdon, but hidden.

The vision as the noon-bell rang.

The bells. Eladora remembers feast days at the village church. Her mother and the other Safidist fanatics took over the church at times, gathering there and praying in frantic devotion, as if whole days of prayer and flagellation could call down sainthood. Once, Silva made Eladora ring the bells for hours, hauling on the rough rope until her hands bled. That village church was small, but even so she remembers the terrible weight and size of its bells.

How large must the bells of Guerdon be? Made, she is now certain, from some black metal. The Black Iron Gods were imprisoned within their own bodies. In the same way one of Ongent's simple thaumaturgical circuits wouldn't work if you scribbled over the magical runes, so too must an embodied deity be rendered insensate by being remade into another form. The

Black Iron Gods have lost nothing of their power – they still hold the soul-energy of tens of thousands of sacrifices – but they cannot express it, cannot move or think. Can't even cry out in agony except once every hour.

Her mother's shade accuses Eladora of blasphemy, of contradicting holy writ. *Very well, mother*, thinks Eladora. *I'll match my textbooks to your sacred scrolls, and we'll see who wins out.*

To the library, her hunger and exhaustion forgotten along with her fear. If the mysterious watcher who was spying on Ongent's office is there, she doesn't see him. She's so eager to prove her theory that she reaches the double oak doors of the library before she remembers the potential danger.

You faithless wretch, how dare you! You must kneel before the gods, not question them! Her mother's voice echoes from a very great distance in Eladora's memory, but, for once, it doesn't make her flinch.

How many churches were built in the Reconstruction? A hundred? More? Did the victorious Keepers re-forge all the Black Iron Gods at once, or was it a slower process? Did they only re-forge the gods into the simple mould of a bell, or is any large metal object from that era a potential prison for an evil deity? Did they only use churches, or did they hide the gods elsewhere? She guesses that all the Black Iron Gods must have been concealed in high places, towers, spires, not underground. Not with the Ravellers still lurking in the depths.

She starts by rereading familiar books dealing with the Reconstruction, then delves into the church archives. Some of the civic archives were destroyed when the House of Law burnt, but for most of the last three hundred years Guerdon was run by the church of the Keepers.

The House of Law. Originally, she recalls, a church. The alchemists had to take charge of the remains after it burnt. Some lingering taint from the weapons used to destroy the building, or a magical discharge from the destruction of the bell there? The timing fits – the House of Law was originally the Church of Divine Mercy, where repentant servants of the defeated Black Iron Gods were allowed to plead for their lives before a jury of fiery saints. It was constructed sixteen years after the fall of Guerdon – and, she discovers, the bell tower was finished nearly two years ahead of the rest of the structure.

The seven great churches of the Reconstruction – the three Victory Cathedrals on Holyhill, St Storm down by the harbour, watching over the fishers and sailors, the Holy Smith in the shadow of Castle Hill, the Beggar in the Wash, and the House of Saints, where her mother had brought Eladora so many times. She remembers walking barefoot along the stony path to the entrance of that church, listening to the bells toll high above. Is that, too, one of the hiding places of Black Iron?

Do you see it now, Mother? Not the invisible hands of the gods, reaching down to bless the faithful, but another Godswar, a secret one. Across the sea, living gods use their worshippers as weapons, blessing them with hideous powers and unthinkable sainthood, hurling warped titans at one another. Everyone in Guerdon always says proudly how the Godswar has never reached their shores, how the Keepers are kind and loving and civilised deities, unlike the mad tyrants of other lands. But what, wonders Eladora, if Guerdon already fought and won its lesser Godswar, and for three hundred years they've been living in an occupied city?

All the seven great churches date from the first fifty years of the Reconstruction. She dives into the church archives that are stored in labyrinthine vaults beneath the main library, dusty corridors lit only by the occasional flicker of a primitive aetheric lamp. Soot marks on the ceilings trace the paths of long-dead monks and scribes. The records of the Keepers are exceedingly thorough and well-maintained. In her digging, she turns up account books tallying the cost of building materials, of labourers, of the various specialists and craftsmen employed in the building. She finds copies of letters written long ago between master masons and priests, discussing the ornamentation of the houses of the divine. She finds blueprints of the secure capstones for the corpse shafts that fall into the depths below several of the older churches. She finds letters and other documents describing the strife over that bargain with the ghouls, how the faithful wept when the Patros declared an end to cremation for all except ordained priests. She finds copies of Safid's original sermons.

What she doesn't find is any reference to the making of the church bells. That absence is her proof.

Seven churches, plus the House of Law. The temples of other faiths might have many bells in a church, but the Keepers usually have only one doleful note. So, she's accounted for eight bells, eight Black Iron Gods. There were, according to all the tales and testaments, between twelve and twenty monstrous divinities in Guerdon before the fall. That means there must be more out there. Eladora doesn't hear the porters in the library above ringing their little bells, warning that the building is closing for the day. Surrounded by books and lit by artificial light, she pays no heed when night falls across the city, nor when the sun rises again eleven hours later.

Where else? High places, connected to the church, built in the first years of the Reconstruction. She compiles a list, weighs possibilities against one another, makes educated guesses. Sometimes, the answers are clear – the Bell Rock lighthouse, for example, is such a clear candidate that she feels like she's being mocked by some long-dead priest. They started building that tower a year after the end of the war, and it has not only a light but a bell for warning ships away from the shoals. Other candidates are more speculative. There's a chapel in the old fortress on Castle Hill, for example, that dates from the right period but she can't find any references to it having a bell. The seminary building – the very seminary where Ongent's office is, where she's worked every day for the last two years – has an old bell over the archway, but she guesses it's too small and too low to the ground to be a likely place for a hidden god. The old monastery on Beckanore is even more of a stretch. It was almost entirely abandoned in recent decades, but, back in the early days of the Reconstruction, it was much more important. The fleets of the Keepers marshalled there before they blockaded the port. And before that, it was a fortress of the Black Iron Gods – its fall was one of the first victories of the rebellion. And that monastery did have a bell.

No, she thinks. *That can't be one.* It was razed by the army of another city state, Old Haith, as part of a minor territorial skirmish. And that was more than a year ago, wasn't it? Long before all this began. If there was a bell there, if the bells really mean something, then what happened after Beckanore?

She reads and writes like a woman possessed, like a saint blessed, like an undergraduate on the night before a final exam. It's only when she stands to stretch her aching limbs that she realises how long she's been down here. She's lightheaded from lack of food.

Eladora discovers that she's still angry about that soup. She made soup for herself and Carillon, last night – no, two nights ago now. It's a small and petty thing, but it still rankles. She tried to welcome her unwelcome cousin back into her house. A second intrusion by Carillon, really – the first long, long ago, when the Thays sent their youngest daughter to live in the countryside. Eladora barely remembers those days; she was only a few years old, and Carillon even younger, but she recalls the mix of excitement and resentment she felt at having a new almost-sister sharing everything in the country house. And now, again, Carillon forcing herself into Eladora's new life, the one she made for herself in defiance of her mother. Eladora trusts Professor Ongent, more than trusts him, but why bring Carillon of all people into the house on Desiderata Street?

"You were right," says Cari in Eladora's memory, "I'm a saint."

That memory stops Eladora dead. She started with Carillon's visions, and from that starting point sprang her theory that the Black Iron Gods are still present in Guerdon, only transformed and limited by their present incarnations.

If that's true, though, that means that Carillon is a saint of the Black Iron Gods. If that's true, then Carillon is . . . immeasurably dangerous.

"It's all right," Cari's memory whispers. "You'll be fine."

She needs proof before she can make such an accusation. Proof that she's on the right track, proof that her speculation about lost gods and hidden bells isn't utter nonsense. Proof that her cousin is or isn't a monster. Eladora hastily gathers her notes and stumbles upstairs, blinking in the dawn light streaming in through the windows of the library. A confused porter sees her and lets her out. She walks briskly downhill, out of the university and through Glimmerside, through parts of the city she would never dare visit normally.

The city swims in and out around her, fading like a vision. She can't stop seeing the bones of history everywhere she looks. The names of streets call to mind famous battles, long-lost kings and long-dead politicians; the curve of one road mirrors the deeply buried river that flows beneath it. Carriages rattle past a guard post than seems incongruously out of place, unless you know, as Eladora does, that that particular guard post marks the location of an old city gate. The gate and the walls it pierced have been gone for nearly seven hundred years, but the shape of them remains, a scar left on the collective consciousness of the city.

The massive bulk of the Seamarket rises before her. Like a

beached whale, the city's largest market is a huge edifice of dark and weathered stone, festooned with brightly coloured flags and banners. The smell of fish overpowers even the stink of the crowds. Eladora has only ever come here with Miren or some other friends, never dared to brave the narrow alleyways and aisles between the stalls on her own. The barks of the fishmongers and butchers and other merchants echo off the vaulted roof of the huge building.

It was a temple before it was a market. Everyone who's studied the city's history knows that.

A temple in the middle of the city.

There, above that stall selling wheels of cheese, is that an empty plinth for some titanic statue?

Runnels in the floor carry away fish guts and blood from the butchers, but those grooves are so old and worn they must predate the market by many many years. The flagstones are original to the building – and what sort of temple needs runnels to carry away blood?

In the middle of the market, she looks up. Far, far above her, hanging from the apex of that vast domed roof, forgotten and unnoticed by the thousands who mill through here every day, she sees a black iron bell.

INTERLUDE

A rla lopes across the blasted valley in seven-league strides. Where she steps, the scorched earth explodes with life, sprouting razor grass and vampire trees in profusion. She sniffs the air again, tasting the salt of the ocean and the fainter stench of alchemical engines. Someone is coming! Intruders who seek to defile the temples of her goddess-self, murder the worshippers who are her life's blood. Symbiosis – they are the body of the goddess, and she is their soul.

Arla turns east, towards the coast. Her blessing is a scant green veil on a scorched landscape, a burial shroud, and she weeps.

Where her tears fall, murderous naiads appear. For a moment, they are her daughters, beautiful and joyous, their watery bodies glittering naked in the sunlight as they leap in search of vanished rivers. When they cannot find their homes, they fall into the mud and arise in their war-forms, as creatures of muck and barbed wire, and follow in her wake.

This is what they have done to me, Arla thinks – or has thought for her, through her. Her mind long ago ceased to be solely hers. She is a saint, the channel for her goddess to manifest in the mortal world. To take revenge for the wounds inflicted by her enemies. Once, in Arla's grandmother's time, the goddess blessed the valley with good harvests and kind weather, and the people of the valley were thankful. They offered her sacrifices of fish and song, and she was pleased, and made her joy known through the young women she chose to be her saints, her priestesses.

The deep-gods of Ishmere took the seas away to fight in their wars. Then the thieves of Haith occupied the valley and took cruel tribute. Then the nameless monsters from afar laid siege to the folk of Haith, driving them away, but they then turned on the folk of the valley. As Arla recites her litany of hate, she bleeds as fresh cuts open on her warped flesh, a millionth ritual scarification.

Her mortal flesh is testament to the righteous anger of the divine.

And the next year, when the goddess blessed the valley with a good harvest, up sprang a crop of spears in the cornfields, and the orchards bore grenades. The kind weather was forged into a single day of searing sunlight, a blazing javelin that concentrated all the heat of the goddess's bright springs and long sultry summers and bountiful autumns into a flash of heat that cut through the battleships of Haith, melting their metal hulls. Grey days from no discernible season filled the gaps in time.

The people of the valley were thankful, but had no fish to sacrifice, and all their songs were sad. Their goddess loved them still, but she was angry, and hurt by the works of the invaders. She made her anger and her pain known through the young women she chose to be her saints, her warriors.

As Arla approaches the shore, and the remains of her holy town of Grena, she releases her war-form. The goddess partially withdraws, lifting the awful reality-warping pressure that maintained the bloated shape of the saint. Arla shrinks down, becoming something closer to the mortal woman she once was.

She notes, and the goddess swallows her fear and pain the instant she notes it, that her right arm is gone again. A cannon blast in the last skirmish with the Haithi, she vaguely recalls. No matter. Already, the green buds of spring are sprouting at her shoulder, and they will grow into new flesh. There is not a scrap of her that has not been reborn in this war.

Her worshippers – the goddess's worshippers, Arla reminds herself – crowd around her as she enters the city. The land can no longer grow food to feed them, but the goddess has not forgotten them. As she walks through the crowd, the starving mob reaches out to touch the hem of her robe. A single touch is enough to revivify the contents of their stomachs. A few seeds or half-digested leaves or – for the lucky – a little scrap of meat all sprout back to life. Others have not eaten in so long that there is little in them for the goddess's magic to work on, but there is always something to be blessed and nurtured, some foreign body or intestinal flora. Bellies swell and the people retch joyfully.

Not all survive her kindness. Some burst from within as a cornucopia erupts inside them. Tall stalks of corn sprout from their stomachs and push out their throats, their eye sockets. Apples and berries spill out of their mouths, choking them. They vomit wine. Killed by fruitful blessings, they stumble after Arla as her entourage or spread out into the crowd to feed those who could not reach the saint. Her bountiful dead.

Her generals are waiting for her in the highest tower. They prostrate themselves before her as she enters.

Arla opens her mouth. Today, her voice is the buzzing of honey bees in the forest glade, the lowing of cattle in the pastures and the rushing chime of mountain streams. None of these things still exist in the blasted war zone of the valley, but the pattern of the goddess is derived from them, and from that pattern they can be brought back into the mortal world. When the Godswar is won and the whole world is valley, there will be honey bees and fat cows and drinking water again.

Now, though, the war.

"Who trespasses in my valley?" she asks. For she – she the goddess, not Saint Arla, there must be a distinction – for the goddess can be omniscient, or omnipotent, she cannot be both simultaneously. She needs her mortals to sustain her with worship, but also to watch for her when she concentrates her power, or to fight for her when she divides her attention.

"A small flotilla of warships. They're not flying any flag, mistress, but—"

"They are the men of Haith!" she declares. Does the goddess know this, or merely assume it? The ships are out at sea, and she is the goddess of the valley. A local deity for a minor people – for now. That is why her loyal servants labour on the borders of her domain, rolling huge marker stones out across the no-gods-land north and south. The valley grows a little every day, and so does she.

The goddess swallows Arla's moment of doubt. They are Haithi.

Haith is in retreat, thinks one of her generals, *they cannot be Haithi*. Thinks it, doesn't say it, but he is in the presence of a goddess in her wrath. She can read his thought before it reaches his tongue.

His lying tongue becomes a snake. His hair, snakes. His intestines, snakes.

She takes his chair at the conference table, brushing away the dust and shed skin from the ruin of the thing that was a man, and begins to weave a long whip from the snakes.

"They are the men of Haith," she says, "and I shall wade out and destroy them before they can hurt my children."

More doubt bubbles through some of her generals. The Haithi invaders are at the very edge of her domain, where her powers are weakest. Arla is already injured – she remembers her missing arm, and realises she's weaving snakes with one mortal hand and one arm made of grape vines and thorns. The Haithi have their own divine monsters, as well as terrible alchemical weapons and legions of seasoned soldiers, both living and undead. Haith is a byword for discipline, for martial tradition.

She lets a little more of the goddess flow into her. She is transfigured.

Some doubts vanish.

Others become snakes.

What does it matter if this saint dies? Arla is one woman. There are more, aren't there? Hundreds, maybe thousands, maybe tens of thousands. "Many" is enough of a reckoning for the gods. Gods cannot die. At worst, she can be diminished if all of her worshippers are slain, but she has her redoubts and her refuges. She has laid up stocks of divine power; she can birth new worshippers from the soil of her valley if needs be.

The folk of Haith will not take her land.

Her weapon made, Arla rises. She leaves the tower, leaves the town, walking down the dry bed of the long-dead river towards the wreckage of the sea.

She becomes the war-form again, grows gigantic. She puts her power into the whip of snakes, and they swell and thrash and hiss, lethal venom dripping from a thousand fangs. She chants a new litany of war. Her words are writ on the land, mosses sprouting on the scorched rocks in the shape of letters. Her priests creep in her wake, scavenging revelations from the hurricane of her passage. They will gather the dead and bury them according to her way, sinking them with holy stones in the bogs of the lower valley, so that the souls will rot and ferment into the wine that sustains her.

The men of Haith hide in iron-clad ships, so she gives her

snakes the ability to poison steel with their bite, to rot it fast as dead flesh.

The men of Haith have alchemical guns, so she girds herself in armour of river mud and stone, impenetrable.

The men of Haith are numerous and doughty, but they are mortal – and in this moment, in this war-form, Arla isn't. The goddess sustains her. No mortal weapon can destroy her.

She wades into what was once the ocean. She can see the ships on the horizon. They are so far away, she has to swim instead of wade. Mud-naiads scout ahead of her, each one clad in their own hermitically sealed shell. It would not be good for her daughters to mingle with these tainted former seas.

The ships do not fire as she approaches. They are so small, like children's toys floating in a puddle, that she laughs. She doesn't need to call on her blazing solid-summer javelin, or sustain her mud-naiads through the deeps. The whip will be more than enough to deal with these little intruders. One slash will be enough to cleave any of these little gunboats in two.

Are they lost, she wonders? Refugees from some defeated fleet, who took shelter in her safe harbour? Once, she might have welcomed those who sought the sanctuary of the valley's bosom, but she can no longer be merciful. The pattern of the goddess no longer admits the possibility of mercy.

Trespassers in her valley must die. Let their screaming shades carry word of her wrath back to whatever gods claim them!

The lead ship turns towards her. A darkness within it. A bomb.

Arla braces herself for the pain, but it is unimaginably worse than she expects. She is flayed, unravelled, seared. *This is it*, she thinks. The time of her death. Even her saintly form cannot endure this blast. The blessing of the goddess cannot sustain her. She feels her limbs cracking and burning, her eyes melting. She dies.

The blast wave passes over her, and Arla's still alive.

Arla hits the water – the water! – hard and nearly passes out from the shock. She struggles to reach the surface, thrashing her legs and her one arm. She's lost the war-form. She's just herself now. Clumps of mud from dissolving naiads rush past her. Everything hurts like she's on fire. *Goddess, help me*, she prays, but there is no answer.

She can't reach the surface. It's too far away. She gasps, swallows water, chokes. Drowning.

A shadow passes over her, as the lead gunboat draws near. Faces peer down at her. Too far away to see who they are, these witnesses to her death.

For the first time in her life, Arla is alone as she dies.

CHAPTER SEVENTEEN

The difference between being a mercenary and a thief-taker was being told who to hit. As a mercenary, there was rarely much of a gap between being hired and getting to smash some bastard's skull in. The old rule about a soldier's life being ten parts sitting around bored to nine parts marching and carrying to one part actually shitting yourself held true in both cases. Sitting around watching and waiting in Guerdon was as frustrating as doing it half a world away. As for the marching part, Jere was footsore after a day of traipsing around the city, chasing down contacts in the Watch. None of them knew anything about the graffiti up at Desiderata Street – or, if they did, they weren't willing to talk.

And then Bolind, the fat fucker, had apparently fallen asleep after coming back from the Beggar instead of fetching more bodies to find Spar and the Thay girl. Jere takes a few minutes to shout in heartfelt frustration at the man before ordering him to go out tomorrow evening instead, trawling bars and cathouses, to rouse the few semi-reliable blades they can trust to search the Wash for the escaped prisoners. More wasted time, and the trail's growing colder. The one mercy was that Ongent's assistant hadn't added to his burdens by showing up at the lithosarium. Maybe her boy Miren had finally oozed out of some alleyway and taken notice of her.

Jere wants to hit someone. No, he wants to be told who to hit. Left to his own devices, he'd thump Bolind in his stupid lazy fat face, and then Miren, just because the boy is the most punchable wretch Jere has ever met – and then maybe he'd take a stroll down the Wash and just start breaking heads. He doesn't even have his favourite head-breaking staff. Yesterday was a disaster, even before he thought about the threat of ancient slime monsters from days of yore or whatever Kelkin and Eladora were on about.

The day matches his mood. Grey rain thunders off the roofs, rattles and floods out of the gutters in a million tiny torrents. The streets are rivers. Cold winds howl, ripping down tiles and screaming at the windows. Out in the harbour, the sea is white with wind-tossed waves, heaving the ships to and fro like toys. Lightning flashes beneath dark clouds, like the wrath of some distant god. The streets are almost empty. You wouldn't send a Gullhead out on a day like this.

Jere wraps his heaviest cloak around him and braves the weather. Takes the high street around the edge of the Wash, the narrow ridge that leads out to Queen's Point and the watch headquarters out there. He'll talk to Ongent, see if the professor can drop some more hints about the Raveller-monster and that book. There is a connection between the thieves' guild, between Spar and Heinreil and what Kelkin actually hired him to do, and all these tales of gods and monsters, and that connection is Carillon Thay.

The cold of wind slips through his cloak like a pickpocket, finding his skin beneath his clothes.

As he approaches the citadel, two guards from the watch spot him. What are their names? Heron and ... and ... Heron and *godsfuck it's too early, just give me coffee and tell me who to hit.* There's a Tallowman, too, as backup, wearing an absurd glass lantern-helmet to protect its animating flame from the winds. It's not that easy to snuff out a Tallowman, though – Jere once saw a drunken sailor grab a burning wick to put it out rather than get arrested. The flame burnt through his hand.

"Jere Taphson?" says the nameless guard. "The chief warden of Guerdon requests and obliges you—"

"Boss wants a word, Jere," interrupts Heron. "They're just about to send out runners to look for you."

"I wish my manhunts were so easy. All right, let's give his grace the time of day."

Heron and . . . Aldras! Aldras is the boy's name. Off a refugee boat from Mattaur a few years ago – fall in beside Jere, obviously glad to have an excuse to come in out of this storm, and escort him up another side door of the watch fortress. Jere glances down at the prison wing; this could be some sort of ruse by Warden Nabur to waste Jere's time so he can't talk to Ongent.

Into the main keep, and up to the warden's palace. Jere wishes he had his head-breaking staff, instead of having to carry his fancy sword cane. The sword cane is too appropriate here, it's elegant and refined and much too clean. Jere carries it when he has to deal with quality. The staff's crude and heavy and leaves satisfying dents in polished wood floors, like these ones. Carrying it in here would piss Nabur off, and that's one of life's great pleasures. The cane makes it look like Jere's dressed up to see his betters.

At least he's dripping all over the clean floor.

Nabur's eating breakfast when they show Jere in.

"Did he come quietly?" demands Nabur of Heron.

Heron salutes. "No trouble, sir."

Nabur's moustache droops. He brushes a non-existent speck of dust off his pristine uniform in irritation. "I've had you brought here, Taphson, as a courtesy."

"You shouldn't have. I haven't got you anything."

Nabur ignores him. "I have had several complaints from my watchmen about your harassment, and your trespassing at Desiderata Street. It is disgusting that you would, ahem, trifle with a tragedy."

Jere tenses, wondering if this is a prelude to them blaming him for the message on the wall.

"I tolerate your bounty hunting and mercenary work because I honestly don't care if one criminal preys on another. Where I become concerned – become *intolerant*, you understand – is where your little manhunts spill out of the lower city and into the places where actual people live."

Does the watch not know who'd written it? Nabur had seen its significance at Mercy Street, at the first bombing.

Jere's mouth moves even as his brain turns over that thought.

"Hey, I was there on personal business, not hunting a thief. Professor Ongent is a friend of mine, and that's his house that got blown up. For that matter, why the hell is he still in custody? He's a victim here."

"His case is still being processed," snaps Nabur. Kelkin clearly hasn't worked his magic yet, then, which annoys Jere. The old man is slipping.

Nabur shuffles some papers on his desk. "You claim you were there on personal business—"

"I don't fucking claim. I was. Or am I under arrest here, oh chief warden?"

"—on personal business," he repeats. "Were any of your recent quarries there that night?"

Jere chooses his words carefully. "Not that I saw."

Nabur pushes a sheet of paper across the desk. It's covered in densely printed legal text and sealed at the bottom with two symbols – Nabur's own seal as warden of the city, and the golden seal of the head of parliamentary committee on law, Mr Droupe.

"You took two thieves from the House of Law. We've decided we want them instead. That's a parliamentary writ to hand them over."

Spar and Carillon. Neither of whom I actually have in custody.

"This is godshit, Nabur. You're running roughshod over my licence, and for what? Two sneaks who don't know a thing about the bombing."

"That is not your judgement to make. The city watch wishes to interrogate those prisoners, and you will transfer them into our custody."

"What if I've collected a bounty on 'em?"

Nabur sniffs. "Neither has come before the courts. If some client paid a bounty on them and didn't bring charges, well, that's highly irregular and should be reported. So, where are they?"

"I'll fight this. Appeal to the magistrates."

"Really?" Nabur seems genuinely surprised, then smiles. "You only have two days left before you have to charge them or release them anyway. Are you really going to put this before the magistrates – put your thief-taker's licence in jeopardy – for two days more time with two burglars who, so you say, don't know anything?"

My licence is gone anyway if they find out I sold one prisoner, who then fucked over me and Ongent and broke the other prisoner out of my own fucking jail.

Jere forces himself to grin. "I'm making a stand on principle." He shoves the letter back across the table. "Keep it. I'll appeal."

"If it turns out that those two know anything about the House of Law bombing, I shall hold you responsible for everything after that."

"Yeah, yeah."

A knock at the door. Enter a young officer in a crisp naval uniform.

"Sir, there's been an accident out in the harbour. A freighter broke its moorings and ran aground on Bell Rock." The officer swallows. "Sir, she must have been carrying weapons. The rock's on fire, and the fumes are blowing onshore."

"Gods." Nabur stands up, wobbles, sits down again. "Send a runner to the alchemists' guild, and ask for their aid. We'll need to . . . to clear the harbour, won't we? And how far onshore? And . . . have there been any messages?"

"Messages, sir?"

THIS IS NOT THE LAST, that's what you're worried about, thinks Jere. The watch definitely don't know what's going on.

"Anything else?" asks Jere.

Nabur looks at him as if he can't remember who he is. "No. No. Get out."

Jere doesn't linger. Pushes his way past the sudden swarms of watch officers and messengers, past the crowd watching the storm-whirled harbour. The black of the storm clouds mixed with a fetid mustard-yellow stain spreading out from Bell Rock. If those clouds reach the shore, who knows how many will die?

He wonders how long it'll be before the city is warned that this disaster is not the last.

CHAPTER EIGHTEEN

Rain drums on the warehouse roof like fingers on a coffin lid. The world's buried alive by clouds.

Rat unfurls from his sleeping nook between two crates and slips towards the side door of the warehouse. He is drawn by the rain. He desires to feel it on his skin, to have it run in secret rivers down the channels of his rot-wrinkled skin, wash away the grime and sewer-stink from his hide. Rain is a thing of the surface world, unknown in the deep places of the ghouls.

His fellow sentries are mostly still asleep – all except old Cafstan, who hasn't slept since his sons died. He sits, staring blind at his bloodied fists. The old man beat one would-be looter half to death when the riots reached Hook Row. Rat has no words for the man, just a quiet discomfort. He feels a loss at the deaths of the Cafstan boys, but for a ghoul it is closer to hunger than sorrow. *I would have eaten them*, he wants to say to the father, *and been satisfied. They looked like good meat.* But he's been on the surface long enough to know that sometimes it's best to keep silent.

Myri the sorceress is gone, and good riddance. The containers from the *Ammonite* went with her, early this morning. Ghouls do not brood; brooding is a function of mourning, and they do not mourn either. They cannot. As soon as the tattooed woman carried the satchel out of the warehouse, Rat put the containers from his mind. Mari didn't stick around for the work of moving goods out of the damaged warehouses. Ghoul muscle and sinew don't tire easily, but after a day of hauling boxes and crates, even Rat's limbs feel sore, and Silkpurse is curled up in a hammock somewhere in the rafters. A few other humans sit around, half snoozing, listening to the rain, glad to be inside. At some point, Tammur's going to call round and whip them into work again. More boxes to be moved. The shit end of Brotherhood.

He steps out into the alley beside Hook Row, takes in a deep breath. There's something strange on the air, an acrid stinging smell blowing in with the storm. It stinks of alchemy. He slinks around the end of the warehouse, sees the yellow stain across the black sky.

"Hey."

A tremendous sense of relief bubbles up in him, lifting a weight he'd carried since Gravehill. The chemical stink in the air masked her scent. The clothes are different. Her face is different, marked with a constellation like freckles, and older than it should be. Even her voice is a little different, like there's a very distant echo, but still he recognises Carillon.

And something else.

In his eyes, Cari's stained by darkness, like dried blood. He feels his fingers stiffen, readying his claws. His mouth feels odd, his tongue running over unfamiliar teeth. Her presence is disconcerting, literally; Rat feels jumbled and confused by the magical whirlpool around Cari.

"What are you?" he demands, trying to make sense of the conflicting impulses. "I can see . . . " Human words fail him, and he hisses a word that even he doesn't know in the secret tongue of the ghouls. A new fear settles on him – he's no longer worried that Carillon might be dead. Instead, some part of him is alarmed at the knowledge that she's still alive.

"Shit. You can tell?" She looks down at herself, as if trying to tell what changed. "When the Tower of Law fell, it marked me." She touches one of the small marks on her face, a slowly healing burn. "It's some sort of sainthood. I don't know exactly. No one does. I've been getting these visions. It's how I found you."

Rat tries to speak, but he still can't form human words for some reason. Cari takes his hisses as a request to go on. She lowers her voice, so her whisper can barely be heard above the storm.

"I'll explain more when I can, but listen: Heinreil tried to kill Spar. He poisoned him, tried to make it look like bad alkahest, but it was a hit. Spar's going to do what he should have done years ago and take back the Brotherhood."

"How . . . ?" His tongue rebels, and he chokes on human speech. Somehow, Cari realises what he was trying to ask, and speaks for him.

"How's Spar?" she says. Rat nods, unwilling to trust his words.

She frowns, rubs her neck. "He's in a bad way. Really bad. I've given him two good shots, but it's not enough. We're going to find out what poison it was, find the antidote, but we need to hit back, too. Spar's going to talk to friends of his father, get them on our side. We need your help – are you in?"

Cari has never been part of the Brotherhood. She's only been in Guerdon for a few weeks. She's not a sworn member. Neither, technically, is Rat, but he's hung around them for years and knows their ways. He knows that Carillon's proposal is, on the face of it, madness. Heinreil took over the Brotherhood smoothly, from within, after carefully demolishing any opposition. It took years, but Heinreil had patience. He didn't need to cut throats.

Spar's starting from next to nothing, and Cari doesn't have patience. There's no way this ends without blood on the streets.

But they're his friends. He fights that fear, cracks its bones and shoves it down his throat.

"What do you need?" he says thickly.

"Get a message to Tammur. Tell him that Spar wants to talk him. Tell him we'll meet him in the back room of the Bull of Ashur tonight. The thing is, Heinreil has someone keeping an eye on Tammur. One of the dock workers, dark hair, big ears with a chunk taken out of one of them. Smells of onions, wears a key on a chain around his neck."

The description matches one of the other guards. Rat doesn't know the man's name, hasn't exchanged two words with him. He wonders how Cari knows that this man is Heinreil's spy, or how she has such a detailed description but lacks a name.

"Bull of Ashur tonight. All right. I'll tell him."

Cari impulsively hugs him. The ghoul flinches; he doesn't like to be trapped, but, more, he is suddenly terribly aware of the strength in his limbs. One squeeze, and he could snap the girl's spine. One twist of his head, one snap of his jaws, and her throat's open, heart's blood gushing over the alleyway, mixing with the rain that pours down off the warehouse roof. And with these alien thoughts, the sudden and overwhelming urge to descend into the depth of the world, to submerge in the oblivion of darkness and warren and pack, to taste the fleeting souls of the dead and grow strong on them.

"You come, too," she whispers, "I'll let you in a back door."

He doesn't do these things. She's his friend. He returns the embrace, gently, anchoring himself to the surface world.

The storm howls on. Cari shivers, and whispers, "I've got to go. Before the bells ring. I need to be ready."

Rainy days belong to Stone Men. No matter how cold the rain or biting the wind, Spar scarcely feels it. There are Hordinger whaling ships that are crewed almost completely by Stone Men. When Spar first contracted the disease, he considered going away to sea with them, living out the few years of mobility left to him amid the ice and snow. Perhaps, he thinks, he might have met Cari out there in the wide world instead of here in Guerdon.

After days walking in endless circles around the perimeter of the little island in the lithosarium, the freedom to stretch his legs is strange, unreal. He feels adrift and uncertain. He had his plan – a terrible plan, a doleful plan, but a plan nonetheless. He was going to die in custody, to hold his tongue against all the tricks and tortures that the thief-taker or the watch could muster. He was going to hold his tongue until it too petrified. Dying stony and silent like Idge, like his father. Spar, the living monument to Idge's famous refusal.

If he has to die of this disease, he wanted it to be on his own terms. To do it with dignity and a certain amount of poetry.

Now his plan's gone, dissolved in the caustic poison of Heinreil's murder attempt, and he's running on Carillon's plan. He has no idea if it can work. Does his father's name still carry as much prestige as it did? Everyone in the Brotherhood pays lip service to Idge's great sacrifice, but will loyalty to Idge count for anything more? Spar knows he doesn't look much like his father any more, not with this mask of half-formed stone over what was once his face.

The storm has emptied the streets of the Wash, so it's easy to avoid people who might recognise him as he goes about his errands.

All night he's been tilling the dirt, as Cari put it. Visiting houses, bars, shops, smoke-dens, bookmakers, whorehouses. In each place, a variation of the same speech that Spar's been practising since he was twelve. *I am Idge's son. You remember the good days when my father was in charge, when the Brotherhood meant something, when we kept the industrial guilds and the parliament from grinding the poor folk into the ground. When the Brotherhood provided for many instead of enriching a few.* And then, depending on who he was talking to, he'd reminisce about his father, or condemn Heinreil's assassination attempt, or talk about the future. When he faltered, he'd hint that he had some secret advantage, a new angle that was going to change everything.

It might even be true, all of it.

He cautions everyone he speaks to say and do nothing for the moment, that he's just sounding them out, but he knows that word will get back to Heinreil. Some will let it slip, others offer it up in the hopes of future reward. Still, there's a lot of dissatisfaction with Heinreil's leadership, and over and over they grasp Spar's hand – his stone-warty hand, his diseased hand – and shake it and tell him that they've been waiting for someone to have the courage to stand up to Heinreil.

Pride and ambition are fire. Feed them, and they grow. Spar spent the last few years of his life, ever since he got sick, stamping down those fires, trying to smother them beneath stone and doubt. The disease had eaten his flesh, so he'd allowed it, even encouraged it, to eat his ambitions, too, until he was cold and hollow.

For the first time in as long as he can remember, Spar allows himself to dream.

His next stop is Dredger's yard. Mother Bleak's grandson, the apprentice alchemist, will meet him there. There are lots of other Stone Men working at the yard, and one more can blend into the hobbling grey crowd without drawing attention. He passes by a small break-yard between two outbuildings, shielded from the rain by a canvas awning, where Stone Men in ones or twos inject themselves with the morning's ration of alkahest.

Some of those working here are relatively healthy, despite

their plague. They have the protective stony hide, second-stage, but beneath it they're almost wholly flesh, still. Like Spar used to be. One shot of alkahest every month or so is enough to arrest the further progress of the disease. You can last years like that, if you're lucky.

Others are nearly gone. Third or fourth stage. Shambling statues, the disease eating away at their innards, transmuting guts and lungs and heart to stone. They need alkahest just to stay functional for another day or two, before they seize up completely and must rely wholly on the charity of others or go out to the Isle of Statues.

The last cruel trick the disease plays on them is giving them strength. Stone Men get stronger and stronger as they turn to stone. Spar's seen dying men topple buildings, smash through walls. All that strength, but blind and deaf and crippled and unable to use it. Dredger, the owner of the yards here, puts them to work as dray horses, dragging huge loads of scrap metal around the docks. Cheaper than alchemy engines or raptequines.

One grey-face stumbles out of the shed right into Spar's path. Fumbling blindly, pawing at him, moaning something. He can't make out a word, it's like stones grinding when the other Stone Man – or Woman, he can't tell – tries to speak. The gesture is clear enough, though. The Stone Man extends his arm as far as it will go, and turns over its flipper-like palm. The fingers have fused together. A deep groove cut into the stone of the palm marks where this Stone Man grips the metal chains of the scrap trucks. Clutched in that groove is a vial of alkahest.

The crippled Stone Man proffers it to Spar.

"You want me to inject you?" asks Spar. His own fingers are stiff and slow, his leg suddenly numb. He needs a shot, too, sooner than he'd hoped. Injury hastens the disease, and that poison is still burning in his veins.

The Stone Man grunts helplessly, angrily. Moans again. Spar realises that the Stone Man is completely blind, that his eyes have scabbed over. Spar takes the alkahest shot and puts it in his pocket, in case one of the other workers tries to steal a precious second dose. He could walk off with it himself – the thought has crossed his mind – but it's not the Brotherhood way. Don't take from those in need, help them instead, we're all in this together – and the latter is certainly true. For all his sickness, Spar isn't the worst case in this yard.

He grabs the blind man's head in one hand, and – as carefully as he can – pinches the stone over one eye, peeling it away. It's not solid yet, more a sort of rubbery scab with rocky scales embedded in it. Exposed, an eye peers back at Spar from the rock face. It widens in horror as the Stone Man doesn't recognise him, and suddenly fears that Spar will take the alkahest.

"It's all right." Spar takes out the vial again, careful to make sure it's the full syringe of alkahest and not the sample of poison. "I'll fix you." He twists the Stone Man's neck to the side, finds the deepest crack he can, and then drives the needle home. Spar's strong enough to bend iron bars, but he has to struggle to push the point through the other man's skin.

The rush of alkahest, from the other side. Spar's hand shakes as he gives back the empty vial. He'll need another shot today, he decides.

The other Stone Man grinds out a word that might be a thank-you, but then an air horn blares, announcing a shift change. The Stone Men stagger and scrape and limp out, a cave floor of stalagmites on the march through the grey curtain of the rain.

Bleak's grandson works in the labs at the far end of the yard, right by the sea. Spar trudges through the mud towards the long, low building.

The sky beyond it is stained yellow, despite the storm. A

mustard cloud rises from a small island in the middle of the harbour. The Bell Rock. There's an old lighthouse there, he remembers. The lighthouse is invisible at this distance, and the island itself is a dark blur, but the plume of yellow gas is coming from there. A small crowd gathers on the pier behind the labs, masked alchemists in leather overalls alongside stony longshoremen and sailors, looking out at the bizarre cloud.

Commotion. From one of the buildings behind Spar two men emerge. One is squat and wears a rubbery suit with a brass helmet that hides all his features. For a moment, Spar wonders if it's a monster like the Fever Knight, Heinreil's notorious thug, but then he remembers stories about Dredger. A very different sort of monster. The other is tall and bearded and – godshit it's Jere the thief-taker!

Spar freezes, gives thanks to whatever gods are listening that he left that distinctive staff back on Bleak's boat. There are other Stone Men here, many of them, and visibility is down to nothing in this rain. He stands, still as a statue, just another one watching the storm break over Guerdon.

Jere and Dredger hurry over to the pier and vanish down a stairway. The roar of a boat's engine over the storm, and they're off, heading into the teeth of the wind and waves.

Spar uses the distraction to slip in the back door of the labs. Bleak's grandson, Yon, pale and stringy, a mouthful of stained teeth from sucking on the rubber hose of his breathing mask.

"In here, in here," he urges, gesturing towards a small storeroom. He follows Spar in, careful to avoid physical contact despite the close quarters. "Nan said you've got a sample you want tested?"

"Yeah." Spar hands over the battered syringe. A little of his blood and grit still clings to the end of the needle. The alchemist wipes it clean, then squeezes the last few drops into a glass beaker. The liquid is the pale milky-blue of alkahest, the same pungent smell.

"Well, then," says Yon, holding the beaker up to the light, "that's not good."

"Why so?"

"Most compounds, you mix them with alkahest, they get broken down. Universal solvent, innit? Inject it, and you might get a bit sick, but you'd scarcely notice on top of the usual shit you get with alk." Yon looks at Spar warily. "Did you . . ."

"It hurt like fire used to."

"Right." Yon puts the beaker on a shelf and produces a handful of vials of liquid from his pocket. "There aren't many things you can mix with alkahest that would still work afterwards — and most of those would just kill you outright."

Heinreil wanted Spar to suffer.

Yon pours one of the reagents into the beaker, and the blue liquid turns dark and rancid. He lets out a low whistle.

"What is it?" asks Spar.

Yon looks at the floor rather than meet Spar's gaze.

CHAPTER NINETEEN

Somewhere, fifty fathoms or more beneath Dredger's boat, lie the remains of Jere's Great-uncle Pal. He was a fisherman, in the days before the harbour of Guerdon wasn't so poisoned with run-off from the alchemists' factories that they have to import fish from fifty miles down the coast. He went out one night to check lobster pots with his friend Otho, who told Jere this story. A fog blew up, so thick they couldn't see the light from the lighthouse. But they could hear its bell, ringing in the murk. All they needed to do was tack so the sound of the bell grew fainter, telling them they were sailing away from the Rock and all its reefs, but there was some devilment in the air that night. No matter which way Pal turned, he thought the bell was getting louder and louder. He dragged the tiller left and right and left again, each time losing his nerve and turning again as that cursed bell tolled closer. In the end, Otho claimed, Pal went suddenly mad and hurled himself over the rail to drown. The fog lifted straight away and Otho brought the boat to shore, but Pal was never seen again.

Today, at noon, the murk is thicker than any natural fog, and they can't hear the bell.

Dredger, hunched over the controls of the launch, roars something at him. Jere can't make out the words through the rubbery breathing mask he's wearing, so he clambers closer, climbing over coiled ropes and chunks of piping and other debris that litters the deck.

"Goggles, in the box there!" shouts Dredger, waving a gloved hand at a locker. It's just out of his arm's reach, but in these seas he dare not leave the wheel for an instant.

Inside the locker are two pairs of heavy goggles with a complicated assembly of lenses. One of them has an even more complicated pair of attachments on the rear, designed for eyes that have more in common with light-bulb sockets than anything human. Jere hands those to Dredger, who clips them onto his helmet and adjusts them. Light flickers in the glass.

"That's better," he shouts over the wind, "maybe we won't die right this minute."

Jere puts on the other pair, sliding them over the eyepieces of his own mask. The yellow murk of the waves and fog turns to a sickly transparent green, scarred with thousands of little sparkling snowflakes. He can see rocks both above and below the surface, although the goggles make the churning sea into an even more chaotic whirl that hurts his head. He still can't make out the Bell Rock, but if they keep heading into the densest part of the cloud, they'll find it there.

"There's a reason, Jere," mutters Dredger, "that I collect salvage after the battle, not during it."

"This isn't a battle," says Jere, but he's not so sure. He came rushing down from Queen's Point and demanded that Dredger take him out to Bell Rock, into the heart of the gas cloud. This is the third catastrophe to strike Guerdon in a week. *THIS IS NOT THE LAST*, left scrawled after the two previous ones. If there was a single intent behind all three events, then Jere wanted to get to the site of the latest one before the watch, before the Tallowmen, before anyone except the perpetrators.

At least, half an hour ago he wanted that.

Here, now, he's not so sure. The protective mask Dredger loaned him is ill-fitting and reminds him of his last days in the army, before he decided that the Godswar was no longer a place for mere mortals to fight. Dredger's launch seems tiny compared to the swell of the waves, and the stench of the clouds is overpowering.

He strains his ears, listening for the sound of the bell over the howling of the wind, but he can't hear it. He starts to wonder if they've overshot the mark and gone right past Bell Rock and out into the open ocean, and at the same time Dredger turns hard to port.

"Over there?"

The goggles, whatever they are, seem to show metal objects better than anything else. Dredger's solid as ever in Jere's vision, but his own hands are ghostly, and it's hard to tell stone from sea. There's another boat in the distance, a bigger one, keeping station or maybe run aground, Jere can't tell. And is that another vessel there, on the island's shore?

"Get me closer!" he shouts to Dredger.

"I can't see the—"

Their launch suddenly lurches and scrapes off some submerged obstacle. Jere holds his breath, but another wave lifts them off and throws them down in open water instead of slamming and shattering their hull on the rocks.

"Rocks," finishes Dredger. "This is madness."

For a moment, though, through the goggles, Jere spots the distinct edge of the Bell Rock, and the little jetty used to service the lighthouse.

"Come back for me after the storm," shouts Jere, and before Dredger can argue he jumps into the sea.

Shocking cold, and his mask fills with seawater almost

instantly. He pulls it off and grabs the strap with his teeth. Powerful strokes bring him closer to the shore. Here, in the lee of the island, the waters are slightly calmer but he's still half drowned by the time he reaches the shore, bleeding and bruised after being dashed against the rocks.

Struggling out of the water, he takes a deep breath that nearly kills him. His chest burns with poison. He struggles to get the mask back on. If it weren't for the winds, he suspects that would have been a lethal lungful. A dunk in seawater hasn't improved the state of the mask, and the breathing apparatus gurgles whenever he inhales.

The goggles' eyepieces rapidly become covered with a paste of yellow dust and seawater, so he has to make his way across the island half blind through the poisonous murk.

The Bell Rock is a mostly flat shelf of rock, barely above the surface of the ocean on a calm day. Right now, with the storm dashing it, it vanishes beneath the waves with every breath. If Jere were on the far side of the island, facing the brunt of the storm and lower down, there's no way he'd be able to avoid being sucked down into the depths or smashed against the stones. Certain death, as opposed to merely risking death with every footstep on this sheltered side.

There's a walkway of sorts, a narrow spit of concrete with iron railings, running between the supply cove where he landed and the lighthouse. He finds it, more by touch than sight, and drags himself along the railings. The fog gets thicker, a yellow haze that quickly turns to mustard mud in the rain. The higher parts of the exposed rocks are leopard-dappled, their yellow coat dotted with the marks of wild sea spray. His boots slip through a sludge of dying seaweed and yellow-brown slime.

This was a fucking terrible idea.

A giant shape looms. The lighthouse. Thank the gods. Rather

than going for it, though, rather than hurrying forward to the shelter of the doorway, he crouches down and watches. Waves rush over him. Icy cold water shocking against his chest, hammering the breath from his lungs. Harder to breathe through the mask now.

He can see figures moving through the fog. Insect-headed, with bulbous eyes – masked, like him. Hurrying away from the lighthouse, moving east in the direction of the second boat that Jere glimpsed. Suddenly, they disappear behind rocks.

And then the lighthouse explodes.

Chunks of rubble cascade through the yellow fog like meteors. The island seems to tip to one side, and Jere's caught by the waves, falling, drowning. Then the thunderclap hits, and he's deafened.

He's back on the battlefield, in the Godswar. The wrath of a warrior saint. Divine vengeance raining down all around him.

He thinks he might be screaming as the waves grab him again, pull him further across the rocks, tearing his flesh to ribbons. His mask threatens to slip, he grabs at it, and then a third wave finds him while his hands are fumbling with the straps. He can't grab on, and the wave carries him

Over the edge.

Jere's caught before he hits the sea, grabbed by a strong arm and hauled up on onto a rock. There's someone else there, pressing him down, dragging him onto a stable foothold. A familiar shape, but almost invisible through the rain and the slime on Jere's goggles. At first he thinks it's the thief girl, Carillon Thay, but then he recognises Miren.

Jere stares at the boy in confusion. What is the professor's son doing on this speck of an island in the middle of a storm, in the middle of a cloud of poison? He can't have come on the other boat. For that matter, he's not wearing a mask. He should be vomiting up his lungs.

There's a crack from the direction of the lighthouse. Jere glances over and sees that the explosion didn't completely destroy the building, merely tore a hole in its upper stories. Now, something cracks and breaks in there, and comes smashing down, landing with a titanic splash and a clang on the rocks. Dented, misshapen, but still intact: the black bell of the Bell Rock lighthouse.

When he looks back, Miren's gone.

Lightheaded, wondering if he's dying or mad, Jere creeps closer to the ruins of the lighthouse once more. The fog's clearing a bit, as the winds of the storm rip away at the cloud. The masked men cluster around the bell, tie cables to it. They're stealing it. As Jere suspected, they have another launch, like Dredger's but bigger, newer, docked at the closest point on the island's coast to the lighthouse. They drag the bell over the rocks and onto the launch's deck.

There's another ship, wrecked and run aground, between Jere and the other launch. She's a small freighter, dwarfing either launch. She's the one that broke her moorings in the night. Her timbers are swollen, bloated, and the poisonous yellow cloud belches from her hatches and the rents in her hull. Gas from a rotting corpse.

The launch departs, heading out to sea at high speed, vanishing into the darkness of the storm, the battered prize hidden under a tarpaulin scrawled with wards and warning symbols. Jere is alone on the island.

He staggers towards the ruins of the lighthouse, thinking vaguely he can find shelter there. Maybe Miren went there. Maybe he can find something that the masked intruders left behind, some clue to their identity. Anywhere's better than out in this storm. The yellow poison cloud diminishing now, blown inland by the winds that tear at his soaked clothing. Nothing between him and the angry black sky.

He gets maybe halfway towards the lighthouse before it explodes again. This blast is even bigger – it levels the place. Jere flings himself behind a rock as the cloud of dust and debris reaches him. He's hit twice at least, pain in his side, his foot, but he can't worry about that right now. The explosion keeps burning, like a volcano, shaking the island. *Phlogiston bomb*, he thinks, just like the one that destroyed the Tower of Law, but this one's unfettered.

There's a secondary blast, a wave of fire blazing through the torrential rain. Fires burning lurid green on the surface of the water as the poisonous dust burns. The centre of the island is death, nothing can survive there. Jere retreats to the edge, caught between the roaring rushing seas below and the burning, poisonous alchemical shitstorm that used to be a lighthouse.

Step forward and die like the other lads in the mercenary company, burnt by alchemical weapons and the wrath of the gods. Die screaming in fire.

Step back, and die like Uncle Pal, cold and black and silent.

Or, thinks Jere, *to the abyss with all that*. Step to the fucking side and climb down to the wrecked freighter. The poison cloud is thickest there, but it's much diminished from what it was, he's still holding onto his gas mask, and there might be something he can use.

The explosion erupts again – what the *fuck* do the alchemists put in their bombs – and there's a crash as part of the cliff shears off into the ocean. The whole freighter shifts on the reef. She's going to slip off and sink or break up before the storm blows out. Parts of her slough off, sliding off the rain-slick deck to fall into the sea or crash onto the beach. Jere peers through the murk, trying to make sense of what he's seeing through the goggles. He can see the freighter's anchor more clearly than anything else, and close to it—

A rowing boat, more or less intact.

A prayer of thanks to the watchful Keepers comes unbidden to his lips. He dashes across the poisoned beach and clambers onto the dying ship. Holding his breath the whole time – he has to plunge into the thickest part of the poison cloud to get to the rowing boat, and his breathing mask is already depleted – he cuts the boat free, kicks it into the water and rows out.

The storm drags him away from the Bell Rock, spins him around so he can't tell where he is. Surrounded by swollen mountains of black water. The waves tear one oar out of his grip, so he drops the other and lies face down in the boat, trying to use his bodyweight to keep it from capsizing. He rolls back and forth for an eternity, drowning and spitting as rainwater or seawater or both fills the little cup of timber that holds his life.

And then there's the piercing light of a searchlight, and shouting, and someone's grabbing him, and he thinks that Miren's somehow come back, but it's Dredger, Dredger and some of the workers from the dockyard, pulling him onto the launch.

Dredger's yelling obscenities and threats in Jere's ear but he's out of the storm and he's not going to die today, so they sound like music.

CHAPTER TWENTY

The bells of Guerdon ring many times every day. All the churches sound the turning of each hour, their chimes are the city's heartbeat. Some bells have their own special duties. In the morning, and again at twilight, the Bell of St Storm rings to mark the change of the tide. The Bell of Holy Smith heralds the opening and closing of the city gates – gates no one uses anymore, because the walls were torn down centuries ago, and the city's expanded twentyfold beyond those original limits. Up on Holyhill, they ring three times a day to summon the faithful to prayer, and sometimes they ring out, too, for funerals and weddings. Grim tolling as the body is given into the care of the monks who'll carry it to the Keepers, and wild joyous peals.

There'll be more funerals than weddings in the days to come, guesses Cari. The poison cloud rolled in with the storm-swollen tide. By the time it reached the shore, it was too diffuse and weak to do much damage in itself, but the panic was worse than the choking vapours. Cari saw at least two bodies in person – a sailor, knocked from her ship and drowned as the crew fled down the gangplank, and a child trampled as they evacuated the Seamarket. She saw a dozen more when the bells talked to her.

Saw, too, men sounding the alarm. Saw them running along

the quays, shouting that a poison cloud was coming. How did they know? She marks their faces, searches for them in the chime-engendered visions.

All day, she's moved through the city's secret ways with purpose, exploring the limits of her gift. Armed with a newspaper filched from a gutter, the list of weddings and funeral announcements rain-soaked but legible, she's pushed against the invisible world that opens to her when the bells ring out.

She's learned that if she's too close to one bell, it's hard to hear what it's trying to show her. If she's too far, then they all press on her at once, and it's an indecipherable cacophony.

She's learned that she can't go near Holyhill. Too many churches, too many bells. Even when she's anticipating it, the psychic shock is overwhelming. She retreated from Holyhill this morning, vomited her breakfast into a gutter and cried as incomprehensible visions of furnaces and pipes drove through her brain like hot metal spikes.

She's learned that the Bell of the Holy Beggar is malicious and secretive, and more aware than the others. She fears that she somehow woke the indwelling spirit of the bell when she touched it. Ever since, it's been calling her by name when it rings. Howling her name across the rooftops. If anyone else in the city shares this gift, they know who she is now.

She's learned that the Bell of St Storm is designed to swing free in the wind, and so it starts screaming at her when the wind picks up. Even before the yellow fog rolled across the docks, she was flinching at every peal of thunder and shift in the wind. The St Storm bell, she suspects, has forgotten whatever it once was — straying too close to that church left her with a map of weather patterns across the harbour seared into her skin.

She's learned that the Bell of the Dowager Chapel up in Bryn Avane remembers the Thays. The visions there are tangled with unwanted and unexpected memory-fragments. She went looking for Heinreil's secrets, and came back with the knowledge of how her father smoked on the balcony at the back of the Thay manor, or how Aunt Silva – Aunt Silva! – danced until dawn and then crept in the back door so no one noticed she'd been out without a chaperone.

She's learned a new-found appreciation for the dedication of the city's bell-ringers.

What she hasn't learned, though, is everything she needs to know. There are blind spots in her visions, people and parts of the city she cannot see. Frustratingly, Heinreil is one of them. He's elusive even to her borrowed divine sight. She kicks shingles off the roof in frustration. She could try getting close to the Holy Beggar again, but she's scared of being *recognised* by the bell, which is the stupidest thought she's ever had, but one she can't shake.

She finds it hard to spy on Professor Ongent. Glimpses of a prison cell, spartan but much cleaner than any jail she's ever spent time in, and him just sitting staring out of the window back at her, like he knows she's watching him. Her vision flickers away to some new vista whenever she tries to focus on him; even though it's as if she's got a dozen giant eyeballs on spires across the city, she can still only see Ongent out of the corner of her eye.

Miren's as elusive as Heinreil, but in a very different way. With Heinreil, it's like she's trying to see herself. Whenever she senses him – whenever the bells sense him, she reminds herself – she looks, and he's gone. Miren's the opposite – she sees him too often, in places he can't be. The visions aren't, well, vision, they're not really *seeing*. Sometimes they are, but other times they're jumbled impressions, tastes and sounds and feeling like she's there, or she's the building, Cari's identity dissolving and fracturing with every ring of the bell. Images of Miren get superimposed on top of everything.

She once heard of a Severastian captain who offended a plague god in a southern temple by giving medicine to a dying woman. The god's priests threatened the captain, saying that the god would send the Hunting Fly after him. Terrified, the captain leaves the southern town and sails north. Next morning, he takes out his telescope and looks to see if he's being pursued, and he sees this gigantic fly in the distance. The Hunting Fly is after him. He looks north, and the fly's there, too. He sails west and east and every which way, but no matter where he goes, every time he looks through his spyglass to check, the fly's still there, big as a thundercloud and ugly as the sins that birthed it. The ship goes around and around in circles until the crew starve and drop dead.

And then the little fly hops off the end of the telescope and goes to lay its eggs in the eyes of the dead men.

Miren's the fly in her vision.

It's almost a relief when she manages to seize control of the flood of visions and make the bells show her other people. Eladora, for example. Cari spies on her working in the university library. Her cousin looks so exhausted and scared that Cari feels sorry for her. Through the vision, she can feel Eladora's shallow, half-panicked breathing, the unaccustomed hunger in her stomach, and the elation mixed with terror she feels as she searches through old books. It reminds Cari of the day she herself ran away from Aunt Silva's, the mix of happiness and apprehension she felt when she was twelve, as she scrambled down the sun-baked slopes towards the little harbour, towards the first ship that would carry her across the sea to the wide world.

"It's all right," Cari tells Eladora in the vision, "you'll be fine."

Then snapped away, at the speed of thought, to other visions. She struggles to regain her control, to push away the flood of images of the yellow fog and narrow alleyways and men arguing in parliament and fishermen huddled in doorways waiting for the storm to pass and preachers in the Seamarket and screaming infants in the City Hospital and a concert in the theatre on Silverstrand and a mercenary recruiter training farm boys near the Dowager Gate and a million million million—

And the sun goes down behind the hump-back of Castle Hill, and, one by one, the bells fall silent across the city as night lays its cloak across Guerdon. The echoes are all that Cari hears. The echoes have no power in them, no supernatural voice or visions. She lingers on the rooftop, watching the lights come on across the city. Alchemical lamps glow like little stars in the richer districts; elsewhere the lamplighters trudge through the streets on familiar paths, lighting the gas lamps. Other parts, like the Wash, fall into their own darkness, lit by a scattered few lanterns and the cluster of lights along the harbour.

She's more tired that she can ever remember being. Her limbs haven't ached like this since she was living in the Dancer's temple, and spent whole days caught up in the god's mystical ecstatic dance. Her hands have no strength to grip the drainpipe as she climbs down. More than that, though, her soul feels frayed, stretched. It's hard for her to shrink herself down, restrict herself to the form of the woman who now walks hurriedly, head bowed, hands in pockets, down towards the canals.

Cari wonders how much of herself she left stranded on rooftops and gutters across the city. Her consciousness expanded to cover all of Guerdon, tugged this way and that by the angry, demanding demons in the bell towers. She doesn't think she came away unscathed. It's been an impossibly long day. Time slows down in the visions; she lives lifetimes between chimes.

She finds the visions linger in the back of her mind long afterwards. Passing a print shop, she glances up at a closed window and knows that the owner secretly prints a seditious newsletter criticising the corruption of parliament, knows this because he stores them in a graveyard within sight of St Storm.

She sees a woman carrying a basket of washing, and knows that her husband is having an affair with her niece, that he's with her now in the back room of a nearby inn, naked bodies pumping and gasping, and for some reason she thinks of Miren.

She stops to buy a snack from a limping street vendor and recognises him. Knows where he lives, where he goes. Knows that he came on a refugee ship, fleeing from the Godswar. Knows that he wakes up screaming, and that part of his right leg was turned to living gold by one of the deities of Ishmere, Blessed Bol, a god of prosperity turned militant. That he bought passage for his family by cutting off his transmuted foot and selling it, still warm and golden-bloody, to a merchant captain. His stall doesn't make enough money to pay the protection fees demanded by the Brotherhood, so once a month they send a Gullhead with a hammer and chisel to cut off another strip from the stump.

Cari knows all this. It's too much for her, too much to fit inside her skull.

She hands over a coin, he gives her a plateful of slop and fried fish, bundled inside a day-old newspaper. Like she doesn't know everything about him from the inside. He prays to the Keepers these days, instead of the gods of his homeland. Blessed Bol is mad, and so is Fate Spider and Lion Queen and even High Umur the Conqueror, but at least they listened. Only the bells listen to his prayers in the churches of the Keepers.

Keep it together, she tells herself. Every time the bells ring, she gets more control over what they show her. Soon, she and Spar will have the power to break Heinreil. The thieves can't say no to a girl who can see inside every house in the city, spy on everyone, know all their secrets.

And then . . . then she can leave the city again, and never have to hear its bells.

Doubled vision as she approaches the canal. What she can see warring with what she remembers seeing from a dozen different perspectives. She kept watch on the canal boat as best she could in the visions, and is sure the Brotherhood haven't found them yet.

Mother Bleak's on deck, smoking. Keeping her own lookout.

"You didn't need to buy that Ishmerian muck," she says, "I'd have cooked you something."

"Tomorrow, maybe, if we're still here," says Cari apologetically, although she's glad to have something to eat with a little bite to it. She developed a taste for spice while travelling. "Is Spar back?"

"He's having a lie-down. Hadn't eaten a thing, poor dear."

Cari touches the handle of her knife for reassurance. A lie-down? Stone men don't lie down if they can avoid it. Stillness is death, that's what Spar drummed into her. Anytime his body settles, it calcifies. Something's wrong.

She hurries past Mother Bleak, heading towards the stairs down into the houseboat's cabin.

"Don't forget the gloves!" calls the old woman. Hanging just inside the door like grasping hands are the two pairs of industrial gloves. Cari brushes past them angrily; she lived with Spar for months in quarters almost as confined as the houseboat and never got the plague.

Spar's lying where he was last night, in the open space between the bench and the little galley.

"Cari." He doesn't look at her as she comes in, just stares at the ceiling.

"What's wrong?"

"Nothing." He rolls over, wincing. "I'm just tired."

She offers him her hand. "Well, get up. We're meeting Tammur tonight. Rat's coming, too."

"Give me a moment," he says, unmoving. She's seen him in this mood before, when he's hurting. He shuts down, acts like an automaton. Gives in to the stone more than he should.

Tonight, she has no patience for it. "We don't have time. You told me how important Tammur is — he's the only one of Idge's old gang who still has any power. We need him, so get up."

"Is there any alk?"

"No, there fucking isn't. You had a shot last night. Come on."

He tries to rise on his own, and fails, slipping back down with a crash that rocks the boat. Cari kneels down and lifts, but Spar shoves her away.

"Don't touch me! I can get up myself."

"Fine." She turns her back and furiously ignores him as she gobbles her fried fish. Doesn't listen to him heave and groan as he wrestles himself upright.

Cari turns around. Spar's standing, staring at his own stone-encrusted hands. "Did Bleak's boy tell you anything useful?"

"No. Come on, let's go and see Tammur."

"Right. Right." He steps out of the houseboat's cabin and straightens up to his full height. Grabs a half-cloak and throws it around his shoulders. "Let's go."

If the waitress in the Bull wonders at the strange group assembled in the back room, she shows no sign. Tammur pays her double anyway. She still scowls at Rat as he scurries past her, wrinkling her nose at the ghoul's stench.

From the way the old man greets Spar, you'd think that it was Tammur and not Rat who'd been friends with the Stone Man for years. Although, Rat muses, Tammur has known Spar for even longer – knew his father, whatever that meant. Ghouls don't have family like humans; their pups are born after three months, the size of rats, and mature in the darkness of the tunnels below.

Rat has no idea who his father was, and all he remembers of his mother is her scent. Neither means anything to him.

Spar, he can tell, is trying to impress Tammur. Admitting no weakness, no disability. Striding in, not limping. Ordering wine in a fragile glass, not the iron cups they usually reserve for Stone Men. It's an act, but Spar's putting everything into it.

"Now, my boy, where is it to be? This cursed weather has thrown everything into confusion, and gods below know when any of my ships will actually set sail. You'll have to lie low in the Wash for another—"

Spar interrupts him. "I'm not here about passage. I'm staying."

"You just escaped from the thief-taker. You're a wanted man, Spar. If you'd gone to trial, then maybe we could have done something – bribed a magistrate, got a lesser sentence, had someone else plead – but you broke out."

"I had no choice. Heinreil tried to have me killed."

"That," says Tammur thoughtfully, "is not something said lightly."

"We – all three of us – were at the House of Law," says Cari, "Heinreil sent us in to steal property records or some shit. We were a diversion while his lads blew up the Tower."

"The Brotherhood had nothing to do with that," says Tammur. Then, as if fishing the thought out of some deep pool in his brain, "At least, so Heinreil told me. And what would it profit us to destroy the Tower – or kill you?"

"It doesn't!" says Cari. "He's running his own scheme. He's just using the Brotherhood, screwing you all over—"

"Sweet girl," snaps Tammur, "you're not a Brotherhood member. I don't know if you're fucking Spar or just here because you got kicked out by whoever took you in, but I am having a conversation with my godson, so shut up."

Cari goes for her knife, but Spar's hand closes around her wrist in a flash. "Don't." His hand is so much bigger than hers, he can make a ring of stony fingers around her slim arm without touching her skin. To Tammur, he says in a voice like a gravestone, "Carillon saved my life. She's the one who broke me out of the lithosarium. And she's . . . "

"A saint," says Rat, licking his muzzle. "She can see things, Tammur. Knows all the city's secrets."

Tammur glances at her suspiciously, brow furrowed, like a fence appraising stolen goods, judging quality and value against how hot they are, how perilous. He raises his hands. "All right. I'm sorry . . . Carillon, isn't it? I misspoke. Please, show me your gift."

"I can't. Not right now." Cari feels her cheeks burn.

"Let's start again, shall we? What do you want?" asks Tammur.

Spar hesitates. His jaw moves, but no words come out. Carillon speaks for him. "We're going to expose Heinreil. He's murdering Brotherhood members and selling out the rest of you."

"We? Or you, Spar? If you want the master's chair, I want to hear it from you."

"I want it," says Spar thickly. His shoulders hunch. "I'll challenge Heinreil. Gutter court." The thieves' court – a gathering of the whole Brotherhood, the rough justice of the downtrodden. Named for its preferred method of execution; those found to have offended against the Brotherhood were, in ages past, hung from gutters as a public warning.

"Gutter court," echoes Tammur. "If he did try to kill you – without good reason – then you have the right, certainly. But you'll need more than . . . " He pauses, as if the word is distasteful, "these 'visions'. No one likes Heinreil, but that doesn't matter when everyone's getting paid."

"The Brotherhood's about more than business."

"Idge should have gone into parliament – though they're bigger crooks than any of us. No one's going to turn on Heinreil out of principle. You'll need support."

"That's why we came to you," says Cari. "You're second in the Brotherhood – or should be. You've been running things since Idge's day."

"Don't lecture me." Tammur glares at her. "This isn't your business."

Cari sits back down and closes her eyes. She's looking inward, Rat guesses. Curious, he stares at her, remembering his violent reaction to meeting her earlier. Now, as he watches, he can sense invisible powers moving around her, circling around Cari, reaching for her. Involuntarily, he starts to growl. Tammur glances at him, snorts dismissively.

"Tammur," says Spar wearily, "can I count on you?"

The older man takes a drink. Washes around his mouth like trying to chase out a bad taste, then swallows. "No," he says finally. "At least, not yet – and out of loyalty to your father's memory, I'll tell you why. You're trying to put together a coup against an established and secure master in, what, two days? Three? Your name counts for something. You've probably got some hotheads on your side, too. It's not enough.

"You say you want this, but I don't believe you. You want to be Idge. We had Idge. And they hanged him. We don't need another one. You want my advice? Leave. Go to the Archipelago or sign up with a mercenary company or go down to Dredger's yard and ask for work on ships. I'm telling you this for your own good."

Spar stands up, wincing as he does. There's an audible crack like someone broke a cobblestone with a hammer. "I didn't ask for your advice, Tammur. I asked for your help and your loyalty. Heinreil tries to murder me, and betrays the Brotherhood, and your advice is to suck it up and walk away? No." He points towards the door. "Get out."

"You think you can order me around, you entitled little shit? I raised you like my own son until you—"

The unseen pressure in the room breaks like a storm, crashing in Rat's ears. Cari speaks: "You threw a dying man into the harbour at Hook Row nine years ago and watched him drown. Your grandson has a blue blanket, and you hit his mother when she couldn't keep the babe from crying two nights ago. You nearly hit the child, too, but instead you threw one of his toys across the room and broke it. You're taking pills for your nerves – your doctor's cheating you."

Tammur looks gut-shot.

"You hoped the sea-witch – Myri – would sleep with you," says Cari, her eyes still shut. "In an upstairs room in a house on Valder, it's twenty-seven nine thirty-two four—"

"Gods below," says Tammur. "Shut her up."

Spar doesn't move. Rat leans forward and – *rips her throat out, letting her blood spurt out across the table* – tugs on Cari's arm. "Cari, come back. Shut them out," he hisses. She nods, bites her lip, grips his gnarled hand. The psychic pressure around her fades.

"See?" says Cari. Blood wells up from her lip and rolls down her chin. What else did she see, wonders Rat, that she dared not reveal.

"It's still folly," says Tammur, but he's rattled. "Still fucking madness. Give me time to think about it, all right?"

"Don't think too long," says Cari, giggling like she's drunk. "Seventeen."

Tammur thumps down the stairs, stumbling and crashing. The noise of his passage like the distant thunder of the retreating storm.

"A combination?" asks Rat. He backs away from Cari, watching her closely. His own unnatural bloodlust diminished at the same time as she dropped her connection to whatever gave her the visions. The room's much too small for him now; he wants to be outside again, in the rain. The room's so small it feels like a tunnel.

"Yeah, to his safe." Cari wipes her chin. "I could see it even when the bells aren't ringing. I need a fucking drink, though." She grabs Tammur's wine glass and drains it, then starts on her own. "That actually went well. We get Tammur to bring in everyone who'll listen. We find that alchemist, trace the poison back to Heinreil. That's our proof. They give us the numbers we need to win in gutter court." She raises her glass as if making a toast. "That fucker's going down."

"Cari," says Spar, but she doesn't listen.

"Spar Idgeson, master of the Brotherhood. Carillon, the saint of thieves. And Rat, we'll come up with a title for—"

"Cari," says Spar again. "I can't move."

CHAPTER TWENTY-ONE

INTERROGATION OF PRISONER #9313.

I: State your name for the record.

P: Aloysius Ongent.

I: Address?

P: The old seminary.

I: But you are also the lessee of number eight, Desiderata Street?

P: Yes.

I: Occupation?

P: I hold the Derling Chair in History at the University of Guerdon.

I: Do you practise sorcery, professor?

P: I dabble, a little. I have a licence, of course, and all the paperwork should be in order.

I: You dabble. You would not consider yourself a powerful adept.

P: I wouldn't consider any human a powerful adept, these days. Sorcery has moved on. The work done on reification in the last two centuries means that it is vastly safer and more convenient to approach sorcery through physical means – alchemy, fetishes, aetheric engines, proxiates, vat-grown adepts and the like – than it is to attempt spells using old-fashioned methods. The average journeyman in the alchemists' guild, for example, can command sorceries that dwarf almost anything attempted in—

I: You would not consider yourself a powerful adept, then?

P: No.

I: Three nights ago, you were on Desiderata Street. Tell me what happened that night.

P: How many more times must I go over this? This is, by my count, the sixth time I've been asked that question. Seventh, actually. Twice by the watch, once by Jere then by some little fellow from parliament, then another time by the watch, then by Magistrate Qurix yesterday morning – and she said that I'd be free to go after that. Why am I still here? Are you from the watch, or . . . ?

I: Seventeen people vanished on Desiderata Street, Professor. Twelve Tallowmen were damaged beyond repair, and twice as many were maimed. You will be answering these questions for a long time to come, either here or elsewhere. Tell me what happened that night.

P: Oh, for heaven's sake. I was dining in the staff common room at the seminary, when my son Miren arrived and warned me of a disturbance—

I: Why did he go for you, and not call the watch?

P: The Tallowmen were already there. He assumed I would be needed in the aftermath, not that I would have to actually, well, intercede.

I: What did he tell you?

P: That there was a brawl going on in the street outside between the Tallowmen and an intruder.

I: Did he tell you what the intruder was?

P: No. He didn't know what it was.

I: You are the professor of history at the university.

P: Yes.

I: Do you know what it was?

P: No. Should I?

I: "For there hastened from the deep places the unmaking, and they swallowed the hosts of the living, and took from them the hame of form, and offered up their souls to the Black Iron Gods."

P: Pilgrin's translation, isn't it? I've always preferred Mondolin's, myself. "And from the deeps they called the Ravellers, eaters of form, who fell upon the armies of the blessed and caused great confusion, for those who fell rose again in semblance, for they were hollow shells." Do you mean to say that the creature was one of the fabled servants of the Black Iron Gods?

I: You tell me.

P: According to the histories, they were all destroyed – gods and monsters alike. That said – have you read my paper on post-Ashen cloacal architecture? Our ancestors in the period immediately after the war were very, very concerned about the security of underground places. There are gates and fortresses of tremendous size deep beneath the city. Why do you think the old castle was abandoned as a defensive structure, and they built this new citadel out on a narrow peninsula? It wasn't just to control the harbour, now, was it? It was because Castle Hill was compromised, worm-riddled with tunnels. But I think you know all this.

I: Did you recognise the creature when you arrived?

P: Dear fellow, I barely saw it. It was fighting all those Tallowmen. All I could see were knives and dancing flames. I wasn't going to stop to examine it.

I: What did you do then?

P: As I said, I dabble. I know a few, ah, vigorous invocations. Sound and fury, really, more than anything else. I'd never cast any of them before, but my home and my wards were at risk, so I—

I: Your wards? Your home was magically warded? What did you expect?

P: [sighs] Wards, as in young students in my care. Eladora Duttin, for example.

I: No one else?

P: My son, Miren, also lives there. Other students, from time to time. Undergraduates, flitting in and out like mayflies.

I: Was there anyone else present that night?

P: I don't know. Possibly. College friends of Eladora, maybe.

I: Professor – dabbling is tolerated. Deception is not. Nor is consorting with forbidden powers.

P: Consorting! What utter bunk! You have no standing here! Go back to your wizened masters in the church and tell them that if they threaten me again I'll bring them before parliament!

I: You have fewer friends there than you think. It is not the Keepers who threaten you. Tell me, Professor, do you remember Uldina Manix? She remembers you.

CHAPTER TWENTY-TWO

The room swims around Jere, spinning and lurching like an eggshell in a drain. He suspects that he must be dead and disembodied. Blown to pieces by the explosion. As though the artillery bombardment that killed so many of his mates in the Godswar had struck again, delayed by ten years and off target by a thousand miles.

He stirs. Everything hurts, but he feels it through a morphine fog. It was someone else's body that had had the shit kicked out of it. He feels a little sorry for that guy.

There's a bandage or blindfold over his eyes. He reaches up to pull at it.

"I don't think you should try to move." A woman's voice. Hesitant.

"Where . . . " he manages. His mouth is dry.

"Where what? Um. Your man Bolind is in the other room. Should I fetch him? Where are you? Back in your office in the" – the distaste in her voice betrays Eladora's identity to Jere – "lithosarium."

"Water."

"Oh! Of course." A moment later, she presses a cup to his lips.

"I can do it myself." He grabs the cup, spilling half of it over his chest as his hands shake. He wrenches off the bandage. Gods below, his eyes sting. Yellowish goo mixed with tears rolls down his cheeks. Eladora dabs at his face with a handkerchief, but he shoos her away.

"Don't fuss over me."

"Sorry." She flinches and withdraws to the other side of the room – of his room. He's back in his bedroom at the office; little cot, travelling chest, greatcoat hanging on a peg by the door, alongside where his sword cane usually hangs. Down in the sea, now.

"How did I get here?"

"This strange man in a helmet—"

"Dredger."

"—brought you to the door. He had a doctor with him. Well, she said she was a doctor. She left some medicine for you." Eladora sounds doubtful. "She said you were lucky to be alive. They didn't say what happened to you."

"Took a little trip out to Bell Rock to see what the problem was."

"Oh!" Riffling of papers. "And what did you find there?"

Memory of masked figures in yellow fog. The bell crashing to the ground.

"I'm not sure. The gas leak was cover, but I don't know who the fuckers were." He pauses, trying to sort actual memory from some fever-dream. "Have you seen your boy? Miren?"

"No. Did you see him? Is he all right?"

"Never mind." Jere struggles to sit up. Doing so dislodges something in his lungs, and he chokes, spits up gobbets of gritty yellowed phlegm. Eladora waves her handkerchief from the far side of the room, as if that's helpful. "Fucking hell."

"Here, take some of this. The doctor said it would help." A mouthful of bitter medicine; it dissolves the gritty gunk in his mouth, and probably a layer of tooth enamel, too.

"When you didn't show up – was it last night? – I figured Miren or the professor had come back. No sign?"

Eladora wrings her hands. "No. The professor – he's been moved. I don't know if he's still under arrest, but he's not in prison at Queen's Point anymore. And I haven't seen Miren. And it wasn't last night – it was the night before. You've been unconscious for nearly fifteen hours."

"Bolind!" roars Jere.

No response from the other room. Eladora crosses to the door and checks. "He's not here," she says.

"Useless lump of lard. What about the others?"

"Others?" echoes Eladora. "There's no one else here. I haven't seen anyone except you and Bolind in this horrible place."

He'd told Bolind to rouse the street crew and send them off to look for Idgeson and the Thay girl. Maybe they're all out, shaking down informants and looking through the slums for the Stone Boy and the thief. Or maybe Bolind's an even more useless lump of lard than Jere fears, and still hasn't done as he was ordered. Has the big man lost his nerve?

"Godshit. Right. Hang on, I've lost a night. That means I'm supposed to meet Kelkin this evening at nine."

"It's after seven now," says Eladora.

An inarticulate roar of frustration and yellow spit. Jere struggles to get up, fails, sinks back down coughing. There's a bandage on his ribs that's red and dripping, another on his left hand taping broken fingers together. And his guts feel like a Tallowman's innards, as if all his organs have partially melted and stuck together.

"Oh gods—" His oath is lost in another bout of vomiting up yellow slime. He takes another swig of the medicine, then reconsiders and downs half the bottle. He manages to sit up on the side of the little cot, weak as a child.

"Would you help me dress?" he asks Eladora.

*

They find Bolind in the cell occupied until recently by Spar. The big man walks with a surprising grace, climbing nimbly around the slick rocks, hands moving like a diviner.

"What the fuck are you doing?" roars Jere from the doorway.

Bolind lifts his head and swivels it around in a way that reminds Eladora of an animal. A snake, maybe, lazy but dangerous.

"Looking for clues."

"Thinks he's a detective now," mutters Jere to her under his breath. Then, loudly: "Any word from the old crowd?"

Bolind blinks, slowly. "No. They're still looking. The gas leak made things harder yesterday."

"I've got a meeting with Kelkin. I'll be back in a few hours."

"I'll come with you," says Bolind. "Got some stuff to talk about."

"And you smell a free dinner. All right, but keep your mouth shut. And that goes for you, too, Miss Duttin."

Eladora of the present day wonders what the Eladora of a week ago would think of her. A week ago, she'd never have dared go into the Wash at any time. Now, she's walking the terrifying dark streets at twilight, hardly flinching at the distant shouts and cries – and, gods, is that *gunfire*? Little sparks of fire race across the rooftops, Tallowmen drawn to violence. Flames drawn to moths.

The Eladora of a week ago would have frowned at her clothing. She fled Desiderata Street without any of her belongings – *Carillon has more of my things*, she thinks sourly – and hasn't risked going back for so much as a change of clothing since. No money to buy clothes either. She's had to make do with what she could scavenge in the lithosarium, so she's wearing a leather jerkin and trousers. She wonders who owned them – some criminal caught by the thief-taker, she guesses. They fit well enough, and when she catches a glimpse of herself in the broken glass of a shop window, she's struck by how much she looks like Carillon.

She looks almost dangerous. If the Eladora of a week ago met her, she'd cross the street to hide from this armed ruffian of an adventuress.

Bolind walks behind her, a silent shadow just like Miren used be. Miren, though, is young and slim and broodingly handsome and smells of rosewater; Bolind is huge, and his astounding ugliness is underlined by a rose-coloured bloom of bruises on his cheek. He smells of stagnant water.

Jere, beside her, is the only one of them who looks like he should be attending dinner in the house of a gentleman. She found a good suit in his wardrobe. A few years out of date, and it needed a good scrubbing to get several unidentifiable stains out of the trousers. Jere called it his court suit. He swaggers as he walks, forging ahead of them. This part of the Wash is crowded, there's a sort of tent city springing up here, people who fled the poison cloud of the previous day crowding into lean-tos and flophouses. The watch said that the cloud was mostly harmless by the time it reached the shore, and that there's no reason people can't return to their dockside homes. Swaying tenements for refugees from the Godswar. Some of them, she knows from her recent studies, were built as divine decontamination centres, where newcomers to Guerdon could be held until they were proved free of dangerous miracles. There's a theory that the Stone Plague was brought out of the early Godswar. Now, there's an internment camp out in the bay, on Hark Island.

Jere makes a path through the crowd for her. No one wants to cross the infamous thief-taker. It's only when they pass the Tallowmen sentries at the entrance to the subway station, when the crowds suddenly melt away and they're left alone on the stairs, that Jere suddenly slows and coughs, leans on Bolind while he catches his breath. The bottle of medicine he got from Dredger's doctor is empty, but he refilled it with medicinal liquor, and he takes a hit. He offers her a sip, which she refuses, as does Bolind.

On the train, she reviews her notes. She turns to the page where she listed likely candidates for the hidden Black Iron Gods and draws an asterisk next to the Bell Rock lighthouse, matching the one next to the Seamarket. She places question marks next to the three cathedrals on Holyhill and the Beggar's Church. Her pen pauses next to the Beckanore monastery. It was destroyed more than a year ago, but may still be relevant. She makes an indecisive squiggle.

"What do you have there?" asks Bolind, leaning in.

"Never you mind," snaps Jere. "As soon as we're done at Kelkin's, you're going back down to the Wash to find Spar. If we don't have him by tomorrow night, we're fucked. Nabur's got a bloody writ for both of them."

Bolind is unmoved. "I'll find him."

The train rattles out of the tunnel mouth, over the Gravehill viaduct. The city's graveyard is a black void beneath them, a starless gulf between the lights of Castle Hill behind them and Bryn Avane ahead.

Alighting, they take a carriage. Only servants walk in haughty Bryn Avane. The driver frowns at Eladora's clothing, and she cringes, but Jere just taps his stick on the roof and mentions Kelkin's name, and they're off. In the cramped carriage, she's pressed up against Bolind, and something about his touch makes her flesh recoil. He grins at her, showing a mouthful of alarmingly sharp teeth.

She looks out of the window instead, watching the mansions and walled gardens and galleries. The sigil of the alchemists' guild marked above half the doors – the new rich in this richest of districts.

"If Kelkin asks," whispers Jere, mindful that the Bryn Avane coachmen are notorious for eavesdropping, "tell him we know where Spar and your cousin are, and we're just waiting for an opportunity to pick 'em up. Otherwise, fill your gobs with his food and keep quiet. Let him do the talking. He's in parliament — he likes that."

"Mr Kelkin's house," announces the driver.

It's a big mansion, old and overgrown. Rusty iron railings hold back a thick and ill-kempt hedge. The mansion sprawls blindly; most of the windows are shuttered and haven't been opened in years. Eladora guesses that three-quarters of it is unused and wonders why a man famed for his penny-pinching would own so many empty rooms.

Jere rings the bell at the front door, making Eladora flinch. It echoes away in the depths of the big old house. Shuffling. An old footman opens the door a crack, just enough for the three of them to squeeze in. A single lamp burns in the immensity of the hallway. Threadbare red carpets, stairways climbing away into the shadows. A ticking clock in the darkness.

The footman clears his throat. "Mr Kelkin is unavoidably delayed and sends his apologies. If you would follow me ... "

He limps down the hall, and they follow after, passing by prints of Guerdon's skyline, of towers and spires and factories. Even the lithosarium has its pride of place. The pictures seem wrong to Eladora, but it is only when they come to a doorway that she remembers why.

"I've been here before! This is the Thay mansion!" The memory of that door has been part of her mental furniture all her life, a keepsake she never understood. It was bright then, and seemed so much bigger, but she remembers toddling through that door, laughing as the nursemaid chased her, then bursting into tears when her grandfather glared at her. Even now, so many years later, Eladora is suddenly nervous about stepping through into the next room.

The footman inclines his head. "Mr Kelkin purchased the house from the estate of the late Jermas Thay. The servants, too – I served your great-grandfather, Ms Duttin, and your grandfather after him."

"Oh!" Eladora wonders if she should curtsey. The ancient servant's rheumy eyes are hard to read.

"I thought everyone in the house was killed," remarks Jere, "when the Thays were murdered."

"Everyone in the main house, yes. On the night in question, I was sleeping in the servants' quarters that adjoin the main building. The connecting door was locked from the other side. By the time we were able to break it down, it was too late to do anything except fight the fires."

Jere glances around the hallway, examining it as he would a crime scene. Eladora follows his gaze, imagining the intruders smashing through the front door, sweeping through the house with knifes, butchering everyone they encountered, setting fire to the family wing at the back of the mansion.

Her mother Silva was gone by that point, married beneath her station to a country farmer. The love match strained relations with the rest of the family. That visit to the city that Eladora remembered was a mostly happy memory to the toddling child, apart from that brief meeting with her terrifying grandfather. But when her mother Silva recalled the evening – usually when she was drunk – she recounted the humiliation of going to beg Jermas for money. Silva hadn't known it then, thinks Eladora, but by then Jermas was deep in debt, the family fortune squandered on bad investments and ships that sank. The Godswar ruined them from afar, as trade gods gone mad turned to war and hammered coins and scales into swords.

"Please, sit down." The footman opens the door into a well-appointed drawing room. "I am sure Mr Kelkin will be home promptly. I shall inform you when he arrives."

"Mr Kelkin," says Jere, "keeps a bottle of good brandy in that cabinet there."

"Quite so," says the footman. Glasses clink. He places one in front of Eladora first. She never drinks, it makes her sick, but that was the Eladora of a week ago, and she lets the footman pour a measure into her glass. The liquor is both slick and sticky, running down her throat and leaving warm fire behind in its wake.

Jere stretches out his legs, wincing as he does so, shifting to get comfortable. He gulps his drink. To dull the pain, she guesses, and sips her own again. She wonders what Miren would say if he saw her now, so unlike the prim postgraduate student he knew. Of course he wouldn't say anything, not him, but maybe he'd look at her differently.

Bells chime in the distance. Kelkin's late.

The bells make her think of Carillon. She was three or four when the rest of the family were murdered. She had been sick, some complaint of the lungs, and the doctor had recommended fresh country air, so they'd sent her to stay with Silva. A child coughs, Eladora reflects as she stares into the warm amber of her half-finished drink, and everything turns out one way. It's not that she'd prefer it if Carillon had stayed here and died along with the rest of the Thays, but if there was no Carillon there'd have been no attack by the Raveller and the professor wouldn't have been arrested, Miren wouldn't have vanished and she wouldn't be here.

Wait, no. The Raveller was already at large, wasn't it? She'd eavesdropped at the professor's door when he was talking with Miren and Cari, and heard that it was eating people in the Holy Beggar before the attack. They learned about it through Cari, and it followed her or Miren back to Desiderata Street.

Still, though. She finds her glass empty and reaches for the bottle to refill it. Jere catches her hand.

"That's enough for you. This is work, remember?"

"Not my work," she says.

"You're here at my sufferance, and you're sleeping under my roof tonight. It's close enough."

"You might think that," retorts Eladora, and pours another splash into her glass. Jere snatches it from in front of her and drains it.

"Thank me later," he says, mockingly. Eladora doesn't know how to respond, and just stares at him.

"He's here," mutters Bolind, rising. The sound of hooves on cobbles, rattling wheels slowing to a halt. Eladora stands and tries to look presentable, despite being dressed as a common cut-throat. She's glad that Kelkin changed all the paintings on the walls. She could not bear the feeling of being watched by judgemental ancestors, staring down at her from their gilt frames.

Outside, an argument. Kelkin berating the old footman. A storm crashing against an old weathered rock.

The parliamentarian throws open the door. "Who is that?" he demands, looking at Bolind. Beside Kelkin is a small dog on a leash, straining and snarling at the intruders. The little ball of fur and teeth struggles to get close to Bolind.

"One of my men," replies Jere mildly.

"You'll vouch for him?"

"He's been with me for years."

Bolind steps aside and gestures to the seat he's just vacated, and the untouched drink on the table beside it. Kelkin hands the dog's leash to the footman, who – with some effort – hauls the little beast out through the door. They can still hear it scraping and snarling from outside.

Kelkin sits down and Bolind melts back into the shadows like the city's best servant. Kelkin empties the glass in one swallow and refills it.

"The majority consensus of the public order committee, as reflected in their recommendations to the city chamber, is that we're all going to be murdered in our beds by a mob of blood-thirsty scum led by spies and assassins from Old Haith. Some of the younger, stupider members actually proposed locking us all in Parliament and surrounding the building with soldiers 'until the crisis abates'."

Kelkin spits in the vague direction of the fireplace, and the gobbet of thick whitish phlegm lands next to Eladora's foot. It looks like Holyhill to her, a white mound rising from a red sea.

"They found more of that graffiti near the mooring for the freighter that crashed onto the Bell Rock. I didn't see you there," says Kelkin to Jere.

"I was on the Bell Rock."

That shuts Kelkin up. He sits back and gestures to Jere to continue.

Eladora notices how Jere lingers over his descriptions of the physical peril he'd put himself in, and how Kelkin's probing questions push through to the facts of the matter. It reminds her of Professor Ongent skewering some unprepared undergraduate.

Halfway through, the footman enters and reminds Kelkin that dinner is waiting. The sound of the dog whining through the open door. Kelkin declares that he isn't moving, and that dinner can come to him. Now, the small side tables and even the floor around the four of them are crowded with plates and dishes, mostly untouched.

Jere reaches the part of the tale where he describes how the intruders removed the bell of the Bell Rock and carried it away.

"The bell?" snaps Kelkin. "What the devil do they want with a bell?"

Eladora can't stop herself. "I-I-I've been doing some research on that matter."

Kelkin raises a finger. "One moment. Jere, anything else of note?"

"They blew up the rest of the lighthouse to cover their tracks. I was nearly blown to bits; I was as close to the blast as I am to your front door, so—"

"So you survived and came here. Very good. Next. Duttin, what did you discover?"

Jere tries to interrupt, to complain about the head of the watch and some legal harassment, but Kelkin ignores him. "Facts first."

"I'm not sure if these are f-f-facts," says Eladora, "but the evidence is compelling." She lifts her bundle of papers, fumbles for the marked page in *Sacred and Secular*. Shows them the illustration of the Black Iron statues, the hungry gods given physical form. Embodied hatred.

She begins as she would a university lecture. "The q-question of the eventual disposition of the captured a-a-avatars of the Black Iron pantheon is a vexed one. I began by looking at the works of Rix and Pilgrin, but found them to be primarily concerned with the mystical and theological implications of mass conversion to the faith of the Keepers after the war. Pilgrin, for instance—"

"What does this have to do with the bell at Bell Rock?" asks Kelkin. His hand shakes as he asks the question.

"My thesis is that the Black Iron Gods were reforged into bells and concealed – in plain sight – around the city."

"The Tower of Law? The Bell Rock?"

"Both were constructed within ten years of the defeat of the Black Iron Gods."

"What could you do," asked Kelkin, "with one of those bells?"

"What could I do?" Eladora wavers. "N-n-nothing."

"Not you, then. A sorcerer. A worshipper of the gods."

"I don't know. I'm not an expert in thaumaturgy. Professor Ongent – he's done some work in the field, and he might – if you got him out of prison . . ."

"Ha. His name came up in the public safety meeting. Your professor associated with a very questionable crowd in his youth. Unlicensed thaumaturgists, relic-hawkers, archaeotheologists. He's under suspicion of being an agent of foreign powers."

"That's absurd," protests Eladora.

Kelkin refills his glass again. He ruffles his moustache, smooths it out again. A nervous gesture. Then he says:

"There's another matter that may be connected. This is military intelligence, mind you, although no doubt it'll be all over the newspapers in a day or two. Old Haith has taken the Grena Valley."

The name means nothing to Eladora, but from the way Jere sucks in his breath she guesses it's a significant move in the Godswar.

"They can't hold it. They've tried before. The local goddess is a vicious bitch. She's—"

"Dead," says Kelkin. "Completely dead. No fallout, no skyquakes. Just snuffed it."

"Gods can't die," says Eladora. "Not like that." Ongent described a god as being like a river channel, a course for flowing spiritual energy. The river might grow and diminish, burst its banks and flood the land, or be diverted to power a mill, or dammed to water farmland. People might drink from the river – or drown in it, like saints.

Block the river at its source, somehow stop the rains that feed it, and maybe, over time – over a long time – it'll diminish down to a trickle, a muddy stream of bitter, aborted divinity.

But a river doesn't just stop.

"There are reports that there was a gunboat in the bay," adds Kelkin.

Jere says, "If Old Haith has a gods-bane weapon, then it's over. They've won the war." The war's lasted so long because gods are hard to kill – all you can do is grind them down, deform them and diminish them until they're nothing but ghosts. The other option is to have one god fight another head-on, and that's arguably worse. A century of grinding, vicious fighting, or a day of hellfire and madness beyond contemplation – pick your poison.

"The committee's convinced that we're a month away from a Haithi invasion force showing up on our doorstep. That the attacks on the Tower of Law and the Bell Rock were acts of sabotage and terror by Haithi agents in our midst. I had to fight to stop them ordering the watch to intern every foreigner in the city." Kelkin swirls his drink, and glares at an etching of Parliament atop Castle Hill on the wall as if he could destroy his political enemies with sheer anger alone. "Forty years of progress, and they try to turn it all back overnight."

"You don't think the attacks are from Haith?" asks Jere.

"That's what I pay you to find out, you dolt!" roars Kelkin. "But no – it doesn't make sense. The House of Law might be a valid target, and I suppose they might take advantage of an unrelated attack by trying to convince people they too were responsible for Desiderata Street. But stealing the bell from Bell Rock? No, put that together with . . . ah, Eladora's research and it points squarely at something to do with the Black Iron Gods."

"What are you going to do?" Bolind whispers. Eladora had forgotten he was there. So, it seems, had Kelkin.

"I've had enough of that from the committee. Asking 'what is to be done' and not giving any bloody answers, because it's not the right question." Kelkin picks at a cold chicken leg, snapping it to get at the meat. "Jere, was there anything at all that might identify who was on the Bell Rock? I assume any evidence that might have been left got destroyed along with the lighthouse?"

"They had gasmasks and alchemical bombs. Could be sappers from Haith all right. They were human, or something close to it. Maybe Haithi walking dead? I'm guessing those Raveller-things wouldn't be too bothered by a poison cloud either. We could trace the wrecked freighter back, see who owned it. Maybe something there."

"I've waited nearly two years for you to bring me Heinreil's head. You'll forgive me if I lack confidence in that solution."

Jere ignores the barb. "It still all goes back to the Tower of Law. That's where it began, and it ties Heinreil to the whole thing."

"That's not where it began," argues Eladora. She flips through her notes, finds her list of likely places where they might have imprisoned a Black Iron God. "Beckanore monastery. There may have been a bell there."

Kelkin groans. "And that brings Old Haith in again. It would explain why the Haithi took Beckanore, if there was a bell there and they knew about it. Makes more sense than the naval base nonsense. Maybe it is Haithi spies. Gods below, I'm not walking into that bloody committee and telling those runts they were right."

"It's giving a lot of credit to Haith, isn't it? From what I recall, they're strictly old-school wizardry and a bunch of death gods. Not tactically flexible."

Eladora turns a page in her book and lays her finger on the robed cultists of the Black Iron Gods. "Could – well, if one of their monsters survived, couldn't some of their worshippers?"

Kelkin stares at her, then laughs. "I needed to be drunker before I have that conversation with you," he says. He refills his glass and drinks half of it.

Jere counts on his fingers. "So, the Beckanore bell, assuming there is one – that gets stolen. The monastery fell without a fight, right?" Kelkin nods. "And then they blow up the Tower of Law, destroying that bell. Maybe they made a mistake. Dredger – my expert on military hardware – tells me those bombs are tricky, maybe they got more bang than they expected."

Kelkin sneers. "If some Haithi spy can steal a giant bell from the middle of my city without being noticed, then to hell with it, I'll hand over my house keys right now."

"All right, I don't know. But then the third bell, the Bell Rock, that one they get right. The freighter breaking its mooring looks like an accident, and the poison cloud hides them while they get the bell. Then another blast to destroy the lighthouse completely. If anyone bothered to sort through the wreckage . . ."

Wreckage. The carts of hot metal on their way through Glimmerside. Dredger complaining about the guild and their prices. The phlogiston bomb, expertly modified—

Jere slams his fist into the table, startling the dog, who starts howling again outside the door. "It's a damn salvage operation! The whole thing – they're extracting something dangerous but still useful from the bells. Gods below, Effro, it's the alchemists' guild."

Kelkin doesn't speak. He stands, starts pacing.

Eladora feels frozen. Even from her sheltered position in the university, she knows the power and reach of the guild. Their wealth funds half the university's departments. Their trade in weapons fuels Guerdon's economy. Their City Forward party has a majority in parliament. They own the newspapers, the printing presses, the hospitals. They make alkahest and the other cure-alls and reagents that modern medicine and thaumaturgy depend on. Guerdon's navy doesn't sail anymore – it's driven by alchemical engines and armed with alchemical guns. They make the Tallowmen. If they're the ones attacking Guerdon, she's not sure what can be done. Who can stand against them?

This must be what the Godswar feels like – to have the

great invisible forces that hold up the world suddenly turn mad and cruel.

She raises her hand, fighting the fear that she's betraying Professor Ongent's trust. The thought that she's about to make trouble for Jere doesn't occur to her. "There's something else. My cousin, Carillon. She's ... connected to the bells. I think she might be a Black Iron saint."

"That's not – oh, to the abyss with it!" Jere gives up on trying to interrupt. "She's the thief girl I arrested at the Tower of Law, Kelkin. She's another Thay."

Kelkin grimaces, but there's no sign he's surprised.

"She had some sort of seizure while in custody, said she had a vision. Professor Ongent took her off my hands – he thought she might be useful to his studies. She didn't know anything useful about Heinreil, so I didn't think she meant anything. I swear I didn't know she was involved in this mess until ... "

"Until when?"

Jere runs his hand through his hair, winces. "Until she broke Idge's son out of my jail. I'll get them back, I've got men on it, but—"

Kelkin stares at him.

"Look, I'll find her, all right. I just need more time."

"There isn't anymore time." Kelkin sighs, picks up his glass, moves back to the fire. Weighing his words. Then he speaks.

"This doesn't leave the room, understand?" demands Kelkin.

Eladora nods.

Kelkin begins, "I met Jermas Thay in the seminary ... "

CHAPTER TWENTY-THREE

It took a dose of alkahest injected straight into Spar's spine before he could feel his legs again. With a second, he was able to stagger to a chair. A third got him down the stairs of the Bull. He took a fourth when they were nearly at Mother Bleak's barge, and insisted on having a fifth to hand before he would go aboard. Cari had found some back-alley alchemists who supplied the drug at a hideous mark-up – quadrupled, no doubt, because they needed to get Spar off the streets before someone tipped Heinreil or the watch or the thief-taker off. They could get money off Tammur, she thought, but they'd have to do it quietly, not advertise Spar's weakness.

The barge looked very small and fragile in the dawn light when they arrived. Mother Bleak wrinkled her nose at the sight of Rat, but said nothing and instead fussed over Spar, helping him lower himself onto a few cushions that she spread on the floor, ignoring his protests that he was made of stone and a cushioned floor felt no different from a bed of nails to him.

They slept, exhausted, Cari curled on the bench, Spar lying on the floor. If Rat slept, he did so in the fashion of ghouls, outside on the deck, eyes open and staring into the darkness of the little cabin. The city awoke around them, gulls crying overhead, shouts from the docks and the markets. Fishermen returning from up the coast, maybe, discovering the city's newest tragedy as they came to docks empty of people, coated in the yellow stains left by the poison cloud.

When Cari wakes Mother Bleak is gone, but the smell of hot curry from the pot on the stove fills the little room She shakes Spar awake, calls Rat in. Serves breakfast at twilight. Spar manages to stand up on his own, but can't manage to lever himself into position to sit on the bench. His spine's frozen again, and once again they're out of alkahest.

Rat breaks the silence.

"It's the poison, isn't it?"

"Yes," says Spar.

"Shit," curses Cari. Without Spar, there'll be no rallying point for opposition to Heinreil. Spar's popular in the Brotherhood in his own right, but, more importantly, he's Idge's son, a symbol of how things used to be.

She doesn't let herself think of Spar actually dying. Doesn't think that her only real friend in the city might possibly leave her all alone, exposed to the incomprehensible wordless fury of the bells. She has to focus on practicalities, cling to them, or she'll be lost. "All right. It's all right. We can work this. There's got to be an antidote."

"There isn't. Yon said there's no counter-agent." Spar closes his eyes. "He said there was no way to tell how fast the poison would work. He said it could take weeks, but that it'd probably be a lot less."

"How quick?" asks Rat.

"A few days, maybe." And then, in a low voice. "Sorry."

"This isn't your fault," says Cari. "Heinreil fucking did this, and we're going to pay him back. Don't you dare apologise for that—"

"That's not what I'm sorry about. I'm sorry I didn't insist that you get on a ship and leave, Cari. I'm sorry I let you drag Rat back into this. I'm sorry that I ever entertained for a bloody moment that this was a good idea, any of this, that I could—"

"Could what? Could take what you wanted? Could be who you were born to be?" Cari springs up from her seat. "What did you think was going to happen?"

"It doesn't matter."

"You thought you could be master! You thought you could make this city better, right?" Cari's eyes sting with angry tears.

"Yes. And I shouldn't have."

"For fuck's sake, Spar! What's the point of just lying there?"

Spar shrugs. "I thought I was sick, and that I'd turn to stone and die. Turns out, that's exactly what's going to happen." He sighs. "I just wanted to leave something behind. Some legacy. But it's not going to happen."

"That's just ... " Cari seethes, trying to find the words to convey just how frustratingly stupid her friend is being.

"Cari," cautions Rat quietly, "this isn't about you or your ... situation. Or your plans. It's Spar's decision."

"I never said it was about me," says Cari.

"All this happened because of your visions," hisses Rat. "Not the poison, but all the rest, Spar going after Heinreil, trying to take over the Brotherhood. If he'd rested after getting out of prison, then maybe he wouldn't have got worse. Everywhere you go, things go to hell. I look at you, and I see ... " His voice trailed off into a growl.

"I didn't ask for this."

"For 'this'," echoes Rat. "You don't even know what this is. Sainthood? From what gods? Who do you think is sending you these visions, Carillon? Why you?"

"It's the bells. They're dead gods."

"They're not dead," whispers Rat. "The ghouls know."

"Enough!" says Spar. "None of it matters. None of it matters. Rat, leave her alone, and drop the mystic ghoul nonsense. It doesn't suit you. Cari, maybe he's right – that professor tried to find out what's going on with you, and you ran. You went up to the Holy Beggar, and tried to find Heinreil rather than anything else. It's not a tool or a gift. It's ... I don't know what it is, but neither do you."

He's trying to drive her away, Cari decides. He thinks she's not strong enough to watch him die, to watch him calcify cell by cell, limb by limb, until he's nothing but a few living organs in a tomb of stone. It's a horrible way to die, and he's right, her instinct is to run away. But that Cari died when the Tower of Law fell on her.

Bells ring very far away, but she's not sure if they're in her memory or out in the city.

"I know someone who can help," she says.

Cari takes the same route as a week ago, although she is not the same woman. Down to Phaeton Street Station, and a rattling train ride over Glimmerside to Pilgrim Street. She kicks herself for dumping the student robes; she sticks out among the crowds of students on this train, like an alley cat amid a flock of pigeons. A Tallowman twists its neck around to stare at her as she passes, head rotating like an owl, jointless and rubbery.

Desiderata Street is empty, closed off. The hole in the road is gone, scabbed over with fresh concrete, but the street's houses are all abandoned and boarded up. A bored watchman patrols up and down, coughing, huddled in an overcoat against the chill of the night.

Professor Ongent doesn't actually live here, though. He just owned the house, kept it for the use of his son and his students – and his lab animals. He lived closer to the university. Cari takes to the mews and alleyways behind Desiderata to make her way up the slope towards the grey towers of the university.

This isn't how she wanted to do it. After she left Bleak's houseboat, she found a safe place to hide and waited until the turning of the hour, when the bells rang. Demanded they show her Ongent, but they didn't cooperate. She saw the professor in a small room, but it was like looking through broken glass as it was being forced into her eye. Fragments that made her bleed when she looked at them, the vision cutting into her. He's alive, but she couldn't guess where. Last time she looked, he was in a jail cell in Queen's Point, but she figured they'd have let him go by now. In Cari's experience, the quality don't stay in prison.

At this time of night, the university campus is quiet. A few lights burn in high windows, but all the libraries and lecture halls are locked up. She pauses outside the window to the professor's office, remembering the experiment. The thaumaturgic skull exploding in her hands, the feeling that she was a dam holding back immense powers. Now, she wants to repeat the experiment, use that power.

Saints are supposed to be able to heal people with a touch, according to Aunt Silva's stories.

Cari's not a very good saint, but she can improvise.

A cough, the flare of a cigarette in the distance. Across the lawn, in the shadows of the medical school, someone's watching her. She glimpses a thin face, balding, a big silver ring on one hand. She keeps walking, adding a little sway to her steps like she's a bit drunk. Just some student taking a short cut across campus back to her dormitory.

She turns the corner around the side of the history department. The side door that leads to the stairs that goes up to Ongent's office is shut and locked. She keeps walking, hears the crunch of footsteps behind her. She keeps moving, but she reaches for her weapons.

Her hand closes around her knife.

Her mind reaches out. The bells aren't ringing right now, but she's found that she doesn't always need that. The powers that have blessed her, tried to claim her, are always out there, in their roosts or prison cells across the city, and she can rattle their cages if she concentrates.

She stumbles.

It's like she's in two places at once.

She's walking along by the side of the history building, hand brushing against the rough stone wall to keep her balance in the darkness, but she's also watching herself from the top of Holyhill, from the bell tower of one of the cathedrals. So far away, but she can see with perfect clarity through the darkness, through the intervening buildings, see her tiny fragile body like a flickering white flame, and the dark shape approaching from behind.

She's never seen him before, but she's seen him before. A flash, a trailing memory. He's talking to Ongent. In the jail cell at Queen's Point. Interrogating him. The professor full of bravado at first, then hunched, flinching. The man doesn't hit him. Doesn't need to. He has leverage.

The trailing edge of the vision: he's got a gun. She can taste the bitter chemicals in their chambers, feel the shape of the bullet.

"Carillon Thay," he calls out, and it brings her back to her body, as surely as naming a demon binds it to a single form in the stories Aunt Silva used to read her at night. She grips her knife tighter and breaks into a run. The archway ahead runs through the old seminary, over to the main quadrangle. There'll be people. He won't dare shoot her there.

He's running, too, thumping footsteps close behind her, coat billowing like wings, but she's faster. The arch opening before her, with its promise of safety.

The second watcher steps out right in front of her from his hiding place in the shadow of the archway. She bounces off his chest. Hard rings of mail armour beneath the coat. He catches her before she can go sprawling on the ground, hands grabbing her forearms like manacles, spinning her around.

The first man, the interrogator, slows down. The gun goes back in his pocket.

"I haven't done anything," she protests.

He ignores her. Steps forward and shoves his hand down her top, gloved fingers roughly grabbing at her neck, collar, breasts.

"Fuck off!" she starts to say, but a hand closes across her mouth.

"Doesn't she have it?" The second one, the one holding her, is surprisingly soft-spoken. Hot breath on her ear as he holds her, pinned down. The only thing she can think they might be looking for is her amulet.

"Get her inside," orders the first man. Cari is dragged to a door in the archway tunnel. It opens onto a corridor. More university offices, the theology department. They force-march her down to the third door, push her inside, follow her in, lock the door behind them.

"Where's Professor Ongent?" demands Cari.

"The alchemists took him. He's an idiot. He should have brought this to the professionals."

"And that's you?" asks Cari.

"We've been doing this a long time," says the interrogator, looking around the office. A heavy desk, a few cabinets, some chairs, a fireplace with a rug in front of it. "Over here."

Cari doesn't move, so the second guy twists her arm behind her back. Pain. A kick, and she's down on the rug.

The interrogator takes out his gun. "If you'd just stayed away from Guerdon . . . Gods forgive me." He aims the gun at her forehead. Grotesquely, the other man breaks into quiet song, a hymn to the Keepers that Cari recognises from her child-hood. A prayer.

The door smashes open as someone throws themselves against it, full-force. A dark shape, small, male, that's all she sees. The interrogator's aim wavers, just enough, for Cari to duck forward. The gun goes off just behind her, deafening her. A thunderbolt at the back of her skull.

Her knife is in her hand, and she slashes with it. The gun falls to the grate, suddenly splattered bright red. Next to it, fin-gers. The interrogator doesn't even blink. His boot catches Cari square in the chest. Ribs crack and she goes sprawling in the corner, winded.

Sees her rescuer and the second guy wrestling.

Miren. It's Miren. His stiletto knife stabs, once twice thrice, but, like the interrogator, the other man is wearing armour beneath his coat, and isn't cut. He's double Miren's size, too, so when it becomes a wrestling match it's all over. He grabs Miren like he did Cari, picking the boy up like he's a child, and slams him into the desk. Miren goes limp.

"Do them both," orders the interrogator. He picks up his gun with his good hand and sticks his maimed one into his coat.

The second guy also draws an alchemical pistol. He closes the broken door to muffle the sound of the shot.

Miren slides off the table, groaning and lands next to Carillon. He grins. His hand grabs hers.

And they vanish.

Kelkin clears his throat and starts to talk. It's not like his speeches in parliament, which are peppered with fire and venom. His voice is low, confessional. Eladora has to strain to hear him.

"Back then, the Keepers ran everything in the city. Keepers, feh. They kept Guerdon in the dark ages. Other religions were banned. Taxes for the upkeep of church roofs and saints' tombs. We were like Old Haith's little brother – a backward theocracy.

"I was blind to it. I came here to be a priest, can you believe that? I was clever enough, I suppose, for a spotty stammering boy, but the only book in the village I came from was the *Testament of the Keepers*, so I knew nothing. I entered the seminary with the full intent of becoming a faithful Keeper and perpetuating the church's wise and beneficent policy of keeping Guerdon in chains.

"That lasted one week. They let you into the library after your first week."

Eladora smiles at that – she remembers the thrill of her own library key, of all that knowledge opening up to her. Jere's watching Kelkin and not paying attention to her so, greatly daring, she steals another glass of the brandy.

"The library then, by the way, was only a shadow of what it is now, but I was still able to read beyond the approved texts. They opened my eyes, and I wasn't the only one. There was a whole generation of us, young and clever and stupid at the same time. The city was ready for change. The old order was starting to melt away, and we swam in the meltwater.

"I stopped going to sermons on the virtues of the gods and started attending meetings with free-market theologians, traders, thaumaturges, transmuters, radical reformers. There were whispers out of applied theology that they'd made great advancements in alchemy, but that the Keepers had banned them from continuing their research. We started protesting, demanding they lift the ban.

"It all seemed part of the same change. The thaumaturges took the old mysticism of sorcery and tore it apart, putting a rational framework on it, just as the reformers wanted to take the Keeper's parliament, with its empty ritual and its rotten practices, and tear it apart and make it rational.

"I met Jermas at the back of one of those reformist meetings. I can't recall what that particular meeting was about, and it didn't really matter. Same crowd of faces at every one anyway, no matter what the speaker was rambling on about – abolishing the index of banned books, or reform of the voting act, or thaumaturgical engineering. We got to talking about the reformist party in parliament. There was a reform party back then, the priests' concession to what passed for democracy. The dignified and respectable opposition, a toothless dog that growled on command. We wanted a real reform movement, but we knew the church would crush us if we tried.

"So we hit on the idea of reforming the reformists. We'd hide our real agenda inside them. I quit university, started working as a scribe and then speechwriter for Turcamen Gethis. He was perfect – wonderful speaking voice, full of conviction, but so senile he had no idea what he was saying, so he just read what was put in front of him. And a safe seat, to boot.

"Jermas provided the money. I did the work. Our first success was getting the ban on alchemical research lifted. The alchemists founded a guild. I gave a speech at the ceremony. Stammered my way through it, and it's deservedly forgotten. I wonder if Rosha remembers that I was there when her bloody empire started. Everything she has, she owes to me!

"Feh. No matter. This is all fifty years ago."

Jere frowns. Nothing Kelkin has revealed so far is scandalous or controversial. "Come on, boss. What's all this got to do with the goddamn bells? Why the secrecy?"

"Bloody context, all right? It's only natural disasters and plagues that come out of nothing – it takes time for people to fuck things up. She understands," snaps Kelkin, stabbing a finger at Eladora. "This has been brewing for a long, long time."

Jere grunts, clearly impatient, but he settles back in his chair and makes a show of being attentive.

"Where was I?" mutters Kelkin.

"The legalisation of the alchemists," offers Eladora.

"Yes, yes." Kelkin's voice grows stronger as he talks of his glory days. "The alchemists needed traders. Traders needed an open port. An open port meant they couldn't keep out other religions. And once that went, the Keepers didn't have much left. We dropped the old reform party, called ourselves the Industrial Liberals, and went to work.

"I pleaded with Jermas to stand for parliament, take a more active role in the party, but he refused. Set himself to the business of making money. We drifted apart – his donations to the Ind Libs came in like clockwork, but we spoke less and less. I thought little of it.

"Reform did not – must not – stop at the church door or the gates of Parliament. I was determined to improve the whole city. I brought in the Land Acts, reformed the navy, ended the church tithes." He thumps his chest as he recites the litany of his deeds. "Let the ghouls out on the surface. Fought organised crime, too – thirty bloody years ago there was Idge. Now there's Heinreil. Scum, fouling my city.

"I kept us out of the war, and kept us neutral even when it became the Godswar. I stopped the fucking Stone Plague.

"I was busy. Jermas would ask me for a favour now and then, and I'd help him if I could, but nothing out of the ordinary. I knew he was involved in the alchemists' guild, in the weapons trade, but so was half the city."

Kelkin pauses. His bluster fades, his voice drops. Eladora leans towards him to hear better; so does Jere. Only Bolind seems unmoved.

"Then, I got an unsigned letter. It claimed that Jermas Thay was part of an underground cult, that he's summoning demons and conducting all sorts of rituals. The letter's descriptions were detailed. There were lists of names – not just Thays, but rogue thaumaturgists, dissidents, even criminals. Defrocked priests. The letter writer said that he or she simply wanted to draw my attention to the matter, but the threat was clear – if they went to the watch, or the newspapers with this, I'd be ruined. Even though Jermas and I were no longer close, our careers were inter-twined. A public trial for heresy or illegal sorcery would have dragged me down, too.

"There was no mention of blackmail, though. Nor any demands. I had no idea what the letter writer wanted. I waited, and no second letter came. I hoped it might be an oddly well-informed crank, but the danger was too pressing for me to do nothing. I started working through the list of names, and found a linguist named Uldina Manix. She was reputable, solid, of good family. She confirmed the letter's contents, told us that Jermas had hired her to translate some books that escaped burning during the Black Iron War. Manix had seen things in this mansion, heard things, and Jermas paid her off to keep quiet. When we put pressure on her, though, she found her conscience and started talking. Gave us more names.

"Jermas Thay was . . . I'm still not sure if he worshipped the Black Iron Gods, or if he thought he could use them somehow, but he was still doing unthinkable things. Human sacrifice. Worse.

"I knew that if I went to the watch, it was all over for him and me. I could have gone to Jermas myself, but what good would that have done? Nothing ever changed that man's mind once he was set on a course – no matter what it was. Even this unholy madness.

"So I did the only thing I could do. I did what we're going to do tonight."

CHAPTER TWENTY-FOUR

K elkin insists on driving the carriage himself, and he drives it like he's hoping to crash, hurtling round the steep slopes of Gravehill and through the narrow streets of lower Glimmerside at terrible speed. He uses the whip with abandon, slashing at the scaly flanks of the raptequine to drive it onwards until it screeches in pain. Inside, every rattle over the cobblestones sends a new jolt of pain through Jere's battered bones. Eladora's face is white with fear. Only Bolind seems unmoved, although his big belly ripples obscenely in time to the carriage's rattling passage.

They're not heading for the crest of Holyhill, as Jere thought they would. The palaces of the Keepers are all up there, high above the city, but Kelkin takes the road that circles around the foot of the hill. Through the window, Jere can see the smoke-stacks of the Alchemists' Quarter, and the shining palace of their guildhall. Somewhere in that industrial wasteland is Professor Ongent. Somewhere, too, are the remains of the bell from the Tower of Law, and, if they're right in their suppositions, the bell from the Bell Rock.

Gods and monsters. At least, thinks Jere, Guerdon's strange local Godwar has been contained so far. Even his experiences on the Bell Rock weren't as terribly, terrifyingly unnatural as the things he saw as a mercenary. By all accounts, the Raveller is a ghastly horror. Jere hasn't seen it himself. He tries to imagine a horde of them besieging the city, but his only mental image is the illustration in Eladora's history book, and that just looks like ink spilled across a picture of some old battle with swords and spears.

The way Eladora talked about Desiderata Street, though, told him enough. It was the same way other veterans talked about the war.

The Thay girl is a saint. A crack in the world that these Black Iron Gods can widen until it's big enough for them to crawl in. Ongent saw it before Jere, before anyone else. The sickening thought that all this is somehow his own fault is born in Jere's brain, and crawls down his chest to settle in his stomach, freezing his heart as it slithers through him. If he'd kept the Thay girl in custody, then they could have contained this threat. It wouldn't have stopped the bombings, but Eladora's account suggests that Carillon is somehow connected to the Raveller. Maybe if they kill the Raveller, it'll all be over before it really begins. Scare the Black Iron Gods back into their bells.

"Hey, Bolind."

The big man doesn't stir. Jere pokes him, and Bolind opens one eye. Was the bastard actually sleeping at a time like this?

"What?"

"Did you bring that hand cannon of yours?" Bolind favours an absurdly big pistol, enough to put a Gullhead down with one shot.

"Nah."

"What did you pack?"

Bolind says nothing for a long moment, then holds up clenched fists and grins – an old joke of theirs, but right now it just annoys Jere, right down to the way Bolind's too-wide smile gleams.

The carriage takes a sharp turn to the left, down brickwork canyons. Industrial buildings, then yellowed stone as they rattle to a stop. "Early Reconstruction," says Eladora, pointing to an old doorway. "Built just after the war with the Black Iron Gods."

Kelkin hitches the raptequine to a post and gives it a feedbag. Scraps of red meat splatter on the ground below.

"This way." He hurries them over to the old doorway and pushes on it. It's unlocked. As soon as they're all off the street, he closes it behind them. The doorway leads to a small courtyard, surrounded on two sides by tall windowless buildings, and on the third by the cliff-steep wall of Holyhill. There's another archway there that looks unpleasantly like a sewer entrance to Jere.

"We're going in there, I presume."

Kelkin grunts.

"Oh joy, oh rapture," mutters Jere with all the enthusiasm of a man climbing the gallows.

The gate is also unlocked. The tunnel beyond is dry and cold, and heads straight into the mountainside, running under Holyhill. Kelkin squares his shoulders and marches into the darkness. Eladora shivers and goes after him.

To Bolind: "Stay here, all right? Watch the carriage, make sure no one bothers us."

"I should come with you."

"Now's not the fucking time for this conversation." Bolind needs a good kicking to remind him of why Jere employs him, and that it's not for his sparkling wit or tactical nous. But not right now. "Stay," orders Jere, like you'd tell a dog, then he follows Eladora into the tunnel. He glances back to see Bolind standing there at the archway, a deeper darkness against the twilight of the yard.

Up ahead, Kelkin holds a lamp. The swaying beam catches the walls; dead-eyed saints watch over them as they walk.

"Stop shivering, girl," snaps Kelkin at Eladora, "there's nothing down here that's going to eat you."

"These are ghoul tunnels," she says, and Jere wonders at that. He doesn't know anything about architecture or art, but he knows that ghoul tunnels are full of shit and carrion and covered with those creepy green-stone carvings they make with bits of bone. This tunnel reminds him of a church crypt.

Another light, up ahead, answering Kelkin's.

They emerge into a circular room, a crossroads under the hill. Three other tunnels running off in the other three cardinal directions.

Waiting there are two priests. Old and young. The young one holding a lamp, the older one huddled on a little bench by the side of the corridor.

"Rejoice, oh brother," says the old one, "our lost child has returned. Have you heard the truth of the Testament, Effro?"

Kelkin ignores the mocking greeting. "Is this everyone?"

"For the moment. We sent an emissary below, but she hasn't returned yet. What do you want, Mr Kelkin?"

"This is Jere Taphson, thief-taker, and Eladora Duttin, historian. They've been assisting me in my enquiries into the recent attacks."

The old priest stands slowly, peers through the gloom at Eladora and Jere.

Kelkin continues: "Ms Duttin was also present at Desiderata Street. She identified the creature that killed seventeen people and a number of Tallowmen as a Raveller – a servant of the Black Iron Gods."

"And we keep the city safe from thousands of them. There are gates in the depths, Mr Kelkin, which must be constantly guarded lest the hordes break through. This is our vigil. One of our watchmen is coming; you can hear his assurance from your own lips that no Ravellers have escaped."

"I saw it," protests Eladora, but Kelkin hushes her.

"A more pressing matter," he says, "is the Black Iron Gods themselves. Your predecessors concealed them around the city. One was in the Tower of Law; another in the Bell Rock."

The two priests look at each other. The younger priest – Bishop Ashur, Jere suddenly recognises the man's pugnacious face – scowls. "Why not? Let every sacred mystery be dragged out and sold in the marketplace. This is your doing, Kelkin. You tore us down, wounded us, and now you worry when jackals come to pick at our carcass!"

Kelkin bristles; he and Ashur are old enemies. "You hid bound demons around my city and kept that a secret for three hundred years. Don't you dare try to turn that into a virtue! You know what I sacrificed for your church, what I did to keep the city safe. What's the difference between you and Thay anyway?"

The older priest raised his hand. "Enough. How can you be certain our assailants know about the bells? We were told by the watch that the Bell Rock was an accident. A freighter carrying alchemical weapons got loose and exploded on the reefs."

"I was there," says Jere. "They came in and took the bell intact, then blew up the lighthouse to cover their tracks."

"Who did?" demands Ashur.

Jere pauses, and Kelkin fills in the silence. "The alchemists' guild."

Jere finds that he's hoping that Ashur rejects the suggestion as preposterous, that he shouts Kelkin down, that there's no way at all that the alchemists might be responsible. Jere has no love for the alchemists or their creatures like Nabur or Droupe – or hell, for their actual creatures, like the Tallowmen – but the guild is one of the pillars of the city. If he's right and they're behind the attacks, then it's going to get much, much worse.

Ashur says, slowly, "Guildmistress Rosha came to the church, some years ago, with a proposal. They offered to buy the monastery at Beckanore. They said they wanted to build a research station there, a testing ground. They even offered to move the chapel and the bell tower back to Guerdon at their expense, out of respect for our traditions. She proposed that the bell be installed in the guildhall church." He spits. "Treacherous bitch."

"Patros," says Kelkin, addressing the older priest. *Gods*, thinks Jere, *that's Patros Almech, the Master Keeper himself.* "I can fix this. It's not the same as what happened with Jermas Thay. We can have a public inquiry, go through parliament. Arrest Rosha, if we have to. Hells, they'll be begging to be put in chains – better a trial than the mob tearing them to pieces in the streets. Do I have your support?"

Almech clasps his hands. "You cannot reveal the truth about the Black Iron Gods. That secret we must keep."

"And if it comes to a confrontation, if Rosha resists, we'll need your saints to counter her Tallowmen. How many do you have on the rolls?"

"One."

"One!?" roars Kelkin.

Ashur rounds on him. "What did you expect? Sainthood is a gift of the gods, and ours are so very, very weak. Kept Gods are what we promised, and Kept Gods are what we have. We keep them starved and quiescent, give them just enough to sustain them and no more. You knew this – and still you opened the city to other gods, divided an already paltry supply of souls among all the rutting lust-cults and barbarian faiths!"

"You sent a dozen against the Thays."

"Twenty years of neglect and starvation have gone by since then."

"We could muster another four or five from missions overseas and from the hinterlands, given time," says Almech, "and perhaps, with prayers and sacrifice, beg for another blessing. But no more."

"Well," says Kelkin, "we had best pray that Rosha does not resist the demands of parliament, then."

"What about the Raveller?" asks Eladora again.

And suddenly Jere feels like he's being buried alive, like there's this clogging weight of cold earth pressing against his head, his skin, forcing his lips open, icy cold pouring down his throat. His mouth moves on its own.

"IT DID NOT PASS THROUGH THE BLACK GATES."

Kelkin swears and backs away from Jere. Eladora lets out a frightened yelp.

"It's all right," calls a woman's voice, "it's just this fucker."

Approaching from another tunnel branch are two figures. One's a woman, human, armoured, holding a lamp. The other is huge, hulking, bigger than a gorilla, twice her height, loping on its forelimbs. Dog-like muzzle, glowing green eyes, the stench of rotten meat: an elder ghoul.

Green eyes fix on Eladora, and the terrible pressure relents, releasing Jere. The ghoul transfers its attention to Eladora, and Jere sees her throat tighten, panic flood her eyes as it speaks through her. It's horrible to hear that gelatinous, groaning voice issue from her throat.

"THIS ONE IS BLOOD KIN TO THEIR HERALD."

It's talking about Carillon. Jere tenses, but he realises there's nothing he can do. That elder ghoul is gigantic, fearfully strong. Its stench fills the narrow corridor like a miasma. If the monster does go for Eladora or Kelkin, Jere has no weapons except a small concealed pistol. He could holler for Bolind, but this is the one time the fat idiot didn't bring that oversized gun of his.

Eladora freezes, a rabbit before a wolf. She just makes a whimpering noise, over and over, until the ghoul grabs her voice again. "SHE IS BY THE WATER. A STONE MAN IS THERE. HE IS SICK AND DYING." The ghoul leers obscenely, as if pleased with itself. "I WILL GUIDE YOU."

THE GUTTER PRAYER 309

A Stone Man, with Carillon. Somehow, the ghoul knows where they are. Spar hangs around with another, younger ghoul, doesn't he? Mouse or Rat or something. Clearly, the younger whelp sold Spar out.

Kelkin's thinking along similar lines. "I welcome you to the surface lands, old one. Your assistance in this matter is most beneficial, and the long friendship between our peoples shall endure forever."

The ghoul answers him with Kelkin's own lips, as the priests warned. "SEND US THE MARROW OF YOUR FATHERS AND MOTHERS, AND WE SHALL BE SUCH GOOD FRIENDS. WE WILL STRANGLE YOUR GODS, OLD AND NEW." Kelkin turns purple with indignation and struggles to speak. The armoured woman thumps the elder ghoul on the hind leg, like she's telling a dog to get down and stop scrabbling at a houseguest.

"Hey, enough of that." The ghoul growls at her, the first sound it's made with its own mouth since it arrived. "Beastie can talk, I swear. He just likes scaring people." She places a hand on her own chest.

Kelkin composes himself. "Aleena Humber, isn't it? Saint Aleena of the Sacred Flame."

"For my sins, aye."

The Patros turns to the elder ghoul. "Are you certain that this Raveller did not get past your watch?" The ghoul inclines its head in a gesture of both respect and agreement. "Praise be to the gods," said the Patros. "It must be a survivor from the dark times, not the start of a new invasion. Our saints slew many such fugitives in days gone by. Perhaps this is the last."

"It's drawn to the girl," says Ashur. "Find her and we'll find the abomination."

Kelkin snorts. "Good, good. If, ah, our ally is willing, he can show my men where the Thay girl is." Aleena looks to Bishop Ashur, as if seeking confirmation, and the priest nods. "We'll take her back into custody. There's an emergency meeting of the public safety committee first thing tomorrow. I'll present all this there, and send Rosha an ultimatum. She can't stand against me, the church *and* the mob she's stirred up. Oh, this is a fight I've been spoiling for," says the old man with glee, eyes bright, envisaging Droupe and the other supporters of the alchemists' guild being torn down in parliament. His excitement is contagious – Jere imagines that a scandal this big could bring down the guildmistress and break the monolithic power of the guild. Kelkin could swoop in again, take back control of parliament. Rise high again, and bring his supporters like Jere with him.

Hell, they could come out of this *winners*.

"What about the Raveller?" asks Eladora.

"Arrest the Thay girl and Idge first. Idge's son," Kelkin corrects himself. "Then we'll hunt it down."

"I can kill it, dear," adds Aleena. "Haven't met the thing I can't, yet."

Somehow, that's the best thing Jere's heard all week.

Ashur raises some technical or theological objection to Kelkin's plan, and the argument starts, the old politician and the young theologian squabbling, interspersed with the occasional mordant interruption from the elder ghoul, but Jere knows that the bones of the plan are there. There'll be a few minutes of bartering before they finally agree. The tunnel is stifling with ghoul stench.

Jere takes Eladora's arm. "Come on. Let's get the carriage ready." She hesitates, looking back towards Kelkin. Jere pulls her along. "It's done, it's done. Not the whole thing, but Kelkin will sort it out."

"Fresh fucking air," mutters Aleena, following after them. "Second time in a week they send me down to talk to the bloody ghouls. I ask you, is it that hard to run a sodding aethergraph line down through Gravehill? Did you know the Crawlers have their own private train line? Those fucking grave-worms have their own transport, and I have to walk all the way from Holyhill to the shitty bottom of the city, and back again. Do you have any sodding idea how many stairs there are down there? Ghouls love their eldritch mysterious stairwells descending infinitely into fucking shit-and-mushroom town. Next time I'm going to have them cut my throat and fucking throw me down a corpse shaft." She grumbles on as they walk back towards the courtyard. "At least that big bastard met me halfway this time. Halfway to the shitty bottom of the sewers, mind you, but still."

Jere's mind races. Spar and Carillon back in his cells – gods, it'll be worth it just to see Nabur's expression when he comes with his writ. Kelkin, running the city again. Ongent, out of jail and owing Jere a huge debt. Hell, maybe he can even get Dredger a cut – like he said, this is a salvage problem.

"What was that thing talking about, when it talked about the marrow of our fathers?" he asks Eladora.

It's Aleena who answers. "You know they eat our dead, right? If you have a church funeral, after the weeping's done and everyone's fucked off to the pub, they lower you down a big shaft and the ghouls eat their fill. Eat the marrow and the soul residue. It's a sort of tribute, you see. In exchange, they watch over these sodding huge gates down below, where the rest of those Raveller bastards are trapped until doomsday."

"Oh." His memory flashes back to his mother's funeral. Had he known that the kindly nuns who took custody of her body were about to feed her remains to the ghouls – he shrugs. The old church teachings echo in his mind, reminding him that the body's just a shell. And being eaten by ghouls is a better end than some of the things he saw in the war.

Aleena shrugs. "They don't talk about it much, these days. Not since Kelkin let the other faiths into the city. It's a bit . . . " She waves one hand, vaguely. "Off-putting, I guess."

"Priests are burnt, though," added Eladora. "And Safidists. It's more traditional. In the oldest verses of the Testament, the fire-sprites carry the souls of the dead into the heavens."

"Safidist tossers, praying for sainthood. If they knew what being a saint had done to my knees, they'd sing a different . . . " Aleena trails off.

Then the flames erupt from her drawn sword, and the tunnel blazes with holy light. She roars in a voice that's like dazzling sunlight breaking through cloud: "WHAT THE FUCKING SHIT IS THAT?"

The thing that charges them has Bolind's body, more or less, but it's got the face of the raptequine that drew Kelkin's carriage, and a mane of delicate golden hair, and claws, and tentacles blossoming like a flower's petals. Eladora screams and screams, recognising it from Desiderata Street. The Raveller.

Jere doesn't have his staff, or his sword cane. Just a regular cane. He drives it like a spear, aiming it at what might be the Raveller's throat. The creature twists, dissolves, streams past him. One of its tentacles brushes his outstretched arm and . . .

Blood everywhere. Pain.

He's on his knees, cradling his shattered arm. He can't tell if he still has a hand, it's just this mess of flayed skin and bone and blood spurting. The pain is a distant thing, a vast continent of agony and he's floating offshore, detached and remote, but he knows it's there and the tide's carrying him towards that shore of broken glass.

The Raveller got past him, got past Aleena, too. Shouts. Screams. The guttural roar of the ghoul. Thunder echoing up the tunnel. Heat of fire. All these sounds, sensations, are so far away he thinks that the tunnel has grown immeasurably long and is still growing, carrying him away.

Jere is, he suspects, one of the people screaming.

Eladora dragging him, pulling him, half carrying him out into the night air. Blood-slick he slips from her grasp, and she looks in horror at her red hands. The Bloody Handed God's troops are coming, warns Marlo, and they've got to dig in here. Jere's lost his pack, his rifle. He has to tell Marlo that he's lost his rifle.

No, that was the Godswar, far far away and long ago.

More explosions. Alchemical bombs exploding nearby. The artillery has our range, warns Marlo.

Eladora pulling at him, but his legs are a thousand miles away, and Jere can't move. He tells her to run, but he can't speak because his lungs are full of water.

Kelkin. Kelkin was in that tunnel. And the bishops. What happened to them?

He should go after them, find out, but he can't. His limbs don't move. He slumps over, watches the gush of blood from the ruin of his arm. Like the tide, gushing and receding. Gushing and receding.

Come down into the waves with me, says Uncle Pal.

Time passes. The gush from his hand slows, then stops.

Movement. Candle lights. More distant shouts.

Hands – stronger hands, smooth and horrible to the touch – pick him up. The courtyard's filling up with people. A Tallowman picks him up, a dying dog run over by a carriage, carries him towards a cart. Jere's head lolls back, and there freshly written on the wall is the last thing he ever sees.

THIS IS NOT THE LAST.

CHAPTER TWENTY-FIVE

U nwilling to risk sleep, Spar tries pacing, but his weight tips the wallowing houseboat this way and that, sending filthy canal water sloshing over the sides. Mother Bleak's hospitality doesn't go that far, so Spar clambers back onto the shore and walks the streets of Guerdon, Rat by his side, scuttling from shadow to shadow. Conscious of watchful eyes, they walk down towards the docks, to neighbourhoods half abandoned by those who fled the poison cloud of the previous day.

Spar draws a borrowed cloak around himself, but still he's recognised. Furtive hand gestures, a thieves' code, cheering him on. He responds as best he can with hands like slabs. Others just pass him by – did he go unseen or did they see him all too well? Heinreil's tenure as master did nothing to help these people – the poverty of the Wash is an even more glaring contrast to other parts of the city these days, much more than it was when Spar was young. And that doesn't take the refugees into account, the thousands who crossed seas or god to escape the horrors of war.

"You're walking better now," mutters Rat, "how's the pain?"

"Painful. But good. If it hurts, it's flesh."

Rat snorts in amusement. "We should get off the streets. Too many eyes. Head up to Gravehill, maybe. We can hide better up there."

Spar lifts his face to the skies. A light rain's blowing in from the bay, spitting down on the roofs, washing away the poison left by the storm. The rain's wonderfully cold, and as the droplets run down his face and chin he can tell which patches of his skin are still alive and which are stone. "Nah. This way."

Up the hill, towards his flat. He hasn't dared return here since escaping the prison, as it's likely to be under surveillance by the watch or by Heinreil's men. Right now, though, he's in a fey mood. An angry nostalgia, almost, that overrides both his own caution and Rat's fretful whispers. As they climb, the streets get busier. More gestures of support – from faces at windows, from young hoods lurking in doorways, from dollymop girls by the taverns. He acknowledges each one with a nod.

Rat notices them, too. "Tammur put the word out, I guess."

"Ah well." *Idge had it easier*, thinks Spar. All he had to do was have courage, to refuse to yield, to endure threats and torture. At any time, he could have chosen to give in and betray the Brotherhood to the magistrates, but he chose instead to hold on and deny them their victory. Despite all the pain, the choice was his. Spar doesn't have a choice. No matter what he decides, no matter how strong his will or how much courage he musters, the time of his death is determined by the blind progression of his disease.

Rat signals Spar to stop at the next corner. The ghoul sneaks around, almost invisible in the shadows. Spar waits, shifting from foot to foot, flexing his hands to keep them supple. He needs to be careful – as his body calcifies, his strength grows. He could break someone's ribs by brushing past them on the street, although any native of Guerdon gives a contagious Stone Man plenty of space anyway. It's another reason they can't stay at Bleak's houseboat much longer.

Rat returns. "Clear," he growls, suspicious that there's no one watching Spar's old flat.

A week ago – only a week – the three of them met there to get ready for the House of Law job. Spar remembers crouching in the alleyway across Mercy Street, watching the Tallowmen patrols go by, two by two, all his attention focused on the side door. Knowing that if his friends didn't open the door in time, he'd be caught. He put his trust in Rat and Cari then, to open the door for him. He feels a flash of frustration – with Cari's new power, there's every chance he could have beaten Heinreil, become master. Achieved his dreams.

Another thing eaten by the plague.

They cross the street. The door's unlocked, and it's clear that the room's been hastily searched. Belongings scattered across the floor. It could have been anyone – the watch, Heinreil's men, kids from the street, maybe even Cari came back here. None of Spar's stuff has been taken, obviously. He didn't have much stuff, for one thing, and no one wants things that have been so close to a Stone Man. Cari's clothes lie strewn across the floor, and her big shapeless bag has been torn open and its contents spilled onto the ground.

All Cari's little treasures are gone, keepsakes from a lifetime travelling. Spar remembers her showing them to him, shyly, one by one, once she'd come to trust him a little. A bracelet of amber stones sacred to the Dancer. Coins from Lyrix. A playbill from some theatre in Jashan. A shiny flat stone she swore blind was a dragon scale. The crown jewel was her amulet, sent to her by her family.

Now that he knows who her family were, it makes more sense that Heinreil would take the amulet from her. A gift from the Thays might be worth a fortune.

All gone now – but Cari isn't the only one who hid treasures here.

Bending painfully, Spar leans down and scrapes away the rushes and the dirt of the floor, revealing a heavy stone with a ring set in it. He salvaged it from a dock when it was demolished. It's easier to lift the stone than it used to be, and he's able to pull it up with one hand.

From the little hollow beneath, he retrieves a vial of alkahest, a few coins and a handful of papers. A handwritten manuscript, started by his father, and almost finished by Spar. He can trace the progress of his disease by the handwriting, by when he switched from pen to some tougher implement, the letters becoming bigger and more childish as he lost dexterity in his petrifying fingers.

He wonders what Idge would have made of the city now, stranger and more monstrous than it used to be.

Rat sniffs the air in the room, then scoops up one of Cari's shoes and inhales. Spar chuckles.

"What?"

"Nothing." *Ghouls are ghouls*, thinks Spar. To keep one as a friend, you have to remember that they're only half there, the other half is a predatory, scrounging creature driven by instinct.

"See, she even smells different now," mutters Rat. "Saints are fucking trouble all round."

"She could have run, you know, instead of coming back to break me out of jail."

"Still might."

"If she does, I don't blame her. She should go. Get away from this sainthood. You're right – it's dangerous." Spar pauses, flips through the manuscript. "I had a lot of time to think about this when I was in prison. Had some ideas on how to finish it. How's your handwriting?"

"Shit."

"Maybe I'll ask Cari when she's back," decides Spar. He looks around the apartment, looking for some reason to stay. Not finding one. "I'll wait for her at Bleak's, then move on tomorrow."

As they emerge from the tenement, Rat glances up the street. "I should get back to the warehouse," he mutters, and with that he's gone, scuttling away. That, too, is the nature of ghouls; they're survivors at all costs. Rat's keeping his options open by working at Tammur's warehouses. If Spar's coup fails, Rat will be able to slip back into Heinreil's service without any remorse or regret. Rat will be all right.

They need to move on tomorrow. To where? Some other hide-out, maybe somewhere seen by Carillon in a vision. Spar envisages himself being dragged across the city from attic to sewer, his path dictated by the ringing of bells and the availability of backstreet alchemists. It's not what he wants. What he wants is in the words his father wrote, about the Brotherhood and what it might mean to the common folk of the city.

Papers and alkahest clutched in his hand, Spar descends towards the docks. The rain's heavier now, a downpour that empties the streets and births rivulets of dirt. The water threatens to soak the precious manuscript, so he stops at a victuallers. The shelves are emptier than normal; panic buying coupled with the harbour being closed. Good weather for smugglers.

Other customers taking shelter from the rain peer at him curiously, watching him through the gaps between the baskets of limp vegetables and rotten potatoes, or the big square glass jars brimming with some red liquid the alchemists insist is a chemical food. Stores like this often ban Stone Men on the grounds of health, but the owner here is a friend of the Brotherhood, another friend of Spar's father. Still, Spar doesn't push his welcome, and doesn't touch the produce himself in case he taints whole baskets with his touch. He calls over one of the shop boys to fetch a sack, and has the boy bring what Spar wants. A few onions, some carrots, and some of the misshapen, discoloured vegetables the alchemists grow in tanks that have never seen natural soil, nor natural light.

Feeding Guerdon is a constant worry for parliament. The city used to import food blessed by the gods, but the war put paid to that. They had to ban produce from Grena, recalls Spar, after the divine vegetables were found to bear a curse and turned to poison at the touch of anyone who supplied weapons to the folk of Ishmere. Now, the only safe food is domestic, and some of it is almost inedible.

As the shop boy hands Spar the bag, he whispers "Fever Knight's looking for you." Spar nods and shoves the papers and the alkahest in on top of the food. Spar's clashed with him before. It's not surprising that Heinreil would send the Knight out to look for Spar after the poison failed.

An ache in Spar's stomach reminds him that the poison hasn't failed yet. How long, he wonders, before he needs that shot of alkahest in the bag? And how many is that in the last week? Nine? Ten? That should have been the best part of a year's supply.

Perhaps that's why Spar takes the bag and walks down the hillside, head held high, no longer trying to hide his face. Standing straight makes his leg hurt less, makes him limp less. He strides back towards the canal.

The Fever Knight waits for him by Bleak's houseboat with two other thugs, humans. One holding Mother Bleak at knifepoint, the other on the boat, searching it just like they searched Spar's flat.

As Spar approaches, the second man jumps to the shore and throws something small into the boat behind him. A flare. The houseboat catches fire in an instant, burning bright, flames of green and blue as the blaze eats at the coloured paint of the cabin, sickly blueish lights dancing across the polluted surface of the canal. Bleak keens like a boiling kettle.

The Fever Knight hisses when he sees Spar. Armour clanking, life-support tubes bubbling as he inhales. His skull-faced helmet swivelling to stare at Spar, lenses in the eye sockets dancing with reflected flames. Stories of the Knight's atrocities run through Spar's mind. They say that the Knight made a man eat his own wife, force-feeding him chunks of her raw flesh until the man paid his debts. That the Knight's articulated armour conceals any number of blades and weapons, illegal ones – flash ghosts and worse – and he chooses the means of execution that you fear the most. That the Knight is so wracked with disease and acidic humours that he'll explode when he dies, that if he bleeds on you you'll die on the spot from the poisons in his blood, and that's why no one dares fight him.

Unless you're already dead, thinks Spar. He puts the bag down on a capstan, like a wreathe on a grave.

"Idgeson," hisses the Knight, "come quietly, and we won't need to gut the old woman." Mother Bleak's eyes are tightly closed, and she's shaking. She's pitifully thin in the brute's grasp, limbs like old sticks.

Spar takes a step forward, feeling the unaccustomed strength in his own limbs. The Stone Plague's ironic curse – the closer you are to petrification, the stronger you become. He's slower than he likes to be, clumsier, but so very strong this night.

He looks up. Faces stare down at him from the surrounding buildings, from behind twitching curtains and from distant balconies. No one breathes a word, or wants to admit they're there, but there are many witnesses to what's about to happen.

"Go back to Heinreil," says Spar, advancing towards the Fever Knight, trapping the warrior between himself and the waters of the canal. "Tell him I'll see him in gutter court, in front of the whole Brotherhood. Tell him that we won't stand for bully-boys like you treating people like that."

"Bleed her," orders the Fever Knight.

Spar takes another step, driving his foot into the ground, making it tremor. Ripples in the canal make little waves, splashing against the banks, the hull of the houseboat. "Hurt her," says Spar, keeping his tone light, almost mocking, "and I'll pull your arms off."

The thief's hand shakes. He looks to the Fever Knight for reassurance, for strength. Irritated, the Knight half turns towards his henchman—

—and that's Spar's opening. The Stone Man breaks into a lumbering sprint, covering the short distance between them in a heartbeat. The Knight grunts and brings his sword around, his armour hissing as syringes automatically plunge into his skin, disgorging some other drug. Spar adjusts his charge minutely to put one of the toughest of his hide's stony plates between his still-vulnerable living flesh and the point of the blade. He slams into the sword, deflecting it, feeling it skitter across his body, finding no purchase. An instant later, he smashes into the Fever Knight, and they both go toppling backwards.

Falling into the wreck of the burning houseboat, breaking through it, down into the cold.

Most of the canal isn't that deep. Even when it was dug, it was only eight feet deep, and these days it's silted up and filled with rubbish, so there's only two or three feet of stagnant water in most places. Here, though, it's close to where the canal meets the waters of the harbour, so it's deeper, and the combined weight of Spar and the steel-clad Fever Knight are enough to sink deep into the mud.

The Fever Knight claws at him, like an animal, thrashing in terror. Spar endures, keeping his arms locked around his enemy. He remembers the submerged statues in the lithosarium, their arms up stretched towards the surface, drowned where they froze. He'll be as remorseless as stone.

He imagines he can feel the heat of the Knight's diseased body through the armour, through the water.

He can't see a thing, but he can tell that he's on top of the Fever Knight, a dead weight, pushing the other man down into the cool mud.

The Knight's thrashings grow more violent. His head smashes into Spar's cheek, cracking the rock of Spar's flesh. Kicks hurt his already lame right leg. Spar endures, like his father endured, even though the whole city saw Idge's grand refusal and no one can see Spar's martyrdom in the murk of the canal.

Something splashes in the water nearby. Then another thing, and another, like rain.

The Fever Knight makes one final effort to throw Spar off. Maybe he finds purchase against the solid bottom of the old canal, lost for centuries in the murk and mire. He nearly succeeds, forcing them both back into the light from the fires above.

Spar glimpses a face like a bleached skull, mottled in purple, eyes bulging. The Fever Knight's fingers claw at Spar's flanks, his shoulders. The waters of the canal must be turning blood-red, he thinks, as they wash away all the blood on the Knight's hands.

Spar's own lungs start to burn and freeze at the same time. He knows what that means – he can't breathe, and soon he won't have lungs to breathe with even if he could, just two hollows in the stone of his chest. *Sorry, Cari*, he thinks, *I won't be around to be what you want me to be.*

The Fever Knight stops moving. Spar lets go, tries to get his feet under him, but he slips in the mud and sinks like, well, a stone, falling again. The canal muck must be like a soft bed.

Something else splashes nearby. The end of a hooked pole. Jere's staff, the one Cari stole, salvaged from the ruin of the boat. It catches on his arm and pulls him towards the edge. Hands, grabbing him, lifting him up. His face breaks the surface of the water, and he gulps air. A crowd has appeared on the banks of the canal, a host of saints. The people from the tenements, dragging Spar from the water.

Two more splashes as they throw the other two thieves into the water. Unlike their leader, they float instead of sinking, but the hail of stones and refuse thrown at them must make them wish they could. One of them's driven into the blazing wreck and screams as he burns.

They get Spar to the edge, where he can hang onto the bank and eventually drag himself out. They cheer as he stands up.

A gang of mudlarks – the children of the canals, who search the slime for coins and scrap and other treasures – grab the hooked staff and go fishing for the corpse of the Fever Knight. They drag the horrific carcass to the bank, nimble fingers pulling at his armour. One of them yanks the Knight's helmet from his ghastly head and gives it to Spar as a trophy.

He lifts it, and the crowd chants his name, just like they chanted Idge's name twenty years before.

It's not like falling or flying. It's being squeezed.

The pressure on Cari's head expands, intensifies, until her whole body is crushed to a point. She can't see the office room in the seminary, can't see the two attackers anymore, because – she assumes – her eyeballs have exploded like ripe grapes being squished. She feels the whole weight of the city on top of her.

Miren's there, too. She's aware of him, knows she's not alone as the whole city spins and crushes her.

She should panic. She should scream. She doesn't have the ability to do either.

Spin. Lurch. And then vomited back into reality. Cari stumbles as she falls into existence, barking her knees against a wooden locker. The smell of dust. Low ceilings, junk – the attic of some big house, maybe. A little aetheric light burning next to a bed.

Miren lets go of her hand, backs away from her. His face is flushed. More animated than she's ever seen it before. She's breathing heavily, too. She feels unsteady. Half wonders if she was put back together properly, like she left something back in the university, or got mixed in with Miren as they . . .

"What the fuck was that?" she manages to ask.

"It's a trick my father taught me," says Miren, watching her warily. "It doesn't always work. Sometimes, I can sort of step in and out, but only when the city lets me."

Cari's no expert on thaumaturgy, but she knows that teleportation isn't something that can be done easily. She saw fakirs in the markets who pretended to be able to walk through walls or jump into one basket and fall out of another, but that was just sleight-of-hand. Actually jumping in and out of reality is more the realm of saints and gods than mortal sorcery, as far as she's aware.

Her clothes feel uncomfortably tight, like she's come back slightly wrong. She adjusts her shirt, catches Miren staring at her breasts like he's never seen a pair before.

"Where are we?"

Miren scrambles away from her, losing his customary grace in his haste to get out of proximity to her. Stumbles over to the bed and opens a locker next to it. Bandages, healing salves, neatly arranged and labelled bottles of pills. Most of the attic is crammed with junk, strewn haphazardly around the big low room, but Miren's little island is organised with military discipline. Hospital corners on the bedsheets, medicines lined up like soldiers on one shelf, knives on the other.

"I'm not sure," he answers with his back to her. "I've never seen it from the outside. I think it's one of the older houses in Newtown, up off Store Street. No one ever comes up here. I found it by accident. I don't always control where I go. Usually, I go where I want, but sometimes it's like a wave washes in and carries me with it."

It's the longest speech he's ever made in Cari's presence.

"I've never been able to carry anyone before," he adds, still looking at her strangely, as if seeing her for the first time. He bites his lip, and Cari tastes something unfamiliar in her mouth, like she can taste his blood. "I . . . I just knew it would work with you."

"How'd you find me?" she asks. Aunt Silva always told her not to question the blessings of the gods, but Cari feels that if the gods send her a gift horse, then the gods are probably running a horse-trading scam.

"I was watching you," answers Miren.

That's not reassuring.

"Why?"

"My father told me to find you after you ran off. I didn't find your trail until last night, and followed you back to that houseboat."

"Where's Eladora?"

Miren shrugs. "I don't know. I was looking for you."

"Couldn't you get your father out of prison?" She needs to talk to Ongent; in fact, this revelation about Miren makes it even more urgent. Maybe sorcery can cure Spar; the professor's clearly more of an expert than he pretends to be, and Cari's got access to enough magical power to—

—actually, she doesn't know how much is locked away inside the bells. That's another thing she wants to talk to Ongent about. Her head's swimming, her skin's crawling. She strips off her jacket and boots, feeling the welcome chill of the night air on her skin.

Miren shakes his head. "I tried! Like I said, I can't carry other people with me normally – and, anyway, he wouldn't leave the watch prison. He's done nothing wrong, and wanted to, to, to wait until they let him go." He pulls off his cloak, takes out a pair of knives and lines them up with the others on the shelf. Refuses to meet Cari's gaze, but shoots her wary glances as she comes closer, like a nervous animal. Licks his lips.

Incorporating unexpected factors into her plans gets easier with experience. Everything's a weapon if you're willing to use it, she tells herself. "The alchemists have him now," says Cari, following him over to the bed. "I'm getting better at controlling the visions. Maybe I can work out exactly where he is, enough for you to teleport in. Or teleport us both in. Or . . . " She's not really interested in talking anymore. She's tired of making plans, of trying to keep her head together under the pressure of worrying about Spar, about the future, about the weird turn her life's taken. She's always been more comfortable acting on impulse, and the impulse running through her now – through both of them – is much too strong, too primal, to resist. She jumps him, carrying him down onto the bed with her. Breaking apart only enough to wriggle out of their clothes, grappling with each other, like they're trying to get back to that point of unity. The bed creaks under their weight, and at the back of her mind she really hopes that there's no one awake in the house below, because she's about to make a lot of noise.

Miren is fumbling, inexperienced, but she guides him in and out, finding their rhythm in time with the ringing of distant bells.

CHAPTER TWENTY-SIX

For as long as she lives, Eladora will never remember the intervening time between the moment when the thing in the tunnel lunged at her, and when Aleena found her and carried her, effortlessly, into the back room of a ghastly tavern somewhere in lower Glimmerside. The saint thumps two tin mugs of something brown and foul-smelling in front of Eladora.

"Drink," Aleena orders, and follows her own advice, draining her cup in one swallow. She grimaces at the taste. "Get it down you. It'll bring your stomach into balance with head and heart. They'll all be equally fucked."

Absently, the saint pulls her cup to pieces, ripping the metal with her fingers like Eladora might pluck petals from a flower.

"It's dead," says Aleena. "The Raveller."

Eladora tries to say something, but all that comes out is a sob. She tries again. "That's what . . . before . . ." Desiderata Street.

"Properly dead. When I fucking stab something, it stays stabbed. And burnt." Aleena throws another piece of metal onto the table from her cup. "The big ghoul's dead, too."

Clink.

"So is his holiness, the Forty-Second Patros of Guerdon, Master Keeper of the True and Merciful Gods, Almech the Well-Beloved."

Clink.

"So's Taphson. I'm sorry."

Eladora feels too hollow to cry. True, she barely knew Jere, but he was kind to her when she felt abandoned and he'd listened when she'd begged him to help the professor. It wasn't right that he should be snuffed out like that.

"I don't know about Bishop Ashur, or Kelkin. I think they're still alive, maybe. The tunnel partially collapsed. They might have been on the far side of that. Or else they were under it, in which case . . . "

Clink. Clink. "Are you going to finish that?" She points at Eladora's untouched drink.

Eladora slides it across the table. "Why did you come after me?"

Aleena takes a drink. "They kept hawks near where I grew up. There were these woods full of game, and nobles would come and go hawking there. When I was a girl, I used to think they were magical animals. I'd watch them from the hedge – we weren't allowed into the field – and see them soar. Like they were going to catch the sun and bring it down. Strong and fast, yeah, but also wise and beautiful." She glances at Eladora, who's too confused and exhausted to interrupt. "When I was . . . oh, fifteen? Younger than you are, anyway – the gods of the Keepers chose me. Storm Knight leaned down out of the highest heaven and anointed me with fire and lightning. Saint Aleena, the invincible. I don't know why they chose me. Safidists—"

"I'm not a Safidist," mutters Eladora, instinctively.

"Safidists talk about faith and good works and aligning the soul with the will of the gods. I didn't do any of that. It just happened. Blessed be their divine wisdom.

"Anyway, I became a fabled fucking heroine, right? Invited to all the fanciest parties, got to go hawking with all the lords and ladies." Aleena sighs. "It turns out hawks are fucking thick. Filthy mouse-shitters who'll peck your eye out if you get too close.

"The gods are like that. From a distance, you think they're wise and strong, but . . . our gods, the Kept Gods, they're fucking dumb as hawks. All instinct, all reflex, no forethought.

"Or maybe like cows. Beautiful cows made of spun sunlight and silver wire and crystal made of souls . . ." Aleena's voice chokes. "You can't see them like I do. They're so fucking beautiful, it breaks my heart, and so fucking stupid, I want to smash them. And we made them that way, kept 'em dumb and weak and dependent on us. It's the right thing to do, I know, I know. Better a Kept God than a wild one, right? But . . ." Aleena trails off. Takes a gulp of Eladora's drink, then adds. "Fuck it all."

"That doesn't answer my question."

"No, it doesn't. I just wanted to dispel any illusions you might have that I'm, I don't know, blessed with a special wisdom or insight or anything. I can kick the tenebrous shit out of Ravellers, but the gods aren't telling me what to do. I'm making this shit up as I go along, just like the rest of you."

"So why *did* you come after me?"

"Three reasons," Aleena holds up her left hand, extends her index finger. *There could only be three reasons*, thinks Eladora, *or she'd need another hand to go along with her maimed one*. "Reason one. You know what the fuck is going on here as much as anyone else. Bells and alchemists and Black Iron Gods, yeah? I don't have the full picture. Neither do you, I guess, but you've got bits I don't."

Aleena finishes the second drink.

"Which brings us to two. I got out of there because the place was crawling with watch and candlefuckers, not church guards. And from what I hear the watch is in bed with the alchemists.

That means that we're going to have to go above their heads. Committee for public safety, right?"

"Aren't there – I mean, isn't this what the church is supposed to fight?"

Aleena catches the bartender's eye and two more drinks appear. She picks one up and swirls it around speculatively. "The church guard has seen as much action in the last thirty years as the Patros' holy cock. And, yeah, I'm the chosen one of the Kept Gods, but look at me – I'm just one woman. What am I going to do, march down to the alchemists' guild, kick the doors open and storm the place single-handed?" There's a light in Aleena's eyes that unsettles Eladora.

"The committee's meeting first thing in the morning," says Eladora.

As it turned out, the committee met before that. An emergency session, the clerks tell them when they arrive at the Parliament building before dawn, in response to the events of last night. Runners rush past Eladora and Aleena, messengers sent to fetch Effro Kelkin and the other missing committee members.

"Shit. Wait here, all right?" says Aleena. Her breath stinks of booze, and Eladora wants to tell her that's inappropriate when intending addressing a parliamentary sub-committee. The saint vanishes down a side corridor where Eladora is quite sure the public aren't supposed to go.

Eladora sits on a hard bench in a lobby in the labyrinthine building, conscious of how inappropriate her clothes are, of the disapproving glances of the clerks and ushers. She sits as demurely as she can, head bowed, hands folded neatly across the copy of *Sacred and Secular Architecture* that she's dragged across the city.

She discovers that, at some point, blood was sprayed across the book's cover. Jere's blood. She covers it with her elbow and smiles at a passing clerk. It's important to be here, she tells herself. She has to tell them about the Black Iron Gods, about the importance of the bells, of the suspected treachery of the alchemists' guild. About Professor Ongent's unjust imprisonment, about Jere's sacrifice. She wishes she had pen and paper, so she could put the shape in some of her thoughts and discoveries. Bring order to the chaos that's erupted around her in the last week.

She shifts on the hard seat and finds that her sleeve is sticking to the cover of the book.

"Do you need this?"

Eladora looks up. A woman offers her a handkerchief. Eladora touches her own face, discovers it's wet with tears. She fumbles for her own handkerchief, but the street leathers that Jere loaned her don't have such a thing.

She takes the woman's handkerchief, dabs it at her eyes. "Thank you."

"Not at all." The woman smiles. Eladora can't guess her age – her skin has the waxy sheen of alchemical treatments. She is elegantly dressed, her simple robe accented by a guild member's chain, long red hair braided and stacked in an elaborate design, held in place by a golden pin. "Please, is there anything else I can do? You seem terribly upset."

"No – no, it's nothing. I'm fine. Thank you."

The woman clucks her tongue. "You're clearly not. Still, the offer stands. What are you reading?"

Eladora carefully crosses her arms over the book. "It's a history of architecture."

"Histories," the woman declares, "are mostly written by idiots or frauds. The preconceptions of others will lead you astray. Study the city yourself, draw your own conclusions."

A clerk glides up. "Guildmistress, the committee wishes to speak with you."

Guildmistress, thinks Eladora, suddenly recognising the woman. Guildmistress Rosha, the head of the alchemists' guild and the most powerful woman in Guerdon, rises from the bench, brushes down her skirts and walks into the council chamber. Half the people in the room follow her, an entourage of scribes, lawyers, advisers and bodyguards.

Eladora starts to follow, too, without thinking. Maybe she can accost Rosha, reveal what she's doing with the Black Iron Gods, or just ask for Ongent's release. She doesn't know what she's going to say once she gets to Rosha – but she never gets there. Aleena appears out of a side door and grabs Eladora's arm.

"Change of plan. Walk."

It's not so much walk as be dragged by a freight train. Eladora suspects that if she tried to pull away from the saint's iron grip she'd break her arm.

"What's happening?" whispers Eladora.

"Fucking fuckers fucked us." Aleena leads Eladora through yet another door in this maze of a building, closes it, then casually rips the handle off it to prevent anyone following them. "The public safety committee folded without Kelkin to give them some death-lizard approximation of a backbone. 'Recommend that existing proposals to hand over non-essential duties of the watch be implemented' – they've fucking sold the city to the alchemists. Admitted that the watch is shit at absolutely everything, so they're letting the candlefuckers have the run of the place. Martial law, to be enforced by the Tallowfucks. Everyone off the streets to prevent rioting, everything barricaded up – and the alchemists can grab any remaining bells without so much as a by-your-leave."

"But ... you killed the Raveller! And it was the alchemists who blew up the Bell Rock! And maybe the Tower of Law, too."

"Yeah. Unfortunately, everyone who could have fucking done

something about that just got fired and replaced by a bloody psychotic walking nightlight. Well, nearly everyone."

They come to a door, heavy, bound in iron. Eladora blinks in surprise. She's seen it before; there's a sketch of a door just like this in the book she's carrying. One of the doors that leads into old tunnels running beneath the city, doors that were fortified and warded after the defeat of the Black Iron Gods.

"BLOODY OPEN ALREADY," roars Aleena in the voice of an angelic chorus. Her sword blazes white, and the door shatters. Sulphurous pops of spell-wards discharging. "Are you coming?" she snaps at Eladora.

She pauses on the threshold, remembering that third reason. Then follows the saint down into the darkness.

"Reason three," says Aleena the night before, "I murdered most of your family."

Rat is unsettled. Ghouls don't sleep like humans do, but he was unable even to curl up in some dark corner and rest his bones. He's hungry, and the leftovers he can scavenge don't satisfy him. He hears Spar in the next room, shuffling papers around, grunting in pain every so often. Equally sleepless. Spar's very public defeat of the hated Fever Knight won them many new friends – everyone who owed money to the guild for a start.

Mother Bleak's houseboat could not be salvaged. She's gone to her grandson's. Spar's kipping down in one of the tenement rooms. The building's overcrowded, ten or twelve to a room, but they've got the place to themselves. Honouring the hero of the hour, or staying away from the diseased and dying Stone Man – either way, Rat welcomes the quiet after hours of visitors and supplicants. Killing Heinreil's henchman brought Spar's rivalry with the guild leader out into the open. No going back now.

Tammur has arranged a meeting in a restaurant with some other thieves. Not the full gutter court yet, but near enough. Spar and Tammur talked for hours, talked so long Rat could hear his friend's jaw clicking as it calcified. More alkahest, injected right into Spar's neck. Money borrowed off Tammur.

A pinkish light in the east outlines the spires of Holyhill. It's the still hour before dawn. A part of him wonders where Carillon is, but he's in a ghoul mood and he's not capable of worrying. It's an abstract question, cold and detached – and very much secondary to his own hungers.

Food. Rat unfolds, pads down the stairs and out onto the street. Down towards the docks, into a line of buildings deserted when the poison cloud from Bell Rock reached the shore. He's not sure what he's looking for. A dead seagull, maybe, or a cat, stiff as a brush. Something whole and dead.

Snuffling among the trash. Picking through abandoned and nearly empty rooms. Rat finds a rat under the floorboards of one room, body contorted, fur yellowed from the poison. He brushes it off and takes a bite. The meat is foul and stringy, and he remains unsatisfied.

Footsteps nearby, soft as shadow. Thick perfume masking rot. Silkpurse is here. She's dressed in her full finery – a discarded, patched-together ballgown, a huge floppy hat, even a lady's fan. Her feet are bare, though – no human shoe would fit on her half-hooves.

"It's a rat-eat-rat world," she says as she sees his meal.

He throws down the half-chewed corpse and hisses a greeting.

"You had some excitement last night?" she asks.

"The Fever Knight came for us. Spar killed him." Rat's stomach rumbles at the thought of the Fever Knight's corpse. They shoved it back in the canal after stripping it of its armour, but maybe he can fish it out.

"Oh, good! Horrible fellow. So, your friend's going to gutter court?"

Rat nods. Suspicious – Silkpurse never takes much of an interest in Brotherhood politics.

"And you'll stand with him?"

"Yeah."

She fans herself, thinking, then says, "Are you peckish? Come with me."

She brings him down to a cellar and pulls a canvas-wrapped bundle out from its hiding place. Inside is the corpse of an old man. Untouched.

Silkpurse touches the body's face, its crinkled eyelids, its pale, lined cheeks with reverence. "His heart gave out. He hid down here from the poison." She uses the fan to hide it when she licks her lips. "I haven't touched him. I'll share, if you like."

"No corpse shafts round here," grunts Rat, and reaches for the man's arm.

Silkpurse slaps his hand, scolding him. "With respect! We're not carrion eaters. I don't eat mouldy dead people just because I'm hungry, and neither should you."

"What else is there?"

"Psychopompery." Silkpurse peels off her gloves and places them daintily on a broken chair. Rolls back her sleeves. Produces a napkin from her purse, spreads it across her lap. Then she digs her claws into the man's ribcage and pulls. It splits like a ripe fruit. She sifts expertly through bone fragments and muscle and lung tissue to find the heart. She offers it to Rat.

"Just a little from the heart and brain," she says as she starts peeling the skin off the skull. "It's respectful. Don't eat too much. And when you're finished, we shall have tea in the sunshine on Lambs Square, like surface people."

"Busy," mutters Rat around the chewy meat. Silkpurse is right, though – the fresh dead thrills him, feeds a deeper hunger than mere sustenance. Down in the tunnels beneath Gravehill, the head and heart are reserved for the elders; he's seen older ghouls carrying sackfuls of tribute from the shafts to the deep places below.

As his hunger fades, he can think again. Heinreil knows where they are now. Rat's instinct is to find another hiding place for Spar, in case Heinreil sends more trouble their way, but the time for secrecy may be over. Spar's declared openly against the master, and has enough support to mount a challenge. Heinreil has to either meet them in gutter court or risk war on the streets, and that'll push more support into Spar's camp.

"See you at gutter court?" he asks Silkpurse. The ghoul woman doesn't have much sway in the Brotherhood, but every vote counts.

"Not really my scene. And . . . don't take this the wrong way, but that poor sick boy should go to the Isle of Statues, not rock the boat with this foolish challenge. I'm surprised Mr Tammur's even giving you the time of day."

She doesn't know about Cari's visions, of course, their secret weapon. Rat feels that strange flood of anger again. His side aches, suddenly, a sharp pain that quickly passes. He rubs his chest, wondering what he's feeling. The other ghoul doesn't notice.

He picks stringy muscle strands out of his teeth as he half listens to Silkpurse prattle on about her human friends.

Back at the room in the tenement, he finds Spar bent over Idge's notes again, sifting through them. He leaves the Stone Man to his work.

Carillon finds her way to the new hideout around noon. He wonders if she found them through her visions, or just asked someone where Idge's son was. Rat smells her while she's still out in the corridor. An unfamiliar smell with her, young and male, perfumed to mask fainter scents of blood, alchemical reagents, flashwater, attic dust.

Rat blocks the doorway when she tries to enter, snarls at the stranger. The man doesn't recoil, just smirks.

"Rat! It's fine. He's fine," says Cari.

"Who's this?"

"Miren. He's the son of the professor I told you about. He can—"

"You're fucking him." The sex means nothing to Rat, but he's learned that humans generally associate it with strong bonds. And he's decided that he doesn't like the stranger.

Cari scowls. Humans prefer to rut in private, he recalls. "Uh, I guess so. Look, he can help us. I need to talk to Spar."

"Just you." It's an effort of will for Rat to step away from the doorway, to let Cari past into Spar's room. When she's too close to him, he can taste his teeth, feel his claws unsheathe. Something in Cari's new power doesn't sit well with him, and he gets the same feeling when he's close to Miren. A murderous instinct.

Rat smiles widely at the newcomer. "I'm Rat," he says, positioning himself across the doorway again, barring it with his arm.

Miren shrugs. "I know. I've watched you at the warehouse on Hook Row," and with that he twists, quicker than any human has a right to move, and ducks under Rat's elbow and into the room beyond. Turns his back on Rat, saunters after Carillon into Spar's room.

Rat wants to claw Miren's throat open – see if a fresh kill is just as satisfying as the corpse Silkpurse showed him – but he swallows his anger and follows the boy into the room.

"The professor can cure you," says Cari. "We just need to get him out of prison." She's prowling up and down, full of energy, brimming with fragments of insight from her visions. Spar sits on the ground, unmoving, deep in thought.

"Not prison." Miren's taken up a perch on the far side of the room from Rat, close to Cari. "The Alchemists' Quarter."

"Not any easier," mutters Rat. The Alchemists' Quarter is a city unto itself, forbidden except to the alchemists and their creations and servants. He's never even been inside it, although he's spied on it from rooftops, and crawled through the sewers and pipes beneath.

"Maybe." Spar closes his eyes. "Cari, you've seen where they're holding him, right?

"Sort of. It's . . . it's like looking into a dust storm."

"Describe the building."

She does so, as best she can, trying to put the alien perspective of the bells into words.

"What's next to it to the east?"

"Loading yard."

"Give me details."

They go back and forth, building a picture of the area. Spar has a gift for architecture, a Stone Man's grasp of space. You have to know how many painful strides it takes to cross that courtyard, which passageways are too narrow to use without brushing against another passer-by and risking contagion. Cari gets frustrated with the interrogation, and shouts that they're wasting time, but Spar is thorough, unyielding. Describe the yard again. Describe the gate. Describe the distance between windows. How many paces to that door, to that archway? How much cover?

Rat loses interest in the words, just listens to the voices of his friends. In his reverie, they sound like they're speaking from somewhere above ground, and he's far below.

The voices fall silent. Spar just lies there, deep in thought.

They wait, and Rat's stomach rumbles.

They wait, until, with the creaking of stone, Spar pulls himself upright.

"Rat," he says, "we need you to go back to Gravehill."

Spar explains the plan to him, and he laughs, this long slow deep laugh, and he can't shake the feeling that the dead man he just ate is laughing, too.

CHAPTER TWENTY-SEVEN

"This," thinks Spar to himself, "is where it all goes wrong."

He pushes his cart towards the alchemists' gate. His stony limbs, newly shot full of alkahest, do not feel the weight of the overloaded cart.

The Alchemists' Quarter of Guerdon is like a new city, a new fortress. It used to be land given over to tanners, to dyers. Lepers and ghouls, too, the foul and unwanted of the city. Now it is the engine that drives Guerdon into the future. The guildhall is the cathedral of this new quarter, gleaming marble and glass, but not ostentatious. Its bulk, too, is carefully hidden behind walls and the surrounding buildings. The architects took care to ensure that the spires of the guildhall did not overshadow the Keeper chapel that stands next to it. Its size and beauty can only be seen clearly when you're up close to it.

The alchemists do not need to boast.

Behind the guildhall, spilling down from the high knoll down to the shore, are the factories, smokestacks and chemical works, the construction yards and munitions plants. And the waxworks, of course. The rendering plants.

The target is a side gate, so Spar avoids the main road through Glimmerside. He can hear shouts and commotion from there; the distraction may be useful. Carillon warned him that her visions aren't accurate inside the Alchemists' Quarter, so she doesn't know exactly where Professor Ongent is. Finding him may take longer than they hoped.

Maybe longer than they have. For Spar, that's a small sacrifice – without the cure that Cari believes the professor can provide, he guesses he'll be dead in a week. Or worse than dead, locked in the coffin of his own body. It's the others he worries about.

He spots Rat out of the corner of his eye. The ghoul makes a hand signal.

It's time.

Spar pushes the cart around the corner, into full view of the gate. It's huge, made of riveted steel, tough enough to give a Stone Man pause. Guarded, too – not Tallowmen, just humans with rifles, watching him from a walkway atop the curtain wall. Half a dozen, with more nearby – and plenty of Tallowmen, too.

One of the guards atop the gate calls down to him. "What do you want?"

"Alk. Alk," grinds Spar, locking his jaw like a Stone Man in the last throes of the disease.

"The guild isn't a charity," laughs the guard, "try the church."

In response, Spar peels back the canvas shroud on top of the cart. A dead Tallowman lies atop a pile of garbage. It's the one that chased Rat into the catacombs under Gravehill, so it's intact and undamaged apart from its snuffed-out wick.

Tallowmen are expensive. They have many virtues, being inhumanly fast, utterly loyal and virtually indestructible. Remake them every few weeks, and they're good as new. To create one in the first place, however, requires a human being to be melted and remade in the vats. You make them by rendering people down to their base elements. Condemned criminals, trespassers in the Alchemists' Quarter – even the sick and dying, trading the last few days of their life and an eternity of madness and horror for a paltry payment to their families.

"Where'd you get that?" snaps the guard. "Damaging guild property is an offence!"

"Found. Like this. Alk?" grinds Spar.

Another guard, an officer, nods. "Bring it inside and we'll get you a shot of alkahest as payment." He signals to someone inside the walls. A siren blares, and there's the hiss-roar of an alchemical engine. The gate shudders and begins to move, sliding along metal rails, opening a gap wide enough for Spar to push the cart through. He does so.

On the other side of the gate is a large open courtyard, flanked by industrial buildings of some sort. Tanks and pipes straddle and penetrate the brickwork like brass insects, giant metal ticks feeding in the sunlight. On the far side, beyond a huge windowless structure that might be a warehouse, a road leads down towards distant cranes that remind Spar of stick insects. He's seen them before from the seaward side, towering over the alchemists' private docks. To his left, there's another narrower lane that Cari's visions claim leads up to the guildhall itself.

"Back," orders one of the guards, not wanting to get too close to a contagious Stone Man. Spar complies, stepping a few feet back.

Now.

Inside the cart, concealed beneath a second canvas, Cari lights the Tallowman's wick. At the same moment, Rat stands up on the rooftop opposite, right in the Tallowman's line of sight.

As the wick catches fire, the Tallowman comes back to life. Stone-hard waxy skin softens into vile animation. Its head burns again, and inside it a chemical approximation of consciousness flares.

To the Tallowman, it's still a week ago. No time has passed for it since Rat trapped it in a tomb under Gravehill. As far as it's concerned, it's still the night that the Tower of Law burnt, and it's still chasing Rat.

And it sees its quarry just across the street.

The Tallowman springs to life, knife flashing. Everyone knows that you don't get between a Tallowman and its target, but that's exactly where the unfortunate guards are standing. The lucky ones are just scattered like ninepins as the Tallowman leaps out of the cart and springs across the street to pursue Rat. The unlucky ones are slashed and stabbed as it passes.

Two things happen in the confusion.

First, the cart topples over to the left, and Cari and Miren tumble out. Cari saw in one of her visions that there was a row of crates just to the left of the gate, and the two vanish into the gap between wall and crates before anyone spots them. They're in.

Second, Spar takes one more step back and then stamps down hard on the metal rail that guides the gate. The impact travels up his leg until it hits his hip joint, and he feels the pain and sudden numbing cold as it calcifies a little more. The rail gives way, bending, preventing the guards from closing the gate.

Spar plays dumb and rocks for the next few minutes, not letting his worries show on his face. He doesn't look back over his shoulder, to watch the Tallowman chasing Rat across the rooftops of Glimmerside. He doesn't glance into the shadows where Cari and her new lover went. He just stares dumbly as the guards shout at him.

For that matter, he doesn't twitch outwardly at the thought of Carillon sleeping with someone else. Sex hasn't been a physical possibility for Spar for a long time, but he'd enjoyed the unexpected intimacy of sharing a small space with a woman when living with Cari. Their friendship had deepened more quickly that he'd thought possible. He takes the memories, tests them like a knife against his nerves. There's a distant, dull pain, nothing more.

It doesn't matter, he tells himself. He pushes the thoughts away for now. He's probably dead in a few days anyway, and even if he escapes that fate he's still stone.

The guards shout at him, demand to know where he found the Tallowman, then talk about him like he's not there as they argue about how to fix the gate. Spar offers to bend the rail back again, and lumbers towards the gate again. More guards cluster round to restrain him. Onlookers cluster around the scene, peering into the guild's private precincts. More guards, more guild officials. Rumours start in the crowd about escaped insane Tallowmen. Horse-drawn carts and cars arrive, but the gate's frozen shut.

All the confusion to draw attention away from Cari and Miren. All Spar needs to do is stand here and keep the distraction going.

Another cart rattles into the yard, coming down the side lane from the main entrance, followed by a second and a third. All of them bear the same livery, the mark of the city watch. Spar recognises them instantly – they're prison vans, for transporting prisoners. They brought his father to the House of Law in one. All three are full to bursting, overcrowded with prisoners.

The convoy heads towards one of the factories on the far side of the yard. A big door opens as it approaches, and Spar glimpses huge bubbling vats, smells acid and molten wax. It's the rendering plant, where they make Tallowmen.

There aren't that many condemned prisoners in all of Guerdon. They must have emptied the jail cells at Queen's Point, he realises, grabbed every pickpocket and drunk and beggar and shipped them across the city to be rendered down to fat and candlewax.

One of the alchemists tosses him a vial of alkahest. "Go on, get out. Stop gawking. You've caused enough trouble." He points towards the open gate and hits Spar with a stick, like a farmer herding a lost cow. "Move, you dolt!"

Slowly, very deliberately, Spar drives the alkahest needle into his own side. Presses down the plunger, feels the solvent work its magic on his frozen joints. Then he starts to walk through the crowd. The guards they have here are also human – the alchemists don't like to show their monstrous face to the city unless they have to – and they can't stop him, anymore than they could hold back an avalanche.

He breaks into a run, crossing the yard with thunderous footfalls, like the tolling of some bell of doom. Too late, the guards realise what he's doing. The guns click and sizzle, and he has a split second to wonder how bulletproof he is these days before the shots strike home.

He staggers under the hail of fire, but keeps going. His back is raked by rifle shot, but he doesn't feel any real pain, just the chill of more calcification. The bullets are bouncing off his stony hide, but the impact's damaging the flesh beneath, turning more of him to stone with every hit.

He reaches the middle prison cart and sinks his fingers into the metal, ripping the side off it. He swipes his other hand across the chains holding the prisoners in place, popping links or ripping them wholesale from the bolts that held them to the floor. Prisoners spill out into the yard. Some fall, some run, some break for cover. One brave woman tackles the driver, pulls him down. She comes up again, chin red, the keys in her hand and the driver's ear in her teeth.

Spar points to the hindmost cart, roars at her to get the prisoners there, then charges to the one closest to the rendering plant.

He tears the cart open.

A young girl, covered with the filth of the gutters and the prison cells, maybe seven or eight years old. She looks him at him with hollow, despairing eyes. Too tired to scream. He rips her chains apart.

"Run," he says, and then he leads the charge back towards the open gate. Another hail of rifle shot, but he takes the brunt of it – better him than anyone else. He can endure.

Maybe, he thinks for a moment, he can even win.

And then come the shrieks of the Tallowmen, dozens of them, maybe hundreds, swarming out of the rendering plant. The same stiletto knife in the hand of every one of them.

A Tallowman lands in front of him and drives the knife into his chest, unerringly finding the gap between two of his stone plates.

The Alchemists' Quarter will haunt Cari's nightmares for years to come. Pipes hiss and gurgle like the intestines of a flayed man. The air is hot and thick with fumes. Through portholes lined with thick green-tinted glass, she can spy on the things growing inside the vats – embryonic Gullheads, raptequines, disembodied organs. A thing that might be the heart and circulatory system of a man swims past one viewport, like a ghastly jellyfish that squirts blood with every spasm of its artery limbs. In another tank, hundreds of stalks grow from a nutrient-rich carpet on the floor, like ropes of seaweed. It takes Cari a moment to recognise them as a crop of spinal cords, ready to be twisted into wicks and dipped in tallow fat to make more Tallowmen.

Worst of all, though, is the vertigo. She doesn't know if it's some side-effect of her sainthood, or just a measure of the sheer intensity of the arcane pressure churning in these machines, but she feels dragged this way and that by invisible waves, like she's drowning in unseen energies. Miren feels it, too, she can tell by his suddenly laboured breathing.

"I think it's this way," she says, indicating a ladder. Trying to reconcile her fragmented visions of this place with the physical reality. Miren follows her up the ladder.

"Getting a good look?" she whispers to him as they climb.

He frowns, doesn't reply. Cari snorts with amusement. Eladora might be enchanted by Miren's sullen air of mystery, but not her. *He'll have to be a better conversationalist*, she thinks. *He can't coast by on fighting skills and a nice body and the power of teleportation and, gods below, the sex last night—*

She misses a rung and nearly slips, barking her knee against the ladder. Miren steadies her with one hand.

"Quiet," he hisses.

They leave the realm of the tanks behind as they climb. A window ahead lets in natural light, and through it she gets a view of the courtyard far below. Spar's easy to spot, and he's surrounded by guards. The distraction's working.

The ladder ends in a hatch that brings them through a place that's called, reassuringly, the decontamination room. *It's a bit late for that*, she thinks. Out into a corridor that reminds Cari of the university. Little rooms crammed with books and papers. Some are empty, but there are people working in most of them. Low, muttered conversations mixed with chants, but they're all so intent on their work that slipping past them is easy.

One level up, another corridor, but this one's much emptier. The rooms here are bigger and smell of money. She guesses that those ledgers are crammed full of accounts, profit and loss – mostly profit – instead of the alchemical symbols in their counterparts downstairs.

Another window lets her get her bearings again. The view of the harbour from this window is familiar enough to trigger a sense of déjà vu – she's seen this sight, or something very like it, in her visions. They're very close to Professor Ongent, and that unsettles her. She'd prefer if the professor was being held in some dank cell. Keeping a prisoner in luxury doesn't make sense to her.

Miren grabs her sleeve, points up ahead. A guard stands sentry outside one of the rooms. Human, again, which both reassures and worries her. The professor, according to the rumours flying around the city, blasted the Raveller and a whole squad of Tallowmen with explosive sorceries. Surely that would warrant a Gullhead or something at the least, instead of one human—

—who is suddenly sprawled on the ground, with Miren standing over him. Cari didn't even seen him move. She can't tell if the guard is dead or just unconscious, and, right now, she doesn't care.

Miren tries the handle. It's locked. "Father," he whispers urgently through the keyhole, "stand back. I'm going to smash it open."

Cari frisks the guard (unconscious, it turns out, and the red mess oozing from the back of his skull suggests he won't be waking up soon) and finds a key. She stops Miren from bringing both the door and every other guard in the plant down on them – or, at least, every other guard who isn't arguing with a Stone Man down in the yard outside. She's particularly confident in that aspect of the plan – anything that depends on Spar being stubborn has to work.

The key clicks, and they're in.

The professor looks little the worse for wear for his incarceration. His eyes have lost some of their lustre, and he wobbles on his feet like he's slightly drunk. A burning brazier hangs from the ceiling, out of reach, and the fumes from it make Cari's head spin. Some sort of sedative, she guesses.

"You found her!" he says to Miren. "Well done, boy!"

Miren says nothing, but his face shines in the light of his father's approval.

"Can you walk?" asks Cari. She pulls the unconscious guard

into the room, with the intent of shoving him under the bed to hide him, but he's leaving a bloody trail across the floor so she just drops him like a dead rat.

"Ever onwards," says the professor, tottering towards the door. Miren darts to his side and takes his arm. She follows the Ongents out into the corridor.

Everything's going according to plan so far. Next, they're to find their way to the back of the Alchemists' Quarter. There's a high, virtually unclimbable wall there that runs along the side of Dust Alley. Unclimbable from the ground, anyway, but they'll be starting from the top and Miren has a length of rope slung over one shoulder. No one ever goes down Dust Alley, so their chances of being seen are minimal. Then it's a quick slip down to a jetty, where one of Rat's pals is waiting with a rowing boat.

A window ahead blazes with a sudden fiery light, and something scuttles past it, moving down the wall outside.

"Tallowmen," Cari warns the other two.

She overtakes the Ongents and peers out of the window.

Fuck.

The yard outside looks like a bonfire. Dozens of Tallowmen converging on what looks like a riot. No: she corrects herself when she spots the overturned prison carts – a prison break. And there's Spar in the thick of it, big boulder-fists flailing. There are too many Tallowmen between him and the gate, far too many.

"What is it?" asks Miren.

"Can you, um, teleport?" Talking about his strange power is just as awkward as discussing her visions.

"Not here, and not with father."

No time to argue. No time to think. Cari bites her lip, tastes blood.

"All right – you keep going. Get the professor out."

Miren nods and scampers off without a backward glance. She's not sure if he has confidence in her ability to get out of this place without him, or if he just doesn't care. Nor is she sure which she'd prefer to be true.

The professor gets agitated when he sees they're leaving Cari behind. She can hear him getting flustered, insisting that they have to go back for her. Cari leaves the drugged old man to Miren and races down a different corridor, trusting in some combination of her fragmented vision and blind luck. Up, she thinks. I need to go up.

Racing through the maze of buildings that surround the courtyard. Every window she passes gives her a glimpse of the chaos in the yard below. She runs, abandoning all pretence at stealth, hurtling through doors and scrambling up stairs.

She crosses a glass-walled bridge, a walkway between two buildings. Through the window she sees a metal ladder that runs up the outside of the next factory structure, up to a flat roof. And up there – if she can get up there, maybe she can save Spar, save everything.

The door at the far end of the bridge is locked, but, as she comes to it, it opens as a masked alchemist emerges, wearing a protective helmet and warded metallic robes. She ducks past him – sees his eyes behind the glass, wide with surprise – and races into the room beyond.

It's huge. A vast factory floor, strung with walkways and gantries. No windows, lit from below by lakes of molten metal bubbling in crucibles. Hanging in the void before Cari, suspended by rune-inscribed chains like flies in a spider's web, are two bells. One is in a thousand twisted pieces, reconstructed scrap by scrap like a jigsaw. The other is intact, though dented and damaged. Both are made of a black metal, just like the one in the tower of the Holy Beggar.

One from the Tower of Law. The provenance of the other she cannot guess, but she can smell the sea for an instant.

To the left of the two bells, the broken and the intact, is another spider web that must have once held another bell. This one hangs empty, the chains trailing loose in the fumes from below. That prisoner is gone.

Beneath the two remaining bells, in the middle of that ocean of fire and alchemy, is a mould, like the one the alchemists use to turn mortal flesh into the hideous Tallowmen. Scores of alchemists work like ants on gantries below the intact bell, assembling some sort of frame around it. The alchemists are all dressed in protective clothing, warded, careful not to get too close to the trapped god within the bell.

They have swaddled the bell's clapper with thick blankets, so the god cannot scream when they lower it to the flames.

Cari sees all this in an instant. She keeps running – it's too big for her. She knows, instinctively, that if the two gods in the room see her, their combined attention, their demands for rescue and release will drive her insane. She doesn't stop to think, she just keeps running.

All that molten metal. All those furnaces. That means there's a risk of fire. That means they're ready for something to go wrong.

Through another door, then another in quick succession. The building's double-walled, a containment vessel, and now she's on the outside, on a precarious balcony high above the yard. There's a ladder going up to the roof. She glances down, through the metal grille of the balcony, and sees Spar surrounded by Tallowman sparks. Someone's screaming far below her, a scream that's abruptly cut short by a knife.

She climbs. The metal rungs are rain-slick and icy cold. Her foot slips once, twice, but she recovers as if supported by invisible hands. The partial attention of something other than angels.

Now she's on the roof, and there it is. A great big tank, like a cistern for catching rainwater, but closed to the sky. Its smell is familiar – it's full of the foul, lung-clogging foamy gunk the alchemists use to fight fires. Pipes lead down into the building below, but there's a long rolled-up hose. Cari drags some of it free, cuts the rest off with her knife. She doesn't need precision for this.

She finds a valve and turns it. The tank gurgles, the hose convulses and then the fire-quenching slime cascades down onto the courtyard, a high-pressure spray like a waterfall crashing onto rocks.

The Tallowmen don't even get a chance to scream. They just stop. The slime snuffs them all out in an instant. They fall in droves, crumpling to the ground to be entombed in the slime. Escaped thieves slog through the green-foam drifts, making for the still-open gate. There are still Tallowmen down there – she can see their lights clustered at the entrance to the tallow-vat factory, where they gather at the open door, snarling and slashing at their foes but unable to set foot outside.

She hears Spar shouting below, marshalling the thieves, telling them where to run.

Cari leans back against the cool metal of the tank, grinning. She's done it. The hose goes limp as the tank runs dry.

Then the first Tallowman appears at the top of the ladder. Its grin is hideously bright as it steps over the hose, almost daintily avoiding the little chemical pools. Cari slashes at it with her knife, but it's too fast – candle fingers close on her hand, pinning her. There's another Tallowman, and another, both grabbing her and holding her down.

A woman follows the trio of Tallowmen. Middle-aged, with reddish hair, and a dress that really isn't suited for clambering around rooftops. The wind catches it, threatening to drag her off the edge and hurl her down to the courtyard below, so she holds tightly to the railing.

She raises her voice – it's rich and cultivated, commanding but not unkind. "Carillon Thay?" The woman doesn't seem surprised. "My name is Rosha. I run the guild. I need to talk to you. If they let you go, will you promise not to do anything foolish?"

Cari nods, and the Tallowmen release her. They stay standing around her with their heads bent at weird, inhuman angles to keep their candle flames sheltered from the sudden wind.

"I know about you, Carillon. About your connection to the bells. Do you know what they are? They're the remnants of the Black Iron Gods. The church defeated them and captured them. Recast them as bells to imprison them." The woman Rosha takes a step towards Carillon, hesitant as though she's scared of her. "We're approaching the same problem from different ends, Carillon. I've found a way to destroy the Black Iron Gods, to do what the church couldn't manage. To safely dispose of their power. You can help. Help me. It will free you from these visions, and I'll make you rich."

Cari glances at the courtyard below. "You turn people into these candle-fuckers."

"I won't do that to you. Or to your friends. Ah." Rosha pauses for an instant, as if she's listening to something Cari can't hear. Cari spent a few weeks as a part of a theatre troop, and she recognises the look – Rosha's being prompted by someone. Some voice in her ear. "Your friend Spar will have the best treatment for his condition. All the alkahest he needs. As for your crimes – I own the city watch, dear, you don't need to worry about them."

"And in exchange? What do you need me for?"

"It's hard to explain."

"Fucking try."

Rosha gestures with her hands. "You've travelled. You've seen the Godswar – not directly, I believe, but you know how horrible it is."

She's right. Guerdon's an island of sanity compared to some of the things Cari has heard about, in lands where the gods have gone mad with terror or bloodlust.

"You can imagine what it will do to this city if it comes here. We've developed a weapon that can strike directly at the gods. Kill them in the spiritual realm instead of massacring their worshippers in the physical. It's so much cleaner. But I need you and your connection to the Black Iron Gods to draw out their power, to optimise the yield. We conducted a test firing a few days ago, and the results were positive but at the low end of our projected effectiveness. It was enough to destroy a demigoddess, but with only a dozen or so bells we need to get them up to pantheon-yield as soon as possible."

"You blew up the Tower of Law to get at the bell inside."

Rosha spreads her hands wide, indicating that she was a victim of circumstance. "The church refused to listen. We had to take drastic action to protect the city. Guerdon's neutrality is precarious – the war's getting too close for us to stay out forever. We need those weapons."

"You did this to me. These visions only started after that fucking Tower fell on me."

Rosha shakes her head. Her hair is weirdly unaffected by the wind, as if it's glued to her head. Not a strand out of place. "No, Carillon. The incident, ah, anointed you, but you were born to this power."

The Tallowmen chuckle at that. Rosha frowns in irritation, waves them back. "Everything can change for you, Carillon Thay. Help me. You can awaken the energies in the bells more efficiently than the methods we've been using, coax the Black Iron Gods into partial wakefulness before we remake them."

Carillon opens her mouth to speak, but before she can say anything the bells on Holyhill sound the hour. Cari braces for the vision that builds at the edge of her perception, but then the world tears right in front of her and Miren is there, between her and Rosha.

Without hesitating, he drives his knife right into Rosha's chest. Stabbing again and again, wildly, penetrating her a dozen times. There's no blood, and the guildmistress seems unharmed. Miren then slashes her throat open, and white wax flows from the wound. She gurgles something, but all that comes out of her mouth is more white wax. Rosha takes a step back and falls off the edge.

The Tallowmen advance on Miren. He's fast, but there are three of them, and there's nowhere to run. He's dead if Cari doesn't do anything.

So she charges forward, ducking between the Tallowmen. Grabs Miren's hand, shouting at him. He doesn't react fast enough, and the Tallowmen close in. There's only one way out.

Cari steps off the edge, pulling Miren with her.

They're both falling now, falling after Rosha. The guild-mistress splatters on the courtyard ahead of them, shattering like a dropped candle. No organs, no blood – just a wax duplicate of a woman.

The vision engulfs Cari at the same time as Miren wraps his arms around her and *jumps*.

CHAPTER TWENTY-EIGHT

"Come on! Come on!" Rat slithers down from a rooftop and darts over to Spar's side. The Stone Man's right leg can no longer bear his weight, so Rat helps support him. "You've been cut," he adds, seeing the deep wound in Spar's chest.

"It's nothing." The flow of blood has mostly stopped. Little chips of stone white against the red. Soon, the wounded flesh will petrify entirely. Of course, if they've nicked a lung, then that whole organ will go soon, too. Spar has to remain philosophic about this – the poison will kill him in a few days anyway.

The pair stumble downhill as quickly as they can, down steep alleyways towards the harbour. In the distance, the whoops and shouts of freed thieves, running through the streets to the safe anonymity of the Wash, leaving trails of alchemical foam behind them like broken chains.

They come to a jetty. Twilight has closed in around them, making footing treacherous. Spar hesitates at the edge, mindful of the suddenly deep waters. Rat pulls a small lantern from beneath a pile of rags, lights it and waves it in a bobbing pattern. It's answered by a matching signal from one of the boats out in the bay.

Spar staggers, leans against a cast-iron capstan. He knows that he should stay standing, keep moving to ensure his leg doesn't seize up again, but he's exhausted. Adrenaline becoming heavy as lead in his veins.

"I saw what you did," says Rat. "They'll be telling that story for years."

"What else could I do?"

Rat shrugs. "Most folk could just walk away. Say that horrible shit happens. I'm a corpse-eater, dependent on a certain degree of fatalism, you know? But ..." The ghoul licks his tongue over his teeth, then extends his hand for Spar to shake. "But that was brave. And stupid. Mostly brave."

Spar accepts the handshake, careful not to squeeze too tight. He can barely feel the pressure of Rat's fingers on his, and could not distinguish between the ghoul's scaly, clawed hands and those of a soft-skinned woman. "I owe Cari after that. Everyone does. Did you see her get away?"

"Aye." Rat seems about to say something more, about Cari and Miren and the boy's literally miraculous rescue, but the noise of an alchemical engine approaching makes conversation impossible. The motor launch pulls up alongside the jetty. Mother Bleak's grandson Yon at the helm; he borrowed the boat from the salvage yards, insisting that it wouldn't be missed. There are three other thieves on board, Tammur's lads, and there, huddled in a blanket, eyes twinkling with excitement, is an old man who must be Professor Ongent.

No sign of Cari or Miren. If things had gone according to plan, they'd be here, too.

Spar slumps on board, nearly capsizing the launch. One of the thieves yells at him to crawl to the middle, but doesn't dare touch a Stone Man. Spar drags himself over, ends up next to Ongent. The boat engine roars, and they're pulling away out into the bay.

"You must be Spar," shouts Ongent into Spar's ear. "Carillon talked about you! It's very good to meet you!"

Spar nods, unsure what to say. Ongent works with Jere the thief-taker, and Spar guesses that he said a sight more about the Stone Man than Cari ever did. Cari knows when to keep silent.

"Miren described your proposal. It's going to be interesting!" continues Ongent. "Applied thaumaturgy! Have you ever read the *Transactional Analysis of the Khebesh Grimoire*?"

The boat slides through the dark waters, lightless and unseen. There's no sign of pursuit from the Alchemists' Quarter, nor from the city watch. They've got lucky; no need to break out the stolen weapons hidden beneath tarpaulins on the launch. Yon steers the boat across the bay, aiming at Dredger's yard at the seaward end of the Wash, to the left of St Storm's spire.

As they approach the dock, a searchlight stabs out at them. A dozen armed figures wait for them on the docks, silhouetted against the blinding light. Most are unrecognisable, but the one in the centre is inhumanly bulky in his armour. Dredger, the yard owner.

"That's my boat, Yon," he calls. "Kindly park it before I cut your fucking fingers off, you little thief." Yon pales, glances back at Spar for guidance. Dredger hefts an alchemical cannon so big that it wouldn't be out of place on a warship.

"Try running. I've been wanting to test-fire this fucker."

Yon hesitates. The launch bobs up and down, a few feet from the dock.

"I don't know if you lot are working for Heinreil or Tammur," continues Dredger, "and I don't care. Into the fucking barrel of black lye with you all. Whichever boss will buy you a new skin, that's the one to follow."

One of Dredger's men points at Spar, says something too quiet for anyone else to hear, but it's clear he's recognised the Stone Man.

"You in the back! Stand up. Stand up, I say!"

Spar stands. The muzzle of Dredger's cannon moves to point straight at Spar's chest.

"So it is! The son returns! Don't worry, I'm sure they have your old cell ready. Yon, if you've got the other one on board, the run-away girl, then maybe you'll get to keep a thumb or something."

"Ah!" Ongent struggles to his feet, ambles forward. "Mr Dredger, is it? We have a friend in common. I am Aloysius Ongent, Professor of History. We both work, I understand, with Mr Taphson. May I have a word?"

Dredger gestures. Yon brings the boat close to the shore, and two of Dredger's men step forward, ready to lift the professor out of the boat and deposit him on the dock. As Ongent shuffles towards the rail, he stumbles and falls against one of Tammur's men. From his perspective, Spar sees the professor's grab some-thing from the thief's belt, but the sleight-of-hand is hidden from Dredger. Spar doesn't move, conscious of the gun trained on him. The weapon looks big enough to kill him, even now.

They take the professor out of the boat. The little old man looks absurdly small and fragile next to the armoured bulk of Dredger, a crumbling wooden shanty-hut next to a wheezing, smoke-belching factory. Spar catches the name Taphson again, and mutterings about money. He's trying to bribe Dredger, which might have worked for a lesser offence, but not for this. Dredger's irritated, he starts to shove the professor away – and Ongent moves nimbly, sidestepping and slipping a knife in between Dredger's armour and one of the tubes that run over its surface.

In that snake-like strike, Spar sees a real family resemblance between Ongent and Miren for the first time.

The professor doesn't cut the tube, but he twists the knife so that it's raised, exposed, ready to be cut with the slightest pres-sure. When one of Dredger's guards moves towards him, Ongent raises and clenches his hand in an arcane gesture – there's a sudden thrill in the air, a crackle of power – and the guard freezes mid-step, eyes bulging in sudden terror as the spell holds him in place.

"No," says Ongent, "I *insist* that I recompense you for the use of your little boat. In fact, we are done with it, and we now return it to you. Intact, as you can see." He waves his clenched hand at the boat, a gesture indicating that Spar and the others should disembark immediately. Yon and the thieves flinch as the glowing fist points at them. "Come along, gentlemen. Be quick about it."

The knife at Dredger's neck tube doesn't waver.

Dredger makes this gurgling sound, like he's dying, and Spar wonders if the professor's hand slipped in the darkness, cut something vital. Then he realises that it's the alchemist's laughter.

"Fuck it," says Dredger. "Tell Taphson he can bill me. Go on."

A climbdown to save face. Spar allows himself to imagine Heinreil making a similar concession to preserve the Brotherhood, but it's more likely the old bastard will cling to power for as long as he can. That's a problem for tomorrow, though, so he turns his attention to the more pressing issue of getting out of the launch without capsizing the whole thing. His right leg is completely immobile now, and his left shoulder's locking up, too. He ends up leaving the impression of his right hand in the dock as he drags himself out, fingers sunk into its tarry surface. A sneak-thief he's not. The impressions start to fill with rainwater immediately.

Ongent keeps up his dotty old academic routine, talking to Dredger as though he doesn't have a knife at the man's throat, like he's not holding a guard in invisible chains.

Spar comes up beside him and takes the gun away from Dredger.

"The Brotherhood done business with you in the past, sir, and I don't think either of us want to change that arrangement. Like the professor says, we'll pay for the rent of your boat, and walk out of here making no trouble. All right?"

Dredger's eyepieces clack and whir as he examines the Stone Man. "You can't even walk, boy. Your word won't count for anything in a day."

"It counts tonight." Spar ejects the alchemical cartridge from the gun, a little glass ampoule of phlogiston cradled in wood and spiralled with dampening runes. He hands gun and shot back to Dredger – a gesture of respect – and then limps across the yard towards the exit, and the streets of the Wash.

They march back to the tenement block, which has become a headquarters for whatever this thing is, this thing with Spar at its head. A splinter Brotherhood, a memorial to Idge's ideals, a shelter from the city's chaos. An ongoing wake for the Fever Knight, maybe. Spar has to move slowly down the alleyways, dragging his lame leg, stopping every few minutes to catch his breath or to meet some supporter.

Rat runs back and forth, carrying messages from Tammur and the other thieves. He can make the journey in a fraction of the time, racing over rooftops. Most of those who escaped the tallow vats are on their way down here, swelling the ranks of Spar's supporters. Some of Heinreil's henchmen have switched sides – they can't be hoping for a better deal under Spar, so they must have decided that change is in the air. It smells like the sulphurous residue of the Bell Rock cloud.

Rat returns again, tells Spar that Cari's back ahead of them. Carried out of danger by Miren. Rat growls as he delivers the news, making his opinion of Carillon's new lover clear. Spar feels an unexpected spike of jealousy. Loneliness kills Stone Men quicker than the plague does. Driven mad by the inability to touch, to feel another's touch, they stop talking precautions and get injured. Or go to the Isle, or just give up and walk into the ocean. Intimacy of any form was something else stolen from him by the disease, another part of his life frozen and broken by the plague.

Cari, in her strange combination of self-centred heedlessness and kindness, hadn't feared him. No matter how often he or the city reminded her to treat him as a walking infection, a stony cancer that could destroy her, she persisted in treating him as a friend. (He wonders now, briefly, how much of her strangeness can be attributed to her connection to the bells, to the Black Iron Gods. The waking visions are new, but he cannot count the number of sleepless nights he spent pacing, listening to her cry out in her troubled dreams.)

He didn't dare embrace her – she may not have feared the Stone Plague, but Spar long ago vowed never to pass on this curse to another living soul if he could avoid it; even when doing enforcement for the thieves' Brotherhood, he was careful, even solicitous, of those he threatened. If he ever delivered a beating, which was seldom needed given his strength, he was always careful to keep his stony hide away from broken skin. He never embraced Cari. Maybe, he thinks, he should have.

He takes the pain of jealousy and loss and cherishes it as he walks; his heart, at least, has not yet turned to stone.

They come to the bank of the canal and turn left, following the stagnant waters down towards the harbour. They pass the blackened ruins of Mother Bleak's houseboat. The Fever Knight's grave.

Perhaps drawn by the mention of Carillon, Ongent comes up alongside Spar. Smiling like this is an organised tour, an anthropological expedition to see how the other half live. Toddling along in his robe like some senile old man, a forgetful grandfather who slipped his minders. Between Desiderata Street and the way Ongent handled Dredger, it's clear that Ongent is much more than a clueless scholar. Still, the growing pain in Spar's chest reminds him that he still wants to live, and for that he needs the professor's sorcery.

"Well," says Ongent, "that was invigorating, if I may say so. How long do you think the thieves' guild can shelter us from the alchemists?"

"Not long. And it's the Brotherhood." Ordinarily, it might be possible to lie low, to submerge in the Wash or Gravehill or some other poor quarter of the city. They have any number of safe houses and hiding places, a host of allies and supporters who'd help conceal them. But now, with the Brotherhood divided between Spar and Heinreil's factions, there's every chance that the Tallowmen are already on their trail. Hell, they might come to the tenement and find it ablaze with candlelight.

"Well then," says Ongent, "to business! I'm told that alkahest is no longer an adequate treatment for your ... ailment." The professor waves his hand vaguely at Spar's calcified shoulder. "And that young Carillon has, ah, volunteered me to assist using sorcery. That is a mark of how much she esteems you, my boy! She ran away from my house and went straight to you – I rather wish she had asked for my help then, instead of, ah, precipitating events to this degree. But no matter! We shall let bygones be bygones."

"Right," says Spar, manoeuvring both himself and the professor around a large pile of raptequine shit which Ongent apparently hadn't noticed.

"Oh! Ah! Thank you! Now, in my career I have given some thought, a great deal of thought to be frank, to the topic of channeling divine power through thaumaturgical constructs, and I believe it is feasible, at least in theory. It is, however, not without quite considerable risk. For her, for you – and for me. Are you familiar – I would assume not, not to cast aspersions on your education – with the Theory of Forms?"

Spar went to an excellent – and expensive – school, at his mother's insistence, while they lived at Hog Close. "Gods have more power than mortals can contain, and Cari's got a direct line to the Black Iron Gods. You're hoping to draw a small fraction of the gods' power through that line and use it to cure me." He stops. "No one's forcing you to do this, you know. If you walk away now, I'll let you go. You have my word."

Ongent claps his hands excitedly. "Nonsense! I wouldn't miss this for the world. It's going to be fascinating! However ... I do have, shall we say, a favour?"

"Go on."

"Should we all survive, I'd like to continue working with Carillon. Her gift offers an unparalleled way to, ah, explore the city's history. I worry that her instinct will be to vanish again, to run off rather than deal with an unpleasant or trying situation. She'll listen to you, though, if you ask her to trust me."

Before Spar can answer, they're spotted. Escaped thieves, glad to be alive, glad to have escaped the tallow vats, swirl around them, laughing. The crowd pushes them towards a warm light. A drink is pressed into Spar's hand. They'd carry him shoulder-high if they could lift him. Instead, he's whirled away into a large room in the basement of the tenement. Ongent is lost in the crowd, replaced by Tammur, nervous and sweaty in the uproar, trying to tell him something about the shift in the city's underworld. Support is flowing to Idge's son, the only man who's stood up against the alchemists, against tyranny.

Tammur urges Spar to address the crowd, but he can't. There are too many people, but, more than that, he feels detached from them. Like they're ephemeral, things of gossamer and spirit, a different order of being to him. He has nothing in common with them, and they have interpreted his acts of desperation, his perverse death wishes, as something else entirely, a gesture of defiance or a move in a war. His mouth is full of pebbles.

"You have to say something," urges Tammur.

With a supreme effort, Spar stands. Speaks. Words force their way past the dam in his mouth, gritty and clogged, coming out in bursts. He has no idea what he's saying, but they love it. Love him. The tale of how he led the charge into the Alchemists' Quarter, how he rescued the prisoners in the cages, is already legend. Idgeson! Idgeson!

He limps out when there's a lull in the celebration, finding his way to his room by memory alone. His eyes are watering, and the water has little sharp specks of grit in them. His left tear duct has calcified, he realises, and his left eye is going. Every time he blinks, he can feel the dust scarring his eyeball, and the eyeball becoming encrusted with a thin film of marble.

There's no bed. He lowers himself to the floor, feels around for alkahest. He can jam the syringe into the corner of his eye, maybe save his vision on that side.

The pain in his chest spikes.

CHAPTER TWENTY-NINE

E ladora follows Aleena through the tunnels. The older woman is tireless, her stride like a metronome, heavy plodding footfalls carrying her through the darkness. Eladora's exhausted and thoroughly lost. They've been going in circles through these tunnels for hours, days, longer. The city above has surely crumbled to dust. The sun is a memory.

The ghoul tunnels in this part of the city have been colonised by the surface. Some have been turned into cellars or storerooms, locked away behind wooden doors. Others are being used as shelters – Eladora doesn't see anyone else, but there are ragged blankets, the ashes of cooking fires, graffiti. She guesses it's mostly newcomers who actually live down here; locals wouldn't trespass in ghouldom, not even this far-flung province so close to the surface.

She's sick of ghoul tunnels. She flinches every time they turn a corner, somehow expecting Jere to stumble out of the darkness, holding the red mess that was his hand out to her, like she's expected to fix it. Or to see the Raveller, congealing out of the shadows like cooling fat in a frying pan.

Aleena's muttering to herself, or communing with the gods. Eladora doesn't dare interrupt her, not even to ask her to stop for a minute.

Now that she's had much too long to think about it, Eladora isn't sure she made the right decision. Where is she going with this murderous saint? Aleena's confession – that she killed the Thay family, murdered Jermas Thay and all his children and grandchildren in that mansion now owned by Kelkin – is almost too big a fact to fit in Eladora's consciousness. She tries to reconcile her memories of her uncles, her grandfather, with Aleena's accusation that they were servants of the Black Iron Gods, but can't hold the two ideas in her head at the same time. It's unthinkable that her family's tragedy should even be an approximation of justice.

News of the murders is the first thing that Eladora remembers from her childhood; memory of her father barring the doors of the farmhouse, of her mother ashen-faced but not crying, kneeling in the middle of the kitchen and praying. And Carillon, three or four years old, running and playing. Eladora remembers resenting her cousin's laughter, feeling that it was inappropriate in the face of tragedy. Eladora didn't understand the murders either, of course – for weeks, she believed that everyone in Guerdon had been murdered, maybe everyone in the world, and that there was nothing left in existence beyond the farmyard walls.

For years afterwards, her fears took the shape of assassins and thieves, creeping in her window with knives to rob and murder her. She has a new shape for her fears now, a shapeless shape. The Raveller, all teeth and darkness.

She could, she thinks, go home. Go back to her mother. Run to the safety of the old house.

This time, she understands the danger, at least a little. The Black Iron Gods and their host of Ravellers. War on the streets, between the church and the frightful Tallowmen and gods know who else. And beyond and above it all, across the sea, the Godswar. The possibility – Professor Ongent would say the inevitability – of some belligerent deity reaching out for the city, reality melting under the horrific *attention* of the divine. But what good is understanding without the ability to do anything to help?

"All right," says Aleena. They've reached a junction in the tunnels. The air from the left-hand path is noticeably fouler, and the ground slopes down sharply. "In the absence of divine revelation, I can't think of anything better to do than go back down into the land of shit and carrion, and fetch up another elder ghoul. I don't know if the bastards will listen, though – not after the first one got killed as soon as he fucking arrived. I'll have to go back."

The horror must be evident on Eladora's face, because Aleena laughs.

"Oh, I'm not taking you down with me. The question is, what to do with you?" Aleena raps her fingers on the hilt of her sword in thought and appears to settle on a decision. "All right, this way."

Right, and up, and up – a long and exhausting climb along steep stairs that wind through the stone. Eladora's long since lost track of where they might be in the city, but they climb for so long that they must be inside one of Guerdon's great hills, inside Castle Hill or Holyhill. They can't have gone farther than that, she reasons. They come to another reinforced door, warded and locked, blocking the stairs. Aleena has a key to this one. Rusty hinges squeal.

"Where are we going?" Eladora manages to ask. Her mouth is drier than the dusty tunnels.

Aleena leads her through a cellar, and up into, weirdly, a clothes shop. Through large glass windows, apart from the one that's shattered and boarded up, Eladora can see it's still night-time. They've been hiding in the tunnels all day. The piles of clothing on tables, the sewing machines in a row, the store mannequins in their finery are unconscionably sinister at this hour. They remind

Eladora of a storybook she read as a child, before her mother took it off her because it was no longer considered spiritually uplifting by the Safidists. One story concerned little goblins who crept into a shoemaker's workshop by night to cobble shoes for him. She suddenly worries about disturbing tailor-goblins, and imagines them turning on her with their sharp needles and scissors. Strangling her with thread.

Aleena goes through one door, comes back out again almost immediately. "He's not here. Must be at Sinter's place." She glances around the room. "Do you want to grab a change of clothes? Take what you need, but be fucking quick about it." She moves to the front of the shop, where she can keep watch on the empty street outside without being seen herself.

"Without paying?"

"I know the owner," says Aleena. "Gods below, do I know the owner. He's one of the church's little fixers. He works for Sinter, the bastard we're going to see. This shop's just a front, which I guess makes it church property. Holy ground."

Eladora looks around the shop in a panic, unable to decide. The leathers and street clothes she borrowed from Jere are more suited to running around tunnels and alleyways than anything here. She ignores the fancier clothes – not that she has any interest in such fripperies, being a serious-minded academic, and grabs a fresh scholar's robe. Aleena stuffs it into a sack and hands it back to her.

"Come on."

Out onto the street. They're somewhere in Glimmerside, high up on the flanks of Holyhill. They can't be more than a few streets away from the University District, thinks Eladora, no more than a few hundred yards from Desiderata Street, but she doesn't recognise the buildings or the shops. Distant clamour from the direction of the harbour. Lights flooding the sky above the Alchemists' Quarter.

"Sinter's a Keeper priest. Doesn't minister to the faithful, of course, not unless it involves leg-breaking as a penance. He runs their spies, their dirty tricks, their inquisitions. Fucker wanted to run me, too, when they started running dry on saints. But he's on our side, right?" Aleena sounds almost like she's trying to convince herself.

Aleena hustles her through more back alleyways, to another door. A tall man lets them in, peering suspiciously at Eladora as she passes. The man reminds her of Bolind – the same solidity, the same fearsome strength. But Bolind was the Raveller in disguise, so the resemblance isn't reassuring.

Upstairs to a larger room where there are others, two men and two women. The windows are shuttered, the air thick with smoke. There's a gun on the table next to one of the women.

"Shit," says one of the men, "it's her." He's looking at Eladora, not Aleena, and he looks terrified.

"No, it is not," snaps the other man. "It's Ongent's assistant, Duttin." Eladora recognises him – bald head, broken nose, glittering eyes – he's the one who was watching the professor's study, the Keeper spy. He gestures to them with a heavily bandaged hand. "Come in, Aleena. We were discussing the death of gods."

Cari wakes, drowsy for once. Usually, she's quick to wake up, but right now she stretches, cat-like, still half asleep. Her leg pushes against Miren's. He grunts and rolls over in the little bed. She lies back, slips one hand over to caress his flank. Smiling as she remembers the night. Again, teleporting created this strange intimacy with Miren, this timeless sense of union that she desperately tried to recapture as soon as they emerged from wherever he'd brought her. She hadn't managed to get there, but the attempt brought its own pleasures.

She can hear the distant noise of the celebration downstairs.

Part of her is furious at Spar for taking such a risk in the alchemists' guild, but it's paid off. He's proved that he's ready to fight for the Brotherhood. It's more than Heinreil has ever done. Cari guesses that if she listened for the bells, if she let the Black Iron Gods carry her consciousness across the restless city, she'd see more thieves making their way down to the Wash in ones and twos and threes. Coming to pledge themselves to the new master of the underworld, the only one who could possibly shelter them from the unleashed Tallowmen. She remembers Heinreil's weasel face smiling at her as he ripped her mother's amulet from her neck.

Heinreil won't be smiling for long. She'll watch the master fall from every church tower in the city.

Cari doesn't want to leave the warmth of the bed, but she wants to join the celebration downstairs. She rolls over, looks at Miren's sleeping face. Softer now, younger. She wonders which is closer to the truth – the innocent face of the sleeping boy, or the quiet bodyguard and assassin he becomes when serving his father. Or something else, the thing she glimpses when he carries her across the city, like a physical counterpart to the visions.

Part of her brain screams at her to run, to stay away, but there's an undeniable connection between them, a kinship she can't understand. And she needs to save her energy for other fights. So don't think about it, she tells herself, just enjoy it.

Her hand moves down his flank. She pushes the blanket back, letting the moonlight shine on their naked bodies. She lifts her leg across him and—

His hand closes around her throat, shoving her away from him. She chokes and falls back on the bed. In a flash, he's standing by the bed, eyes bright with fury.

"What are you doing?" he hisses. His gaze darts for a moment towards his knives, neatly arranged next to the tangle of their clothes on the floor.

"I wanted more," says Cari hoarsely, rubbing at her neck. She can tell it's already bruised. "Fuck, you hurt me."

"Well, don't touch me," says Miren. He grabs clothes, starts dressing.

"It's the middle of the night. Where are you going?"

"My father's here." With that, Miren's gone out of the door, his precious knives vanishing into his sleeves like a conjurer's trick.

Cari wraps the blanket around herself and lies back down, shivering with anger. She's furious with Miren, but angry at herself, too, and she's not sure why. Embarrassed, furious, full of restless energy. She rolls over, rolls back, gets up and half dresses, locks the door, goes back to bed. Gets up again – she remembers grabbing a bottle of wine earlier, when they first arrived, a celebratory drink to mark Ongent's successful rescue. It's bad wine, but improves by the third or fourth mouthful.

She could go down and join the party, go and find Spar and Rat, celebrate with them. Listen to Spar insist that he acted on impulse, that he never considered what he was doing until he'd actually done it. She knows it's the truth, but it doesn't change the fact that her friend has a knack for making friends, for inspiring others. He may have rescued the thieves out of compassion instead of calculation, but it was the right thing to do on both scores. Rat would tell him that, always watching from the sidelines. Seeing things others missed. Rat saw her, found her in the streets when she was stranded here desperate and alone.

And Rat doesn't like Miren. She raises the bottle to her absent friend, toasting his perspicacity as she rubs her neck.

She's waiting, she realises. Waiting for the turn of the hour, when they'll ring the bells to mark the time. She can spy on Miren and Ongent then, if she wants, or look for Heinreil. Or look for Rosha, the alchemists' guildmistress. Is there a real Rosha, a flesh-and-blood Rosha out there, a model for the wax duplicate that fell from the roof? Did she somehow turn herself into tallow? Or turn herself in a *mould*, so she can stamp out infinite copies of herself? The thought of Rosha gets tangled up in thoughts of the bells – is she the body that fell from the roof, or an inhuman thing of cold metal, remote and loathsome, projecting herself into the world through a human mask?

She herself, Cari realises, is waiting to leave her body and walk with the gods. The same gods who made the streets run with blood, who made the Ravellers. Still hungry for blood and sacrifice even in their confined, truncated forms.

The bells start to ring.

She scrambles up, half falling out of the bed, slamming the window shut. She wraps the fallen blanket around her head to blot out the noise. Grabbing at the floorboards, at the legs of the bed, trying to hold onto the ground, anchor her soul against being plucked up and hurled across the skies, flung from belfry to belfry, stretched and torn by the metal fingers of cold black iron.

BLOOD OF MY BLOOD HERALD OF OUR RETURN SIBLING CHILDSELF

"Go away," she screams, or tries to. Hot vomit in her mouth, skull in a vice. An overwhelming sense of panic – flash-vision of men with pickaxes, hacking at stone. The Holy Beggar church surrounded by a cage of scaffolding. The bell – the god – being lowered to the ground below.

Flash again. A circle in the darkness. A gate. And beyond it, a churning sea of chaos. The Raveller host, thousands of them, reaching out for her.

"Go the fuck away!"

The hour turns. The hammering in her head replaced by hammering at her door.

"Cari?" Rat's voice. "Open the door, now."

"Wait a moment."

"Spar needs you. We've got to go now."

Tammur, speaking to her in low, urgent tones, warning her how much they need Spar – how precarious their situation is. How he's risked everything for this bid against Heinreil. The way he talks, you'd think Spar was a racehorse that had suddenly fallen lame. Or a ship, a thing that had to be repaired. They found Spar when they noticed he was missing from the revels. He'd collapsed in his own room and was scarcely breathing. They thought him dead when they first found him, until Rat arrived and heard the faint grind of one working lung. There's no time to waste.

Ongent, pottering around with wires and paintbrushes, drawing binding circles and warding runes on the floor of the washroom they've annexed for what he refers to as a second experiment. Absurdly cheery, as though they're still in his office back in the seminary, and all the chaos of the last five days hasn't happened at all. Miren in the corner, ignoring Cari, giving no indication that he's shared her bed for the last two nights, almost invisible in the shadows. She guesses he's told his father, though, from some comments Ongent makes, innuendos.

Rat, pacing nervously. Fighting the urge to flee, she guesses, but sometimes he moves his head in this heavy way that's most un-Rat-like, his gaze becoming old and ponderous, and there's a light in his eyes that scares Cari. Before long, he slips out of the room, unwilling to stay for the actual invocation.

And Spar, lying on the floor, choking. His right lung has entirely calcified, and his left is partly stone. She can hear it – every time he inhales, there's a crackling, scraping sound; a paper bag of pebbles being dragged over rocks. Talking's hard, but he manages a Stone Man's smile for Cari when she kneels by him. She clasps his hand, leans down and whispers in his ear.

"Trust me, okay? Not the gods, not the professor. It's me. I'm running this show." His hand tightens on hers, careful despite the pain not to crush her bones. She straightens up, turns to Ongent. "Ready?"

The professor gestures to a spot on the floor in the middle of the diagram he's drawn. Cari asks, "Should I kneel, or sit, or . . . ?"

"Kneeling would be, ah, a little too like supplication. We come to the Black Iron Gods not as worshippers, but as thieves, to steal their power and use it for our own ends, yes? I think standing right there would be best. Unless you feel faint, in which case – ah, thank you, my boy." Miren's moved over to stand next to her, ready to catch her, his feet nimbly picking a safe path across the runes. Cari scowls, but doesn't argue. Miren, for his part, is expressionless.

"All right. Carillon, this invocation is really the same as the experiment we tried last week. Do you recall?"

"Yeah. You had a skull thing. It exploded."

"In this revised experiment, I am both invoker and channeler. The spell will make it easier for you to access the accumulated arcane power of the slumbering Black Iron Gods, and open a connection to me as well. I can then channel that power through you into my own sorcerous constructs – in this case, a spell of healing. Curative spells are extremely inefficient and rarely provide lasting benefits, but in this case we should have access to a source of power immeasurably greater than anything I could channel myself."

"And if it's too much?"

The professor taps his own forehead. "Again, a skull thing will explode." He rolls back his sleeves. "Let us begin."

"Wait." Spar whispers. "Cari."

She kneels down next to him again. Speaking is immensely hard for him. He has to inhale for every word, force it out past frozen lips and throat. "Just cure ... poison. Not ... stone. Don't ... too far."

"But if we can make you whole ... "

"I'm ... Stone Man. Just ... don't want ... to die ... undone." The last effort is too much for him. His left eye flutters closed; she can't see his right beneath the pall of stone.

Cari straightens, takes her place in the diagram, wishes Rat would come back in. She takes a deep breath. "All right. Do it."

CHAPTER THIRTY

E ladora can't tell if the house is small or large, or if it's a house at all. The door on the street below was modest, but the building seems to go on forever. Rooms open onto other rooms; corridors turn off at unexpected angles. She guesses that they've connected several houses to make this secret warren.

One of the women brings Eladora to a kitchen and makes her help assemble plates of food. Eladora's hands shake as she piles hunks of black bread and fruit onto a tray. The woman – "call me Isil" she said, in a way that makes Eladora sure that whatever her real name is, it isn't that – counts the knives before and after. Eladora feels like she's made an embarrassing faux pas; should she have tried to steal a knife, to arm herself? Carillon certainly would have grabbed one.

"Please, I'm terribly tired," says Eladora, "where am I to sleep?" It's true – she's exhausted and filthy from a day traipsing around tunnels with Aleena, and the night before she spent dozing in the back room of a tavern – but, really, Eladora wants to know if she's a prisoner. If they show her to a cell or a room with no way out, she'll know.

The woman just shrugs. "Bring those bottles, too," she says, pointing at three bottles of some amber-coloured liquid on a high shelf. They're too high for Eladora to reach, so she grabs a small stool to stand on. The stool wobbles and she slips to the ground, twisting her ankle. One of the bottles smashes to the ground and shatters.

"Fuck," says Eladora. Something inside her breaks, too. "Fuck fuck fuck fuck." She's sobbing now, tears pouring out of her like she's a cracked vessel. Crying for her old life in the university, for Ongent and Miren and the life she's lost, crying for being dragged around the city like unwanted luggage, crying out of sheer terror and exhaustion. Liquid from the broken bottle crawls out of the cracked glass and crawls across the floor towards her, like the Raveller in the tunnel, a black tide ripping Jere and the Patros apart in the tunnels under Holyhill. The terror of the gods catches her, and she shakes uncontrollably.

"Stop that!" snaps Isil. "Be quiet." She stands over Eladora, unsure of what to do. "Stop that!" she says again. "Stop or I'll hurt you."

"Try-try-try," moans Eladora – trying even to say 'trying' is beyond her in this flood of terror. Isil grabs a wooden spoon and raises it, then reconsiders and drops it back down. She grabs one of the trays and marches out of the kitchen, leaving Eladora alone.

Try to escape, part of her urges. Get up and run! But she has no idea how to get out of this part of the rambling house, let alone escape onto the streets. She has nowhere to go, anyway. Even the safe places like the seminary are corrupt now. Sinter and his spies watched her there.

She has nowhere to go, and no one is coming for her, and there's no point in crying. She gets up and composes herself. Takes the surviving bottles off the top shelf and carries the second tray into the other room.

There's another stranger there when she returns, a pock-faced man with reddish hair who Sinter introduces as Lynche. He stinks of chemicals, like he's been swimming in the polluted waters of the bay, and the only free seat in the room is next to him. Eladora instead sidles up to Aleena and stands behind her.

"All right?" mutters Aleena to her.

"No."

"Fucking true, that."

Sinter rises, a note in his bandaged hand. "Word from our masters. Bishop Albe's the acting Patros, and he doesn't have the balls to act. He's permitted the alchemists to put Tallowman guards on all the cathedrals in Holyhill."

"They've surrounded the Holy Beggar and St Storm, too," adds a thin woman with one eye.

"How many . . . how many other bells are there?" asks Eladora. "How many Black Iron Gods?"

Sinter chuckles. "If you'd asked that a week ago, I'd have had to kill you. Still might." He looks at the letter in his hand in bemused disgust, then crumples it up and throws it aside. "Thirteen, altogether. Eight here in the city, now that the Tower of Law and the Bell Rock are gone. The seven old churches, plus the Seamarket. And that means the alchemists can make lots more of those bombs."

Isil raises her hand. "Boss – is that the worst thing? The Patros is dead. Parliament's in the alchemists' pocket. Why fight it? Is it that bad if the alchemists use the Black Iron Gods – the gods of our enemies – to kill a bunch of insane foreign gods? We've all seen the war – no one's going to weep if it ends."

"True enough," says Sinter, "but I'm not going to hand over all power in this city to Rosha. The church of the Keepers made this city, and it's our job to protect it."

"And how long will it take 'em to make more of those bombs, eh?" The speaker is a little man with the accent of the Archipelago and blue tattoos crawling around his wrists. The smell of his cigarettes burns Eladora's eyes. "Soon as the gods find out who struck the Valley of Grena, they'll be coming for us. Fuck, Ishmere already knows, I'll bet, if they were paying any attention in Beckanore. Our neutrality is fucked worse than a temple dancer."

"We need leverage," says Sinter. "Suggestions?"

"We attack," says Isil. "Get the navy on our side – they'll follow the banner of the church if we fly it high enough. The alchemists don't have that many Tallowmen, not if they're rounding up every crippled beggar and footpad in the Wash to turn into more candles. Take the Alchemists' Quarter and the remains of the bells."

"The thieves got in," says a big man sitting next to Sinter. He's very soft-spoken. "But not very far."

Aleena perks up. "What thieves?"

"Ones from the Wash. They tried breaking in to the Alchemists' Quarter. Freed a passel of prisoners earlier this evening."

"Since when is Heinreil fighting with the alchemists? He's Rosha's man," says Isil.

"'Twasn't Heinreil," insists Lynche, almost angrily, "it's Idgeson's lot, from out of the Wash."

Sinter shakes his head. "The alchemists showed they were willing to use alchemical weapons within Guerdon when they blew up the Bell Rock. Why'd they hold back when the thieves hit them? Why just use Tallowmen when they could have broken out withering dust or a flash ghost or—"

Eladora speaks up, reluctantly, "Idgeson and Cari are f-f-friends. If she was there—"

"Carillon Thay," says Aleena, and Sinter nods. "She was there. And Rosha needs her."

"She's the linchpin. She's our leverage." Sinter turns to Eladora. "Tell me everything you know about Carillon Thay."

*

Cari's outside herself, seeing things in the same detached, fly-on-every-wall perspective as before. This time, instead of her consciousness being smeared over a whole cathedral, or dragged wide enough to perceive the whole city, it's pulled out only a little, to encompass half this basement room under the tenement. She is, in this timeless moment, the totality of the diagram drawn on the washroom floor and everything inside it. Ongent, Spar, Miren, Cari – she sees all of them from every possible angle. She tries to look at herself, but feels that she's falling back into her own body – truncating herself down to fit inside her little skull, as the Black Iron Gods were hammered down and squeezed inside little bells. She looks elsewhere.

Miren's dimmer because he's technically outside the spell. She can see him, inside and out. She can see him as he is, see him naked, see the muscles and veins beneath his skin. See his bones, make him a skeleton standing behind her like a vision of death. Go deeper, even, follow the silver filigree of nerves and brain until it exposes what must be his soul. Impression of burn marks, branding. Scar marks, sutures.

He knows she's watching. He moves, and her vision's blocked. She registers surprise, but it's Cari's surprise, and somehow that's harder to hold onto.

Ongent, in her vision, is wreathed in colourless fire. Words scuttle from his mouth, his brain, like seething scorpions. Shapes boil around him, echoing – no, defining – the framework that now houses her consciousness. *I'm seeing magic*, she thinks, and that thought visibly ripples across the field of her mind. *I am magic* might be more accurate. Here, within the diagram, her soul blends into the elemental chaos of the arcane field. *The soul is an epiphenomenon*, she thinks, and it's not her thought at all.

Spar. A leaden lump. Ongent and Miren are pillars of flame, but Spar's a blackened ember. There's more life in the walls of the building than there is in parts of Spar's body. She can see his mind there, his soul, and it's much more contained than Ongent's or Miren's – or her own, she guesses. It reminds her of what she sees when she flies over Guerdon in her dreams, only it's more beautiful, more complex and harmonious. Spar's thoughts are palaces and boulevards, shining marble and lush green trees in parkland.

The spell changes. *I'm invoking them now. Hold fast.* Is it Ongent who's speaking to her, or is he speaking to herself? How many of these perceptions are hers, and how many are his – and how many are *theirs*, because she senses them now, far away. The Black Iron Gods. Like dark wells hanging above the city, impossibly suspended. Vile tesseracts, containing infinitely more malice and suffering than their physical dimensions would suggest. She rejoices that it's only a few minutes past the hour, and they are still and silent. If they were agitated into half-awareness she knows they would be able to swallow her, swat her away. Ongent's right – she needs to be a thief for this. To steal their power without them noticing.

She can look at herself now without falling back into the prison of her own body, although there's still a dragging sensation, a sort of elastic tension that would pull her mind back if she let it. Sees herself from the inside and out simultaneously, watches the play of muscles beneath the skin, sees the cords and tendrils of magic that connect her to the body, or the body to the diagram that's now housing her soul, or however that works. There's a tangle of energy around Carillon's neck, the lines of power are all bunched and distorted. Her vision focuses on this point, just below her throat.

Where her mother's amulet should be.

She'd already suspected that the amulet was connected to all this, that it's blocking her ability to spy on Heinreil. Now, though, she has proof. What did he take from her? Was the amulet protecting her from the visions? Is that why she didn't have them until recently? Anger. Her attention flickers to Spar for an instant, and he grunts in pain. She glares at the crust of stone; soon, they'll tear it away and cure Spar, and then he'll bring down Heinreil. That's what they're here for.

It's getting hard to focus. She keeps slipping, floating away. Forgetting who she is. Like a ship, battered by currents. The shallows and reefs of Carillon's body; the distant, ominous storm clouds of the Black Iron Gods, a hurricane she cannot survive. Whirlpools and hidden rocks. She glimpses, for a moment, the woman's right shoulder. Wounded and bandaged, but she can see beneath the bandages to the skin, and the wound's infected. A stain beneath the skin. Well, that's what they're all there for, isn't it? To steal the god's power for healing magic. She touches the wound—

She's Cari again, back in her own body. Everyone's shouting, even Spar's trying to sit up, reaching for her. The smell of burning, strong hands – Miren – tearing at her clothes, her jacket. His knife cutting at the ties. "I'm all right, I'm all right," she insists, even though she doesn't know what might be wrong.

The pain hits her a moment later. Her shoulder feels like it's on fire – and then Miren shows her the blacked patch on the jacket, a scorch mark right over the wound.

"Did I do that?" she asks.

"Yes," says Ongent. He's pale, eyes watering, leaning heavily on the wall.

Cari takes the jacket off Miren and looks at the burnt area. The scorch mark is about twice the size of her palm, but when she touches it five smaller areas flake away. She puts her fingers through the holes, and they match perfectly.

"Gods below," she says, but then flexes her shoulder, and there's no pain at all. "Hey, it worked!"

"Carillon," says Ongent gravely, "do not do that again, or anything like it. You could just have easily set yourself on fire – or destroyed this whole building."

"The Godswar," echoes Tammur. "You're talking about the Godswar. Direct divine intervention, miracles." He swallows, stares at Cari with terrified eyes. "That was a miracle you did there."

Ongent nods. "None of us have ever been so close to death as we were a moment ago."

"But it worked!" protests Carillon. Miren shrugged, as if to say she got lucky.

Tammur makes his excuses and hurries off. Cari wonders how far he'll go. She'll worry about that later. "All right, let's try again," says Cari. "Anyone else want to leave?"

"Not ... an option," says Spar from the ground. Miren moves back to stand behind her, which really doesn't reassure Carillon.

Ongent double-checks the protective runes around his feet, then coughs, wipes his eyes and shakes his hands like an actor getting back into character. "Forth rode the faithful, into the formless host."

Again, the feeling of disconnection. Cari becomes untethered from her body, a ship slipping its moorings. The Black Iron Gods on the horizon, a bank of storm clouds. She can't make out any distinct features, or tell one from the other. They're all just roiling, chaotic power and hatred. She should ask Ongent about them, find out what they were before the Keepers captured them and melted them down, but the thought makes her nervous, as though, if she knew their proper form, so would they.

Herald of our return, they keep shouting at her.

This time, she heeds the professor's warning and just watches. Without moving, Ongent builds these paths of glowing light, rune-warded channels, running between him and Cari, and then another one between him and Spar. They're frail, ethereal and empty. No power flows through them.

Next, he conjures a complicated shape. It reminds Carillon of a big clockwork from Old Haith, or maybe an architect's model of a cathedral. It hovers in the middle of the diagram, over Spar. Hovers might be the wrong word – somehow, it's more real and solid here than anything else, than Spar or Cari or the building around them. This isn't an illusion, she reminds herself, or a dream. It's another perspective on what's real.

Power flares in the channels between her and Ongent. The professor's trying again, invoking the gods again.

The storm's closer now. The Black Iron Gods stir, their terrible attention probes the city as they search for this irritation, this theft. Flash-images of shapes like sharks, like lions, moving across the sky. Cari freezes, tells herself not to move, not to run, no matter how much she wants to.

The flow of power becomes a torrent as the gods whirl around her. Light, intolerably bright, flares around Spar, as though Ongent is using an alchemical cutting torch. She laughs at that thought, or would if she had lungs or a mouth – that he'd have set up this whole mystic ritual, only for Miren to sneak in and cure Spar with a cutting torch and a pair of pliers while she was high on sorcery.

The building shakes. The wind becomes the roaring of angry gods. How can the others be so calm? Can't they hear the storm? It's all Cari can do not to fling herself to the ground, to hide or prostrate herself before the Black Iron Gods. The whirlwind tears at her vision – now she can only see the diagram, the aetheric fields and constructs of magic. The physical world is lost to her. She's suddenly terrified that her body's gone entirely, ripped away by the fierce winds, and she's left disembodied as a ghost, an eternally conscious bodiless perspective. She wants to look over to check where her physical form should be, but any change might disrupt the healing spell, or let the gods in.

She has to stay still.

It should be easy. She's disconnected from her body, unaware of any physical sensations. Seeing without blinking, without eyes. Existing without breathing. Increasingly, though, she has to fight to stay in the ritual space.

The metaphor shifts – she's not a ship anymore, she's just a sail, a square of cloth hung on a mast of bones, straining to contain the howling force of the Black Iron Gods. She's hauling Ongent's ship forward, and its anchor is skipping along the seabed, catching and tearing up rocks. Every time the anchor catches, the pressure on her becomes agonising, intolerable.

Her soul's fit to rip and burst.

She can't see Spar anymore. Somehow the light's so bright it's become all-encompassing darkness.

The winds howl through her. She feels something rip inside her, but she can't tell if it's in her body or her soul. Panic rises, and that's definitely physical, a desperate fluttering inside her chest and throat like a flock of trapped birds, her heart pounding.

She tries to ask the professor if they're done, if they've stopped the poison, but she can't find her way back to her mouth to speak it. How could she be heard over the wind, anyway, or the booming brass voices that ride on it, whooping and roaring and shouting as loud as earthquakes. There's more ripping.

"Hold steady," says the professor's voice, weirdly distorted. Cari feels Miren's arms around her, keeping her in place. His hands locking around her arms, gripping so tightly she guesses it would hurt if she could find her way back fully to her body. She tries to flinch away, but he won't let her move. He's screaming something in her ear, but she can't make out the words.

He's drawn her attention back to her physical form, though,

reminded her where she is. She clambers down towards her skull – that's the only way to describe it – towards the shell that no longer quite fits whatever her soul's become. She sees herself, for a moment, caught by Miren, and it reminds her instantly of that gate far underground, the one that imprisons all the defeated Ravellers. Horror held back on the far side.

She finds her throat, her mouth. "Stop," she shouts. Miren twists to hold her tighter, and she struggles against him.

The door smashes open, splintering. It's Rat, eyes blazing with murderous rage. He leaps straight towards Professor Ongent. Quick as a snake, Miren drops Cari and tackles the ghoul in mid-air. The pair roll across the floor. More people come in, Tammur and more thieves, grabbing at Rat, at Miren.

Ongent sways, unsteady, face flushed, contorted with rage. It's the first time she's ever seen him angry, and it's terrifying. He raises his hand, and lightning dances around it. He aims it at Rat.

Cari steps – stumbles, really – forward, positioning herself between the professor and the ghoul. "It's all right! We're done! We're done!"

And they are. Spar's sitting up, groaning, but breathing easily now. Hauling himself upright without wincing or too much stiffness. Better than she's ever seen him.

"We are not finished," hisses Ongent.

"I'm not doing that again," says Cari.

As if to underscore her words, a peal of thunder breaks right above the tenement, so loud it shakes the walls. It's the Black Iron Gods, Cari knows. Shaken into awareness by the spell, as surely as if they'd rung the bells with wild abandon. That awareness, that ability to act, fading now, expending its strength with terrible force above the Wash. There's a series of lesser thumps on the roof far above, that she knows are dead birds falling to earth, casualties of the wrath of blind gods. There will, she fears, be more deaths on the upper storeys, on the heights, caught when the gods reached down from the bell towers and spires of Holyhill to fumble around the rooftops of the Wash.

She's very, very glad they performed this ritual in the basement.

Miren shakes himself free from the crowd. Snarls at Rat, then rushes to his father's side. The fight and fire goes out of Ongent, and he flinches at the sound of thunder. Miren helps him stumble out.

The thieves crowd around Spar, cheering his resurrection. Tammur puffed out, like all this was his idea. They had to blackmail him to help, but now he's telling everyone that Spar's his protégé, his adopted son in all but name. He had to step in after Idge's sacrifice, you know.

Everyone stays clear of Carillon. The diagram at her feet is dead now, the runes and channels no longer afire with stolen divinity, but none of them are willing to cross it, none except Rat. He hovers nearby, studying Carillon for a moment, then makes this familiar, sharp-toothed grin and nods.

"Still you?" he asks.

"Not doing that again," she echoes to herself.

The trains have stopped in the city of Guerdon for the duration of the emergency. Tallowmen stand watch at all the stations to ensure no one enters. In the quality parts of the city, people lie sleepless in bed and listen for the sounds of riot and explosion. In the lower quarters, Tallowmen sweep the streets. Arresting gatherings of more than two, arresting anyone they deem suspicious or dangerous. They cordon off the refugee tenements and shanty towns, drag men out of tents and flophouses, march them off to the Alchemists' Quarter. They work with terrible industry, going section by section, building by building. Ensuring that one neighbourhood is processed without warning spreading to the next.

It works passably well for their first few sweeps, but there are other ways to move around the city. Sewer lines and tunnels, secret streets and secret doors, rooftops and walkways, crawls and wynds. Rumour trickles, then floods down these hidden channels: that the Tallowmen are taking refugees, taking known thieves, taking anyone they can to build their numbers. That they're looking for someone in particular – for Idge's son, some whisper. Others talk of a seer who prophesies ruin for the city, who knows everything the alchemists and parliament want to keep hidden.

They organise through these secret channels, crystallise around catalytic incidents. When the Tallowmen swarm around the much-beloved Holy Beggar and workmen demolish its spire, it becomes an assault on the people's faith. Even the newcomers, who worship a hundred other gods or none at all, know that if the new regime can attack one house of worship – a church of the Keepers! – their own temples must also be in danger. When one woman refuses to go with the Tallowmen and they murder her with knives, she is transmuted into a martyr and inspires a hundred others to resist.

The stopped trains, too, are a symbol of the alchemists' attempt to take control of the city. To break down and analyse Guerdon as they would any other compound, to dissect the city like a specimen sedated and bound on an operating table.

All the trains are stopped – except one line.

Trains rattle down that line that is not on any map. Down and down and down, the line spirals in a tight descent towards the under-city. It terminates at a misplaced, impossible station in the depths, near the ghoul kingdom under Gravehill.

One by one, the trains disgorge their passengers. The Crawling Ones disembark in human form, gliding with sinister grace in their black robes and porcelain face masks, speaking to one another like philosophers or judges, heads bowed as they talk of abstruse matters.

One by one, they come to a pit, a bowl that's already overflowing with fat white grave-worms. As each Crawling One reaches the lip of the bowl, they let robe and mask and human form fall away, and their woven-worms unravel and join the rest of the swarm. Now, they speak to one another in a more subtle language, a writhing unspeech of chemicals and slime and soul-fragments. Every worm in this vast throng grew fat on the dead of this city, competing with the ghouls for the unburnt dead. They are not psychopomps, carrying the souls down to the elder ghouls or onto some distant god. They have grown fat on soul-stuff, fat and powerful.

Sorcery ripples through the worm-mass.

At last, one more Crawling One arrives. This one does not surrender his human form; he kneels by the bowl and places one hand in the writhing mass. In his other hand, he clasps a scroll. His worm-fingers unknot, joining with the wriggling mass. His will contends with the rest.

For the Crawling Ones, there is no martyrdom. No symbols to accrete around. No higher meaning to be found. Only the cold declension of the memories of the unburied dead, only the chill hunger for more.

The newcomer is victorious. He imposes his will on the rest.

They rise from the bowl. Some return to the trains. Some follow their leader on another errand. But the rest, the great majority of the Crawling Ones, march down the lightless greenstone tunnels, towards the kingdom of the ghouls.

March to war.

CHAPTER THIRTY-ONE

"Coffee?" offers Tammur.

"Gods below, yes." Spar hasn't dared drink coffee in months. If he burnt his throat, it might calcify and throttle him. This morning, though, he feels like a new man. Even the ache in his right leg is gone.

Late morning, he mentally amends. He slept like the dead last night, and woke to find his bed littered with thousands of flakes of stone. He can still feel the trailing edge of the wave of sorcery, its heat sinking deep into his bones. It feels good, like strong alkahest.

Tammur sits down heavily, puffing, and starts pulling apart one of his pastries. "I don't intend to ask what happened last night. Sorcery is too perilous for my tastes, in general."

Spar nods and smiles inwardly. Rat mentioned that Tammur had been leching after some southerner woman who turned out to be a sorceress, and one of Heinreil's creatures to boot. What was her name? Myri? Clearly Tammur's still smarting from the betrayal. Spar files the name back in his memory in case he needs to bring Tammur down a little. Spar needs the older thief's reach and contacts – and his money – but he doesn't want to be Tammur's puppet either.

"I don't fully understand it either. I trust Carillon, though, and the healing spell worked." Spar flexes his arm as proof. The coffee tastes wonderful, and he can smell the fresh pastries, too. He wonders where Tammur got them – there's nowhere in the Wash that bakes such delicate sweet things, so he must have smuggled them in from elsewhere in town.

"And what about the university professor? Can you trust him?"

"I don't need to. We broke him out of the alchemists' gaol – he's not going to go back to them."

"He might buy a pardon by turning us in."

"He wants Cari and her gift." Spar doesn't mention the Black Iron Gods. "And the alchemists' price for forgiveness would be too high."

"The alchemists are going to be a problem," mutters Tammur. "I'd trade one Tallowman for six of Nabur's guards. We'll be lying low for years. Maybe move operations to the Silver Coast for a while."

"We're not going to abandon Guerdon. I think the alchemists have overreached themselves. People are scared of the Godswar, but that's still far away. Tallowmen on their doorstep, that's something else. The city's going to turn against the alchemists. We just need to keep our heads above water until it does."

"They have parliament. There's no one pushing back against them."

"Then we will," says Spar. "Cari!"

Carillon slips into the room. She looks exhausted, but brightens when she sees Spar – and the pastries. "Hey, breakfast!" She attacks the food like a starveling cat.

"No ill effects?"

"I had to haul Rat out before he killed Ongent, or Miren killed him, and I don't have a fucking clue what's going on there. I'd say that Rat's been weird since the Tower of Law, but . . . " She trails off, waves her hand in a gesture that encompasses her scarred face, her visions, the Black Iron Gods, and Spar's rejuvenation.

"I'll deal with him," says Spar. "Cari, I don't know Professor Ongent or Miren, but if you say that we need them—"

Cari snorts into her coffee. "You're under the delusion that I have a plan. I had a plan. You're it. Now it's all up to you."

"Thank you for the vote of confidence."

"Confidence and miraculous resurrection. A whole day or two extra of life, before we get shanked by Heinreil or the Tallowmen."

"Miss . . ." begins Tammur, and then hesitates.

"Just call me Cari," says Carillon, at the same time that Spar says "Thay". Tammur fails to conceal his surprise at the revelation of Cari's family name, but he passes over it.

"Miss Thay. As I was telling Spar, I've made contact with some members who I suppose we can count on in gutter court. Others are proving harder to find – they're in hiding from the Tallows, of course, and our normal lines of communication are broken. Can you use your sorcery to find them?"

The mid-morning light blazing in through the windows comes from a cloudless sky, but last night there were angry gods in the sky above the tenement. After the ritual, Ongent warned Cari not to risk drawing the attention of the Black Iron Gods again without his protective spells, to avoid agitiating them. Carillon takes a gulp of coffee.

"Sure. I'll need descriptions, and we'll need to wait until the hour changes . . . " She trails off again, suddenly remembering the silence of the morning. "I didn't hear the bells this morning." She had seen scaffolding around the Holy Beggar's spire, but there are many other churches in Guerdon. They can't all be silent. She needs them.

"The alchemists have stopped the city bells from ringing. They're having their Tallowmen announce curfew instead."

Tammur leans towards Carillon, studying her. "You need the bells for your gift, I take it."

"They make it easier. An awful lot easier." She takes a pastry and tears it to pieces, scattering the crumbs on her plate, shoving them around as if she can read the entrails. Her stomach has abruptly contracted to a sick knot. "Have you heard if they're doing anything else?"

"There are Tallowmen surrounding the Holy Beggar church. Some altercation with the church, I believe. The building's been deemed unsafe."

"Shit. Spar, they're taking the Black Iron Gods. They're going to recast them, use them as bombs. I saw them do it in the Alchemists' Quarter."

Spar looks at her quizzically. "Shit, I didn't tell you. I had a vision last night, before we did the ritual." Hastily, words tumbling over one another, she describes the sight of the Black Iron bells being reforged into weapons, and her conversation with Rosha.

"You turned her down?" asks Tammur.

"I pushed her off the fucking building."

"I've heard rumours about a battle in the Grena Valley. They're saying that the Haithi killed a goddess there with some sort of new weapon."

"God bombs," says Spar. "They're making bombs that can kill . . . gods, that can win the Godswar."

"And they need the bells to make these? That gives us leverage over the alchemists. They've got the Beggar surrounded, but there are other churches. If we get hold of some of the old bells maybe we can cut a deal, or sell them on."

"I'm more worried about reprisals. If the foreign gods know that Guerdon can kill them, then our neutrality won't mean a thing. The Godswar will come here. And Cari . . . what happens to you if they start blowing up the Black Iron Gods?"

"I don't know. Let's talk to the professor." Cari has to grip the side of the table to stand. Spar can tell she's exhausted beyond all measure. The last time he saw her that pale was when Rat brought her to his doorstep.

"This is not a secure base of operations," says Tammur. "Too many entrances, too many eyes. We should move to my warehouse on Hook Row. There's an—"

Cari interrupts him. "Upstairs room that you've fortified. I've seen it. Yeah, that'll work."

Spar shakes his head. "No. I'm not running or hiding anymore. We stay here and gather support until gutter court. People need to see I'm willing to stand my ground." He swirls the coffee around his cup. "They need to see I'm able to stand, too. We'll move to Hook Row when we're ready."

Shouts from outside. Running feet.

A ghoul. Not Rat; she's wearing a veil and a white frock. Silkpurse. "Heinreil's here," she says. "He says he wants to talk."

It's not just Heinreil, thinks Spar. He's brought an entourage. He recognises some of the faces – old thieves, in good standing with the Brotherhood. The sort of people Tammur hoped to sway. Others he doesn't know, but he guesses they're Brotherhood, too, from other districts. The sorceress, Myri, is at Heinreil's left hand. To his right, there's a big man, dark-skinned, with two crescent-shaped knives at his belt. Heinreil's replacement for the Fever Knight.

Spar realises that his side has unconsciously lined up in a mirror of Heinreil's group, with Cari facing Myri, him facing the bodyguard, and Tammur opposite Heinreil, like this is Tammur's challenge, not Spar's. He needs to break that pattern, so he steps forward and crosses the room. The bodyguard tenses, draws those knives, but Heinreil waves dismissively and the guard steps back.

"Spar," says Heinreil, "you're moving well."

"Like a new man." Spar towers above Heinreil. He's not sure if Cari's magical cure has diminished his plague-granted strength at all, but he's certain that he's still strong enough to smear the master across the cobblestones.

"Thanks be to the gods." Heinreil surveys the crowd opposite him. His eyes light on Cari, but keep moving, noting the faces arrayed against him.

"We shall settle this dispute at gutter court, master," says Tammur loudly, addressing the whole room.

"I'm not here to settle anything. I just want a quiet word with some of you."

Heinreil's voice is low, mild, but somehow reaches every corner of the room. He reaches up and grips Spar's shoulder. "We should have done this long before now, Spar. There's always been a place for you in the Brotherhood. Your father's place, even. We could have sorted all this quietly."

"You poisoned me when I was in prison," says Spar. He tries to keep his voice equally mild, but his throat turns his words into the grinding of stone.

"That's a lie! Who told you that I gave the order?"

"You set us up in the House of Law! Rat and Cari and me. You sent us as a distraction, hoping we'd get caught."

"The Tower was a mess, I'll give you that. They were only supposed to crack the damn vault open, not bring down the whole building. The second team let you down, but they paid with their lives. And the way I've heard it, you could have made it out – Rat did – only you stopped to go back for Carillon, and she lingered to pull one of the guards from the fire." Heinreil spins around and addresses Cari. Somehow, the conversation's shifted from a private word between him and Spar into a stage play, a performance for the assembled thieves of Guerdon. "That's admirable charity, Miss Thay, but not very wise."

"You didn't tell us about the second team," growled Spar.

"No, I didn't. I tell you what you need to know. I'm the damned guildmaster. And I'd have got you out of jail, too, once you came before a magistrate. I didn't poison you, and I didn't tell anyone to silence you, either. I watched Idge hold fast – and I have faith in his son."

There's cheering at that, from both sides of the room. Spar feels like he's standing on quicksand. "You're in league with the alchemists!" he shouts, and the room goes silent. "You blew up the Tower of Law for them. Maybe the Bell Rock, too – you planted the poison gas on that ship, the *Ammonite*, and your sea-witch magicked it out into the bay and ran it aground. How many died when the poison cloud rolled in? How many of our brothers and sisters got sent to the tallow vats?"

Heinreil's face contorts in fury. All his bonhomie falls away, and he spits out his words. "I'm surprised you didn't count 'em from the high ground you've made from the corpse of your father! Yes, I work with the alchemists. In case you haven't noticed, that's where the money is! I've put coin in the pocket of every one of you, haven't I? Kept the Brotherhood going even when the city tried to break us, time and time again! Seventy-four thieves, that's how many went into the tallow vats. It would have been one hundred and fifty if not for your fucking heroic gesture, and they'd have kept it at one hundred and fifty. Now they've got to come for us, you bloody idiot, now that you've hit them in their own bloody stronghold!"

"You admit that you sold us out," shouts Tammur.

"I tried to buy your safety! One hundred and fifty was the price I had to pay to ransom the rest of us."

"And there it is," says Spar. "Selling people. Selling us out. And you say you put coin in the pocket of all of us, like a few pennies are recompense for all the sufferings. My father wanted the Brotherhood to provide for the common folk. He saw that Guerdon was becoming ruled by greater forces, by craft guilds and churches and—"

"It's always been that way," says Heinreil. "And you're a fool if you think it can change."

"And he wanted the Brotherhood to be better than that. If the city wouldn't reform, then stealing was the only way to give people what they deserved, to get their fair share of the city's wealth. How many here – how many here think they have their fair share? How many here think the Brotherhood benefits them?" The room erupts in shouts, cheers, roars of approval or jeers of condemnation.

"Let's settle this now!" Tammur waves his hands for silence. "I call for a vote on who should lead. Speech! Speech!" He's playing kingmaker – or is he hoping for a tie so he can be crowned as a compromise?

"All right." Someone fetches a box for Heinreil, so he can be seen above the crowd. He's a head shorter than most, whereas Spar's inherited his father's lanky frame. A few voices in the back cheer as Heinreil climbs up, but far more are calling Spar's name, and even Myri and the others who arrived with the master look subdued.

"You know me. You know what I've done for you. If you think I've steered us true through the bad times, then vote for me. If you think I've done you wrong, or that children's stories of a city where we're all merry outlaws giving to the poor will serve you better, then vote for Spar." Heinreil stops, as if he's about to step down, then adds. "I knew Idge. I was there when they hanged him. And thank the gods they did, because if he'd stayed master we'd all have ended up in the noose or the vats. Great man, great thinker he was. But he was a fool, and if you follow his son, you're fools, too."

A few cheers, quickly swallowed by the voices calling for Spar. He steps forward, suddenly nervous. His tongue feels like it's turned to stone. He turns to look at the crowd. Thieves he's know all his life, thieves he grew up with. Strangers, newcomers to the city who arrived with nothing, and turned to the guild to survive. Those who've always been poor, and others who've slipped down into the Wash, cast down as the wheel of fortune turned and brought the alchemists up.

All of them look to him to speak for them, to fight for them. That was Idge's vision – to put a knife in the hands of the poor, to make the struggle a fair one.

Fragments of Idge's manuscript float through his mind, and he grabs them, starts reading out loud. He has no idea if what he's saying makes any sense at all, but he keeps talking until the crowd drowns him out.

"IDGESON! IDGESON! IDGESON!"

Blood pounds through his veins unhindered. He feels as though every inch of him is afire. Their cheers are alkahest to his soul, dissolving his fears, restoring new life to calcified dreams.

The crowd surges past him then, towards Tammur and the tallies.

Cari slips out of the crowd as soon as the speeches begin. Heinreil's presence here discomfits her. She was ready to face him at the gutter court in a day or two, when she had time to prepare. Her instinctive reaction to a surprise is to run away, and she can't run away now. Not when Spar's putting her plan into action. So, she flees as far as she can without leaving the hall, to the fringes of the crowd. Keeps an eye out for Rat or Miren; she wouldn't put it past Heinreil to have some sneak in the crowd here to stab her, and she's not armoured like Spar.

The silencing of the bells took her edge away. Now she's ragged

and unsure. Spar's voice rises above the roar of the crowd, talking
about how he'll fight back against the alchemists' guild, take back
the city from them, but she can't judge the mood of the crowd.
Even if they win here, though, she's not sure if that's enough. The
Wash is already on Spar's side, but the Wash isn't the whole city.
There are more thieves in other parts of the city, and they might
still be in Heinreil's pocket.

There, pushing through the crowd, is Heinreil's bodyguard.
Cari draws back into cover, worried that he might attack here.
but he's there just to open a path through the throng. It's Heinreil
who sidles up beside her. The man has slumped, become smaller
than he was when he walked in here. He looks very, very tired.

Her own knife is in her hand. His ribs are just there.

A truce, she reminds herself.

"Ach, Cari," says Heinreil. "Is it true you can see everyone's secrets?"

"Pretty much."

"Not mine, though." Dangling from his finger is her amulet,
her mother's amulet, on its silver chain.

Cari wore that amulet around her neck for twenty years, never
letting it go for an instant until Heinreil stole it from her. Now,
though, she sees it as if for the first time. Beneath the worn
enamel, it's made from some dark metal she was never able to
identify. It burns dark in her sight, blazing with hidden power.
She knows that it awoke at the same time she did, that it somehow
shared in her baptism at the Tower of Law.

She snatches for it, but he's faster, and it vanishes inside his
shirt. "I thought so. I may not have your gifts, but I knew there
was something off about you when I first caught your skinny
carcass stealing from me. I know all about you, Carillon Thay."

"You don't know anything. If you did, you wouldn't be dealing
with the alchemists."

"And what are you dealing with? You know where your visions come from, I think. We both made deals with devils." He sighs, rubs his head. He looks exhausted. "I didn't want this, you know. I loved Idge, and I took care of his son. They wanted to throw him out of the guild when he got sick. I stopped that. His sickness doesn't mean he's not useful. I mean, look at him. Look at him! Less than two weeks, and you've wounded *me*. That's a credit to you both."

"Give us another week, and we'll take you down."

"Counter-proposal. You convince Spar to withdraw his challenge. Blame Tammur for giving you bad advice – that's got the virtue of being true. Spar becomes my right-hand man, takes the Fever Knight's place. I'll protect you. We work together, get back—"

Spar finishes his speech, and the cheer is deafening. Tammur stands on a table, waves his arms and calls for a vote. The crowd surges forward, casting tokens into a pot. Little squares of black cloth for Heinreil. Stones, predictably, for Spar.

"And who'll protect you?" says Carillon. "Here's my proposal – give me back my amulet, and maybe we'll be merciful."

"That's that then." Heinreil shakes his head. "Can't say I didn't try."

He turns away from her, walks slowly towards the front door. Something terrible is going to happen, realises Cari, and she chases after him, knife in hand. Heinreil's bodyguard catches her, throws her against the wall. There's shouting, a scream. The bodyguard expertly pins her, one hand gripping her wrist so tightly that it goes numb in a flash, and she drops the knife. A curved blade against her throat. Foul breath in her ear. "Speak and you die, witch."

Then the call goes up. "Jacks! Jacks!" Through the front door, through the side door, wriggling in through windows, a waxy army, a tide of tallow. Hundreds of Tallowmen swarm into the tenement, so many that the few thieves watching the door are overwhelmed in an instant.

They blinded her for this, Cari realises. If the bells of the city hadn't been silenced, she might have seen the Tallowmen marching down from the Holy Beggar church, been able to warn Spar and the other thieves that the tenement wasn't safe anymore.

"Don't move!" shouts Heinreil to the thieves, "For fuck's sake, don't fight 'em, or they'll kill you where you stand. Everybody, fucking stay still."

Hundreds of pairs of eyes look to Spar. Fight, or . . .

It's not just thieves and cut-throats here, though. It's everyone who lives in the tenements, people like Mother Bleak and her grandchildren. The Cafstans. Others, wholly innocent. They're under the knife, too. Spar bows his head, extends his hands, and two Tallowmen spring forward. They bind his stony hands in cords of alchemical rope.

Another Tallowman stalks through the crowd. Shit, she recognises this one – his features were hardly distorted at all by the tallow vats, but his beard is now a solid mass of carved wax, and his right arm is weirdly smooth and featureless, like a baby's flesh.

Jere the thief-taker. Now Jere the Tallowman. He takes Cari away from Heinreil's bodyguard. He opens his mouth as if to speak to her, but all that comes out is a hissing noise and a spray of milky-yellow liquid that stings her eyes. She tries to break out of his grasp, but there's no escape. She looks around, praying she'll find something, some edge she can seize to her advantage. Rat to lead a counter-attack, or Miren to teleport in and steal her away. Or Ongent to throw some of his sorcery around.

But there's no sign of Miren, and Ongent's exhausted after healing Spar. And Rat's not here. She glimpses a hooded figure in the back of the crowd, then two, three more, but they came in with Heinreil. They stand back with their heads bowed, not getting involved.

More guards arrive – Tallowmen again, but dressed in the livery of the alchemists' guild, not ragged tunics of city-watch blue worn by the rest. They're the honour guard for Guildmistress Rosha. She follows them in, seemingly none the worse for having been stabbed and shoved off a building by Cari less than twenty-four hours earlier. Jere drags her along and drops her to the ground in front of Rosha.

Heinreil comes forward. As he passes Cari, he shrugs, as if to say *what else could I do?* She's close enough to hear what he says to Rosha.

"The bargain stands, right?" he says to her. "One hundred and fifty total for the vats, and I'll throw in Cari here as recompense for Spar's foolish attack on your guildhall. But you let me choose, and the Brotherhood stays. You'll call off your Tallowmen and end the curfew."

"Our bargain was made under very different circumstances, Heinreil. You must see that. When I first hired you, I needed to work in secret and avoid the attention of parliament, the watch and the church of the Keepers. Now . . . " she spreads her arms, indicating the scope of her triumph, "the church is in disarray, the watch is mine and no one is left in parliament to oppose the wisdom of my policies."

"Don't do this, Rosha," mutters Heinreil, glancing to his left.

"I think I must," she says, "after all, it would be terribly negligent for me to allow a notorious criminal like the head of the Brotherhood of Thieves to go free. It's only fitting, really. The last nail in Effro Kelkin's coffin."

"Don't. You've got what you want. You'll get the fucking Black Iron Bells, and good riddance to them. Take your victory and walk away."

"I thought you understood, Heinreil. It's a new era. All the old powers are obsolete."

"Ah, well." He reaches into his pocket and pulls out something small. Not the amulet – it's a worn stick of chalk. He flips it into the air, lets it fall to the grounds and break into a dozen shards at Rosha's feet. "Ah well," he says again, and then, under his breath: "Myri."

Cari tenses – Myri, she knows from her visions, is Heinreil's sorceress. The alchemists have their own counter-magics, though, dampening rods and ablative wards, so one spell caster isn't going to have any effect.

At the back of the room, the hooded figures shuck off their cloaks. Crawling Ones, every one of their ten thousand wormy mouths chanting an incantation. Lightning crashes through the crowd. Gobbets of hot wax explode, followed by sprays of red blood and meat as some unlucky thief gets in the way. The air is thick with sorcery.

It's not one spell caster. It's a crawling host of them, and they make Ongent's display at Desiderata Street look like a child throwing firecrackers.

A blast hits Tammur, and the old thief splits like an overstuffed sack, his fat belly bursting and his bones cracking as the spell smashes through him. Cari's half blinded when Guildmistress Rosha turns into a pillar of flame. Rosha doesn't scream as the blue fires engulf her, she just stands there glaring until her wax eyes slide down her cheeks and her head flops over into her shoulders.

The heat from the blast softens Jere's fingers, and Cari manages to wrench herself free. She runs forward, dodging around the bonfire that used to be Rosha. Unable to see, searching for the cooler air outside. *It's like the Tower of Law again*, she thinks as she stumbles forwards. Again, Heinreil's trapped her in the flames.

Hands grab at her, but she slips free. She gets a fleeting glimpse of Heinreil reaching for her, shouting at her, but she slashes at him with her knife and – joy of joys – she cuts him and he stumbles back. Other pursuers – Jere? – keep after her, though, so she puts her head down and sprints blindly, leaping over dismembered and splattered limbs, over dying thieves.

Somewhere in the carnage behind her, she hears Spar roaring. The cheers of the crowd have turned to screams, but he's taking charge, telling people where to run. There's a wall of burning Tallowmen and spell-flinging Crawling Ones between her and Spar, though, no way for her to return to his side.

The ground disappears beneath her pounding feet, and for an instant she's in free-fall. The canal. She twists in the air, but still hits the foul waters badly, knocking the wind out of her. Her lungs burn as she dives into the murk, trying to pull herself so deep that she'll leave no trace on the surface.

Later, she'll piece together what happened. Heinreil brought Crawling Ones with him, at least a dozen of the horrors, and each of them a powerful sorcerer. He kept them in reserve, hidden in the crowd or the nearby alleyways, until Rosha broke her word and tried to arrest him. And then the carnage began. The alchemists and Spar's thieves took the worst of the sorcerous blasts, but Heinreil's faction suffered, too. His new bodyguard, for example – they found his curved knives afterwards, next to a blackened skeleton with bones so leached of strength by the death-spells that they crumbled to dust when touched.

Later, much later, she'll walk numbly through the ruins of the tenement, looking at the devastation and knowing that she shares in the blame for this.

She swims underwater for as long as she can, and then another two three four strokes, pushing herself beyond her limits. Her hand closes on the slick stone of the far bank of the canal, and

Cari pulls herself out of the water. Otter-quick, she slithers up and runs into the welcoming shadows.

The tenement is an ant-hill that's been set on fire. Figures running this way and that, outlined against the lurid flames of sorcery. The surviving alchemists, not the Tallowmen but the ones that might be human, are fleeing back towards the Holy Beggar. Whistles and shouts – the watch are coming, battalions marching down from Queen's Point. Carriages rattling through the streets at speed, fleeing the scene. She can't tell how many of the thieves made it out or where Spar is, assuming he's still alive.

Tallowmen move through the darkness, searching for her. She can see the one that used to be Jere Taphson, his balding pate now gaping open and a candle flame burning within. He stands by the canal bank on the far side, bending low to the ground, searching for some sign of Cari. Then he flexes his wax legs and leaps across the canal, clearing it in a single bound.

Cari runs down the slope of the Wash, stumbling and slipping in the darkness. Her lungs, seared with toxic fumes from dying Tallowmen, ache as she gasps for breath. Trash slithers underfoot; wet cobbles betray her and she sprawls, picks herself up again.

Candlelight blazes on the rooftop to her left as a Tallowman – not Jere, a candle that was once a woman – leaps up there. The monster spots her and throws back its head, emitting this inhuman squeal like the sound you get when you quench hot iron. More lights close on her, outlining the shapes of the tenements and shacks around her in a dozen false dawns.

If she can make it into the tangle of buildings around Sumpwater Square, then she might be able to lose her pursuers. She knows those buildings well, Rat used to lair there and they're still dark: the Tallowmen haven't got there yet.

Shit. If she continues on this street, she'll pass close to the Church of St Storm. There were Tallowmen at the Holy Beggar church, and if there are more at St Storm she'll run right into them. She needs to get off this street.

Cari finds a low side wall and scales it. One of the Tallowmen tackles her when she's on top of the wall, trying to knock her down into the yard beyond. She twists out of the way, catching her foot on the rough bricks of the wall so she can hang upside down for an instant and the Tallowman misses her, cold mushy hands failing to find purchase on her. It lands heavily in the yard beyond, skidding into a chicken coop. The straw catches fire instantly, and the Tallowman shrieks as it finds itself caught in the burning coop. The hens squawk in terror, and the panicked beating of their wings gives Cari just enough time to cross the yard and scramble over the far wall before more Tallowmen arrive.

Darkness is her friend. There aren't any of the alchemists' monsters where it's dark. And right now, it's still dark over Sumpwater.

She runs down the narrow laneway behind the buildings, an old cattle run dating to when there were farms west of the city. She can hear Ongent's voice in the back of her mind, lecturing her about the history of the city. The bones of the past stick out, deforming the present.

She's nearly there when the cattle run floods with light. They've found her. Tallowmen race along atop the walls to her left and right, footsteps echoing faster than her pounding heart. A third one is behind her, closing on her.

And then Cari runs straight into what feels like an iron bar. She goes sprawling on her back, winded, stunned. Standing over her is a woman. Middle-aged, hefty, rags over what must be armour. Cari tries to speak, warn her to run, but she has no breath.

"No mistaking you, Carillon Thay," says the woman. "We've been looking for you. We need to have a talk, you and I."

The nearest Tallowman hisses and gestures for the woman to

depart, *now*, on penalty of whatever cruelty the Tallowman sees fit. The warrior woman draws her sword, gestures at them to strike.

"Right then. Come on."

Three Tallowmen leap. Three slashes with her fiery sword, and the cattle run is a mess of sticky yellow wax-gore. Cari catches her breath, tries to run, but a fourth swipe, this time with the flat of the blade, knocks her down again. The woman is terrifyingly fast and strong.

"Now, let's have that talk. I'm Aleena."

CHAPTER THIRTY-TWO

Eladora lies in bed, listening to the noises of the strange house. She hasn't slept despite her exhaustion. Every time she hears footsteps, she freezes, terrified that one of the men will come into this little attic room where they've stowed her.

At some unknown hour of the night – the city's bells are silent, so she has no idea how long she's lain here, cold and sleepless – she hears shouting, running feet. Angry voices raised as some other clandestine messenger arrives, another one of Sinter's seemingly endless network of spies. She strains her ears to hear, but gets only half the conversation. They speak of ghouls, of a war beneath the city streets. There's been some disaster in the deeps, some terrible defeat. At first, she thinks it must be the death of the elder ghoul in that tunnel under Holyhill, but then she clearly hears the word *Ravellers*.

Ravellers. Plural. More than one of those formless horrors.

The terror of that thought is enough to drive her from her bed. She crouches down and presses her ear to the floor. A memory of doing the same thing back in Wheldacre, listening for the clink of glasses in the living room that would tell her that her mother's devotions that night were found in a bottle instead of a holy book.

Sinter's voice is cold and quiet, speaking in an unfamiliar tone, ragged with fatigue. "What if they're already here? They steal faces. They could be anyone."

The whole city, like Desiderata Street.

The unfamiliar voice continues, describing testimony pieced together from the gibberings and yowlings of blood-crazed or wounded ghouls, retreating from the calamity below. Eladora listens to the nightmarish account of how the most secret sanctum of the ghouls was destroyed in a surprise attack by a cabal of sorcerers. The sorcerers killed many of the elder ghouls as they slumbered, then broke open an ancient seal in the depths that was maintained by the psychic vigilance of the elders. That seal, the ghouls say, holds back the formless hordes of the Ravellers, the shapeless host of the Black Iron Gods.

Now the ghouls are in retreat, and the Ravellers are free.

The other spies begin to speculate about who these sorcerers might be, but Sinter cuts them off. What, he asks, is the point of guessing? However it happened, the city is now under siege from below, a siege all the more deadly because it is unseen. The Ravellers may have already crawled up through the sewers and train tunnels and out onto the streets. Stealing form and faces from those unlucky enough to meet the slithering tide, taking shape like they took Bolind's form.

She still has that copy of *Sacred and Secular Architecture*. She drags it to a patch of moonlight that streams in through the narrow grimy window, opens it and looks at the too-familiar illustrations. Images of the city as it was in days of myth, when saint-heroes warred with monsters on the streets. The men in the room below are talking of stories, she tells herself, of history that's dead and buried. She can't reconcile those tales of sorcery and horror with the city of coffee shops and timetables and newspapers that she's known for years.

The voices fade away. Footsteps hurry down stairs and vanish in the slamming of doors. She can't tell if she's alone in the house, or if her remaining captors are merely very quiet.

The book is comforting, in its way. Reading it puts her in mind of days in the university. She hears Professor Ongent reading it to her, notes of amusement playing in his voice in counterpoint to the text, glossing every sentence with unspoken questions – *Are you sure you trust this? Where's the proof? What assumptions are you making about the past?* She loses herself in the book, even though she's read it hundreds of times. She hides so deep in the book, taking refuge behind the ink drawings of lost churches and the layered foundations of the city, that she doesn't notice any noises in the house below until it's too late.

The door creaks open, and the man's hand closes around her mouth. It's Lynche – one of Sinter's thieves – she recognises him as he drags her downstairs. They pass through the carnage of the meeting room, stepping over bodies. Isil lies there, a knife in her heart. Another corpse next to her, its face melted by some alchemical powder. Numb, Eladora can't muster the courage to struggle or run. The horrors pass over her, like she's just a glass mirror reflecting them but not containing them.

Somewhere upstairs in the house, she hears shouts, gunshots, a scream. Lynche hurries her out, glancing back as if expecting pursuit, but no rescuers appear. Out into the night air, and there's a carriage waiting for them, drawn by a pair of raptequines in harness. Lynche shoves her in. There are two other people in the carriage. One is a tattooed woman; her face is smeared with blood that's caked around her nose and mouth. Her head lolls back and forth, her eyes are vacant. The other is a small man who takes Eladora's hand and apologises to her.

"Now, girl, you don't want to do anything foolish like running, understand? The streets aren't safe tonight, of all nights."

He leans out and speaks to Lynche. "Make sure they're all dead.

No one on our trail, aye? Good lad." Lynche bows his head, draws a gun, and walks back into Sinter's labyrinthine house.

The smaller man bangs on the roof, and the carriage takes off with a jolt. The woman wakes up, too. She licks her stained teeth and gestures at the windows with outstretched fingers. Unseen forces crackle against the glass. A warding spell.

"I'll miss this city," says the man to himself, peering into the darkened streets outside. Eladora glimpses fires, sees dark shapes moving that could be running figures and could be other things. More gunshots in the distance behind them, and she guesses that Sinter is dead, or Lynche is, or maybe both of them.

"It's not . . . your fault," says the woman. The strain of maintaining the spell is evident; purple motes of light blaze inside her eyes, leaving little burn marks across the sclera, and her nose has begun to ooze blood again.

"Ach, I tried, Myri. I did try."

The man reaches into his shabby jacket and takes out an amulet on a silver chain. He dangles it from his finger for a moment, holding it like a dowsing crystal, then slips it back into his pocket.

"There we are," says Heinreil, "one last stop, and all's done."

Rat is the only living thing in the tenement.

How he knows this, he cannot articulate. But he is certain of it. He knows the sorcery unleashed by the Crawling Ones in their rescue of Heinreil killed dozens of people, that his namesake vermin lie cold and contorted behind the walls and floorboards, destroyed by the psychic shock wave of the spells. He knows everyone else has fled, leaving behind a charnel field.

He picks his way between the bodies on hoofed feet, stepping over puddles of molten wax. There, on the wall, a message written in chalk. THIS IS THE LAST. He sniffs. Heinreil's scent, although the smell no longer stirs anything in him. He is beyond petty grudges now.

He pauses at one broken waxwork and picks up the shattered, melted face of Guildmistress Rosha. With his new senses, he can feel a fading thread of sympathy, a cord of magic that connects this alchemical avatar to whatever remains of the woman who made it. Like him, she has changed under the oblique pressure of the divine, becoming something new.

He discards Rosha's face. The abstract thought sits awkwardly in his mind. A hunger, a literally spiritual hunger, takes precedence.

It is time to eat.

He cracks open the skull of one corpse. The ribcage of another. Sniffing around the third – the body of a pickpocket – he settles on eating only the hands, stripping the flesh from them like a chicken wing. The girl's hands were beautiful beneath the dirt and calluses, she lived on her deft movements. Even as the Crawling One's spell struck her and killed her, Rat knows that she curled to protect her precious hands.

The greatest portion of her soul was in her hands. Now it is in Rat.

Change begets change, like a tunnel collapse. One falling rock becomes a dirt rain, which becomes an avalanche that buries a whole subterranean city. The more he eats, the hungrier he grows. Changes that usually take centuries for a ghoul pass over him in minutes as he gorges himself on soul-stuff. He stops occasionally to vomit up a torrent of meat and bone, filling and purging his stomach more times than he can count. His hunger is not for flesh, but for soul-stuff, and the meat can be discarded. Still, he retains more than he disgorges. He passes through the feral stage of ghouldom in one grotesque feast of fresh carrion.

His skull cracks and reshapes. His body swells. Now the whole building shakes with his hoof steps, and his horns brush against the ceiling. A corpse-light builds in his yellowed eyes.

His ears itch. Irritated, he brushes against one of them, and it flakes off and falls to the ground.

He can hear clearly now, hear the yowling of his siblings under Gravehill. Their laments speak of terrible suffering. An enemy has brought death to the deathless. The Crawling Ones have made war upon the ghouls and slain the elders.

This conflict has been long in coming. Ghouls and Crawling Ones both feed upon the city's dead. Ghouls are psychopomps, consuming corpses and carrying the souls within away to the underworld, taking only a fraction of their spiritual energy and giving the rest to their elders. The worms are unquiet dead, consumers, capturing the soul entire. Both factions are parasites on the city above, profiting from its endless bounty of corpses that must not be given to the mad and hostile gods.

But the Crawling Ones have gone further. They have struck not only at the ghouls, but at the jail they guard. The church sends the dead down the corpse shafts as payment for the ghoul's watch over the prison of the Ravellers. Now that vigil is broken and the enemy is loose.

Rat's remade brain has no capacity for fear. He acknowledges the threat of the Ravellers with detached amusement.

He picks up another corpse. A man, old and fat, his thin beard scorched to cinders by some spell, his entrails spilled. Tammur, whispers some part of him that still remembers. He draws on that memory, examines it dispassionately, like a mortician laying out a body. The choicest cut of Tammur's soul, his residuum, will be in the tongue, he decides, and in the liver. He peels away the jaw bone with one hand and licks out the tongue. His claws, sharper than knives, find the liver. He can see it beneath the skin, pulsing and pregnant with accumulated spiritual energy.

He adds it to his own swollen stock and moves on to the next course of the feast.

As he picks apart the carcass of a child, he hears heavy footsteps. The scrape of a half-lame leg. Smells stone dust and the tang of alkahest. And nearby, a chittering, nervous voice. The rustle of fabric.

Silkpurse and Spar.

The Stone Man enters the room, makes a mouth noise. Rat tries to remember how human speech works, but the memories of language are deep in his brain, buried beneath the accumulated soul-stuff of countless dead. His tongue is now long and snake-like, adapted for licking grey matter out of skulls and sucking marrow out of bones, not speaking. The young ghoul – older than he is, he reminds himself – knows the customs of the surface.

She will speak for him, listen for him. He reaches out with his swollen soul and takes hold of her, just as the elder ghoul did to him.

"Rat . . . is that you?" asks Spar.

"I CONTAIN HIM." He makes Silkpurse chuckle, even though her face is a mask of horror behind her veils. "HE WAS . . . VERY SMALL."

Spar gestures at the stacked bones, at Rat's transformed body. "Why?"

Rat stretches and stands. He's taller than Spar now by more than three feet. He stalks towards the wreckage of the doorway.

"I . . . MY KIND SWORE TO GUARD THE PRISON GATES. NOW THE GATES ARE OPEN, AND THE ENEMY IS ABROAD. THEY COME FOR THEIR MASTERS, FOR THE BLACK IRON GODS." With an effortless swipe of one heavy claw, he flings the door aside and steps out into the city.

Again, he speaks through Silkpurse. "THEIR HERALD MUST BE DESTROYED. SHE IS THE KEY. WHEN SHE IS DEAD, I SHALL RETURN TO THE KINGDOM BELOW

AND AWAIT THE TRIBUTE OF MARROW. TELL WHOMEVER RULES ABOVE, BE THEY PRIEST OR KING OR WIZARD, THAT THE BARGAIN HOLDS AND THE GHOULS SHALL MAKE GOOD ON THEIR PART."

Silkpurse gasps and adds in a small voice. "Spar – help me! I'm going to kill Cari!"

Confused for a moment by the change, Spar glances at Silkpurse, and, in that instant of distraction, Rat leaps, hoofed legs carrying him to a rooftop in a single bound.

The city is strange to him, bathed in the piercingly bright light of stars, full of alien scents, bellows full of breathing. Hordes of living people instead of stacked corpses, their marrow hot and fresh. The buildings, too, are like living things, an infestation of architecture. His mental map of the city is a jumble, mixing three-hundred-year-old recollections of fighting a war on the streets with Rat's own more recent experiences, all covered with a patina of consumed memories and emotions. The ghoul lets his Rat-portion take the lead, calling up the boy's knowledge of the city and of his quarry.

Cari would run towards the sea. Towards the sea, or maybe to the lair she shared with Spar. Either way, she'd have crossed the canal, gone through Sumpwater. He follows, snorting in hurricane lungfuls of night air, seeing her scent.

There.

He cloaks himself in sorcery, becoming invisible as he scrambles from roof to roof, moving faster than a train.

North, across the city, he can smell the enemy rising from below. Slithering out of sewer grates and cellars. Taking faces and shapes, the first victims of this new war. The Ravellers are in Guerdon. He hears their alien calls across the aether, their plaintive prayers as they seek their high priestess, the Herald who will bring back their creator-gods.

But he is closer to the quarry, and he will kill her first.

CHAPTER THIRTY-THREE

"**Y**ou look like your cousin," says Aleena.

Cari double-takes at that; the last time anyone said that, she was six and Eladora was seven. "How do you know her?"

"Oh, I have my ways. She's safe, by the way – or at least as safe as any of us, which is fucking insecure." Aleena spots one waxen limb that's still animated, connected to a burning wick by a thin strand of matter. She squishes it beneath her boot. "What did you do last night?"

"Nothing."

"YE CANNOT DECEIVE ME, SPAWN OF DARKNESS," says Aleena. Her voice rolls off the walls of the alleyway and hammers Cari like the psychic assault of the bells. Cari staggers and half falls into the mud. Blood bursts from her nose and mouth. "SHIT, SORRY. WOULD YOU LOT FUCK OFF AND LET ME TALK normally. Gods below, sainthood's a bloody curse, isn't it?"

"You . . . " says Cari, still half stunned.

"Aye. Saint bloody Aleena, that's me. But my gods don't go around murderin' people, leastways if they don't deserve it. Tell me, girl, do you deserve it?" Aleena puts her sword's tip to Carillon's chest, pricking the skin right over her heart. "What were you doing last night?" she asks again.

"My friend Spar – he's a Stone Man. He was poisoned. Dying from it. We took the power of the Black Iron Gods and cured him." Cari wipes her mouth. "I didn't ask for this, all right? I never wanted to come back here, and I never wanted a bunch of evil bells to start screaming at me. But I use what I find."

Aleena's sword blazes with sudden fire. Cari screams as the hot blade scorches her skin, but Aleena whirls around and throws the sword across the cattle run. It bounces off the far wall and clatters down to land in a muddy puddle. Steam rises from the bubbling water.

"I'm not fucking killing her, understand! Not unless I fucking have to!" shouts Aleena to the sky. "Stupid idiots. I didn't mean to do that, see?" she says to Cari. Helps her up, brushes at the burn marks on her breast – and expertly takes Cari's dagger, with the grace of a pickpocket.

"Hey!"

"Not going to kill you. Not going to let you do aught stupid, either." Aleena grabs Cari by the arm and lifts the younger woman like she's a doll. "You say this ain't no fault of your own, and that's fair enough. But the alchemists want you for their god bombs, and that means I can't let you go. I'm going to take you to the church, see, to a man named Sinter. Now, you've met him before – the fucker tried to kill you day before yesterday at the university."

Cari remembers the ugly man and his accomplice who captured her. She'd be dead if it weren't for Miren's sudden appearance.

"Listen to me!" hisses Aleena. "He's not going to hurt you. I won't let him. You're under my protection, as long as I can manage it. But that means that you're not going to run off, or vanish again, all right? Or do something really stupid, like try to stick me with that little knife. The other option is that I hurt you now, knock you out or break your skinny legs to stop you escaping, and I don't want to do that. What's it's going to be?"

"I'll—" begins Cari.

"I can tell if you fucking lie, by the way."

"I'll go! Just don't break my arm!"

Aleena drops her again. "See, 'twern't so hard. Come on, those wax fuckers are everywhere tonight." She hands Cari back the knife.

Cari gingerly touches the burn on her chest. "God bombs . . . Rosha said something about them. I was going to ask Ongent about it. I saw them melting down the Black Iron bells. They're making god-killing weapons, right?"

"Aye. Fuck it, and the world could do with a few fewer gods, too, if you ask me. But it's the alchemists, and I wouldn't trust . . . "

Aleena trails off and looks back up the cattle run. The darkness behind them is moving. Someone screams, off in the distance, a scream that isn't so much suddenly cut off as suddenly elongated, distorted into a wail that falls into silence.

Both women are saints. Both are divinely blessed with perceptions beyond the merely human. Both, though, serve deities that are truncated or trammelled. Aleena's deities are Kept Gods, kept weak and starving and confused. Cari's the chosen saint of the Black Iron Gods, and they are trapped and limited in a quasi-material form. If either was a saint of another god, if either was one of the superhuman embodiments of divine madness and divine wrath that fight the Godswar, then the darkness would be no impediment to their eyes (if they still had eyes) and they would know, with the certainty of omniscience, what was coming towards them.

To Aleena, the tide of darkness runs with bile and fear. It is everything loathsome, everything that must be destroyed. Her mind floods with the memories of other saints, other heroes of Guerdon. She remembers marching with the peasant army three hundred years before, bolstered by the desperate strength of the gods. Granted the strength to tear down the old walls, the fire to burn her foes. She remembers putting the city to the sword. Remembers the place now called Mercy Square.

To Carillon, it isn't darkness. The things crawling there are her faceless children, her shapeless siblings. They blaze with an unearthly light, stolen faces swimming up from below only to be discarded again. They are her knives, made to flense the useless, confining flesh from her worshippers. Already, they are stained with blood, but they are ready to cleave through the city. Guerdon is fat and ripe for the slaughter, all those souls laden with the strength the gods need to break free of their prison-selves and make themselves anew. All she need do is take the power they offer.

"Ravellers," says Cari. "Run." She pulls at Aleena's arm. The other saint grabs the fallen sword, which blazes even brighter for a moment. She hesitates an instant, then sheathes the sword and nods.

"*Run*," Aleena agrees.

They race down the cattle run, hand in hand. Whenever Carillon slips or falters, Aleena drags her forward. They scramble through debris, over broken walls, still heading for the safety of Sumpwater Square.

Behind them, the Ravellers spread out or subdivide, if there's a distinction between the two actions for the shapeless horrors, slithering into every door and window as they fumble blindly for their missing mistress. They'll devour whoever they find, Carillon knows, eat people so they can learn how to make eyes to watch for her, tongues to ask for her, faces to hide behind while they search for her. Their devotion is worse than the malice of the Tallowmen.

Aleena finds a door, kicks it open with such force that the frame splinters and the lock's reduced to a twisted ruin. "Fucking cheap shit," she complains in the voice of an angel. They run upstairs, through a warren of narrow graffiti-scrawled corridors. Pale faces stare at them in confusion, shout at them or leer at them until they see Aleena's sword.

"Get inside!" roars Aleena. Some of them listen, for all the good it will do them. Cari shudders. What's a wooden door going to do against a Raveller? If their pursuers want, they can consume every living thing in Sumpwater Square in a matter of minutes.

They climb and turn, climb and turn, taking short cuts across narrow walkways suspended fifty feet above the alleyways, spanning the gaps between buildings. From this height, they can see much of the city. There are fires burning across Guerdon, roughly marking the boundaries of the Wash. More fires and smoke from Holyhill.

Cari stops and gasps for air. "Where are we running to?"

"Sinter," insists Aleena. "He's ... aw shite. That way." She points towards Holyhill, but there's chaos between there and Sumpwater Square. Pinpoint flames – Tallowmen, in huge numbers – and the explosions of alchemical weapons. Maybe they can make it. Maybe not.

"Have you tried telling these things to fuck off? You're the saint of the Black Iron Bastards, so their spawn should obey you." Aleena grabs Cari, points at a Raveller slithering through the alley below. "Try."

Cari stares at the Raveller and whispers a command to it, ordering it to stop. She can feel it with her mind, a slithering, slick presence. Her thoughts slide off it.

"I'm trying," she whispers to Aleena. "It's—"

The Raveller twists and springs, its liquid limbs scrambling up the brick wall of Sumpwater, scaling the fifty-foot gap between alley and walkway in an eye-blink. Cari draws her knife, slashes at it, but the blade has no effect on the monster. One tentacle lashes out, razor-sharp, slicing at Aleena. At the same time, a dozen faces sprout from the Raveller's central mass, and a dozen mouths speak in unison, crying out to Carillon in a language she doesn't recognise but, horribly, understands.

MOTHER/SISTER/GODDESS/HERALD/SLAVE!   WHY ARE YOU WOUNDED/UNRAVELLED? THERE IS A HOLE IN YOUR HEART! WHERE IS THE FULLNESS OF YOU? She thinks of the amulet dangling from Heinreil's hand.

Aleena's sword blazes as she swings it in an arc, lightning-fast, batting the Raveller away before it can find purchase on the bridge. The tentacle slashes at her side, cutting through her armour with ease, but skittering off her divinely toughened skin. Still, Aleena's blood splatters on the wood, mixing with the black ichor of the wounded Raveller.

"That way," insists Aleena, pushing Cari across the bridge. Cari stumbles forwards onto the adjoining rooftop, glancing back just in time to see Aleena jumping down into the alleyway. White light flares from below, and the Raveller screams in a dozen voices.

Cari runs across the roof, finds an open door and hurries through it. She's running blind, although memories of her divine visions give her the layout of the building, a patina of stolen knowledge. She knows that if she takes the left branch of this attic corridor, she'll end up at a staircase that goes down to ground level. She knows that a beggar froze to death in the alleyway outside last week, knows the sensation of uncanny warmth as the feeling left his fingers, then his legs, then his chest. She knows that the family who lived behind the door she just passed are from Lyrix, driven into exile when their dragon-matriarch was thrown down in one of that land's endless intrigues. She knows everything about them, but doesn't know if they're still alive – her information is two days out of date, and the city has changed so much in that time.

Out onto the street. The thought strikes her that she could keep going, lose herself in the Wash, but she dismisses it. She can't run from this – there's no place in the world far enough to hide from all the powers that want her dead, or worse than dead. The Tallowmen, the Ravellers, those wormy sorcerers – Cari realises that if she did run, she'd be praying for one of Heinreil's knife-men to find her, give her a human death instead of some divinely ordained horror.

Assuming that she can still have something like a natural death. She can feel the Black Iron Gods on the fringes of her mind, reaching for her in their muffled panic. Trying to drag her down with them. Cari's very soul is exposed.

She turns left, hurries around the building, clinging to the shadows. She can hear Aleena's heavy breathing in the alleyway, big snorts of air like a horse after a gallop. The Raveller's circling her, a one-monster ring of blades. Cari has her own knife, although what good can it do? Ordinary weapons don't seem to hurt the Ravellers.

Sister, it called her. She's got lots of small cuts on her hands from scrambling over walls and rubble. She pinches one, and blood wells out, black in the dim light. She takes her knife, drips blood over the blade.

Aleena grabs a broken wagon wheel and, holding it like a shield in front of her, advances towards the Raveller. The monster's tentacles whittle chunks from the wheel, but it's bound in iron and holds together, and those comparatively fragile tentacles wilt and burn when Aleena's fiery sword comes close to them. The Raveller changes form. Draws in on itself, gathering into a central mass. The creature's shape is a stolen one. Cari glimpses the outline of an old woman, bent and worn, in the midst of those writhing shadow-tentacles and teeth. Thicker, stronger tentacles sprout from this core, resilient enough to survive Aleena's flames.

One blow shatters the wagon wheel, drives Aleena to one knee.

But now Cari has a body to backstab. She darts forward and drives her bloody knife in, and it bites. The Raveller screams, more in surprise than pain, but Aleena takes the opening and the fiery sword goes in. The Raveller burns like a cobweb.

"It's going to be a lovely little stroll, getting to Sinter," mutters Aleena. The bravado has leaked out of her voice, and she's limping now, awkwardly favouring her right foot. "If we have to fight these bastards every step of the way." She spots the bloody knife, rolls her eyes. "Classy."

"Did you hear it speak," asks Cari, "when it jumped at us?"

"It screeched. Was that a language?"

"I could understand it, anyway. Fuck, I don't know. It said I was incomplete, and I think I know what it was talking about."

Aleena snorts. "Go on."

"There's this amulet. I got it from my mo— I've always had it, as long as I can remember. Heinreil – do you know Heinreil, the thief-master?" Nod. "He stole it from me when I arrived. I think that the amulet's connected to the Black Iron Gods somehow." Cari gestures with her hands, wishing she had the words. "Maybe that's why I'm incomplete. Maybe if I had that amulet again, I could do something about all this."

"An amulet. Black, about yea big, heavier than it should be?"

"You've seen it?"

Aleena smiles wanly. "Not in a long time, and not with my own eyes. But, aye, you have the right of it. It's connected to the Black Iron Gods. Heinreil has it – where's he?"

"I don't know," says Cari, "but we can find him."

She points south. Over the rooftops of the low terraces, the spire of St Storm rises at the edge of the harbour.

"That's a terrible idea," says Aleena, "but fuck it, lead on."

*

The carriage brings Eladora and her captors to the east side of Gravehill. It's quiet here, among the uninhabited tombs. The south and west of Gravehill has been colonised and reclaimed by the living, but here in the precincts of the east there are silent and empty monuments to the dead.

The modern tombs are cenotaphs, of course. The dead of the Keeper's church, which until recently meant all the dead of Guerdon, are not entombed as they were in centuries past, nor are they cremated; cremation is an honour now reserved for the priests and certain heroes and civic leaders. Common bodies are given into the care of the church, which disposes of them in euphemistic 'rites of disincarnation'. Most people never inquire further, for who wants to think about the corpse shafts carrying their grisly cargo into the depths?

Even though the tombs are empty now, they are a place to remember the dead and to pay homage – and another way for the wealthy families and guilds to compete with one another. Heinreil leads the two women up along a white gravel path, passing huge marble monuments emblazoned with guild crests and coats-of-arms. Ivy-covered stairs leading up to the tombs of forgotten kings.

"This way," he says, "I think." He points them along a branch of the path that runs through willow trees into the shade of the overhanging rock above. *He looks like a mourner*, thinks Eladora hazily, *with his slumped shoulders and black clothes and sad face*. Kidnappers should look crueller than that unhappy little man.

All the while, Myri stays close to Eladora. At times, the sorcerer looks so sick and exhausted that she's on the verge of falling over. Her coughs leave her hands stained with blood and soot, and her skin's flaking away in places – it flakes around her tattoos, leaving them perfectly intact and visible against the sores and rawness. She's still dangerous, though. Lethal sorcery slithers between her fingers and coils around her wrists like electric snakes, hissing at Eladora whenever she contemplates fleeing.

"Not much longer now," says Heinreil. "Want my cane?" he adds to Myri. She shakes her head.

"Where are we going?"

"Myri and I are leaving the city, I'm sorry to say. A man has to know when to leave the table, and my luck's turned. I'll come back, maybe, in a few years. And you, you're going to buy my retirement and a promise of safe passage. You and this." Silver flashes for an instant in his hand – an amulet. Cari's amulet.

"I won't tell you anything. I won't help—"

"Child, there's nothing you know that I don't, excepting a lot of academic twaddle."

The path twists to the left, and then left again sharply. They emerge onto a little shelf on the shoulder of Gravehill. The view is spectacular – from here, most of whole old city is visible. Castle Hill blocks Eladora's view of Queen's Point, but she can see Holyhill off to the left with its bright cathedrals, Glimmerside and beyond it, the smokes of the alchemists, and there's the heart of the city, Mercy Street and Venture Square and the Seamarket, and there's the ugly smear of the Wash.

She realises that she has seen this view before. She was younger, much younger. Shadow-sensation of clutching her mother's hand, the smell of incense.

She turns and looks at the nearest tomb. It's built recessed into the cliff wall, stately but reserved. Most of it is buried in the stone of the city's foundations, invisible but still utterly present. Engraved above the entrance is a symbol that Eladora saw almost every day when growing up – the crest of the Thay family.

Heinreil grabs her arm and pushes her ahead of him, towards the tomb. The doors open as they approach, and Eladora shrieks at the two masked faces waiting in the darkness. Crawling Ones.

Worms slither from the eye sockets of their white masks, and crawl from under their cowls.

"I've got business here," insists Heinreil. His grip on Eladora's arm is painfully tight; this close to the man, she can hear him breathing shallowly, feel his heart beating wildly. He's as scared as she is. His other hand creeps inside his jacket, closes on the amulet around his neck. Behind him, Myri sways back and forth muttering, the smell of sulphur filling the air as she engages in some sort of unseen magical contest with the Crawling Ones.

"You are expected," says one of the worm-men. She can't tell which one spoke, or if it was both of them in unison, or maybe there's only one creature here, divided into two roughly humanoid piles of worms. The Crawling Ones withdraw into the darkness.

"Don't want to be late for this appointment." Heinreil pushes her over the threshold, into the murk of the tomb. It's much colder in here. Her footing slides on the slimy floor. "Keep going, straight ahead," orders Heinreil. "I can see, I'll guide you."

Eladora walks blindly forwards into the impenetrable gloom, her free hand held out in front of her. She brushes against a corner, finds her way down the central corridor. She came this way as a child, after the death of the Thays – after Aleena and the other saints murdered them, she now knows – but she can't remember the layout of the tomb. She had to mind Cari, she recalls, a child tending a toddler amid the graves.

"This wasn't supposed to be how it went down," whispers Heinreil in her ear. "If you want to blame someone for you being here, blame the alchemists. Blame Rosha. We had it all worked out, she and I, and then she turned on me. You can't bloody trust a sorcerer, that's what I should have remembered. They've all got heads full of gods and magic; can't trust them to act sensibly, see. Can't rely on 'em for business. Not even Myri, I fear."

"Are you going to bury me here?" asks Eladora. At some point,

Heinreil's grip on her arm shifted, and now they're holding hands, like she held her mother's hand the last time she was here. She can almost smell her mother, and Myri's arcane mutterings behind them meld into half-remembered impressions of chanted prayers of mourning.

"Bury you? Where's the profit in that? I'm selling you, I'm afraid; you – and this amulet – command a high price tonight. Seller's market, although the other potential buyer has removed herself from contention on the grounds of attempting to turn me into a fucking candle. There are steps here – there we go."

She remembers the steps. They go down into the crypt, to the monument to the murdered Thays, empty of all those butchered and blasted corpses.

"Of course, it's young Carillon who's supposed to be here," continues Heinreil. "I thought she was just a cutpurse when she first showed up; I took her amulet to teach her a lesson about guild law. You don't steal from me, see? The amulet, though, she said she didn't steal it, that she got it from her mother. I did some digging, some divinations, even went to the House of Law and looked up the civic records – all those watchmen and magistrates, not to mention Jere Taphson, running around, and not a one of them recognised me. I didn't really know what I had, though, not until Nine Moons tried to steal the amulet from me over cards. That brought me here."

He stops without warning and shoves her to the left. She stumbles into darkness. A door shuts behind her, and Eladora's all alone in the pitch blackness. She flings herself back at the door, finds it closed and locked. Her fingers scrabble at it, at the stones around it. The room she's in is small, barely big enough for her and a small plinth bearing a little casket. Gods below, they've locked her in a child's tomb, some ancient anteroom to the main crypt.

She doesn't scream. She's too numb. She stumbles back to the door, presses her ear against it. She can dimly hear Heinreil's voice, but can't make out the words.

An eternity passes in the darkness; a hundred heartbeats. Then she hears footsteps outside again, muffled grunts of effort. Heinreil and Myri, carrying something heavy between them, labouring under the burden. Heinreil pauses outside the door, knocks on it with one knee.

"For what it's worth, miss, you have my apologies."

And then he's gone. She wants to scream after him, to beg him to take her with him, but she's not going to break like that. She doesn't know why she's here, but she suddenly guesses who's really to blame her for her being here. Eladora Thay stands up straight, with good posture. She can't see herself, but she runs her fingers through her tangled hair, wipes her face as best she can. The scholar's robes she's wearing are not the most appropriate attire for such a reunion, but this is a tomb, not the mansion in Bryn Avane.

She's not being sold, she's being ransomed.

CHAPTER THIRTY-FOUR

The square outside St Storm is crowded. Three Tallowmen, heads blazing, stand in a line across the steps of the church, blocking the entrance. Cari spots the beginnings of a scaffolding at one side of the building, and overhead workmen have knocked a hasty hole in the centuries-old stone of the bell tower. Fear of damaging the imprisoned deity in the bell, maybe, or fear of inciting the already terrified crowd.

"More inside," whispers Cari to Aleena, pointing at a stained-glass window that's illuminated from behind. St Storm, his protective hands guarding the fleets of Guerdon. There's another Tallowman inside the church, maybe more than one.

"Over here." Aleena leads Cari around the crowd, towards a townhouse just off the square. Technically, St Storm's part of the Wash, but this is a gentrified neighbourhood, where the quality live. Lower Queen's Point. The one time Cari was here before, she was just off the boat, sick as a dog and reduced to begging and pickpocketing. She thinks she might have asked for alms at the very house that Aleena brings her to.

Aleena hammers at the door. "Hunnic, open up."

A bolt's drawn back, then another. The door opens a crack – a priest, soft features hidden behind a beard that doesn't sit well on his face. A palsy in his hand, which shakes with more than fear. "Aleena, is that you? Thank the gods! Come in, quick, before they see you."

Hunnic, Cari quickly gathers, is one of the priests of St Storm. He babbles, a flood of irrelevant questions about Patros Almech and the Tallowmen and the city watch, but Aleena cuts him short. "We need to get into the church. Up to the bell tower."

"Those damnable alchemists and their Tallowmen – they're vandals. They've smashed up the spire! What's hidden up there?"

"A god," says Cari. No sense in lying to the man now.

"Never mind that," snaps Aleena. "We need to get up there, and I'm too fucking tired to take on all those waxworks at once. Can we take them by surprise?"

"There's another entrance to the crypts," says Hunnic. "It comes out right at the base of the bell tower." Cari figured as much. The city's crisscrossed with old tunnels and ghoul-runs, a smuggler's paradise, although many of them are bricked up or warded. She used to think that the watch did it, to stop the thieves' guild using the underways. Now, she knows what they were trying to keep out, and that it's much too late. The Ravellers are already in the city.

Hunnic shows them to the crypt entrance. After opening it, he gestures down the alleyway towards the crowd. "What should I do? They keep asking me to make the alchemists open the church. They're terrified. But I don't – I mean, those Tallowmen won't listen to me."

"Honestly," says Aleena. "Lead 'em' down to the harbour. There's every chance that everyone in Guerdon will be dead by dawn. Get out while you still can. Someone may as well make it out alive."

*

As promised, the passage leads through the crypt to a trap-door below the bell tower. Cari peeks up, sees one Tallowman patrolling the inside of the church, smells another up the stairs. Aleena pulls her back down.

"Stay here." And with that she's gone, moving quietly for all her size and armour. *Fuck her*, thinks Cari. Aleena may say she's tired, but she's got divine blessings keeping her going. Strength and speed and stamina and a fiery sword – proper sainthood, a taste of divinity, unlike Cari's blessings of migraines and unwanted visions.

She could have all that, though, if she let the Black Iron Gods in. They'd exalt her if she let them; she's seen it in visions. Somewhere, up above in the city, there's a whole army of horrors slithering through the streets looking for her, eager to make her their queen. She toys with the idea of letting them do it, the same way she used to stare into the ocean and thing about jumping overboard in a storm. All the people who want to control or kill her – Heinreil, the alchemists, even Ongent – all swept away in the hurricane of her wrath. The tyrant queen of Guerdon, terrible and beautiful. Make the streets run red with the blood of her enemies. Cast down the Kept Gods, and let the Black Iron Gods rule once more.

She imagines what would happen if she gave in; from what she's gathered, there wouldn't be much of her left if she opened herself to full sainthood. She'd be hollowed out like a Tallowman, her soul consumed in its union with the Black Iron Gods. She imagines Spar looking at her with horror and disappointment in his eyes. It can't happen. So, keep fighting.

She shifts uncomfortably; suddenly, she's thinking of Miren, and a foul-smelling crypt really isn't the place for such fantasies. He could suddenly appear here, take her away from all this, remind her that she's got a physical body, reknit flesh and soul.

Some part of her mind presses on her, flooding her conscious mind with memories of that night in that attic room. The images drive away the chill of the crypt, help her fend off thoughts of the Black Iron Gods, and of what Aleena said earlier. *Everyone will be dead by dawn. Get out while you still can.*

Sex and death; sex as a hedge against oblivion. She'd rather lose herself in screwing Miren than go through that terrifying spiritual union again. Ongent's spell nearly killed her, and now Aleena wants her to try again only without all the magical protections. She can certainly command the Ravellers – by becoming the thing they want her to be. They'll bow to their idiot goddess-queen, the mindless puppet of the Black Iron Gods. She doesn't know if she can control them on her own terms.

The amulet protected Heinreil from her visions. Maybe, she hopes, it'll protect her from the gods. That must be why her mother sent it to her. She wonders where her mother got the amulet. Maybe she too was a thief, robbing some ancient temple, before she got involved with the Thays and their bloody fate. If you could only give your child one gift – and you knew what was going to happen to her, then surely you'd send her protection. The embodiment of a mother's love, something to shield and anchor her again the darkness. It's a comforting thought.

Or she could run. Slip out of the crypt, join Hunnic on his way down to the harbour. The only things keeping her in the city were Spar, Rat and her stolen amulet, and the amulet's already lost to her. For all she knows, Spar and Rat are dead, too, along with her scheme of taking revenge on Heinreil by stealing control of the thieves' guild. Why not leave? She ran away from Guerdon years ago and never intended to return, even though she sometimes wondered about her family and her origins. Now she knows more than enough, and it's nothing good. She could leave again.

But you can know, she reminds herself. You can find out

if Spar and Rat made it out of that building. You can still find Heinreil.

The trapdoor opens again. Aleena's standing there. She scrapes wax off the blade of her sword. "Come on, one of the bastard's screeched before I got to him, so we may only have a few minutes before more come. Or Ravellers, for that matter."

They climb the narrow spiral staircase that winds steeply around the core of the spire. Cari quickly loses track of the number of steps. This spire is much, much taller than the modest belfry of the Holy Beggar.

Aleena stops when they're nearly at the top. Readies her sword, swinging it to judge the distance available for head-chopping in these close quarters. "In case we get company," she mutters, "I'll keep watch here. You go on. Be fucking quick."

Cari emerges into the cold air. Wind whistles in through the hole the alchemists have blasted in the side of the spire. They've knocked through part of the floor, too, leaving only a narrow wooden beam above a vertiginous drop straight down to the church floor below. The Black Iron Bell is still intact, but they've wrapped chains around the bar it hangs from to keep it from moving.

The padlock holding them in place is easy to pick. She lets the chains slither down through a hole, lets them slip into the void and tumble until they clatter like thunder far below. The bell's free now.

Cari takes one last look at the city spread out before her with her own mortal eyes, then gives the Black Iron God a shove.

The sound from the bell ringing right next to her should be deafening.

Maybe it is. Cari's not in her body to hear it.

She glimpses her mortal form as she soars above the city, borne aloft by the fumbling consciousness of the Black Iron Gods. There, beneath her, she sees the city as a tapestry. Thousands of people, thousands of souls, all linked together by shining threads of life. The Ravellers are there, too, like a black stain, a parasitical mould on the fabric of life. One by one, they will tease out those shining threads and weave them into a new form. They will consume all life in the city and fashion those stolen lives into a shape for the gods. The Ravellers cannot be counted, cannot be numbered as they rise from the depths, slithering out of drains and tunnels and subway stations. They sense Cari's presence as her awareness passes over the city, but they don't obey her. They see her as a peer, as another tool for their Black Iron masters.

The Ravellers are – so far – confined to the older parts of the city. She doesn't see any as she passes over Castle Hill, and Gravehill is mostly clear, too. The north Wash, the slopes of Glimmerside, the central district around Venture Square crawl with the monsters, but they haven't pushed into the rest of the city yet. They don't need to – every soul they consume is fuel for the gods, and there are souls enough in this thronged city to sate the thirst of the Black Iron Gods as they rebuild themselves.

Not yet, thinks some fragment of Carillon, even as another part of her – an alien aspect that she is aware of only in this liminal state – looks forward eagerly to that destiny. Part of her wants to be the channel for the Black Iron Gods.

Show me the amulet, she tries to say, but it's like shouting into a storm and she can't muster her thoughts against the hurricane of the Black Iron Gods in their panic and eager wrath. She has to snatch images, memory-fragments, as she's blown hither and yon across the rooftops. Her perceptions are a sickening kaleidoscope of impossible sensations and visions. One moment she feels the cold tendrils of a Raveller stalking across the lead-tile scales of her back as she shares the feelings of the Holy Beggar church; an instant later she's watching people flee the advancing line of Tallowmen – their waxy skin still soft and unformed, candles fresh from the mould as the alchemists desperately field reinforcements. She's a bird, an old woman, a drainpipe, she's a nameless tunnel under Holyhill. Subways tunnels are veins beneath her skin. The slaughter in the Wash is blood pumping through her heart.

She rallies before she's entirely swept away. Spar. Rat. Her friends. She can find her friends. She seizes onto them as anchors.

There – in the cattle run where Aleena fought the Tallowmen. A ghoul, an old one. Hooves scraping through the wax, horned brow heavy with the weight of sorcery. It's much too old and big to be Rat, but as her awareness passes over it, it raises its face to the rain clouds above and sees her. Rat's yellow eyes stare out of the skinned-horse face of an elder ghoul.

Startled, Cari loses her mental grip, and her awareness is blown away again. Suddenly, she's burning, her flesh melting as her bones glow white-hot. Enclosed spaces, walkways, the crackling of elemental sorcery – but familiar. She's in the alchemist's furnaces; she sees them melting her down to make another god bomb. She's the bell of Bell Rock, screaming a lament for her shattered sibling even as her lungs fill with molten metal. (Cari is distantly aware that her real body – her original body, her mortal form, that little scrap of meat and skin – is lying on the cold stone of a distant belfry. Blessed shock of coolness, pushing back against the intolerable heat.)

Rosha is there, directing the construction of a second god bomb. Cari tastes the fear of the Black Iron Gods. She's known them in their anger and in their confusion and in their frustration before, but tonight they're afraid. Until now, the rule was that Gods cannot be killed, only diminished. Death was for mortals. That's not true anymore.

Detonate a god bomb over Guerdon, and what happens? An invisible explosion. Spiritual annihilation. The Black Iron Gods die – even the ones still locked in bell form. There wouldn't be any more god bombs after that, not unless the alchemists find another pantheon that's been trapped in a form that can be easily weaponised. The Ravellers vanish, saving the city. It might be worth it for Rosha but it'd be a huge gamble, especially as she'd risk killing the Kept Gods, too. Guerdon would be spiritually defenceless in the Godswar. Cari doesn't know what would be left of her if that bomb went off – how much of her soul is divine at this point, and how much is mortal. She strongly doubts she'd survive the blast.

The Bell Rock god succumbs to the fire, and Cari's off again. Spar – she sees Spar, in the warehouse off Hook Row. He's still alive. Her emotion makes her buoyant and she soars even higher above the city. She shouts, or wants to shout, but her body is far behind and far away.

Show me Heinreil. It's never worked before, but it works this time. He's in a carriage, rattling down the road that runs from Gravehill to the Dowager Gate. He's leaving the city. His raptequines strain against their harnesses as the coach driver whips them into a frenzy. Heinreil's out of the old city, which means he's out of danger. He's got Myri the sorceress and a host of Crawling Ones to protect him from any danger, mundane or supernatural.

Almost any danger. Cari puts forth her power, reaching for the tiny angry mind of the raptequine on the right. She takes the creature's fierce, frightened soul and squeezes it. The raptequine screeches and convulses, jerking the carriage to the right and ploughing straight into a stone wall. Cari laughs with the voice of thunder as her enemy's dashed against the stone, his body crushed between the wall and the chest of gold.

But he didn't have the amulet.

Cari backtracks, searching for blind spots. And then—

"Eladora?" Cari senses rather than sees her cousin – a momentary impression of rustling robes, books, sniffy disapproval – before she's swatted out of the sky by a blast of psychic force. She's batted clean across the city, back into her body, her soul hitting it with such force it leaves bruises all across her skin. The last thing she sees before the bell tolls a second time is the host of Ravellers opening a thousand stolen mouths in a hymn of homage.

Spar lumbers a few steps forward, but Rat's gone. The ghoul's as fast as ever, despite having swollen to three times his previous size. Spar shakes his head, unable to believe the transformation in his friend. It's even stranger than Cari's supernatural abilities – he's known Rat for years, and the ghoul was always a creature of the alleys and gutters, as far removed from the realm of gods and demons as anyone could be in this age.

He helps Silkpurse to her feet. She frantically smoothes her crumpled dress, gnarled fingers plucking at the fabric to hide its rents and tears. "Is my face all right?" she asks, wiping away a slimy liquid that might be the ghoulish equivalent of a tear.

"It's fine. Are you all right?"

She nods. "The elders can't speak any tongue you'd know, so they borrow the mouths of younger ghouls. I've done it before. It's not too bad."

"Rat's not an elder – can he change back? Can I make him change back?"

"I don't know what he is, or who else is in there," admits Silkpurse. "I warned him, I told him, I did! Stay in the light, that's what I said." She presses her hands to her face again, keening. Spar looks closely – are her features slightly more canine, less human, than they were before Rat spoke through her? He can't tell, and there's no time to waste.

"Go after him. Maybe get ahead of him and warn Cari, or make him see sense . . . do what you can. I'll go and find other help."

Silkpurse looks down at the dress, a ballgown salvaged from some charity shop or Bryn Avane midden, and bobs her head in acknowledgement. She rips at the hem of the garment, exposing her hoofed goat legs, carefully shorn of hair. She skitters up a drainpipe and sprints across rooftops, following the course Rat took.

Spar retreats from the tenement the same way he went earlier, out through a passageway to an adjoining building made by some enterprising thieves in years gone by. It's said in the better parts of Guerdon that you can walk from one side of the Wash to the other without setting foot outdoors if you know all the thief runs. That's not entirely true, as the watch closed off many of the underground passageways, but Spar knows the surviving routes.

The Tallowmen don't, which is a small mercy. He got as many thieves out of the building as he could when Rosha and her monsters attacked. Still, his stony feet are now caked with the blood of his friends. So many dead, Spar's heart is numb as a rock. He walks blindly, one foot in front of another in an automaton's pace. All that's left now is damage control, triage, seeing which parts of his universe are dead and which are dying and calcifying. He's already cut away his dream of taking the Brotherhood from Heinreil – all that's left now is saving the Brotherhood.

He tramples through a pile of papers. Blinking, he recognises his own handwriting. It's his father's manuscript, scattered and torn. He'd left it in his room in the tenement. The Tallowmen must have raided it before they were attacked in their turn by the Crawling One sorcerers. Instinctively, he's about to move on, but he remembers that, thanks to Ongent's healing spell, he's got the flexibility to consider picking something up off the floor.

He bends laboriously and scoops up the nearest page, reading it like an oracle. It's Idge's writing – from the cramped script, it must have been written in the jail cell before they hanged him.

Change is simultaneously a fast and a slow process. The great forces of history are slow-moving and unnoticed by those surrounded by them, visible only in hindsight where they appear inevitable.

The next few lines are torn and missing. Whatever insight Idge had is lost.

But there will come a time when the city is ready for freedom, and on that day there must be an inciting incident to reify that force, to make real the possibility of hope.

Idge thought that by defying the city authorities, he was committing a symbolic act that could awaken the latent desire for freedom and justice. He was wrong; the conditions weren't right. His death was a squib, a spark that failed to ignite a greater fire. Spar never even got a chance to try, and now hope's receding into the conceptual realm of Idge's unreal historical forces. Spar crumples up the paper and drops it.

Miren, he thinks. The boy has power, wherever it comes from. He can teleport – perhaps he can find Cari before Rat does. Spar sent Miren and his father up to the Hook Row warehouse, the nearest refuge to the tenement. He turns that way, hurrying through alleyways and over a rickety bridge that crosses the canal.

The absence of Tallowmen confuses him. Even if the Crawling Ones' ambush destroyed the waxworks that Rosha brought with her, the alchemists have hundreds more. There must be some emergency elsewhere in the city, some other devilry of the Crawling Ones that he's unaware of. The street is weirdly deserted; he glimpses faces at windows, barred doors. Even the taverns are mostly shut. Everyone in the city is hunkered down, hiding from the alchemists' curfew, but there aren't any Tallowmen around to enforce it.

A scream breaks the silence, off in the distance. Without thinking, Spar follows the sound. Ahead, a door bursts open and a woman stumbles out, weeping. She points behind her, through the open door, and there Spar sees another woman, older, a mother or aunt perhaps judging from the clear resemblance.

"It's not Janny," cries the weeping woman. "It's not her."

Unsure, Spar positions himself between the woman and the doorway. The older woman – Janny? – doesn't react. She studies Spar with curiosity, tilting her head as she watches him move. Then she dissolves into a thrashing mess of slime and darkness, and lashes out at him with one tentacle. It's razor-sharp and driven with superhuman strength, and cuts a deep gash in Spar's stony hide, but doesn't wound what remains of his living flesh. Another tentacle sprouts from the thing's central mass, this one probing one of the gaps between plates. It's shockingly cold as it *tastes* him. The pain will come later. The black tentacle shivers and recoils, the last third of it turning grey and withering to dust.

Spar registers that strange reaction even as he's reaching up to wrench the lintel out of the wall. The building collapses down, trapping the Raveller in the wreckage.

The younger woman shrieks in horror. Spar can't tell if she's appalled by the thing that stole her mother's face, or the destruction of her home, or the hideous screeching made by the trapped Raveller. She claws at her face and runs, low to the ground like a frightened, witless animal. Spar stares after her, unsure of what he can do. From what Cari told him, no weapon he has to hand can affect the Raveller. All he can do is pull more of the building down on it, burying it in a cairn of rubble, a stony prison, until he can't hear its screeching anymore.

He turns his face towards Hook Row.

CHAPTER THIRTY-FIVE

Rat hears the little ghoul scrambling behind him, struggling to keep him in sight. He casts his mind back towards her. He's already spoken through her, so they are connected. A grave-dug channel exists between them that he can reopen, even at this distance.

WHY DO YOU PURSUE, FOOLISH CHILD?

The part of him that is still Rat can still think in human language, but he can feel that capacity slipping away from him as he's buried by his larger self, by his elder ghoul self that roars and buzzes and howls with the energy of two hundred freshly eaten souls. That part can't speak, but expresses his irritation at Silkpurse's meddling through a psychic pulse of annoyance that says much the same thing.

The question shoots through Rat's mind, and an instant later he hears it gasped behind him, as Silkpurse unwillingly says the words even as she struggles up another tile-shod roof.

"I want. To. Help," says Silkpurse.

The elder ghoul pauses as it rifles through her mind. Memories – crawling out of Gravehill, stinging sunlight on dark-adjusted eyes. A life in the alleys, scavenging for scraps. Not all the dead in Guerdon ended up in the corpse shafts, especially in the Wash; back-alley knifings, sea-swollen drowned washed up on the shore, old women forgotten in attic rooms, Silkpurse found them all. Running to hide from the watch. Hiding in the pre-dawn half-light, watching a serving girl hang clothes on a line, admiring the way the fabric billowed as the breeze caught it. Admiring the way the woman turned her face up to the light.

It's incomprehensible to the elder ghoul. In his labyrinthine, sorcery drenched mind, ghouls exist only in the dark tunnels below. He cannot grasp Silkpurse's desire to stay on the surface. She dresses herself in the clothing of the surface folk, hides her face, denies her impulses and her destiny. None of that is *useful*. It doesn't help her feed on carrion, or grow strong so that she too might in some future century become like him, an elder, and ascend a hexagonal pedestal in the lowest cavern.

She is irrelevant to him, but still he finds himself stopping. He sinks his claws into the brickwork of a chimney and swings around, hooves finding purchase like a goat on the rooftop eaves. He hangs out over the street, tasting the city's fear as he waits for the younger ghoul to catch up. She staggers up the rooftop and sinks down to straddle the ridgeline.

WHAT ASSISTANCE CAN YOU OFFER?

"I want," says Silkpurse, picking her words like stepping stones across a raging river, "to help Rat."

I AM RAT.

"All right. You told me yesterday – back when you could speak for yourself – that you wanted to stay on the surface. Said you didn't want to be anyone's servant. You want to be free to do as you want, same as anyone else with half a brain." She cringes, aware that she's very close to condemning the rules of the ghouls right in front of an elder, but she presses on. "You've got friends. Surface-folk friends. Spar and Cari. Do you know how lucky you are? I went years without talking to anyone, without a kind world or a restful night. Having friends is a blessing for a ghoul."

The elder ghoul speaks though Silkpurse again, seizing her mouth roughly. She bites her lip as she resists the psychic command, but to no avail. The grave-dark voice grinds from her throat.

IF THE HERALD LIVES, ALL THOSE IN THE CITY ABOVE AND BELOW PERISH. He uses a ghoul-word for *perish*, husk-death, which she's heard before only when discussing the bodies taken by the Crawling Ones. A body whose soul has been consumed before the ghouls get to it.

"But she ain't this herald – or if she is, it's just something they've put on her, same way you ain't an elder. We can choose who we are, Rat. You don't have to be what a dead ghoul tells you to be."

CHILD, YOU KNOW NOTHING OF DEATH. The elder ghoul gurgles a laugh, and shares a glimpse of the slaughter in the ghoul kingdom. Silkpurse convulses as her brain floods with visions; sorcerous blasts explode in the caverns, shredding hundreds of ghouls. The host of the Crawling Ones took them by surprise, a sudden invasion of the ghouls' warren. She shares the memory of an elder squatting on his throne, locked in eternal contemplation of the great seal. Unable to move, limbs old and withered and soul caught in the spell, unable to do anything except watch as the worms closed in. The elders are murdered. The younger ghouls scatter and flee.

Rat watches Silkpurse slide towards the edge of the roof, tangling roof slates and debris in her ragged skirt. Her eyes roll back into her head, her mouth foams with greenish spittle. Rat grabs one of her thrashing limbs and drags her up to a chimney, then wedges her in place. The fit passes and she goes limp.

She can offer nothing to him. He turns back to the hunt. The Herald went this way. He can smell Cari.

He follows her trail down an old cattle run. Things made of wax found her there – *Tallowmen*, Rat reminds himself, but the other half of him is dominant again, and he has to fight to recall the city as it is now, as opposed to the city he remembers from hundreds of years ago. The Tallowmen were destroyed, but not by Ravellers. He sniffs; another familiar scent, familiar to both Rat and the elder he's become. Cari is with the saint, Aleena. He scrabbles in the dirt, looking for signs of bloodshed. He finds none, and growls. The saint has failed him, failed her oath. By the terms of the ghouls' compact with the church of the Keepers, Aleena should have killed the Herald if she had the opportunity.

The two scents mingle. Aleena smells of steel and sweat mixed with rose and incense; Cari is canal water and blood and acrid smoke from sorcerous blasts. Both trails lead towards the Church of St Storm.

He bypasses Sumpwater Square. He can hear the Ravellers feasting within. They kill only a few; the rest they herd together. They did the same in the last days of the siege, when the war turned against the Black Iron Gods. They gathered the people of the city together and marched them to the Black Iron temples so they would all be killed at once, mass sacrifices so profligate that the iron statues were waist-deep in hot blood. All that will happen again if the Herald survives the night.

The bell tolls as he reaches St Storm. He can see one of the Black Iron Gods take shape around the church's spire. The apparition lasts only an instant, for that brief moment when the ringing bell aligns the consciousness of the truncated god with that of its mortal herald, but in that moment Rat senses the thing's terrible power.

He climbs the wall, leaping from buttress to buttress, using the crumbling masonry for handholds. Aleena's scent is stronger here, and he can hear her breathing. He slows, moving with care, silent as a shadow on the stone. She's waiting on the spiral stair that leads up to the belfry. He picks his way across the wall, heedless of the steep drop below. He creeps as he circles the tower until he finds a weak spot in the wall.

Then he drives his fist through the blocks. Stones topple inwards, smashing into Aleena. The saint is stunned and knocked off her feet. He hears her curse as she tumbles down the stairs, half buried. Rat dashes up the stairs, up to the belfry.

The Herald is there, climbing human-slow to her feet. She looks at him in alarm, then recognition.

"Rat?" says Cari.

The elder ghoul steps on the narrow beam leading to the bell. His hooves are the tread of doom as he stalks towards her. Old power wells up within him, the dregs of three centuries of soul-rich carrion, spells wrought in blood and bone, defending him against any possible attack. The Herald draws her knife, but that little weapon wouldn't even threaten Rat, let alone the thing he has become.

This murder is necessary, he reminds himself. The final blow of a long war. When the Herald dies, it will close the one remaining gap in the prisons of the Black Iron Gods. Without any hope of liberating their creators, the Ravellers will have nothing to fight for. And then there will be revenge, long and sure and slow, as every cursed grave-worm in the undercity is ground to mush beneath ghoul hooves. The Crawling Ones have broken their truce and will pay the price.

Another step closer.

The Herald's speaking – pleading? Begging? Cursing? Human languages all blur into an irrelevant buzz, echoing down from the streets above. The only true tongue is the language of the soul, and humans speak that only after death, when the ghouls pull away the meat and bone and free the holy spirit within. That sacrament must be denied to Cari, though – her soul is inextricably entwined with the Black Iron Gods. She is spiritually poisoned, unclean. Whatever existence she finds after life is no business of the ghouls.

Another step. She slashes at him with her knife, cutting into the callused hide of his palm but not deep enough to draw the black tarry blood of a ghoul.

She falls back, crawling on her hands, taking shelter under the bell. Rat bends down, his hunched back scraping against the icy cold metal. He catches her leg, drags her back towards him. She kicks and struggles, but she's only human.

Then he smells the danger. Another familiar scent, suddenly in the tower, and at the same time he feels the Black Iron Gods desperately scrabble at the skin of the world, their unseen metal claws finding momentary purchase. Pinching space so that *there* is for an instant *here*. Miren steps into existence on a narrow ledge that runs around the ruins of the belfry. There's a gun in his hand, already going off.

The world fills with noise and pain.

The elder ghoul has never experienced an insult like this. Alchemical guns are a novelty of the last century, and he has never felt their bite. Rat has, though; glancing shots fired by watchmen after a burglary went awry. In the confusion, the part of him that is Rat slips past the elder ghoul and acts on instinct. He throws Cari like a rag doll across the room, towards Miren.

The smoke blinds him, but he doesn't need eyes to sense that same twist again, that same tearing of distance. Miren has teleported again, and taken Cari – taken the Herald with him. She has escaped him!

He roars in anger and frustration. Claws dig into the ancient support beams and ropes that hold the bell in place, ripping them like matchwood and wet string. Cut loose, the bell falls. The god smashes through the weakened floor of the belfry and tumbles down the inside of the tower, clanging in terror at every turn of the stairs as it smashes through steps and bannister alike, until finally it hits the ground far below and cracks.

He staggers back to the edge of the belfry, probing the damage to his chest. The wound oozes thick blood, already matting the coarse hair of his chest, and he guesses any number of his ribs are cracked, but he is alive. He climbs out of the belfry and looks out across the city, gulping in the night air in the hopes of catching the Herald's scent again.

He doesn't smell her, but he can sense her, feel the strands of the Herald's power knotting together. Far away across the city, beyond Castle Hill, the Herald prepares to open the way.

He snarls and climbs down from the belfry, claws digging into stone. She will not escape him again.

The worms wriggle in through cracks in the doorframe, squeezing through then pooling in two piles. In the time it takes Eladora to draw breath, the piles become trunks, the trunks blend into a torso and that torso sprouts arms, ragged woven-worm fingers, and something like a head. Then, as she exhales, a merciful cloak of shadow descends around the Crawling One, hiding its disgusting form from her. It produces a porcelain face mask and settles it into place.

"Follow," it says. It gestures, and the stone glides aside like a cloud scudding across the sky.

Down they go, down a stair that Eladora remembers from the funeral. Now that her fate is inevitable, she finds she has no fear. All her life, she's fretted and worried, but there's no point in doing so now. She's powerless against even one of these Crawling Ones, and she has no idea how many of them slither through the crypts of the Thay family tomb. As she passes nooks and crypts, she glances at the porcelain masks, wondering if any of them are kin to her. It's the worms, she reminds herself. The worms eat the brain and consume the knowledge of the deceased. Her family, her uncles and aunts and cousins, they're all gone. Even if a worm ate the identity of one of them, that fragment of consciousness would be lost, subsumed in the wriggling slimy totality of the Crawling One.

She knows this, but she also knows with a horrible certainty who awaits her at the bottom of the stairs.

He wears a black cloak like the rest, and she can see the worms that make up his legs and feet as he walks towards her. His mask, though, is made of gold, and is a perfect likeness of how he must have looked in life. She remembers it from portraits and photographs that were old when she was young. Her memory of his face is quite different. She recalls papery skin, yellowed teeth, wrinkles, bloodshot eyes, beard gone white and patchy. The mask captures the sneer she remembers, though, catches the cruelty of the man.

Jermas Thay steps forward and takes her by the chin, examining her. He did the same when he was alive, when her mother first presented her child to the patriarch. Roughly jerking her head this way and that, holding her up to the light to appraise her, to assay the purity of her Thay blood.

The touch of his worm-fingers repels her, and she cannot hide her shuddering. He withdraws as if burnt. "Eladora." His voice, though, is unlike that of the other Crawling Ones. It's like the voice she remembers, sharp and deep, each word stamped out as if by a machine. It's stronger than she recalls, but she only knew her grandfather when he was already very old. "Show respect, child."

"I did," says Eladora, shivering, "w-w-when we buried you. You're d-d-dead."

"You know, you were always one of my favourites. My children's generation disappointed me, and their children – feh. Spoiled brats, for the most part. You, at least, knew how to curtsey and stay quiet. Tell me, how is your mother?"

"You're dead!" repeats Eladora.

The gold mask looks at her with hollow eyes. "That's your father's coarse stupidity in you. A lack of vision. A failing of the line, I fear. No matter. Obedience is all I require." Jermas holds up a familiar amulet. Carillon's amulet, a gift from her unseen mother. In the dim light of the tomb, it looks to Eladora as though the black metal of the amulet is alive, flowing and recoiling in a horrible way that reminds her immediately of Desiderata Street.

"I bought this, and you, for a high price. The last of the family treasure, hidden here until it was needed. I have given everything for this city, child. Family and health, wealth and happiness, even life itself. I had a vision, and it shall come to pass. Guerdon is a city ill-served by its gods. The cruelty of the Black Iron Gods could not be abided, but is the timid divinity of the Keepers preferable? Why should we be held hostage—"

"The Keepers killed you!"

Jermas hisses. "I was betrayed!" In his anger, he can't maintain the simulacrum of his human voice, and it breaks into the distorted concerto of the hive. "Some rogue sold me out to the church, and they did not understand my work. They had no idea how the city was changing around them. Kelkin and I broke the dam of dogma and set Guerdon free to change. We unleashed this city's power! The guilds, the thronged harbour, the envy of the world – we built all that! A second liberation, accomplished without bloodshed on our part. It was out of jealousy as much as fear that they struck me down."

He gestures down at his robed body. "I had made arrangements, as you can see. I knew that I would not live long enough to see my great work come to fruition. Even as an approximation of my former self, I can oversee the last parts of the plan. But the betrayal cost us time. Everything takes longer than it should, child, and I am sick of it. It took too long, too long, to make a suitable conduit. There were many failures. I made some of them, but when they perished I feared that younger seed was needed, so I called on your father Aridon to serve in my stead."

"Aridon – Aridon is Cari's father! I'm Eladora."

Jermas grabs her and drags her over to a tomb – his tomb, she realises. He shoves the lid aside with ease. The coffin inside is open, but empty apart from a few scraps of wormy velvet. "Lie down," he commands, and then he continues speaking as if unaware of his own words. "Eladora, yes. Silva's girl. No, you're entirely human, child. You weren't part of the great work. Where was I? Aridon. My son. He was young enough to sire healthy offspring. I paid off enough of his bastards to know he was fertile, too, and the shape we gave the thing was not uncomely."

He holds up the amulet, and Eladora suppresses a scream as it unmistakably moves.

"See, here she comes now. Behold the mother of my youngest grandchild. A portion of her, anyway, the little we could retain after the conjuring."

Eladora crawls back in the coffin, huddling away from the wriggling thing. "You – made – Carillon? Bred her from . . . is that a Raveller?"

"I made a conduit to the Black Iron Gods. Guerdon is ill-served by its gods. Mad, or weak, or absent. But we need them! The Godswar will not spare us for long. I will not see this city conquered by some foreign abomination, or by the dusty Crown of Haith! We shall have civic gods. We shall have the gods I shall forge from the ruins of Black Iron, the gods of my design. Carillon is the conduit through which they shall be made manifest. I never cared for the child, even then. She cried all the time, wailing and weeping so loudly I could hear it in every wing of the mansion. If I could have used her then and there and been done with it, I would have, but I knew it would take years for her to come into her power. I thought I would have to wait another five years. I thought, even, that I could hang on that long. Instead, twenty years, bitter and wormy. I lost myself in the dirt. I was diluted down until there was almost nothing left of me." He pauses, hanging his head with exhaustion. "I am so far from what I was, child. Sustained only by the plan, and when the plan is done there will be nothing left. I learned . . . I learned. Look! Look!"

He fumbles in a shelf under the casket and thrusts a ragged piece of parchment at Eladora. Confused, she scans it. The language is incomprehensible, although she recognises it as a sacred document written by Keeper scribes, and the seal at the bottom is the personal seal of the Patros himself. The symbols remind her of the scratchings of ghouls. It's a letter from the church authorities to the ghoul kingdom below. "You came back," whispers Jermas, "and they awoke. The plan can still be achieved. The time is now."

One hand grips Eladora's shoulder, the worms biting down, a hundred tiny knives, and her body goes numb. She can feel their poison rushing through her, a wave of cold running down her veins like ice water. The other deftly slips the chain of the amulet around her neck. He still holds the amulet itself, suspending it above her as he stares into its inky depths.

"I'm not her!" says Eladora. "If all this, everything you did, was to make Carillon, then she's the one you want!"

"It would be better," agrees Jermas. "As I said, you always were my favourite grandchild. But the Black Iron Gods are waking, and the Ravellers are abroad. There is no more time. Even without the amulet, Carillon has made a conduit between the gods and the material world. With the amulet, you are close enough to her to open the way."

He drops the amulet onto her chest.

And Eladora sees.

CHAPTER THIRTY-SIX

The thieves do not cheer when Spar enters the warehouse. They hail him, say that it's good that he made it out alive, and a few even clasp him on the hand or shoulder, heedless or uncaring about the risk of infection. But they don't cheer. They look haggard, their voices reduced to scratchy whispers and low tones. There are very, very few left. Spar spots a Cafstan, a few of the younger thieves from the docks, some older men run to fat, pale beneath the red blotches of their cheeks. Hedan, sitting on a barrel, staring at rats as they dart in and out of a hole in the wall.

The camp of a defeated army. They've set up a makeshift hospital that will soon become a makeshift mortuary along one wall. He spots Mother Bleak there, lying on a pallet. Her lifeless eyes stare up at him. Her grandson, exhausted and half asleep, still holding her hand, unaware that she's passed on. A wave of despair hammers Spar, but he has to keep moving. This place will destroy his spirit as surely as the plague destroyed his body.

He scans the crowd; no sign of Carillon or Rat. He finds the stairs and goes up to the small office once used by Tammur.

Miren appears out of the shadows at the top of the stairs, knife in hand. When he recognises Spar, he fades back into his hiding place. Like a sea anemone that Cari once described to

Spar, a predator that waits in cracks in coral reefs and bursts out to ambush fish.

"Master Spar! Come in, come in. I was just taking a moment to rest before heading back down. Coffee?" Professor Ongent's voice is perversely merry considering the disaster all around them.

"Back down?" echoes Spar dully.

"I have some skill as a doctor. It may be wasted effort, though – we don't have long before the Ravellers get here. What news from the street? Have you found Carillon? I've sent Miren off to look for her, but he insisted on escorting me here safely first."

"No sign. And Rat ... I found him eating all the dead back at the tenement. He's changed." Spar briefly describes his conversation with his friend.

"The ghouls are moving. That may be a factor in our favour. They've fought against the Ravellers before, after all, in the last war. History repeats itself. In the last siege of Guerdon, during the battle of Mercy Street, the elder ghouls fought against the temple guards of the Black King not half a mile away from this very spot. The city was much smaller, then, of course, and the old city walls ran – ah, never mind."

Spar shuffles through Tammur's papers, finds a map of the city.

"From what I could see outside, those Raveller things are running riot all through the Wash."

"They'll kill everyone, won't they?" he asks.

"Oh, not immediately. They want souls. Think of them as ambulatory sacrificial knives. Again, history is our guide." Ongent clears his throat and declaims. " 'The people of the city were driven like cattle to the slaughterhouse, and gathered in great numbers in the hall of the thirsty. And the Ravellers drove them, and harried them, and walked among them as knives, so that ten thousand were offered up to the Black King.' Mondolin's translation; Pilgrin's is a little, ah, bloodless, pardon the pun."

Spar stares at the old man, wondering if one or the other of them has gone mad. "They'll corral the people and bring them to be sacrificed."

"Yes, I assume so. Kill them according to the old rites, and feed the gods – assuming they can be fed in their current forms, which may not be true. In either case, they'll need a conduit – that is to say, they'll need Carillon to open the way."

"She could be anywhere. She knows about this warehouse, though, so if she's free she'll make her way here." Spar clings to that thought as the only thing keeping him afloat in the black tide. "If they find her first . . . what will they do?"

Ongent coughs lightly. "I'm a historian and a dabbler, my boy, hardly an expert. I'd assume they'd bring her to one of the bell towers where the Keepers hid the Black Iron Gods. Free one, and that one can free the rest. The bells are the key to all this, as is Carillon."

Spar's breath catches in his lungs. He can't tell if the tightness in his chest is panic or calcification. Outside in the streets, shape-shifting monsters out of children's stories are marching people into death camps. The Wash is surrounded by waxwork assassins made from the corpses of his thieves, commanded by mad tyrants who now run the city and are building bombs to murder gods. One of his best friends is the herald of armageddon; the other has mutated into something ancient and alien. And he still doesn't know what the Crawling Ones were doing when they attacked the guild. He knows next to nothing about the worm-men, and can't even formulate questions for the professor. He clenches his fists, feeling the impossible strength of the Stone Man but not knowing how it can be applied to any of these horrors.

But Idge endured, and so can he.

"All right. You're saying that as long as the Ravellers don't have Carillon, they won't kill everyone."

"Not immediately. Don't think of them as conscious beings — they're emanations, technically, shells thrown off by the gods that have seeped down to the lowest energy state of base matter. But, yes, I think we have a little time."

"Professor, you're our only sorcerer. Cari told me that your house in Desiderata Street was warded, and those wards stopped the Ravellers from entering. Can you redraw the wards here to protect us?"

"They'll be rather slapdash, I fear, but they might help. I'll need ... oh." Ongent hurries over to a window and opens it. "Listen!" A bell is ringing wildly, down by the harbour. "The tide turns, my boy. The hour approaches!"

And the city, and the city, and the city.

Tumbling hillsides of history, building upon building, culture upon culture. Scars and calluses of the flesh of *place* grow in marble and sealstone. People as ants, as droplets forming lakes and rivers, flowing in channels. As above, so below — she can see through the ground, through foundations and cellars and tunnels, to the sewers and pipes beneath, and below them the subway tunnels and the ghoul runs, the subterranean catacombs of the Varithian Kings, the ghoul tunnels, deeper still, past the black seal to the lightless void where the Ravellers dwelt.

And above, above, the bells revealed in terrible glory. She can see them now. The Black Iron Gods aren't black or iron, Eladora realises, they are blood and fire. They unfold as she approaches, shambling, misshapen angels crawling across the face of the heavens. They fumble blindly for the material world, looking for her eyes, her vision to guide them.

One of them flails towards her, and the pain is beyond all measure. She is all disembodied awareness, soaring over the city, but she is still connected to the living body that writhes in the

Thay family tomb behind her. Looking down, she sees her own cells with the same omniscience with which she sees the city. And, like the city, her body is on fire, beset by an invasion of Ravellers. The blind swipe of the god is killing her.

"It's not working!" she screams. Bodiless, her cry manifests in the material world as signs and portents. Rain sweeps across Castle Hill, and her agony echoes in the rattling of rainwater in the gutters. Windows break along Orison, and their cracks are the wave pattern of her voice. Dogs howl in response – but no one in the city below can hear here.

Tonight, there's enough screaming in the Wash that one more would go unnoticed anyway.

Carillon. This is Carillon's destiny, or Carillon's fault. Her cousin was made for this – this is the bitter cup of her sainthood, not Eladora's. But Carillon is the only one who might be able to hear her.

Her vision sweeps across the city, hurtling south towards the sea. Over the Wash, over Jere's lithosarium, towards the Church of St Storm.

She sees Carillon standing in the ruined belfry. Nearby, another presence – Aleena! The thought of the Keeper saint cheers Eladora for a moment, before she remembers that Aleena killed the Thay family to prevent exactly what's happening to her right now. The Keepers were too late – Carillon had already been smuggled away to Eladora's mother's house in the country, to be sheltered like a cuckoo. If only Carillon had stayed in the right place for once in her life!

No. She's being unworthy. She can judge her cousin for many, many things, but Carillon's just as much a victim of Jermas Thay's mad designs as Eladora is. To be *made* with this intent in mind, to be bred for a singular and terrible purpose, is appalling. She has to warn Carillon of what's going on, of Jermas' plan.

Just then, Carillon rings the bell. The god's metal prison swings back and forth, and when the bell sounds the heavens shake. For as long as that terrible note echoes across the city, the Black Iron God is manifest in the skies above Guerdon, and Eladora is caught right in the middle of the god.

Eladora snaps back to her body, back to the tomb. The smell of burning skin and cloth. She can't tell how bad her injuries are – her body is still mostly numb from the venom that Jermas injected into her. The fact that she feels such pain despite that terrifies her.

Jermas looms over her, worms bulging through the eye sockets of his mask. "You are resisting! Insubordinate child!"

"It's not working!" shouts Eladora. "It's killing me! I'm not her."

"You have the amulet, and you are disguised by the spells of the Crawling Ones. To the Black Iron Gods, you *are* the Herald. If you continue to resist, you will not survive this, child."

"Please," sobs Eladora, "it's killing me. It's killing me." Survive this? No mortal could escape unscathed after such close contact with a god, let alone an entire pantheon of mad, imprisoned deities. Even if she doesn't lose her life, what remains afterwards will be far from mortal, far from human. As bad as any god-touched abomination spawned in the excesses of the Godswar.

He reaches down. Fat, slimy-soft form-fingers scrabble at her breast and lift the amulet from her skin. It's left a raised welt on her chest. He removes the amulet's chain from her neck.

"The spell must be adjusted. A moment, and we shall begin again."

"Please no! Gods, if there's anything of my grandfather left, I love you, I love you, I've always been good, please, don't do this to me!" It's half feigned, half real. Her mind feels like a raft of ice, floating on a sea of tears. She is very close to losing her sanity.

"Compose yourself." Jermas slithers away to the entrance to the tomb chamber, where two of the other Crawling Ones wait. The three converse wetly. Eladora can't raise her head to look, but from the way shapes bulge and slither under their cloaks, she can guess how the worm-men communicate among themselves.

She closes her eyes. Bites her lip and tries not to cry. For the first time in many years, Eladora wishes her mother was here to protect her. Silva sheltered the children from the worst of Jermas' tirades when they visited the big mansion, made sure they were seen briefly and not heard from again. Scuttling up to the room they called a nursery, though it was filled with junk and old books instead of toys.

"Why didn't you tell my mother you were still alive? Does your daughter mean nothing to you?" she calls out.

"Quiet!" orders Jermas without looking at her.

Or anyone. Aleena, come back to finish the job. Miren, sneaking in like a shadow and whisking her away like some masked hero in an opera, swashbuckling his way through hordes of Crawling Ones. Professor Ongent, his kindly old face illuminated by the flash of sorcery. Anyone. Even Carillon. Even her father, who's been dead for six years. Hells, if Grandfather Thay can come back from the dead, why not the solid, quiet man who always smelled of sawdust and incense to his loving daughter? *Daddy*, she thinks, *oh kindly gods, send him back to me.*

There is only the slithering of the Crawling Ones, crackling and hissing at the edge of hearing. Jermas' shadow falls across her again. "We must be quick. The Black Iron Gods are very close to breaking through, even without the Herald. They fear the alchemists' weapons. If my allies lose their grip on the Ravellers, the sacrifices will begin prematurely, and they will try to free the gods in their wasteful, hateful original forms, instead of my design. I must be midwife to the new city as well as father to it. The Black Iron Gods must reincarnate in useful forms. Spirits of commerce and trade. Order and strength. All must be in accord with my plans – and if you hesitate, child, and impede me, I shall be forced to cause you pain. I shall take no pleasure in such discipline. It is necessary. Necessary." He stares at the amulet in his hands. "Decades of planning, of preparation, and it all comes down to hugger-mugger and haste. Feh."

If she can stall, if she can resist, then maybe the alchemists can fire their god-killing bomb and stop Jermas, save her life.

She remembers her mother deflecting her grandfather's anger over some childish mistake by asking him questions about politics. Giving Jermas an opening to expound about his strategies and trades was often the only thing that could distract him.

"The C-C-Crawling Ones – what do they get out of this? What happens to them when you remake the Black Iron Gods?"

"We shall no longer need the filthy ghouls to maintain a watch on the Ravellers. The dead of the city will mostly go to maintaining the civic gods, of course – we shall have need of a great many souls, far more than Guerdon presently produces, but there are efficiencies to be made. The balance of the dead shall go to the Crawling Ones. The best, of course – the scholars, the craftsmen, the artists – their knowledge preserved eternally in the flesh of the grave-worm. It is only foolish superstition and childish squeamishness that prevented such an arrangement in the past." He taps the amulet, and actually leans in to whisper in her ear. "Such arrangements would be temporary, you understand. My adoptive kin are not trustworthy."

"Aren't you one of them? You're made of w-w-worms!"

"But my legacy shall be writ in gods. Prepare yourself, child. Do not resist."

Prepare yourself. The thought is so absurd it makes her want to scream. How can any preparation make this nightmare any less horrible? She prays again for anyone to come through the door and rescue her, anyone at all.

The wormy horror that was her grandfather pushes her back down on the slab, drapes the dreadful amulet around her neck again. Chants the words that will tear the soul from her body and make her a channel, a vessel for some crazed rebirth of the Black Iron Gods. In response, she chants her own prayer, a Safidist prayer, one of the many, many devotions that her mother made Eladora practise every day for years until she left for university.

The Safidists believe that by faith, diligent study, and mental and physical acts of self-discipline and abrogation, one can make of oneself an empty vessel for the Kept Gods to fill with their shining light. Eladora knows too much about the true state of the Kept Gods now to think of their light as shining, but even their faltering, wan candlelight is better than Black Iron darkness. Eladora prays to the Kept Gods with a purposeful fervour that would impress even her mother.

Jermas realises what she's doing even as the spell takes hold. As she rises to that divine perspective, she can see the Crawling One clawing at her insensate mortal body. Jermas slams her head against the metal of his own burial casket in a fury, but he's too late. She whispers her message to the Kept Gods just before the Black Iron Gods descend in an uproar and claim her.

Chapter Thirty-seven

Cari and Miren tumble bodiless across the city, hurled this way and that by invisible storm clouds that rise like angry plumes from the bells of Guerdon. They skip across rooftops, their passage marked by claps of thunder without lightning, by window glass that suddenly cracks for no apparent reason, by a sudden wave of heat.

They fall back into reality in Miren's attic hideaway in New-town. As her soul is once again sheathed in flesh and bone and she breaks away from that dizzying divine viewpoint from on high, Cari is again consumed by desire. She desperately wants to be naked with Miren, to press against him skin to skin, to fill the sudden absence of divinity with carnal pleasure. His tongue probes against her lips, his fingers tear at the ties of her shirt, her trousers, tugging at them. The heat of his bare skin against her belly as he pushes her down onto the bed.

And oh, how she wishes she could run away from the world outside and just fuck him until they both forgot who they were, but that's not going to happen. The world outside is burning.

"Get off me!" cries Cari.

Miren ignores her. He's pulling at his own clothing now, his skin fever-hot and perspiring. Cari's lust turns to a sick fear;

Miren has the look of an animal about him, his face is eerily blank and ugly despite everything. She gets an arm free and elbows him in the jaw, and the shock knocks him to the floor. Cari rolls to the other side of the bed and clasps her shirt closed with one hand. Her knife is in the other.

"Not now, all right? All right?" Miren scrambles into a crouch, making him look even more like an animal. His face contorts, and he lets out an anguished squeal, then bites his own arm as hard as he can, drawing blood. Cari stares at him in horror as he sucks at his own blood, nuzzling at his forearm like it's one of her breasts.

And then, like a wave falling back into the ocean, it passes. He stands up, his features returning to their familiar look of sullen boredom, arms held loosely by his side as blood drips from his wound. He scoops up his own discarded clothing and starts to dress. Cari shakes her head, resists the impulse to flee out of the door and never look back.

"Sorry," mutters Miren, staring at the floor. A child's rote apology. Cari's reminded that he's, what, two years younger than she is? More?

Cari turns her back on him, runs through the supplies Miren has lined up like toy soldiers on the shelves. She grabs anything that looks like it might be useful – alchemical cure-alls and painkillers, guns, some money – and stuffs it into a satchel. "How did you find me?" she asks without looking at him. He responds with a shrug, dismissing the question. Kneeling down, he opens a chest by the bed and pulls out a heavy cloak that glistens like lizard scales in the dim light. He throws it around his shoulders.

"Fuck," mutters Cari, thinking about the layout of the city. From her visions, Newtown's behind the cordon of Tallowmen. To get back into the Wash, they'll need to sneak past them, and then get past all the Ravellers and whatever else is loose on the streets tonight, and then they've got to cross the entire width of the district to get up to Hook Row on the far side. On a normal day, the walk from Newtown to Hook Row would take forty minutes or more. With the city in uproar, it's going to take a lot longer.

"Can you teleport again?" asks Cari, expecting – hoping, even – the answer to be no. Miren closes his eyes for a moment, takes a deep breath, and then for an instant he flickers like a candle flame, darting in and out of existence.

"Yes. Tonight, they'll let me."

They, she wonders, but the time it'll take to drag an explanation out of Miren is almost as long as it'd take them to walk across the city. She crosses to him and grabs hold of his shoulder. "Take me back to Hook Row." He takes her elbows, leaving an awkward space between their bodies, and together they step out of the world again.

Hook Row.

The professor somehow senses their arrival before they materialise; they fall back into reality in the upstairs office just as he enters the room. He welcomes them with a wide smile.

"Well done, boy," he says to Miren, ruffling his hair. Then, to Carillon. "Are you all right, my girl? We have much to do, but if you need a moment . . . "

"Where's Spar?" she asks, just as the big stony bulk of the man heaves into view behind the professor. Cari twists out of Miren's grasp and runs over to give Spar a rare hug. "It's all gone wrong!" she whispers in his ear, half choking on unexpected tears. "With the guild, and Rat, and everything." Spar's presence makes her feel safe, and that makes everything worse – as soon as she lowers her guard, even a fraction, the terror of the situation sneaks in and freezes her heart. The impulse to ask Spar to kill her flares in the back of her mind. If she's gone, then the Ravellers have no way to open a conduit to the Black Iron Gods. Spar might do it, too. There's no one stronger.

"I know," says Spar, "but Cari, we need to fix this. We need to find a way to stop the Ravellers."

Cari steps back. Ongent and Miren are whispering to one another on the far side of the room. She catches Miren scowling jealously at Spar, and she rolls her eyes. Her attraction to Miren feels right in the moment after teleporting, but after that he makes her skin crawl. She clears her throat.

"I ran into a Keeper saint. Aleena. She said I should be able to command, to control the Ravellers. I tried, but ... it didn't work." Cari pauses, rubs her back, bruised purple when Rat flung her into the bell at St Storm's. Takes a breath. "I had an amulet that I got from my mother. It's the one Heinreil took from me." Spar nods. "I think it's to do with my sainthood, and the Black Iron Gods. Aleena said that if I had that, maybe I could command them. I don't know."

Ongent smiles encouragingly at Miren, then says, "Many saints use relics to bolster their connection to the gods. It's certainly plausible. How did this Keeper – ah, never mind. Where is the amulet now?"

"Heinreil had it, and when he was wearing it I couldn't see him in the visions."

"Of course you couldn't, any more than you can see your own eye. He *had* it, though. Now it's ... "

"Gravehill. I saw him leaving Gravehill, when I rang the bell at St Storm. He must have left it up there with the Crawling Ones. The graveyard's full of them." Cari pauses. The memory is so incongruous, it's hard for her to believe what she sensed, but there's no reason to hold anything back now. She has to trust the professor. "And I ... Eladora was there. I didn't see her in the vision, but she was there. Out of her body, like me. I guess in the gods' realm."

"What happened to Heinreil?" asks Spar.

"Tallowmen got him. I think he's dead."

"Good."

The professor is interrupted by a shout from below, followed by Hedan stumbling through the door, clutching a broken nose. "Spar, there's some woman here who—"

"Who can speak for her bloody self," huffs Aleena, stomping in. She's flushed and breathless; she ran up from St Storm's church, sprinting across the Wash nearly as fast as Miren was able to step across the city. Her eyes narrow when she sees Miren, and the naked sword in her hand glimmers with fire. "Don't you move, lad. Sinter warned me about your tricks. Carillon, are you all right? That fucking ghoul near broke my neck."

"I'm fine," says Cari. "How'd you find me?"

"Divine fucking intervention. The Kept Gods are screaming fit to burst me head. Got anything to drink?"

Wordlessly, Spar retrieves a bottle from Tammur's desk and throws it to her. "I'm Aleena. I should burn half of you fuckers at the stake and hand the other half over to those candle-sucking alchemists in the name of law and sodding order." She takes a swig, then waves the bottle at Ongent. "You mentioned Eladora. I left her at a church safe house with Sinter, that rancid lump. What happened to her?"

Ongent hasn't moved a muscle since Aleena entered. He's frozen like a mouse hiding from a housecat. He has to lick his lips before speaking. "We are hardly allies, you and us. Your spies have harassed me for years. You think of me as a heretic – and I have no doubt that you are under orders to kill Ms Thay."

"I trust her," says Cari, surprising herself. Like her, Aleena's caught in the grip of unwanted sainthood. Acknowledging the compliment, Aleena hands Cari the bottle. Cari takes a mouthful of the liquor. It burns going down, but makes a welcome warmth as it pools in her stomach. "Aleena, we don't know what happened to her. I saw her in a vision, but—"

"Yah, well, so did I, twenty shitty minutes ago. Having people shouting in your head is your problem, not mine. I'm divinely exempt from hangovers, but this is fucking worse." She pokes Hedan with a booted foot. "I've half a mind to kill this twerp, just to take the edge off."

"You had a vision?" asks Spar, obviously trying to make sense of the bizarre intrusion.

"Eladora. Calling for help through the Kept Gods. How she managed that I don't know. I couldn't make much fucking sense of it – worms and Gravehill and some shite. But she told me to come here, and here I find you. So, what the fuck is all this about?"

Still moving very warily, like a man trapped in a room with a manticore, Ongent rises and circles towards the window. "Carillon, come here please. A little divination is in order, to make sense of all these competing visions."

Any clarity would help, thinks Cari, and she joins Ongent at the window. Outside, the city's lit by fires. It looks like chaos. The professor comes up behind her and places his hands over her eyes. He smears a sticky resin on her eyelids. It feels like stinging jelly-fish floating around inside her eyes. Ongent mutters a few words of power, and power surges through him and into her. "Look," he whispers, and Cari opens her eyes.

It's not like her visions, but it's halfway there. She can see the invisible currents of magical potential that run through the city, just as she did back in the basement of the tenement when they healed Spar. She can still see the lingering traces of that spell, the incantation that connected her to Ongent and Spar so she could channel the power of the gods into a healing spell. Beyond, she can see smaller, chaotic threads of magic, slithering like worms through the city. The sky to her right is on fire with sorcery – it's the glow of the alchemical furnaces reflecting off the clouds. She can dimly see shapes moving beyond the clouds. The Black Iron

Gods, perhaps, although none of the bells are ringing. Have the Ravellers begun their sacrifices? Trying to give the gods enough power to manifest even without Cari.

Ongent whispers another word, and the connection between Cari and the professor flares back into existence. Pressure behind her eyes as he looks out of them, too. Her vision blurs as he tries to make her look towards Gravehill. There, rising from the east side of the twisted hill, there's a pillar of magical energy, blazing bright.

"Jermas," whispers Ongent right in her ear. "That's Jermas' spell. My word." He dismisses the magic, and Cari snaps back to the mundane world.

"Jermas ... you mean my grandfather? Jermas Thay?" Cari steadies herself against the windowsill, trying to recall her long-dead grandfather. All she can summon up are memories of being told to be quiet, of hiding as a tyrannical monster raged through the mansion that was all the world until they sent her to Aunt Silva. The thought that his rage fills the unseen skies over Guerdon makes a sick kind of sense.

"I worked with him briefly, many years ago. He was a visionary man, truly, with some fascinating ideas about sorcery and divinity. I lost touch with him, of course – the early days of liberated thaumaturgical research were a chaotic period, all sorts of groups forming and dissolving, and Thay was very secretive. I knew his theories, though, and I can recognise their application when I see it."

"Did you know when you paid my ransom?" demands Cari. "You knew I was a Thay. Did my grandfather do something to me? Is that why I'm a fucking saint? Did you know when you came for me?"

Ongent raises his hands. "I suspected, yes. But I wasn't sure. I didn't know what you were. Jermas studied the beliefs of the

Safidist sect, the god-aligners, who try through prayer and self-abrogation to humble themselves before the will of the divine, with decidedly mixed success. Jermas – he was always a proponent of efficiencies and the direct approach, you understand – he believed that it would be better to create an entity that was, shall we say, spiritually receptive. I was certain, when I visited Jere Taphson, that you were entangled with a spiritual being of some sort. I feared that it might be the Black Iron Gods, but I wasn't sure. Our initial test indicated that it wasn't some lesser elemental or ghost that had visited upon you, but you, ah, left in haste before I could confirm that you were indeed connected to the thirsty ones." He smiles, but his eyes are dull and tired. "You were an initiate of the Dancer, for one thing, and you were dreaming of the Keeper's churches. There were other possibilities then – there are none now."

"What did this Jermas do to Cari?" asks Spar.

"I have no idea. Jermas himself was only a dabbler in sorcery, but he recruited some brilliant minds. He spent a fortune on his work, but all that research was lost when the Thay family were murdered. Whatever she is, though, she is unique."

"If she's unique," says Spar, "then how is her cousin Eladora involved? And the amulet?"

"Before the Black Iron Gods were cast down by the Keepers and reforged into bells, they were iron statues. These statues echoed and reiterated the spiritual patterns that make up the gods' essential structure in the elemental realm. Reforging them disrupted those patterns and paths, making it impossible for the gods to exert their power."

Aleena frowns. "Aye. We couldn't kill the bastards, but they'd conveniently locked themselves into big ugly lumps of iron, so we just fucked them up by casting 'em as bells. So what changed? Cari?"

"Yes. Her presence agitates the vestigial, damaged structures that were once gods. She is like a candle for them, guiding them back to what passes for consciousness among deities. Now, I fear, Eladora is close enough to Carillon for the Black Iron Gods to use her as a beacon instead – when augmented by the amulet. The amulet, I would surmise, is a relic of great significance to the Black Iron Gods. A holy talisman, marking the wearer as their high priest and herald." He sounds cheery about the whole prospect, as if the end of the world is a riddle he's just solved.

"Why the fuck would grandfather – would anyone – want the Black Iron Gods back?" asks Cari. Unbidden, the memory of what she saw, what she was offered in the Holy Beggar comes to mind: a vision of Carillon as high priestess, an immortal saint-queen ruling the city. Her enemies gutted at her feet. She stamps on the thought, tells herself that she rejects it all – *but you used their power to kill Heinreil*, part of her whispers, *why stop there?*

"Not back as they were. He intended to bring them back in a form he designed. Remade gods, engineered for his purposes. Hubris and folly, I fear, but marvellously ambitious, one must acknowledge. Alternatively, Eladora might be in the hands of someone using Jermas' research, perhaps those who—"

"It doesn't matter who," says Spar. "If we don't stop the Black Iron Gods, then we don't have the amulet. If we don't have the amulet, then we can't stop the Ravellers, and then the alchemists will launch their god bombs to save the city. That will kill the Kept Gods, too, along with the Black Iron Gods and probably Aleena and Cari. All that matters now is getting through the night. All other concerns must be put aside. How do we stop them?"

"The fucking Ravellers have half the Wash corralled down in the Seamarket. There must be thousands of people there," says Aleena. "It's going to be mass slaughter."

"Cari, you think you can command the Ravellers if you have the amulet?"

She opens her mouth to speak, feels the back of her throat burning with vomit, closes it again. She nods weakly. Outside, thunder or some spell crashes across the clouds, and she flinches. Her heart's racing with panic.

"It will be dangerous," admits Ongent. "Carillon will become what Jermas Thay intended her to be – the Herald of the Black Iron Gods, their conduit to the material plane. The temptation to abuse that power might be overwhelming – and even if you resist that, you'll still be in danger. The Ravellers may obey you, but their first loyalty is to their trapped gods. They might turn on you and make you open the way for the gods." The professor sighs, then claps his hands. "I may be of some little service. I was able to wound a Raveller with my spells before."

She nods again and walks across the room to stand next to Spar. The rough floor of the warehouse heaves like the deck of a storm-tossed ship beneath her feet. Ongent keeps talking about protective spells and countermeasures – the same lecture he gave in the tenement after they healed Spar – but she's not listening.

"I'll go and get the amulet then, and young Eladora. She was under my protection," says Aleena, "and I know the tomb."

"Miren," says Ongent, "go with Aleena. Once you've rescued poor Eladora, take the amulet and come to us. My son," he says with a note of pride, "has the gift of teleportation. He can get us the amulet faster than any other method."

"I should stay with Cari," says Miren, eyes fixed on the floor. "I can guard her."

"No. Go with Aleena. Get the amulet," snaps Ongent. "Do you understand?" Miren grunts.

"I'll go with Cari and your father," says Spar. "You'll get to Gravehill faster without a Stone Man tagging along. I'll get some of the thieves to back you up." She takes a deep breath. The thought that Spar will be with her in this madness is heartening. One hand closes around the knife in her pocket, drawing strength from the cold weight of the blade. It's still sticky with her own blood and the ichor of the Raveller. The things can die.

"We have a plan, then," says Ongent.

"We're thieves," says Cari, "call it a heist."

CHAPTER THIRTY-EIGHT

Spar wonders if it is close to dawn.

He's counted time in alkahest for the last few years, and that gave him a remarkably accurate internal chronometer. If his finger joints and neck stopped aching, he'd know that at least a week had elapsed since his last injection. Other symptoms gave him even more precise measurements. A particular plate in his back locked solid around six days after an injection; his good knee started getting stiff three days and six hours after a dose.

After Cari's healing spell, his sense of time is gone. It makes him feel adrift, like he's spinning out of control into some dark future. The city shares the feeling. Everything's uncertain tonight.

He stands at the door of the Hook Row warehouse, waiting for Professor Ongent to finish some sorcerous preparations. The professor's strange son Miren left a few hours, with Aleena and a half-dozen thieves that Spar's almost certain he can trust. Even if there are still some of Heinreil's men in the remains of the Brotherhood, their loyalty is to a dead man. Heinreil is gone. Tonight, Spar is the master of Guerdon's thieves, just like his father. Whatever else, he has tonight.

By now, Aleena and her followers should be nearly at Gravehill. It's not far as the crow flies or as the train runs, but the trains are shut down and the Wash is a war zone. The streets are impassable, and – without a ghoul guide – so are the deep tunnels which are the most direct route to Gravehill. So, Spar sent along two ex-linesmen who'd turned thief, Harper and Gladstone, to lead Aleena's party through the city's suddenly empty train tunnels all the way to Gravesend. If they haven't run into Tallowmen, they'll be at the Thay tomb soon. They'll grab the amulet, and then Miren will carry it back to Cari, and she'll be able to work another miracle.

Spar's watchers on the street report (when they do report back, instead of going abruptly silent) that the Ravellers are still gathering prisoners in the big Seamarket near Venture Square. There must be thousands of people inside the market by now. Thousands of souls to be filleted by the Ravellers and fed to the Black Iron Gods.

The scale of the tragedy is unthinkable.

So, he suspects, is the scale of the victory. Say Carillon is able to command those monsters – what does command mean? She can tell them to stop, and just doing that will be enough to save all those lives. They can go farther, though. The Ravellers are unstoppable by any weapon short of divine magic or alchemical weapons. Divine magic is in short supply in Guerdon, and if the alchemists had a god bomb ready, they'd have used it already. There's a chance, he thinks, that he and Cari might end up at the head of an unholy army.

There are furnaces in the alchemists' guild that maybe could burn a Raveller. They could order the Ravellers to turn on each other, kill each other until there's nothing left. They could tell them to march into the ocean and keep going, or just go back underground. Put the genie back in the bottle, have the Ravellers slither down to that gate beyond the ghouls' realm and reseal it.

Or they could use them. Desiderata Street proved that the

Tallowmen are no match for the Ravellers. Spar could have Cari take down Rosha's monsters with her own. March an army of Ravellers up to the alchemists' guild, and up to the cathedrals on Holyhill, and up to Parliament and demand reform. Put a noose of darkness around the city, and see if they've got a fraction of Idge's strength.

He lumbers back inside. The warehouse is eerily quiet despite being crowded with people who took shelter here. Everyone's afraid to speak above a whisper, as though too much noise would attract the Ravellers.

He passes Professor Ongent, lying stretched out on a pallet. The professor is napping, soundly asleep in the midst of apocalypse, a child-like expression of contentment on his face. Cari's upstairs in the office.

Spar's heavy footsteps sound like gunshots as he crosses the floor and ascends the stairs. He finds Cari rifling through the desk.

"Look at this!" she insists and shoves a ledger across at him. "It's Tammur's accounts. The bastard – look, the fucker bought a consignment of poison from Ulbishe. That's the shit that Yon identified – the stuff that they dosed you with. Tammur was the one who poisoned you!"

Spar laughs.

"What's fucking funny?" Cari's face is almost comically furious and appalled.

"It doesn't matter. It just doesn't. I mean, maybe Tammur poisoned me. Maybe he bought it on Heinreil's orders. Maybe Heinreil planted that ledger, and he was planning on using it to screw Tammur when it came to light. I don't know, and it doesn't matter. They're all dead."

"Of course it matters," she insists, "we have to know."

Spar settles into a heavy chair, testing its strength. "Even with your visions," he says, "we don't know everything. Everyone's in the grip of these tremendous unseen forces, thrown this way and that. Not just gods – they're in there, yes, but they're part of it. Fate, circumstance ... fuck, money and power and family, too. Economics and politics and history. Necessity, maybe. Like the world's on railway tracks. Things happen even though no one sane wants them to happen, when no one involved wants them to happen, but everyone's caught by circumstance. Actually, if we're going to have this conversation, hand me that bottle."

"I don't know what the fuck kind of conversation we're having." Cari pours some of the remaining drink into a cup, hands him the rest. "Should we be getting drunk before we go and save the city?"

"That's the crux of the matter, maybe. Think of it this way – the head of the Brotherhood was always going to try to kill me. There's no choice in the matter. My father's name, my history, that's one force acting on them. Acting on me, too – even if I hated people and didn't want anything to do with them, I'd still be seen as a champion of the poor. Because of Idge."

"Oh gods. I know this kind of conversation. This is the reason you have no friends, you know, not the Stone Plague."

"Idge says—"

She takes a sip of her drink and sticks her tongue out at him.

"Idge says—"

" 'Finish the bottle if he reads the whole page at you'," quotes Cari. It's a drinking game that Rat invented, mocking Spar's devotion to his father's unfinished philosophy.

"Idge says that there are moments when revolution is possible. Most of the time, we're all – everyone, from the poorest beggar out there to the Patros on his golden throne – caught in the gears, controlled by these invisible forces, and if we act against them we're crushed. But there are moments when things can change, when the forces balance and it's possible for people – individual people – to make a big difference. To – realign things. Remake the world."

She scowls. "Who wants to do that? You get it wrong, and then the whole world is your fault. Every bad thing that happens after that moment is on you. How do you live with that?"

"Cari – when you get the amulet and command the Ravellers, what are you going to make them do?"

"Stop." She looks pale.

"And then?"

She puts her unfinished drink down on the table. "I don't fucking know. Make them go away. I guessed that maybe Ongent would know something. If it's up to me . . . if it's up to me, Spar, I don't want it to be up to me. I wanted to run away when all this started, and I still do. I came back to help you, and to fuck over Heinreil, and to get my amulet back." One finger. "You're – I don't know – not cured exactly, but healthier than I've ever seen you." Two. "Everything and everyone in this city is getting fucked over tonight, but at least Heinreil's dead. And three." She extends a third finger. "Once I get that amulet back, it's going in the fucking sea. That's my answer, Spar. I want out. All that amulet ever meant to me was the idea that I once had a mother who loved me, and that I hadn't spent my whole life being a fucking inconvenience to someone. Now it turns out that it's all part of this magical shit, and I don't want it anymore."

Suddenly angry, she snatches up the cup and drains it. "Take your invisible forces and shove them. I want out. The open sea, and a place where no one knows who I am." Her eyes light up. "You could come, too. Saving the city discharges any fucking obligation you can possibly feel to the Brotherhood or anything else here. Gods, Spar, I can show you the world. There's so much out there beyond Guerdon. The Godswar isn't everywhere yet. Come with me."

What about Miren? part of him thinks, but before he can answer, running footsteps. One of the messengers, a girl of no more than eight. She drops a paper on the desk and backs away, unwilling to stay close to a Stone Man. He pushes himself out of the chair, hearing it groan under the strain, and picks up the note.

"Tallowmen are gathering for a push near the Mercy Street cordon, aiming at liberating the Seamarket."

"What are they waiting for?" asks Cari.

"There's a carriage or truck of some sort coming down through Glimmerside right now. It must be the god bomb. It looks like they couldn't fit it to a rocket in time, so they're carrying it right down into the middle of the city."

Cari stands. "As soon as the Ravellers spot it, they'll start killing people. Try to break the gods out before the alchemists blow them up. Fuck, they may have started already. They're assuming all the Ravellers are obvious monsters, but there could be any number hiding in human form."

"We've got to get down there, so we're ready the instant Miren brings you the amulet. I'll wake Ongent."

"Spar." Cari runs around the table and embraces her friend, jumping up so he has to catch her. She kisses him on the cheek, then whispers in his ear. "If you ask me, I'll do it."

And she's gone, running to a side room to grab the last of their gear.

The worms pop beneath his teeth, each one releasing a delicious little burst of soul-stuff. He swallows, then hawks up a gobbet of black slime and spits it out, using the ragged remains of a black cloak as a handkerchief. The elder ghoul smells the air; the Herald is very close now. The audacity of his enemy – to choose *Gravehill* as a final refuge! Gravehill has been the stronghold of the ghouls since they came to the city, and even with the ghoul kingdom in disarray he has *power* here. Elsewhere in the city, or below, these two Crawling Ones might have been a challenge to him, but not here.

He moves through the familiar graveyard. The ancient willow trees know him, and bend aside for him. He scales the cliff-side rather than take the longer, guarded path. The worm-men are looking for him; he can hear them calling to one another in horrible rattles too soft for any human ear to hear. There will be a reckoning, he promises them silently. There was a time that the ghouls were willing to share the bounty of the dead, but they have broken the rules and there will be war beneath the streets. And fire, too. Fat worms frying, a feast for young ghouls.

A familiar scent, and an even more familiar voice. "Bloody thing." He pauses in his climb and scans his surroundings. Over there, cut into the hillside, is a passageway that connects with Gravesend Station far below. An access shaft, cut decades ago and mostly forgotten. The surface entrance to the shaft is sealed and chained up.

He watches.

There's a flash of light from the far side, and the door shakes. It's sturdy, made of steel, and it holds. Rusted shut.

Aleena's voice again. "I can fucking open it, but I don't want to write 'Hey, intruders here, come blast them' in sodding fifty-foot letters of fire across the bleeding hillside. Element of surprise, right?"

A muffled response. Harper, the still-Rat part of his mind reminds him, or maybe Gladstone. A fellow thief. Urging Aleena to hurry, that their only alternative is to blow it open with explosives and that will be even more obvious.

The Herald is near, thinks the elder ghoul. He should leave. Instead, he finds himself drawing closer to the door. His powerful soul ranges ahead of his body, probing the minds of those beyond. This one will be a suitable voice.

"I SHALL OPEN THE DOOR," says Hedan, in a voice like treacle. "STAND BACK."

A swipe of Rat's claws, and the chains fall to the ground. He catches them before they can clatter. With his other arm, he wrenches the door from its frame and pulls it open.

Aleena steps out. She keeps her sword between herself and Rat, but the blade is cold and dark, not fiery. "Might have guessed you'd beat us here."

Hedan stumbles out and falls to the ground, staring up at Rat in terror. His mouth opens. "I MUST KILL THE HERALD. CARILLON."

"Aye, so you fucking said when you kicked me down the stairs, shithead. Listen, it's not Cari who's in there. It's her cousin Eladora – and you're not killing her either. They've got her prisoner, the worms do. They're using some amulet to make her the Herald, or look like the Herald, or – I dunno, I didn't follow that nonsense. We're going to get the amulet, all right?"

"I WILL KILL THIS ONE," says Hedan, gurgling on his own vomit. Rat extends a long, claw-tipped finger and points it at Miren.

"No." The sword doesn't ignite, but it flickers. "He's going to bring the amulet to C— to stop the Ravellers. There's thousands of poor shits corralled in the middle of the Wash, and the Ravellers are going to kill them all unless we get the amulet there quick as a Haithi fuck, see. So we need the teleporting twerp."

"I WILL KILL THIS ONE," says Hedan, and Miren finishes Rat's sentence, "LATER." Miren's eyes blaze with helpless fury when Rat manages to seize control of his voice.

"No time to lose," says Aleena. "They're in the Thay tomb."

"I KNOW IT." They start the march up the shady slope towards the tombs.

"First part of this whole shit-show is easy," says Aleena. "We go in and get the amulet, and Miren takes it out. Smash and grab, right? But it's the second part where we get fucked. All the Crawling Ones on the hillside are going to come after us, and we'll be stuck at the bottom of a fucking dungeon. If you've got ghouls nearby to take some of the fight off us, we might not all die."

Rat chuckles. "THERE WILL BE WAR, OH YES."

"Marvellous." The sword catches fire. "I don't know what I'd fucking do with peace," says the saint.

CHAPTER THIRTY-NINE

R ockets arc high over the city, their glare mirrored in the waters of the harbour. The city watch gunboats that launched the salvo stay well clear of the docks at the end of the Wash, which is still enemy territory. There could be Ravellers hiding among the shadows, or even disguised in rat-form or gull-form. The gunners use the damaged spire of St Storm as a reference point when aiming, a trajectory that goes just east of the church, over the docklands and warehouses, and into the heart of the old city. The rockets howl over the dome of the great Seamarket, so close that the terrified crowds in there scream. Some try to flee, but their Raveller captors won't let anyone go. Hundreds perish in a split second, sliced into bloody chunks.

The rockets land beyond the Seamarket, on the far side of Venture Square. Offices, shopping arcades, covered markets – all are consumed in a flash. There's screaming in the inferno, but only briefly. Too quick to tell if it was human or Raveller.

A second barrage screams in across the city. These rockets are fused to explode in mid-air, showering the area below with a thin spray of flame-retardant foam. It's nowhere near enough to put out the fires – the Wash is burning now, a gathering conflagration bigger than any Guerdon has seen in recent history – but it makes a clear path through the debris, a sudden road between the edge of Glimmerside and the Seamarket, cut through a dozen blocks in an instant.

The Tallowmen advance in a ragged, wild line. Skirmishers. Behind them are heavier troops, more disciplined but fearful. Armoured mercenaries, their services bought with the guns they carry into battle. The city's entirely human and mortal watch, with Warden Nabur at their head, follow after them, a stamp of official sanction on the bombing of the city. Civic necessity – the needs of the whole city must be weighed against a few buildings that were probably empty of anyone important. The alchemists need to get their weapon as close to the army of the Black Iron Gods as they can.

Guildmistress Rosha rides with the bomb. At least, one of her copies does. As long as the mould survives, they can cast new Roshas for all eternity. Still, despite the knowledge that her essence will go on, the wax effigy in the bomb carriage cannot quite control the trembling of her freshly cast hands as she adjusts the weapon she has made. She struggles to ignore the inchoate psychic battering from the remnants of the Black Iron God in the wreckage. This wax body is disposable, but the mould-shrine containing the distillation of her soul is not far away. The god, once imprisoned and truncated, is now mad as well, and full of hate for its tormentor. Rosha knows that if the gods break free from their prisons, the thing in the carriage beside her will manifest as some misshapen avatar of wrath, and all imaginable suffering will be visited on her.

By her reckoning, such a fate is less than twenty minutes away.

Up on Holyhill, the guild engineers who were ordered to safely recover the bells from the spires of the cathedrals now receive fresh orders under Rosha's own seal, commanding them to stop the bells from ringing by any means necessary. One work team, careless and unaware of the true peril, simply remove the ropes and think their work done. They are surprised when the bell begins rocking back and forth of its own accord, moved by invisible forces, and shocked when a presence manifests in the air around the bell tower, the shade of a god not worshipped in any of the cathedrals. None of the engineers survive; the dismembered remains of three of them are found scattered on Glimmerside rooftops over the next week, and the other two are never seen again. In the cathedral below, the icons of the Kept Gods shatter.

Cari hears the explosion of rockets and quickens her pace. The three of them – Ongent, Cari and Spar – climb through a seemingly endless series of storerooms and abandoned offices backstage at the Seamarket. Ongent, though red-faced and puffing, has the most energy of any of them, urging them onwards. He even has the breath to point out interesting architectural features.

"This was the temple to the Black Iron Gods. These would have been priest quarters and ritual chambers where sacrifices were prepared before they were brought downstairs, to what is now the main market. Back then, the Black Iron statues stood there on a dozen plinths, with an altar in front of each of them. There are tunnels and cisterns underground where the Ravellers were kept. When they sacrificed an offering, a Raveller would rise up and unmake the, ah, victim, carrying everything – body and soul and everything else – into the spirit world. It was exceedingly efficient, as these things go. Their high priest – more than priest, arch-saint or avatar is a better translation – shared in their power. A demigod – or goddess." He casts a sidelong glance at Cari.

"If they're down there," whispers Cari, "why the fuck are we up here?"

"This leads up to a ring of balconies overlooking the main

hall," answers Spar. "Fuck", he adds as the building shakes, sending dust cascading from the ceiling. The noise of another blast
rolls over them. "Are they targeting the market?"

"Doubtful." Ongent runs his hand lovingly over a carving that's
half concealed behind the remains of an old puppet theatre. "The
bombing won't kill all the Ravellers, and even one of them is
enough to carry all the souls to the Black Iron Gods. Rosha dare
not offer holocaust within the temple precincts." The carving is
ruined. Worn by the passage of time, hacked by both victorious
crusaders and idle boys, and covered in the graffiti of three hundred
years, but Cari guesses that it once depicted one of the Black Iron
Gods. "We have time," Ongent declares. "We can wait for Miren."

"When they steal the amulet, how long will we have before the
Ravellers here work out what's going on?" asks Spar. "How long
before they start killing people?"

"My boy, those Ravellers are emanations of the gods. They're
not living creatures, remember? Spirits given material form. No,
they know what the gods know. Once the Black Iron Gods know
that the ersatz Herald is gone and that door is closed, they'll start
a mass sacrifice and try to break through by sheer brute force."

"All right, let's get up as close to the balcony as we can without
getting spotted. We want Cari giving her commands right away."
Spar hunches his shoulders as another barrage comes down outside. Cari can't meet his eye; she knows he's thinking about what
command she'll give them.

May as well be hung for a sheep as for a lamb, she thinks, *or an
unholy army of monsters as for cursed visions*. "One sec." She dares a
quick peek at the city entire, opening her mind to the visions.
Flash-image of Holyhill, of Glimmerside burning below, and then
the impression of a great door opening up above Gravehill – but
the door's blocked. Held shut from the far side.

Cari's presence in the spirit world doesn't go unnoticed. *THE*

HERALD tolls one voice. *DIVIDED, DIVERGENT!* says another. The thing in the wagon outside shrieks like some demonic newborn, this keening wail equal parts hatred and raw need. And then, closest of all, a presence. There's a Black Iron God no more than fifty feet away, hanging at the apex of the great domed ceiling of the Seamarket.

It knows her. Knows what she must be.

Transformed, transfigured, made divine.

High Priestess, dark queen, immortal and invincible.

In the vision, the Ravellers bow before her. The crowds, driven like cattle onto the killing floor of the temple, fall to their knees and love her. Some are so enraptured that they willingly hurl themselves on the altars, dashing their brains out against the stone so she can consume their souls. She leaves the temple on wings of darkness, her knife transforming into a blade of black iron. Single-handedly, she destroys the armies of the alchemists. She annihilates the prison of metal that holds a portion of her soul captive with a word, and girded in godbone armour she rises, casting down the cathedrals of the false gods on Holyhill. They fall like marble landslides down the hillside, and she calls up a throne fit for her divine glory, so she might rule over her city eternal. Alchemists, watchmen, Heinreil's thieves, all her enemies are dragged from their filthy hiding places and sacrificed in front of her by robed priests and Ravellers, so she might bathe her feet in their life's blood and—

Cari slams shut the door in her mind. Spar's suddenly beside her, holding her upright.

"A vision?"

"Tried to check on Miren." She takes a gasp of air. Fish mixed with blood and dust. "They're near the tomb, I think. Oh shit. One of them – one of the gods – it saw me."

Ongent pales. "They have enough awareness to recognise you?" She nods.

"Run," says Spar. "Climb!"

Through the door, faster now, no point in stealth. Crashing through rooms and hallways, looking for stairs.

She's the one who finds a locked side door. Spar smashes it open with a stony kick. It leads onto another circular hallway. The right-hand wall is studded with doors every few feet, but the left-hand side has little arched windows that look out onto the market floor below. A strange sound; thousands of people weeping silently, in terrified unison. Cari stares down at that sea of faces. The reality of what's about to happen falls into her stomach like an iron ball – all those thousands of people are going to die if she screws this up. The responsibility is a physical weight, slowing her down, and she hates to be slowed down.

Two hundred feet below, a surging black tide scrambles up the interior of the dome. The Ravellers move as one, slithering towards them.

"This way," shouts Spar. The crowd below ripples in confusion as his voice echoes around the huge dome. Some people must think it's an escape attempt. Cari spots explosions of black-then-red, like flower blossoms, and nearly vomits when she realises what they are. Someone tried to run, and a Raveller reached out and killed everyone nearby. Dismembered in an instant.

She runs after Spar, half blind with tears. Ongent shouts something, a spell maybe. She finds the stairs up, climbs them like a dog, on all fours. The balcony offers a better view of the Seamarket. From this height, it's like her visions. The people below are dots; the distances all seem warped.

It's not enough. The Ravellers are too close. They change shape as they climb, budding stolen limbs and tentacles to grip onto the cracks in the stone when needed. A thing of darkness clambers towards Cari, climbing on the stolen hands of a hundred children, sprouting a hundred eyes as it closes.

We need to get higher, she thinks, but Spar's already ahead of her. He points up. There's the Black Iron Bell, hanging another fifty feet above them. Four ribs, like the horns of a giant's crown, rise up from this level of the building to support the upper dome. She can see two little doors distantly, one at the end of each of two ribs, on either side of that central bell. There's a little ledge – not a balcony, a ledge – running around the circumference of the dome from one door to the other. Iron handholds, recessed into the stone, so you can cling on and not fall three hundred feet to the floor below.

Getting up there is as high as they can go, but she can't see a route up.

Spar turns right and smashes straight through a wall. They follow.

The Ravellers are right behind them now, calling on Cari to come back and join them. Without the amulet, it's a false promise – she'll be consumed by them, hollowed out and used as a mask. They don't need her to have a soul to complete the ritual.

Ongent points to a narrow stairwell that goes up. It must be the access stairs to get up to the bell, she thinks, even as she wriggles through the entrance. Ongent follows after her, groaning as he squeezes in. Spar has to smash away some of the door, and the stairs beyond is even narrower. She hears the scrape of stone on stone behind as her as she climbs.

The stairs go on forever. There's no light here, nothing at all. She can see nothing. All she has to guide her is the feeling of stone beneath her hands and the ever-tightening turn of the stairs. Ongent can't breathe behind her – she can hear the old man wheezing and coughing. She can't hear Spar at all. He's too far behind to be audible, she tells herself, but he's there. They haven't caught up.

The climbing becomes automatic, even ecstatic. She's leaving her body. It's Ongent's spell all over again, when they healed Spar. The three of them, suspended in the void between the city below and the gods above, stealing power from the divine. Surely she's climbed all the way out of the world by now. Or is this some trick of the Black Iron Gods, some last illusion? She imagines an infinite tower, like a thread of black, rising out of Guerdon forever and ever, and she's condemned to climb it for eternity.

Up and up and up.

She can't hear Ongent now either. Her hands are numb, her legs aching with the exertion. All she can hear is her own pounding heartbeat and gasping breath.

And up.

The stairs so narrow now she has to squeeze around every turn.

And up.

Every step brings the terror that this is the one where the Ravellers catch her. Phantom sensation of a tentacle closing around her ankle, dragging her down.

And up, and she's at a door.

Stunned, she grabs the handle, and it's unlocked. It swings outwards, out into the void. She edges forward onto the little stone ledge, inching to the right. A spur of stone runs out to the gigantic bell that hangs before her. It's the largest of the Black Iron Gods, the head of their nightmare pantheon. Unlike the other bells she's seen, at the Holy Beggar and St Storm and in the alchemists' furnaces, the reforging process could not completely erase the thing's features. It has a face, and she will never, as long as she lives, forget the sight of it.

The professor emerges from the stairwell. "Oh fuck," he whimpers at the sight of the fall before him. Weak-kneed, he clings to one of the handholds. "Oh gods," he says, but he has to move to leave room for Spar. He takes two terrified steps to the right, and Cari grabs his hand.

"You're okay!" she shouts to him. "I've got you."

Spar crawls out, covered in the cobwebs and dirt of the stairwell. His shoulders are scraped shiny. Blood wells up between the cracks of his stone plates. He crawls out onto the little spur, kneeling in front of the Black Iron bell. Then, very cautiously, he turns and places his massive hands on the door. "I'll hold it shut!"

It's no good. More Ravellers are climbing up the inside of the dome.

"Miren!" shouts Cari.

Her cry echoes around the dome—

– Echoes off the bell.

CHAPTER FORTY

Eladora's view of the battle is confused. Her soul is like a rag on the wind. At times, she's dragged up to the heavens and is in alignment with the Black Iron Gods. In those eternities, she sees everything – the armies clashing in the heart of Guerdon, the gods moving through the skies over the city, the thieves who have come to rob her from her family tomb. The Black Iron Gods thunder at her, booming with church bell voices, demanding that she be their Herald and let them in.

In those moments, she's transfixed between two immense magical constructs. The Black Iron Gods hammer at her soul from without, trying to use her as a door out of their prison. Jermas Thay's spell claws at her from the inside, from the amulet that is like a burning coal on her chest, trying to force her to let the gods into his trap. His spell would make her soul into a furnace, a second remaking of the Black Iron Gods. The priests trapped them in physical bells; he wants to trap them in abstract purpose.

The pressure to give in to one or both is unbearable, but all she has left is pride in herself. She endures.

She falls back down into her body. She knows, intellectually, that she is badly hurt. She wonders if she is dying. The tomb was very cold, but now it is hot. She tries to focus, and sees fire. A flaming sword, and then there's a Crawling One on fire. Its black robe ignites, roasting the column of grave-worms inside. It collapses into a horrible swarm, but Aleena swings her sword again, low to the floor, and the worms catch fire. Scattering is no defence from the wrath of the saint.

Eladora cannot be sure if these things are happening in the same room as her body, or somewhere far away. The visions have smashed her sense of self. Now, she sees a road. A carriage has crashed here, the raptequines having turned and run head-first into the wall (*Did I do that?* she wonders, and wonders at the thought). The carriage is smashed, overturned, and in the wreckage lies a small man.

And here, approaching him, walking with a jerky stumble, is a Tallowman.

This Tallowman is old-young-old. Old for the tallow vats. Most of those condemned to be rendered are young, but he was old, in his forties or fifties. He can't remember. Young, because he's only two days old. And old, because he's been burnt and blasted and scarred since then, and needs to return to the vats to be remade again.

If you asked him why he was here, when every other Tallowman in the city is back in the Wash fighting the Ravellers, he would be unable to answer you. His mind is a flickering candle flame, burning within the waxy hollow of his skull, but the answer isn't to be found there. It's engrained into his flesh and bone, or whatever's left of flesh and bone after the vats.

He stops and scratches at his beard, which leaves scars in his moulded face. He stares at the encrusted brown-grey wax beneath his fingernails, then laughs to himself. *This is wrong*, the Tallowman thinks, even if he doesn't know why.

His knife – that's wrong. What he needs is a staff. A long staff, six feet long, almost as tall as he is. Shod in iron. There's an iron railing nearby, part of a fence that was damaged when the carriage crashed. It'll do. He drops the knife in the middle of the road and pulls a railing free. It feels familiar in the Tallowman's hand.

Tap tap tap as he approaches the wreckage. He uses the railing to probe the debris. He finds the first body immediately. The coach driver, guesses the Tallowman, his neck broken in the crash. Searching, he finds a bloody handprint on one wall, and bootprints in the mud. One of the passengers survived and got away, stumbling down this alleyway. He puts his drooping nose to the handprint and inhales, then licks it with a half-melted tongue. A woman, and the tingle of sorcery, too.

The Tallowman returns to the wreckage. Large parts of the carriage are still intact, and he hears moaning from beneath one of them. *Tap tap tap.* He finds he's relishing this, in a way that's quite foreign to how he was made. He's supposed to delight in following orders and inflicting pain. This is cruelty, yes, but with a different purpose. His distorted features twist into a smile as he reaches down and lifts off the wreckage.

Beneath he discovers a little man, still alive. Two broken legs, though, and other injuries. Crushed, guesses the Tallowman, by the heavy chest that must have been on the seat beside him. When the carriage crashed, the chest went flying, and crushed the little man. Many, many broken ribs. Perhaps he's dying.

Perhaps he's dead? No. The eyes open, then widen in terror at the sight of the Tallowman.

"Help me," pleads Heinreil. "Bring me to Rosha."

The Tallowman finds his voice. It's not a pleasant one. "You. Can. Thank. Me. Later."

He scoops up Heinreil like a father carries a child, and starts walking towards the blue light in the distance.

"South, you dolt! You're going the wrong way!" Heinreil twists and tries to resist arrest, but the Tallowman's grip has solidified again in the rain and is unbreakable.

Step by step, the Tallowman that was Jere Taphson takes the thief to the sleepy city watch station in Bryn Avane.

For Aleena, every step closer to the Herald takes her back in time and magnifies the power that flows through her.

One step, and she's young again. How young she was! Still unsteady on her feet, still unused to her unexpected ascension from farm girl to the youngest of the chosen champions of the Kept Gods. She's descending the stairs of the tomb, but in the eyes of the Kept Gods she's also walking into the foyer of the Thay mansion in Bryn Avane. She thought it was a holy mission that night, a righteous purpose that the Thays should be exterminated. She was the youngest and least experienced of the saints, but, still, she walked at the head of the company. The others knew the horrors of sainthood, of being taken up and used by vast, inhuman forces that were coldly impersonal or raving mad or both, but she was still innocent then, and that innocence gave her strength. She was never so powerful as she was that night, when all the Thays' bodyguards and magical defences fell before her like wheat before the scythe.

Another step, and it's three hundred years ago or more, and she's riding into the city of the damned. Guerdon has fallen to the vile cult of the Black Iron Gods, and she is some other saint, some previous weapon of the gods – but these are not the frail and nervous Kept Gods that Aleena knows. No, these are the gods as they used to be, when they had all the souls of their faithful to fortify them. They are giants of molten sunlight, and they ride with her as she charges down Mercy Street.

Her lance is a beam of sunlight that blazes so bright it makes Ravellers explode in flame with the slightest touch. Her shield is the dawn horizon, as inviolate and glorious as the sky. She is a war-saint in full wrath, and this is gods war. She knows her enemy awaits her in the gigantic domed temple ahead, and she knows that *he* is more powerful yet. He has the full force of a pantheon behind him, and his gods are dark thunderheads, dark celestial mountains in the shadows ahead of her. She can hear the screaming of the victims as the gods feast, gathering power for the confrontation.

But she is too quick. She was too quick, will be too quick. Aleena remembers how she – how another saint – killed the High Priest before he could let loose his power, work his terrible miracles. And gods cannot be destroyed, so all that stored power went nowhere, stayed locked up in the suddenly dismayed Black Iron Gods. Stayed locked up even when the victorious Keepers turned those dark statues into prisons.

Back in the present, Aleena grows in stature, echoing that triumphant ride down Mercy Street. Her sword becomes a lance, and Crawling Ones burn just as well as Ravellers. There is a shield in her hand where there was none before, and it is proof against all sorcery. Their spells cannot harm her. She is invincible.

She bursts into the inner chamber. *There is the Herald* – no, she reminds herself, shaking her mind free of the Kept Gods' delusions of omniscience, *there's wee Eladora Duttin, because shitty Sinter couldn't keep her safe for one bloody night*. And there is Jermas Thay. He shrieks when he recognises her, loses control of his woven body and half collapses into a writhing pile of disassociated worms. He struggles to rebuild himself as she approaches.

"JERMAS THAY!" roars the saint, and her voice is Judgement, *"HOW MANY FUCKING TIMES DO I HAVE TO KILL YOU? AND WHAT DID YOU DO TO THIS POOR GIRL!"*

Aleena breathes a prayer of healing and transfers a portion of her overbrimming strength to Eladora. Wounds close, bones reknit, as the child is healed.

"*YOU LET THE RAVELLERS BACK IN THE CITY, YOU ASSHOLE*" cry a chorus of angels in Aleena's throat. The lance flares, brighter than the sun, and Jermas Thay – every one of him, all the thousands of worms that fed from him – burns. Some of his constituent worm-fragments slither into cracks and holes in the walls, screeching as the light scorches them, but the rest are consumed in the fire of Aleena's wrath. The gold mask burns like cheap paper.

It's done. The Kept Gods withdraw from her. The divine pressure, palpable to even the surviving thieves, departs. Aleena leans on her sword, which is just a sword again. She's mortally tired, all of a sudden, and really just wants to rest. There's one last thing to do. She plucks the amulet from Eladora's throat and hands it to Miren.

Rat follows behind the wrathful Saint Aleena, loping after her like a dog. When necessary, he stops to counter the Crawling One's sorcery – to an elder ghoul, there's little distinction between the physical and spiritual realms. He can claw their spells apart, bite the throats of their incantations. He conserves his own power where he can; even if they are victorious here, there will be other battles tomorrow. The city will be reshaped by these events, and he has a responsibility to ghoul kind. A generation ago – as humans reckon time – the ghouls were restricted from coming to the surface by day and from holding any sort of job in the city. Things changed, and they will change again after tonight. Rat intends to be among the victors, for the sake of his ghouls.

He laughs. The elder ghoul in him is trapped, outmanoeuvred by Rat. He can't just sink back into the underworld to squat on a pedestal and contemplate occult secrets. No, as the last surviving elder, he speaks for the ghouls and there will be councils aplenty on the surface in days to come. Spar would be proud, thinks Rat, to learn that all those talks about politics weren't completely in vain.

There's a blaze of light as Aleena destroys the Crawling One chieftain. Rat licks his lips – the Crawling Ones are responsible for this crime against the city. Everyone in Guerdon will turn on them, above and below. The ghoul kingdom was terribly wounded by the Crawling Ones' attack, but their revenge will be complete. Not a single grave-worm will be permitted to survive, and that thought is pleasing to the elder.

He casts around for a voice to express his triumph. Miren is the closest. He reaches out, smirking at the thought of humiliating the disagreeable boy. His mind brushes against that of Miren, and he sees the boy's intent.

Rat lunges forward, howling, trying to grab the boy before he teleports away with the amulet. He's too slow. His claws close on empty air.

CHAPTER FORTY-ONE

Like a conjured demon, Miren appears, materialising next to Spar on the stone spur that juts out from the ledge. He's bloodied, scorched, but alive, and in one hand he holds Cari's amulet. In the other, his knife.

"Go on," shouts Spar, "command them!"

Cari stretches out her hand for the amulet. *He'll have to throw it*, she thinks. *It's only a few feet, but if I drop it . . .*

Miren throws it with a smooth motion, hurling it across the abyss, right into Ongent's waiting hands. He continues that same balletic spin, a dancer on the edge of the precipice, whirling around so he can drive his knife with full force into Spar's back.

Spar roars, slips, and Miren hits him again, the thin blade slipping between the rocky plates to draw blood. Spar loses his grip and falls, tumbling head over heels into the air. Falling into the vast void of the dome, falling hopelessly out of reach. Cari watches helplessly as he tumbles down, past the bell, past the Ravellers, past everything, to crash like a fallen star on the hard ground far far below.

Stone dead. Nothing could survive that.

Everything stops – she can't breathe, can't think, her heart might not even be beating. Even the pressure of the Black Iron

Gods in her mind is gone. There's nothing in her except shock and grief and . . .

And she's going to kill Miren. She draws her knife and tenses, a split-second prelude to throwing herself across that same void – or into that same void – and killing Miren. He murdered Spar. He murdered her friend for no fucking reason, the bastard, and she's going to kill him. It's all she can think of, but Ongent's spell catches her before she can move, and she's frozen. Immobilised, like a fucking statue.

Ongent takes the amulet and places it around her paralysed neck. "Let's try this again," he says. "Properly, this time."

She can't move a muscle. The spell has her locked in place so tightly she can barely breathe. All she can think to do is topple forward, to follow Spar down to the killing floor below. She tries, but, before she can fall, Miren appears next to her and steadies her. His slim hands grip her as strongly as his father's spell.

The Ravellers freeze in place, then start to crawl back down. Some sprout black membranous wings to glide down, circling inside the building to land in the midst of the crowd of victims below. Most clamber back the way they came, crawling along the inside of the dome. Cari sees all this; she can't even blink. Her gaze is locked on the grey and red splatter mark on the floor below that used to be Spar.

"I worked with your grandfather," whispers Ongent in her ear. "He was a remarkable fellow, but no respecter of tradition. He saw history like some great engineering project, a process that could be improved on. Gods of trade and justice and profit, marching towards infinity! An accountant's utopia!"

He's lecturing her. Here and now, of all places, he falls into lecturing. "A student of history sees that there is no process, no great purpose. Empires rise and fall, kingdoms come and go. War and disease and time make mockeries of all grand projects. Everything made by mortals comes to dust. I could see Jermas making a grubby sort of golden age for the city – Effro Kelkin writ across the heavens, perhaps – but I knew it would come to nothing in the end, even if he succeeded. A few decades of prosperity, feh!"

Locked inside the prison of her own flesh, Cari screams silently. She tries to reach out with her mind, to stab at him like she struck at Heinreil's carriage, but his spell holds her trapped in the spiritual realm, too. She thrashes and spits, but nothing happens.

"The Black Iron Gods – they were *unlucky*. The Keeper's rebellion should have failed. A bunch of plucky farmers and a few rural harvest deities from the hinterlands try rebelling against a pantheon of fiercely competitive deities? It should have been a slaughter. It was a slaughter, only some Keeper saint got lucky and killed the High Priest. Mischance, nothing more. Empires come and go, but the Empire of Black Iron should have lasted hundreds of years, not just a few decades!

"All I'm doing here is putting history back on its natural course. And I shall see it all."

Ongent inches away from her, carefully feeling his way back along the ledge towards the spur of stone. He risks a glance down at the floor below, gulping in terror.

He reaches the spur and walks gingerly along it. He talks to allay his nervousness. "I thought I'd lost you. I suggested to Jermas that he send you away for safekeeping, just before I told Effro Kelkin – anonymously of course – about all his blasphemies. I intended to be your godfather, your tutor, to prepare you for this. But you ran away. Miren was my backup plan – I tried recreating Jermas' work, although I didn't have a Raveller to work with. Still, there were some successes. He's nearly a copy of you in their eyes. From here, he might be able to serve as Herald – but with you here, he doesn't need to."

Cari tries to struggle. Tries to speak. Tries to stab. Nothing works. She can't even run. She's utterly immobilised, as stuck as a Stone Man. Her helplessness is complete.

"I see the charm in Pilgrin's, at the last," says Ongent to himself. " 'They swallowed the hosts of the living, and offered up their souls to the black iron gods.'"

He shoves the bell with all his might.

It swings, gathering speed of its own accord, and sounds a single note, a signal to the Ravellers below.

The sacrifice begins.

There are hundreds of Ravellers in the crowd, and every one of them is a hundred knives. Razor-edged tentacles whip through flesh and bone; blood sprays drench the floor, which becomes a red lake in an instant. And Carillon sees each death as a burst of energy that is swallowed before it can bloom, as the soul is captured and consumed by the Raveller, to be given to the Black Iron Gods.

Given *through* her.

She can't stop it. She feels the power building around her. If she stood against this flow of power, she'd be annihilated in an instant. It'd be like standing against a tidal wave. She'd be burnt away, leaving only the thing they made her to be, the Herald. Magic rushes through her and into the bell in front of her. It cracks and begins to change. Metal flows and twists, and it begins to take on the outline of its true form. The physical shape of the thing is nightmarish, but Cari can see the spiritual realm, too — see the cage of Ongent's spell, see the bonds connecting her to Ongent, and to the amulet, and to the Black Iron Gods. And now she can see the Black Iron Gods, too. All across the city, they're returning.

The strength from the slaughter in the temple below will remake them, and then they'll have access to their stored power, their tenfold reserves from decades of similar atrocities. And there is a whole city now, three hundred years of growth and change, thousands more souls to feed their hungers.

Two steps more, and she'd have been right under the Tower of Law when it fell. She'd have been crushed to death, and none of this would be happening. She tries again to fall from the ledge, to kill herself that way, but Miren won't let her go. He's kissing her even as she's trying to scream.

Ongent rises. A dark halo of power manifests around him. Years fall from his face, and he steps out into the empty air, levitating. Lightning crackles around his hands. He's crowned with black iron, High Priest of a monstrous pantheon.

BRING THEM BACK, he commands her. His voice is the tolling of a great dolorous bell. There's no way to resist his command, no way she can stand against the power of the gods.

Standing still is death. A thief runs, a thief dodges. A thief steals.

It's like stealing fruit in the market, she thinks. *You make a big show of taking one, the fruit seller chases you, and then your partner grabs the apples.*

She looks for the thread of magic connecting her to Spar. It's still there, frail and fading. The remnant of the healing spell Ongent cast, fuelled by magic stolen from the Black Iron Gods.

Carillon can't move, but she can still do sleight-of-hand.

She concentrates on that skein of sorcery and opens the gates.

CHAPTER FORTY-TWO

Rat screeches in frustration and grabs the mind of the nearest thief. Roughly, heedless of the damage. The man staggers forward and falls to his knees before the elder ghoul.

"HE STEALS THE TALISMAN," roars the thief through bloodied lips. "HE HAS BETRAYED US!"

Eladora tries to get down off the bier and half falls to the floor. Her body is still limp, as if her limbs are disconnected from her will. "Cari. He's bringing it to her. But she—"

"It's your fucking professor." Aleena's face is pale beneath the worm-gore that cakes her features. "Sinter fucking warned me about him, and I didn't pay attention. Shit." She draws herself upright, turns to Rat. "All right. All right. Back across the city. We do this—" nodding to the burning pile that used to be Jermas Thay "again."

The elder ghoul wants to say it's hopeless. It took them half the night to get from the Wash to Gravehill; by the time they get to the Seamarket, it'll be too late. It may be too late already. Even the gods agree – he can sense no trace of the Kept Gods around Aleena. Their saint is out of position, a playing piece on entirely the wrong side of the game board. They bolstered her so she could counter one threat, but now that another has arisen they abandon her.

He wants to tell her that all is lost. That they should lie down and die, and let him eat their bodies and carry their souls down into the dark. If he consumes the flesh of a saint — TWO saints, even! — it will do much to strengthen him, give him a chance to survive the apocalypse now set in inevitable motion. But the words catch in his mind, and he cannot put them into the throat of the thief who sprawls before him, twitching.

Rat discovers he doesn't believe that all is lost.

Instead, he speaks with his own voice, forcing the words out past his warped larynx, his monstrous tongue, his massive fangs. "Spar will stop him," he whispers, wondering at his own faith in his friend. And then he adds, louder, "Crawling Ones. Outside. A great many."

The sorcerers they scattered on their wild charge up Gravehill have returned and gathered outside the tomb. Rat can dimly perceive them through the shut stone door of the chamber, their woven shapes like a skein of silvery slime-trails on the edge of his mind.

"Is there another way out?" asks Aleena.

Eladora shakes her head. "I didn't *see* one." Tears roll down her cheeks; she wipes them away as if mostly unaware of them.

Aleena sighs. "Of course there isn't a shitty back door. All right." She grabs Eladora by the arm and hoists her up, hands her to Rat. She has to strain to do so — her god-given strength has left her. "Get her out." She pulls the surviving thieves to their feet, too, like a drill sergeant. "Stay behind the ghoul, you hear me?"

Outside the door, the low susurrus of worm-spells.

"Church business," says Aleena to herself. "Fuck that."

Rat senses a swell of power with her, and he watches as she reaches up to heaven and *pulls*. Like Carillon does, hauling the gods down to her.

The tomb floods with light once more as Saint Aleena rides out to war.

Eladora clings to the ghoul's back, her face buried in shanks of coarse, foul-smelling hair. She cannot bear to look as they charge out of the tomb. She hears shrieks and screams, explosions of sorcery, the roar of flames and the sizzle of flesh. Despite this, all she can think is *it's going to get worse*. She's seen the Black Iron Gods first-hand now, and she knows that all the stories in the history books don't even begin to describe the horrors that are coming. A reign of divine terror, where you're either a slave of the mad gods, or another sacrifice to be devoured by the Ravellers.

Sorcery blazes around her. All she can hear is the air rasping in and out of the ghoul's huge lungs as he staggers forward, lanky arms raised as a barrier against the Crawling Ones' spells. She can't hear Aleena anymore.

One of the thieves screams as something catches him, a spell that swallows him like an invisible mouth. He just snaps out of existence, suddenly no longer there on the stairs out of the tomb.

A hand made of fat, soft, slithering fingers closes on her ankle. She kicks at it, feels the worms burst beneath her heel, but it drags her from Rat's back. The Crawling One is wounded, dripping dying worms from a burnt hole in its robe. It claws at her, muttering what might be arcane syllables or nonsense, the leavings of a thousand corpse-brains.

Eladora shoves it off her, feels around for a weapon. Her fingers close on a sword. It's still hot to the touch, but no longer flaming. The long blade is blackened and scorched, partially melted. Aleena's sword. She uses it as a club, smashing it into the Crawling One's head mass over and over until the monster lets her go.

Then running, taking the elder ghoul's hand and running up the stairs again, out of the tomb, into the night air of Gravehill.

They are, she discovers, the only two to have escaped the tomb.

She turns, looking back into the darkness for some sign of Aleena and the thieves. There's a flash somewhere deep in the tomb, like a buried thunderstorm, and part of the ceiling collapses. Rat grabs the heavy stone doors of the tomb and slams them shut as dust billows out. The crash echoes out across the silent hillside.

"All dead," she whispers, and she's not sure if they're her words or the ghoul speaking through her mouth. She holds Aleena's ruined sword gingerly, unwilling to set it down.

She stumbles to the edge of the rocky shelf where the tomb stands, to the vantage point from which half the city can be seen. In the distance she can see the huge dome of the Seamarket, outlined by fires down in the Wash. The sky above the city is scarred by smoke trails from rockets. For a moment – and she's lost her borrowed sainthood, so she cannot really see, really be sure – she perceives titanic figures standing all around her. Not the hateful Black Iron Gods, but more familiar, comfortable deities. The Holy Beggar, stooped and lame. St Storm, knight of heaven, with blazing lance and cloak of grey. The Mother of Mercies, crowned in fire, and her face is Aleena's. The Kept Gods bear witness to the death of their last saint, and there is a new sense of purpose in them, an awareness that Eladora has not sensed before.

And then they are gone. They flee like phantoms as a pallid light blooms over Guerdon, retreating west and north across the hinterlands beyond the old walls. They are falling back to their old temples and village churches, ceding the city to other powers.

Eladora's stomach lurches as she hears the bells tolling wildly.

She falls to her knees as she watches the end of the city.

Spar's body blazes with a light that is not a light, so bright it is painful to behold.

The Ravellers are the first to change. They freeze and turn to stone, the plague progressing through them in an instant. Knife-sharp tentacles reach towards their victims, but calcify and shatter before they can draw blood.

Spar's remains explode in a cascade, an eruption, a hurricane of architecture. Stone rushes outwards and upwards, building on itself, a riot of streets and towers erupting within the dome of the Seamarket, vomiting structure. An earthquake in reverse, a cataclysm that builds. Impossible palaces and rookeries boil out of the ground stained with Spar's blood.

Ongent's miracle, a gift of the Black Iron Gods, fails. Screaming, he tumbles into the churning madness of the new city and is crushed between stone walls, ground away to reddish dust. His remains will never be found.

There are few other casualties. Impossibly few. Even those standing next to Spar's remains are spared. Later, they will speak of how the new buildings grew around them, wrapping them in stone, leaving them standing in corridors or great concourses or small private rooms that had not existed a moment before. There will be tales of beggars who fell asleep in alleyways and awoke in mansions.

The wave of making, of building, does not stop with the Seamarket. It roars out of the doors of the great domed temple in all directions, but the strongest currents are west, east and south-east.

West, into the Wash. Here, the miracle surges down the streets and narrow lands. Towers and theatres, all jumbled up, dance along the gutters with the grace of alley cats. In some places, they merge with existing buildings, or, better yet, complete them, the new flesh of the city fusing with the old as if it was always meant to be that way. In other places, they are weirdly ill-fitting. Hovels jostle for space with palaces.

If there is a plan to this spasm of miraculous creation, it quickly goes awry. Many of the new buildings are beautiful, but weirdly misshapen or twisted. Houses without doors. Body parts writ in stone, only magnified hundreds of times. Explorers of this new urban wilderness will find a heart the size of a warehouse in what was Hook Row; others will find streets shaped like words, as if the city is trying to communicate a message to them. Building piles upon building again and again. Stairs and elevated roads struggle to keep up; new structures spring into being to bridge gaps between others. It's mad and wonderful, like the gods have handed over the building blocks of creation to an enthusiastic child.

East, the stone storm engulfs the army of the Tallowmen. Here, there are casualties. The Tallowmen are caught in empty rooms, rooms without windows or doors. Airtight rooms. All across the battlefield, the lights go out. The alchemist's wagon with its precious, lethal cargo sinks into the marble tumult, vanishing into the new streets like a founding ship slipping beneath the waves. The stone seems enraptured – or offended – by the empty side of Venture Square, because here it rises, higher and higher, building in a wild impossible spiral. It leaves a tower taller than the spires of Holyhill, a cryptic monument to this miracle.

It's not done yet. South-east it rushes, along the docks and cliffs. The stone wave is like a running man, now, a sprinter climbing the rocks along the edge of the Alchemists' Quarter. It strikes the wall of the Quarter, but it's not enough to break the wave – it washes over and into the factories. Furnaces explode, towers topple and shatter.

Later witnesses will describe it as being like a stone giant. They will say that, in its last moments, the wave resembled a titanic figure, hundreds of feet tall, falling on the alchemists' factories and storerooms and engulfing them within its being. More than half the alchemical works are consumed or destroyed by this eucatastrophe, this miracle of the gutters.

Finally, the wave rushes over the far edge of the cliff, tumbling down into the sea in the direction of the Isle of Statues. As it falls, new buildings and streets spring fully-formed on the cliff-side. The last creation of the miracle is a shimmering white dock in a sheltered cove, a welcoming place for a ship that crosses the sea.

At the last, stillness over the new city.

EPILOGUE

Y ou stand on a rise, overlooking the new city.

From this vantage, you can see the confusion of the miraculous streets. Magic conjured them into being, and magic has no truck with urban planning. It's a thief's city, a city full of byways and concealed passages, of stairs and tunnels. Hiding places and secret rooms everywhere. In places, you somehow intuit that you are looking at some unspoken memory, where the stone wave froze in unexpected organic forms like coral or petrified wood.

You watch a woman make her way, hesitant and nervous, through the strange streets. Her clothing marks her as a stranger to the new city. She walks with a cane despite her youth. You watch her path with disinterest. Her route will take her through a tunnel that resembles the skull of a horse, carved from the same marbled stone as the rest. Another building, over there, looks like a boat on a canal. If she goes that way, you know she will be ambushed by thieves.

The new city is more crowded every day. In the last month, refugee ships have arrived from Severast and Mattaur and a dozen other lands, an armada fleeing the war. There is safety and a place to live in Guerdon, say the rumours, a city safe from mad gods.

There is a gun in the woman's pocket. She touches it, a talisman against unseen danger.

Street names are still a confusion. There's a parliamentary committee that's supposed to produce an official map of the new city, but the people who actually live here have their own names for the bizarre streets that sprang up overnight three months ago. According to her informants, the woman's looking for the place called Sevenshell Street.

She finds it, with some effort. It's a small row of houses. All the houses in the new city are remarkably – miraculously – warm and dry in the winter. This particular house, though, already shows signs of poor maintenance. There are thick curtains on the grimy windows.

She raps on the door with her cane.

She waits patiently. Two minutes. Three. Another woman opens it.

"Fuck you," says Carillon Thay.

"We know most of what happened in the Seamarket," sniffs Eladora, "from the accounts of the survivors, and from forensic theology. And, obviously, my own experiences. I won't ask you to relieve what must have been . . . well." She sniffs again, dabs at her nose with a scented handkerchief to block the smell from the hovel. "Witnesses said Professor Ongent died in the ruins. He fell from a height."

"I let the gods in. Into Spar. I thought – I don't know, that it'd kill them, waste their power. Like emptying a bottle into the dirt. But it just all came rushing out . . . " Cari shudders. "Ongent – he was flying. He was their High Priest. Said he was immortal. But then when the gods went through me, he was cut off and he just went." She spits on the floor. "Like that."

"The Black Iron Gods are gone, we think. The ones still

imprisoned in the bells. You didn't just channel the energy from those sacrificed that night, but also all their accumulated power." Eladora consults her notebook. "There are theological engineers who are still trying to calculate how much divine power you, ah, disposed of."

"Didn't bring him back, though, did it?"

"I never met Mr Idgeson, Cari," says Eladora, as gently as she can. "But I understand he was a remarkably . . . moral man. For a thief."

"I should have known. I shouldn't have trusted him. The professor. I fucking didn't trust him, and still."

"I knew O-O-On – the professor, a lot longer than you did, and I never suspected either. The church had files on him, extensive files, but he was able to outmanoeuvre them. He fooled many people, Carillon, and under the circumstances you can't blame yourself."

"Watch me."

Eladora crosses to the window, opens the curtains a crack. Cari hisses and moves out of the spring sunlight. She looks many years older, you think.

"Have you seen any sign of Miren?" asks Eladora.

"He's alive?"

"I take that as a 'no'. Yes, he's still alive. He must have been able to t-teleport out before the Black Iron Gods were destroyed. He's been seen since and implicated in several m-m- – crimes. I wondered if he would make contact." Eladora stares out of the window, carefully controlling her expression.

"Because we were fucking?" Cari laughs. "That was the Black Iron Gods trying to cram their two Heralds together. If his skinny ass shows up, he's dead."

"He was always fastidious about cleanliness, so you're certainly safe here in this filth fortress."

"Found your tongue in the tomb, did you?" Cari rubs her eyes, looks up at Eladora. Her cousin's dressed like a guildmistress, but the sharp cut of her jacket can't hide the shape of the gun in her pocket. "What do you want, anyway?"

"I'm working with Effro Kelkin, on the emergency committee. And your friend Rat, too."

"Did you tell him where I was?"

"No," says Eladora. "I guessed that since you haven't made contact with him, you'd prefer to remain in hiding. I think he assumes you left the city – I did, too, for a while. I won't mention this meeting, not unless you want me to."

"Thanks."

Eladora continues. "Part of our remit is dealing with the aftermath of . . . the Gutter Miracle, and ensuring that the instability caused by the new city and related upheavals don't impact the security of Guerdon. It's not going well," she admits. "But we must try – especially in light of all the new refugees. We're maybe the best refuge from the Godswar now."

She reaches into her jacket and removes a small envelope, marked with warding runes. "We found this in the Seamarket afterwards. It's magically inert now, as far as we can tell, and harmless. I thought it might have some sentimental value to you, though." She tips the contents of the envelope, and the amulet glitters in the sun.

"You know Heinreil went to trial, don't you?" asks Eladora, when Carillon makes no move to pick up the jewel.

"I heard. Prison! Fucker should be dead. Or turned into a candlestick."

"The tallow vats were destroyed in the Miracle, and the new guildmaster has promised not to rebuild them."

"Make an exception for him," mutters Cari. She looks at the amulet, then closes her eyes. "Shit. You sure it's broken?"

Again with the notebook. " 'Magically inert'. I think that's the same thing."

"Right."

A long, awkward silence follows, and Eladora is the first to break it. She stands, carefully brushes herself off, and says: "You saved everyone, Cari. You stopped the Black Iron Gods from—"

"No, I didn't! Or if I did, it's just balancing the scale. If I hadn't been there, if I'd never been born, then they'd never have been able to get back in at all! Or if I'd just fucked off again instead of staying, then Spar would still be alive along with everyone else. And Rat – don't use his name for that thing on your committee. I broke everything, El. I broke . . . "

Eladora embraces her cousin. Tears soak into her sleeve. After a moment, Cari shoves Eladora away, wipes her face. "Just go." Eladora leaves a calling card on the table, pristine white against the dust, and departs without a word. She's already late for another appointment.

Cari circles her little house, looking for anything else to do, but finally returns to the amulet on the table. She holds it for a moment, remembering what she thought she knew about her mother. Remembering what she did to get it back.

Remembering what she did to the city and its gods.

She puts it on.

Lays her hand on the wall, touching the stone.

Spar, are you there?

To be continued in book two . . .

ACKNOWLEDGEMENTS

Thank you for reading this book, especially if you've read this far. I always feel the acknowledgements page is like the closing ceremony of a small convention: some people have gone home already, the trade stands are packing up and the venue staff have already begun to stack the chairs and sweep the back of the hall. It's tempting to reconvene in the hotel bar instead of making speeches, but formalities must be observed. Don't worry – I'll run through them quickly.

This is only a partial accounting of gratitude, but a full list of everyone who was integral to the creation of this book would be longer than the book itself. Let's stick to the highlights.

Thanks to editors Emily Byron and Bradley Englert, and the whole crew at Orbit for the warm welcome. Thanks to agent and gentleman John Jarrold, worker of wonders and fielder of nervous emails. Thanks to Richard Ford, fellow survivor of the word trenches, for the introduction and advice.

Greg Stolze gave me great advice on self-publishing, even if fate decided to be ironic about the whole affair.

I'm indebted to the Pelgrane crew, especially this year. The UCC Warps crowd of dear friends and reprobates, thank you all.

At the intersection of those circles: Cat Tobin, and her unfailing inspiration and encouragement.

Allen Varney wrestled my first novel into existence through sheer patience and persistence; in several ways, this book was born out of that one.

Thanks to all those who read *The Gutter Prayer* over the years in various forms, especially Alasdair Stuart, Neil Kelly, Matthew Broome, Sadhbh Warren, Mark Fitzpatrick and Bernard O' Leary.

To Chris Crofts: it was only in the final stages of editing that I realised how much of the book was informed by you. I only wish you were around to read it.

And finally, thanks above all to Edel. This book would not exist without your support and partnership; it definitely wouldn't exist if you hadn't given me the best (and only universal) piece of writing advice:

Finish the book!

extras

about the author

Gareth Hanrahan's three-month break from computer programming to concentrate on writing has now lasted fifteen years and counting. He's written more gaming books than he can readily recall, by virtue of the alchemical transmutation of tea and guilt into words. He lives in Ireland with his wife and twin sons. Follow him on Twitter as @mytholder.

Find out more about Gareth Hanrahan and other Orbit authors by registering for the free monthly newsletter at www.orbitbooks.net.

interview

When did you realise you wanted to be an author and what was your first foray into writing?
"Foray" sounds planned. "Enthusiastic stumble" is more apt.

I had a cunning plan – go to university, study computer science, get a job in programming and write on the side. However, it turned out I wasn't a very good computer programmer, and when I got downsized, I thought I'd try freelance writing until I ran out of money and had to get a real job again. It hasn't happened yet, for which I am profoundly grateful.

Can you tell us a bit about your writing process?
It primarily involves waggling my fingers over the keyboard, and hoping I hit the right keys. I've never been precious about process or conditions – get the words down, no matter what, even if you're putting down five hundred words in the back of a cramped bus or while a toddler's trying to eat your knee.

I tend to edit a bit as I go along, and take stock every ten chapters or so. Early chapters tend to need more revision, as characters are inconvenient gits and don't always let you know how they act until you've written them for a while.

I'm also regularly reminded that my subconscious is smarter than I am, and that minor throwaway bits of background detail in Draft 1 are probably pointers to big plot elements in Draft 2.

Who are some of your favourite authors and how have they influenced your work?

Tolkien got me into fantasy, and still exerts a disproportionate influence, especially in terms of the importance of names. Lovecraft I came to through gaming; the ghouls are obviously lifted from him, but also the ability to look at anything and imagine ghastly abysses beyond it. Tim Powers is a bigger influence on the deities of Guerdon, and I found Le Carré through Powers' masterful *Declare*. I'm a big fan of Jeff VanderMeer, too, both for his fiction and his writing guides.

Also, for functional mysticism and wonderful weirdness, Robert Holdstock's Mythago Wood series, especially *Lavondyss*, for putting human protagonists through nigh-indescribable transformations and experiences.

Where did the idea for The Gutter Prayer *come from?*

I'm not wholly sure. I wrote the first 20,000 words or so, and abandoned it. That initial draft had the three main characters, and the Tallowmen, and the bells, but I had no idea how it all fitted together or that there was a larger story.

I stopped for a few months, started another novel, gave up on that and then went back to *The Gutter Prayer* with fresh eyes. And that second approach carried me all the way to the end, more or less. It was oddly liberating; it felt like I was working off someone else's notes and outline at times, which took a lot of the stress away.

What was the most challenging thing about writing this novel?
Characters are always my bugbear. I cut my teeth on tabletop roleplaying games, where the protagonists are under the control of the players, where someone else is driving the action and I can react to them. The setting and the machinations of the bad guys were second nature to me, but I had to go back and relearn how to write traditional stories.

Carillon came to my rescue – she's impulsive enough to just act and get into trouble, which is a great trait in a character in any genre. And then Spar as a more cautious foil, and Rat as commentary and contrast.

The city of Guerdon feels fully realised and lived in. What was your approach to creating this living, breathing city?
Guerdon's a mash-up of cities I know, mixed with chunks of history both real and fictional. The geography, for example, is mostly Cork; the architecture has bits of Edinburgh and London in it. There's some New York in there too. The trick is thinking in layers, piling on different eras of the city and showing how places evolve and grow over time, how they respond to events and changes in culture.

The Gutter Prayer *has an amazing cast of characters: if you had to pick one, who would you say is your favourite. Who did you find the most difficult to write?*
Aleena's always immensely fun to write; in a book where most of the characters are running around with dark secrets, sinister plots or are in deep denial about something, she's as brutally honest as a boot to the face.

Ongent was dangerous to write – either he'd monologue about history and magic, which was fascinating but not germane, or else he'd be far too dangerous. Nothing's more perilous than a thoroughly lovely avuncular mentor figure who's secretly a manipulative monster.

Spar was tricky, too; he has a few topics he ruminates on a lot, and spends a large portion of the book sitting in a cell, so it felt like every time I went back to him, he was saying much the same thing. It was a relief to get him out and punching the system.

Do you have a favourite scene in The Gutter Prayer? If so, why?
I'm very fond of the interlude in Grena, which was written in a single burst so easily it doesn't feel like I wrote it, and it's a nice glimpse into what the Godswar is like elsewhere. I really like the final action scene too. I had no idea how Cari was going to defeat Ongent for a long time, and I'd rather stacked things against her. Fortunately, it's a setting where you can write "and then, a miracle occurs" in your outline and then have that plausibly happen.

When you're not writing, what do you like to do in your spare time?
At the moment – wrangling small children away from sharp objects. A weekly gaming group. Enjoying the faint memory of sleep. Swearing that I'll stop checking Twitter, and then checking Twitter.

Without giving too much away, can you tell us a bit about what can we expect from the next novel in the series?
The second book's set several months later, as the city tries to come to terms with the events of *The Gutter Prayer* and the appearance of the New City. Eladora's now working for Kelkin as he prepares for the first general election since the Crisis.

With the alchemists and their supporters in disarray, and Heinreil's criminal operations destroyed, Kelkin believes that he can reclaim his former position of undisputed power. But the Godswar is closer than anyone knows, and various powers look to Guerdon as a refuge, an ally – or a target.

if you enjoyed

THE GUTTER PRAYER

look out for

THE WINTER ROAD

by

Adrian Selby

The Circle – a thousand miles of perilous forests and warring clans. No one has ever tamed such treacherous territory before, but ex-soldier Teyr Amondsen, veteran of a hundred battles, is determined to try.

With a merchant caravan protected by a crew of skilled mercenaries, Amondsen embarks on a dangerous mission to forge a road across the untamed wilderness that was once her home. But a warlord rises in the wilds of the Circle, uniting its clans and terrorising its people. All roads lead back to war.

If you enjoyed
THE GUTTER PRAYER

look out for

THE WINTER ROAD

by

Adrian Selby

CHAPTER ONE

You will fail, Teyr Amondsen.

My eyes open. The truth wakes me.

You will fail.

I had slept against a tree to keep the weight off my arm, off my face. My tongue runs over the abscesses in my mouth, the many holes there. My left eye is swollen shut, my cheek broken again, three days ago, falling from a narrow trail after a deer I'd stuck with my only spear.

I close my eyes and listen, desperate to confirm my solitude. A river, quick and throaty over rocks and stones. A grebe's whinnying screech.

I take off one of the boots I'd stolen, see again the face of the man who'd worn them as I strangled him. I feel my toes, my soles, assess the damage. Numb, blisters weeping. My toes are swelling like my fingers, burning like my face. I need a fire, cicely root, fireweed. I have to be grateful my nose was broken clean. A smashed up nose is a death sentence in the hinterlands. If you can't sniff for plant you're a bag of fresh walking meat. You need plant to heal, plant to kill.

If I keep on after this river I can maybe steal a knife, some plant and warmer clothes. These are Carlessen clan lands, the

coast is beyond them. I'm going to live there, get Aude's screaming out of my head, the horns of the whiteboys, the whisperings
of the Oskoro who would not, despite a thousand fuck offs and
thrown stones in the black forests and blue frozen mountains,
let be their debt to me.

The grebe screeches again. Eggs!

I pull on the boot with my right arm, my left strapped
against me and healing, itself broken again in my fall.

I pick up my spade and the small sack that I'd put Mosa's
shirt in, the spade something of a walking stick to help me
along the mossy banks and wretched tracks. Snow was making
a last stand among the roots of birch trees, a few weeks yet from
thawing out. A few handfuls ease my gums.

The sky is violet and pink ahead of the sun, the woods and
banks blue black, snow and earth. I stumble towards the river,
a chance to wash my wounds once I've found some nests and
broken a few branches for a fire.

The grebes screech at me as I crack their eggs and drink the
yolks. I find five in all and they ease my hunger. If a grebe gets
close enough I'll eat well. The sun edges over the hills to the
east and I am glad to see better, through my one good eye. The
river is strong up here, my ears will miss much.

I drop the deerskins I use for a cloak and unbutton my shirt. I
didn't have to kill the man I stole that from. I loosen the threads
to the discreet pockets that are sewn shut and take a pinch of
snuff from one. It's good plant, good for sniffing out what I need.
Feels like I've jammed two shards of ice into my nose and I gasp
like I'm drowning, cry a bit and then press another pinch to my
tongue, pulling the thread on the pocket tight after. Now the
scents and smells of the world are as clear to me as my seeing it.
For a short while I can sniff plant like a wolf smells prey.

I forget my pains. Now I'm back in woodland I have to find

some cicely. The sharp aniseed smell leads me to it, as I'd hoped. I dig some up, chopping around the roots with the spade to protect them. Around me a leaden, tarry smell of birch trees, moss warming on stones, but also wild onion, birch belets. Food for another day or so.

I wash the cicely roots and I'm packing my mouth with them when I hear bells and the throaty grunts of reindeer. Herders. The river had obscured the sounds, and on the bank I have no cover to hide myself in. I cuss and fight to keep some control of myself. No good comes of people out here.

The reindeer come out through the trees and towards the river. Four men, walking. Nokes – by which I mean their skin is clear and free of the colours that mark out soldiers who use the gifts of plant heavily, the strong and dangerous fightbrews. Three have spears, whips for the deer, one bowman. There's a dog led by one of them, gets a nose of me and starts barking to be let free. Man holding him's smoking a pipe, and a golden beard thick and long as a scarf can't hide a smirk as he measures me up. The herd start fanning out on the bank. Forty feet. Thirty feet.

"Hail!" I shout, spitting out my cicely roots to do it. My broken cheek and swelling make it hard for me to form the greeting. I try to stand a bit more upright, to not look like I need the spade to support my weight.

"Hail. Ir vuttu nask mae?" Carlessen lingo. I don't know it.

I shake my head, speaking Abra lingo. "Auksen clan. Have you got woollens to spare? I'm frostbitten." I hold up my good hand, my fingertips silver grey.

He speaks to the others. There's some laughter. I recognise a word amid their own tongue, they're talking about my colour, for I was a soldier once, my skin coloured to an iron rust and grey veins from years of fightbrews. One of them isn't so sure, knowing I must know how to fight, but I reckon the rest of me isn't exactly putting them off thoughts of some games. Colour alone isn't going to settle it. Shit. I reach inside my shirt for some of the small white amony flowers I'd picked in the passes above us to the north.

"No no no. Drop." He gestures for me to drop the spade and the amony. He lets a little of the dog's lead go as well. The bowman unshoulders his bow.

At least the stakes are clear, and I feel calmer for it. He has to be fucked if he thinks I'm going to do a word he says, let alone think his dog could hurt me.

He has nothing that can hurt me, only kill me.

"No, no, no," I says, mimicking him before swallowing a mouthful of the amony and lifting the spade up from the ground to get a grip closer to its middle. I edge back to the river, feeling best I can for some solid flat earth among the pebbles and reeds.

He smiles and nods to the bowman, like this is the way he was hoping it would go, but that isn't true. The bowman looses an arrow. Fool could've stepped forward twenty feet and made sure of me but I throw myself forward. Not quick enough, the amony hadn't got going. Arrow hits my left shoulder. It stops me a moment, the shock of it. He's readying another arrow, so I scream and run at the reindeer that strayed near me, the one with the bell, the one they all follow. It startles and leaps away, heading downstream, the herd give chase.

Time and again I made ready to die these last nine months. I'm ready now, and glad to take some rapists with me. I run forward while they're distracted by how much harder their day is now going to be chasing down the herd. The one with the pipe swears and lets his dog go at me while one of the spears fumbles in his pockets for a whistle to call the herd, running off after them.

Dogs are predictable. It runs up, makes ready to leap and I catch it hard with the spade. It falls, howling, and I get the edge of the spade deep into its neck. I look at the three men left before me.

"Reindeer! You'll lose them, you sad fuckers!" They'll understand "reindeer" at least.

The pipe smoker draws a sword, just as my amony beats its drum. I don't know how much I took but it hits me like a horse just then. I shudder, lose control of myself, my piss running down my legs as my teeth start grinding. I gasp for air, the sun peeling open my eyes, rays bleaching my bones. My new strength is giddying, the amony fills me with fire.

He moves in and swings. He's not very good at this. The flat of my spade sends his thrust past me and I flip it to a reverse grip and drive it hard into his head, opening his mouth both sides back to his ears. I kick him out of my way and run at the bowman behind him. He looses an arrow, and it shears the skin from my skull as it flies past, almost pulling my good eyeball out with it, the blood blinding me instantly. He doesn't know how to fight close, but I'm blind in both eyes now and I'm relying on the sense the amony gives me, half my training done blind all my life for moments like this. I kick him in the gut, drop the spade and put my fist into his head, my hearing, smell exquisite in detail. He falls and I get down on his chest and my good hand seeks his face, shoving it into the earth to stop its writhing, drive my one good thumb through an eye far as it'll go. A shout behind me, I twist to jump clear but the spear goes through me. Out my front it comes, clean out of my guts. I hold the shaft at my belly and spin about, ripping the spear out of his hands, his grip no doubt weakened a moment with the flush of his success. I hear him backing away, jabbering in his lingo "Ildesmur! Ildesmur!" I know this name well enough, he speaks of the ghostly mothers of vengeance, the tale of the War Crows. I scream, a high, foul scritching that sends him running into the trees.

My blood rolls down my belly into my leggings. There's too much of it. Killed by a bunch of fucking nokes. No more than I deserve. I fall to my knees as I realise, fully, that it's over. The river sounds close, an arm's length away maybe. I fall forward, put my arm out, but it gives and I push both the spearhead and the end of the arrow that's in my shoulder back through me a bit. A freezing spike of pain. My senses lighten to wisps, I fall away from the ground, my chest fit to burst, my blood warming my belly and the dirt under me. Why am I angry that it's all over? The sun keeps climbing, the pebbles rattle and hum as the song of the earth runs stretching and drinking. I hum to quieten the pain. It's my part in the song but I was always part of the song, I just haven't been listening. The birch trees shush me. Snowy peaks crack like thunder in the distance. The sky is blue like his eyes, fathomless.

"I'm coming," I says. He knows I'm coming. I just have to hold out my hand.